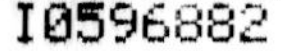
I0596882

J.T. Bock's
Time Trap

An UltraSecurity Novel

PepperLip Press

www.jtbock.com

All rights reserved. This book, or parts thereof, may not be reproduced in any form, print or electronic, without the express written permission of the publisher, except for brief passages that may be cited for purposes of review.
Manufactured in the United States of America

Cover Design by Mike Parkinson © 2018
Interior Design by Mike Parkinson

Cover and Title page image from iStock photo

Edited by Chris Hall and Rachel Daven Skinner

Published by:
PepperLip Press
Virginia

Copyright© 2018 by J.T. Bock

ISBN: 978-0-9888362-6-6

www.jtbock.com

For Karen,
who believed in me when I didn't.

Acknowledgements

Just like my UltraAgents, I couldn't defeat the Big Bad (i.e., finish this book) alone.

Thank you to my mom for instilling a love of movies and adventure at a young age. Thanks to Ma, Mom Barb, and Dad for all your encouragement. It means a lot.

Thank you to my writing friends for hearing me whine while plying me with wine: Karen, Jessica, and Laurel.

Thanks to my critique partners and beta readers for your honest feedback. Thank you to Beth for taking the time from writing your book to read mine. Thanks to Karen, who provided inspiration for TimeTrap and a swift kick when I was down. Thanks to Avi for reading and providing feedback on physics, story, and superhero questions. Thanks to Mike for reading a superhero story that wasn't a comic book. Thanks to Nigel for doing a last minute read of my Aussie slang. Thank you to Stacia and Nick for getting me started and your constant support. To Chris for saying that he enjoyed TimeTrap's character and would read her story.

Thank you to my Morning Glories—Keely, Angele, Jessica, and Geri—for making me accountable for my progress.

Thank you to my content and line editor, Rachel, for your amazing insights and helping to shape the story into something better than I'd imagined. Thank you to my copy editor and proofreader, Chris, for being flexible when my dates slipped again and again and for cleaning up my grammar messes.

Thank you to all my friends who asked about my book and inspired me to keep going.

And, most importantly, thank you to my readers.

Chapter 1

Shenandoah Valley, Virginia
1969

Maxwell Martin Sr. stood in tree pose under the crest of a trickling waterfall that joined with the Shenandoah River thirty-odd feet below. When it rained, the water would gush over the rocks and flood the area. But it had been a hot, dry August. Even the occasional breeze didn't provide any relief.

He shifted his stance, and a flock of birds squawked and flew from the trees above him, unsettled by his presence.

Or maybe they sensed the unsettling presence lurking inside him.

This strange sensation, unbalancing his qi, was the reason he'd sought out his favorite meditation spot on the edge of the peacenik commune he'd founded five years ago. He needed clarity, direction, and most of all tranquility. The latter he'd missed ever since an old friend had trusted him with a mysterious journal and a green bottle containing an odd oily liquid, which Maxwell had sampled in spite of his friend's warnings.

He'd hoped to gain knowledge from this substance. And he did but at a steep price.

He lowered himself into a lotus position, inhaled, and focused his senses deep inside. An hour or so passed when a gust of wind blew through the leaves and over rocks, bringing a cool mist of water along with a sweet song.

Carol, his latest lover, belted out a folksong underscored by a strumming guitar, which was her version of the dinner bell. His chosen brothers and sisters were almost finished preparing the evening meal. The group of them worked together to live off the five hundred acres of land bought by Maxwell. To his ambitious friends in Washington, D.C., fifty-two was too young to retire, but he had been working since he was ten. He'd earned this respite.

The no-nonsense voice of Carol's son, Stephen—the most focused teenager he'd ever met—cut her off in mid-song. Maxwell was too far from the cabins to hear what Stephen was saying to Carol and the group, but he was certain it was important for the young man to interrupt his mother's singing.

Stephen had a bright future, an important path to follow. Maxwell's hunches—psychic alerts (or PAs) as he'd eventually dub them—were never wrong, although they occurred randomly. He had no control over when or where or how much information was granted to him during these PAs.

Mostly they came in dream-like flashes. Other times, there were no images, only emotions that flooded his body until he felt as if they would drown him. He didn't mind the sensation when the feelings were positive. It meant the person near him would go on to do great things.

Like Stephen.

As a small child, the boy relished taking charge in the schoolyard, ensuring the other kids followed the rules, both those of the school's and his own. The teachers had nicknamed him the Little General, and the name stuck even after he grew to tower over Maxwell's average height.

He'd had the first PA about Stephen during a meeting with his father at the Department of Defense before the families had become friends, years before Stephen's father would die in an accident at a testing site that Maxwell had seen coming, but his pragmatic colleague refused to believe would happen.

The Little General had been a toddler, the same age as Maxwell's son, when Carol had brought him to the office to visit his father. When he'd shaken his small hand, a PA occurred, stronger than ever before. One where the Little General was a real general, leading an army unlike any that existed in the present time.

A PA, the most important, life-changing one, had led Maxwell to establish this commune where only those with potential were allowed to reside, those he'd had positive hunches about. They were to be the new world order, the bringers of peace and knowledge to the next generation. He needed to believe this, to support this ideal of balancing out the destruction that had been caused—and would be caused—from the weapons he'd helped build through the Defense Energy Research Science Technology (DERST) lab, which he'd founded.

The sounds of splashing roused Maxwell from his thoughts. Another teen, Hugh, sat several feet below on his favorite perch. His bare feet slapped against the trickling stream. The fourteen-year-old buried his face in a physics book, pages yellow and spine falling apart. Every so often he'd doodle on the rocky surface with a piece of chalk, working out problems on nature's chalkboard. Maxwell made a mental note to buy Hugh a new physics textbook and hire a tutor from the University of Virginia to meet the needs of the boy's expanding mind.

"Government men are here." Stephen appeared on an outcropping above. His clean-shaven face, buzz cut, denim jeans, and pressed plaid shirt were a stark contrast to Maxwell's flowing linen pants, naked torso, and shaggy black hair and beard salted with white.

"How do you know they're government?" Maxwell closed his eyes so he could hear more clearly.

"Fit the profile. There are four of them and all in suits. Pulled up in two black sedans."

"Did they show ID?"

"They stopped at the bottom of the driveway before the hill. Looks like they're debating whether their cars can make it up the dirt road past your bus."

Maxwell wriggled his toes and straightened his back.

"Hugh," Stephen called down.

"Hugh," he repeated, like a parent about to lose patience, when the other teen didn't respond.

Maxwell opened his eyes to find Hugh setting down his chalk as if he had all the time in the world.

"Yes?" Hugh squinted up at Stephen.

"Dinner's ready. Go help your mom. I need to talk to the Man."

Maxwell grimaced. He never liked that nickname, the Man. But those at the commune found it funny to call him that. Both because they saw him as their leader and because of his previous life working with government.

Hugh sighed and snapped his book shut, though he clearly didn't move fast enough for Stephen's taste, because he bellowed like a drill sergeant accustomed to giving orders, "Move. Now."

He leaped to his feet and gave Stephen an exaggerated salute. "Yes, sir. Little General, sir."

The older teen's face turned redder than his mother's tomatoes.

"That's enough, Stephen," Maxwell said before he could berate the younger one.

Hugh smirked at the Little General before bolting through the brush.

Stephen watched him leave, letting a few seconds pass before he asked Maxwell, "What do those government people want?"

"Why don't you ask them?" he replied, not in a sarcastic way but as a pleasant suggestion.

The teen cracked his knuckles. "My mom has drugs. I need to get rid of them. Tell the others to do the same."

Stephen didn't like the idea of hallucinogens. He didn't believe in using them, because he felt the world was not meant to be escaped but faced. It was a waste of time—and one's life—to do otherwise. He wasn't shy about preaching this unpopular opinion to the group either.

Maxwell wasn't going to force the point on Stephen, although he wished one day he'd change his mind, so he could open it and experience the metaphysical as Maxwell had. The supernatural would play a role in his family's future. Stephen needed to embrace it, in order to understand it.

"I doubt they're here for our weed or acid," Maxwell said.

"Then what?"

Stephen didn't distrust the government as the rest of those living in the commune did. He never understood why his mother had left the daily grind after his father had died. According to Stephen, their country would fail if its citizens stopped contributing. What he didn't know was how much his parents and the others in their small community had contributed already. How they'd sold their souls many times over after being duped into believing it had been for the greater good.

The world wasn't safer after the weapons they'd engineered had been released on supposed enemies. Policies hadn't changed. Terrorist groups hadn't disbanded but had grown stronger. Thousands of innocent lives had been destroyed in wars and secret government attacks that should never have happened, and wouldn't have happened, if he and the others hadn't supplied the weapons and engineering power through DERST. So they withdrew from that world to find themselves and carve out new, positive paths for their families.

Maxwell's scalp prickled. Hairs on his arms stood on end. Without turning, he knew a man was approaching, one who wasn't from the government, as Stephen suspected—at least, not any government on Earth.

Maxwell peered over his shoulder. The top of a brown bald head appeared over the edge of the boulder where he sat. Two manicured hands planted themselves on the rocky surface as the man hoisted himself up. His head and face glistened with sweat. His dress shirt was soaked under his bespoke, black suit replete with a bright white handkerchief.

"You used to follow the fashion trends. Since when did you start wearing dark suits to look like every other man?" Maxwell said.

A stick cracked behind him. Hard-soled shoes skidded on the rocky surface.

"Around the same time you abandoned the mission to become a dirty hippie," came the bitter reply.

Grinning, Maxwell turned back to the waterfall and closed his eyes again.

"I'm free, Gabriel." He held his lotus pose and inhaled the scents of dry leaves, aftershave, and gun oil. "And what a rush, man, to finally be free."

"What do you mean, finally free? You walked away from your responsibilities years ago to sit out here on your rock and stare into nothing. You obviously haven't bathed. You smell like a pig rolled in mud." He sniffed the air. "No . . . oh, no . . . not a pig. But something . . . truly foul. Please tell me you didn't—"

"I had to know what it could show me, teach me. And what your kind was hiding from me and my world." Maxwell filled his lungs with the sticky, humid air to force himself back into his meditated calm. But like his favorite wool sweater, his nerves were starting to fray, and Gabriel was tugging on the one thread that threatened to unravel them completely.

"I asked you to hold two items for us. One of which contains an energy that you are not prepared to understand. I surely didn't ask for you to sample that energy. In fact, I recall saying the opposite."

"Both items were stamped with my family seal," Maxwell argued but even he didn't buy it. He had been curious and filled with hubris believing that it wouldn't corrupt him.

"They? Did you write inside . . . no, let me rephrase this . . . After tasting the essence trapped in the bottle, did you spew its so-called predictions inside the journal I gave you?"

"I discovered rudimentary schematics scrawled on its pages. They were similar to weapons engineers at DERST had been trying to build. Then I noticed my name, Max Martin, but couldn't decipher the language." What he left out was the PA he'd experienced when first touching the book. He'd seen a man who resembled his son, with black eyes and a devil's toothy grin, standing alongside a pile of bodies with Gabriel's on top.

"The language is encrypted. Not by the design of the Dark, the substance inside that bottle, but by a natural failsafe that keeps knowledge of the supposed future from us. The Dark, which you consumed and I warned you against, is showing you what it wants, so it can influence future events," Gabriel said.

Future events that impacted Maxwell's family, potentially destroying them and everyone around them. "I needed to know what it said. Besides, the book had my seal on it like my other journals. And it looked almost like them. It was fate, pure and simple."

His two personal journals—filled with his metaphysical journeys as well as alien tech Gabriel had shared with him that he felt DERST wasn't yet ready to tackle—were safe in his home in McLean, locked away in a secret compartment under the priceless Oriental rug his wife had come to admire more than their marriage. He'd hoped one day his son would discover the journals when they needed them.

"That seal is older than your family line, older than Homo sapiens. Humans appropriated it, stole it from us. It has nothing to do with fate."

Gabriel heaved a disgusted sigh, one that seemed to carry the frustration of the world with it. "You've poisoned your body. You've corrupted your soul."

With his back to his friend and his eyes still closed, Maxwell couldn't decide whether his associate was more afraid or hurt over what he'd done. He was about to turn around to read Gabriel's expression when he heard a snap unfastening.

"You must understand, Maxwell, that what you did can never be undone. This won't kill you, not much can now, but it will disable you enough for us to drain that infection from you. I won't lose you to this. You're too important to me in ways you'll never know."

A gun cocked behind his head. A revolver, based on the sound of the barrel rolling then the pin being pulled.

Another sound followed that one. It was the flick of a butterfly blade where Stephen had been standing. He'd forgotten the teen was still there, listening to everything they'd said.

Maxwell's eyes flew open. He jumped to his feet, but it was too late. He pivoted to find Stephen's blade embedded in Gabriel's bicep. The well-dressed man flinched. He swung the gun at the teen standing on the outcropping above them. His finger rested on the trigger.

"Stop." Maxwell lunged in front of the barrel.

His gaze locked with Gabriel's as he ordered Stephen, "Go back to your cabin."

"But—"

"Thank you for your protection. But Gabriel and I have business, which doesn't concern you."

Maxwell lowered his voice so Stephen couldn't hear. "I'll give you the bottle and the book and whatever is inside me. Just let the boy go."

Gabriel lowered the gun and holstered it. Shooting the teen a disdainful look, he pulled the knife from his arm and winced—more at the tear and stain on his sleeve than from the pain of the wound, Maxwell suspected.

Wrapping his fingers around his cut bicep, a golden glow emanated from under his palm.

Stephen uttered a string of curses then took off. His shoes struggled to find purchase against the mossy rocks. He slipped twice before disappearing through the tall green ferns lining the waterfall's edge.

Gabriel wiped Stephen's blade clean with his handkerchief. He tossed the knife to the ground then stuffed the cloth into the pocket of his pants.

"Who else came with you?" Maxwell asked after he was certain the teen was gone.

"The Three, and considering what you've done, I'm glad that I brought them."

Maxwell kept his expression neutral. A hard thing to do with Gabriel's personal enforcers—his sister and her two spouses—near.

"Although the more we talk, the more I see you're in your right mind. I don't have to disable you, yet." Gabriel touched the gun under his jacket to make his point.

"I'll give you whatever you ask. But please don't hurt my family."

"Are we talking about the wife and boy you abandoned in Northern Virginia so you could live a life of freedom—or whatever you call this—with strangers?"

He had to bring up what Maxwell regretted most in his decision to leave his former life. His wife and son were of a different mindset. They were consumed by materialism, blinded by their baser wants, unable to discern the big picture or the world beyond the veil. In his travels—both physically and metaphysically—he had seen not only the guts of the clocks but the clockmaker and found both wanting. He wouldn't be a pawn in his family's or his government's games anymore.

"I want to make the world a better place," Maxwell said, trying to rein in his rising agitation.

"So do we. That's what we've been doing since the dawn of your race, don't you see? Although you wouldn't understand how hard we've labored for your species to survive. For that, I blame myself. You were special at an early age. You were spoiled. It blinded you to what needs to be done."

"On the contrary, I saw the light."

"And I've seen the darkness. I've stared into it, and it is cold and unforgiving. It doesn't give a damn if you feed every single starving child in the world, if you cure cancer, or if you disarm all nuclear weapons. The only way to stop encroaching enemies is to build a good defense. I can only help you so far. Humans need to continue evolving on their own if they want to save themselves."

"At the cost of lives?"

Gabriel chuckled. "That's rich, Maxwell, considering you weren't thinking of this when you built DERST to defend your great nation. If I remember correctly, money was the initial factor. A growing seed that still bears lush fruit for your wife and child and countless other investors."

Maxwell winced. Gabriel's sharp point cut through to his soul. It didn't matter that he'd left DERST. The contracts kept coming. The business expanded into Top Secret technologies of which he was no longer privy since he'd retired.

"If I only knew at the start what I know now." Maxwell took a deep breath until his lungs filled to capacity. Then he let it out slowly, hoping the anger twisting his insides would follow suit, because he hated the way it made him feel and what it made him want to do. He was never a brawler, but his hands itched to punch Gabriel's face, which barely showed a wrinkle to indicate the decades that had passed since they'd met, and since Maxwell had learned what he was.

He folded his arms across his chest. His nails dug into his triceps. "Where's the rest of your gang?"

Gabriel took out another handkerchief from an inner pocket and dabbed the sweat on his head. "The Three are doing a sweep of the property. I told them to meet us at your cabin."

His nails dug deeper into his arm until he felt a pinch as one broke the surface. "Why did you bring them?"

"Why do you think?" Behind his brown-tinted contacts, Gabriel's irises glowed with a soft golden hue, the same color his hand emitted when he healed his wound.

The longer Maxwell remained in the alien's presence, the more unbalanced he felt. Standing close to Gabriel made his blood pump harder and his muscles tense, readying for a fight.

He longed to savor Gabriel's delicious life force.

Maxwell staggered. He shook his head to shake off the disturbing thought.

"I have no clue why you brought the Three with you," he finally replied.

Gabriel squinted as if trying to see through Maxwell's skin to the oppressive force that was now making his arms prickle with gooseflesh.

"I've broken with the Organization," Gabriel announced.

"Why?"

The Organization was a group of otherworldly beings, who had been using Earth for their testing grounds since Homo sapiens first drew breath. They stayed under the radar and blended with humans as they carried out their research. One segment of these researchers included the Custodians, which Gabriel oversaw, and who had been studying earthlings' evolution. Since his days at DERST, Maxwell had known about the Custodians. Recently, Gabriel admitted they were part of a larger group, the Organization, a shadowy, alien version of the United Nations.

The Custodians' rules were strict about not sharing their technology with humans or otherwise interfering with their development. Although Maxwell suspected there had been interference of the sexual kind. He'd seen how Gabriel flirted with earthling women, and he'd shacked up with at least one since they'd met.

During World War II, the Custodians had approached an up-and-coming DERST to combat an alien experiment that had grown out of control. They'd feared it would take advantage of the war that limited the U.S.'s home resources, allowing it to spread terror across the country.

Gabriel had broken with the Organization's code of conduct to work with Maxwell, sharing with him select knowledge to help defeat this danger. He believed the only way humans stood a chance against growing threats—both from another world and Earth—was by kick-starting their next evolution in technology with his help. It was one of the reasons DERST became so successful and won lucrative wartime contracts. Human engineers working for their competitors couldn't beat their alien tech.

Of course, Gabriel shared limited intelligence—only that which could help restrain this threat and provide a foundation for a new tech industry. He didn't want human technology to surge too far ahead too quickly.

"I didn't mention it when I trusted you with the journal and bottle, but in hindsight, I should have." Gabriel paused, eyeing him once more as if he was on guard for any signs that he needed to put a bullet in Maxwell. "The Organization misused the Dark. We sacrificed many lives to get the genie back inside that bottle. One of their members fabricated that book from the skin of the first who had been possessed by the Dark."

Maxwell's knuckles cracked behind his back as his hands wrung tighter and tighter together.

"The book is bound with flesh?" he asked.

Gabriel flapped his hand, dismissing Maxwell's disgust as if it were a normal occurrence to bind a book in a person's—or alien's—skin.

"We kept the drained body of the first. She had been a fellow Custodian. It was such a shame for us to lose her unique talents." Gabriel sighed. "But that's what the Dark does. Corrupts the best of us." He gave Maxwell a pointed look before continuing. "Our tests had shown that we could use what was left of her skin as a failsafe to trap the Dark if the bottle no longer worked."

Maxwell nodded because he knew this fact, even though this was the first time he'd been told about it. After he'd sampled the Dark, a compulsion had overtaken him, guiding him to wrap cloth around his hands before he read the journal. Since then, he wore gloves whenever he handled it.

Another notion that struck Maxwell about this compulsion was the underlying fear he felt from this foreign presence undulating inside him. It feared the consequences of Maxwell's flesh touching the journal. The only thing it appeared threatened by.

Gabriel said, "As we continued our tests, we uncovered its other properties. One of which a researcher with the Organization decided to exploit. He had an extrasensory ability. When he drank the Dark, his ability became stronger, and while possessed by it, he transcribed visions inside the journal pages. He discovered that the Dark could not only tell the future but also control it when these visions were written inside the bound flesh. The Three and I killed him before he could recast mankind's future. However, he was not working alone but under the direction of upper management—so to speak. Hence, by doing this, we broke ties with the Organization. We then drained the Dark safely back into the bottle and stole away the journal, which brings us to you."

"I'm cool, man. I only had a drop." Maxwell tried to brush off Gabriel's fears, but it was a fool's errand as he grew more afraid himself. If he gave shape to the rage burning in his core, he'd find a smoky mass of suffocating ash.

"A taste is all it takes." Gabriel replied.

Then what would happen if Maxwell drank the entire bottle? What if an enemy of his nation (hell, an enemy of the Earth) consumed this evil? It took the aliens, with their technology supported by DERST weapons, to stop the previous attack during the last world war.

By killing this alien researcher, Gabriel had kept it from spreading again, but what would happen next time and the next and the next? They couldn't keep it hidden from enemies forever. At some point, someone would find the Dark and defeat whoever was guarding it.

As he considered this Pandora's box of consequences, Gabriel rested his hand on the handle of his gun. Maxwell took this action as a sign to get moving. He needed to show the alien that all was well with him.

"We've spent enough time jawing. Follow me. I'll give you what you came for, and you can drain this stuff out of me." Maxwell pointed to a path below them.

"I need to climb back down?" Gabriel frowned.

"You should've dressed the part."

"Of a hippie. No thank you. That is one fashion statement I detest. I'd go back to wearing knee breeches first."

"Then use your power to float down to the river. I've seen you do that."

"That young man saw enough. I'm not about to create a spectacle for your camp." He glanced at the rock above them, as if he expected Stephen to be standing there surrounded by a torch-bearing crowd.

"Then follow me." Maxwell climbed off the bolder to a well-worn path, weaving down past the waterfall to the river below. Behind him, Gabriel scrambled to find traction in his dress shoes. Several times, he had to hug a trunk to keep from sliding down the dry walkway.

Maxwell had hoped the constricting anger would subside as he put distance between himself and Gabriel. He'd hoped the hike would distract this force, maybe weaken it. But it became more determined. Although determined to do what, Maxwell didn't know and didn't want to find out.

He took a breath and let it out slowly.

In with the good air, out with the bad. A mantra Maxwell had adopted. If he'd spoken it aloud, Gabriel would know he was fighting against a tide of negative emotions. So he repeated it inside his mind, and that simple action kept the oppressive feelings from spreading any further for the moment.

"What will happen if you leave the Dark inside me?" Maxwell stepped over a fallen log.

"Its power will continue to grow. Slow at first, then eventually consume you."

"What does that mean?"

"It means you will no longer exist, and it will seek to feed on life forces outside your body to sustain itself and grow in power."

The ground leveled out near the river. They continued along the widening path with Maxwell leading the way.

"Then it would be better to destroy this substance than hide it once again for another to find."

"It can't be destroyed."

"Then use the journal to send it to another universe," Maxwell spoke aloud this idea that became more appealing as the toxic energy crept up his neck and spread into his mind. It then gave way to a voice whispering, cajoling him to do unspeakable things to Gabriel. Thoughts ascribed to mass killers, not a man who sought out peace and love and positive modes of consciousness

"How do you know the journal will send it to another universe?" Gabriel skidded to a halt.

"You told me." Maxwell turned to face him.

"No, I said it would trap it," the alien corrected.

"I could've sworn you said that it would be sent to another universe."

"That was one theory which I didn't share with you." Gabriel propped himself against a tree and lifted his foot. He scowled at the dirt caking its sole.

Maxwell wiped the sweat from his hairline, feeling as if he were going crazy. He could've sworn that Gabriel had told him about a portal to another universe hidden inside the journal's binding.

"If that's one of your theories, then maybe we should test it. The longer it's inside me, the less free I become. And the more you reveal, the more freaked out I am. If it stays here, then our universe will be damned—along with my family and everyone we care about," Maxwell said.

"We'll determine the next course of action after we drain it from you. I don't want it in you any longer. Its sour odor is growing by the minute." Gabriel punctuated this statement with an exaggerated cough.

Maxwell picked up a long, gnarled branch that had fallen across the path and used it as a walking stick. He worked hard to project a disinterested calm while his emotions surged and raged. Gruesome images and compulsions infected his thoughts, turning his long-held beliefs on their heads until from this confusion, he blurted out, "The world ends, Gabriel. According to many myths, it has ended and been reborn hundreds of times."

"There is no rebirth after the darkness is unleashed again. That is why it's imperative we contain it and the ideas it spreads."

Maxwell set his jaw and took one breath after another to quell his anger— or maybe not his anger but this thing he'd consumed. He paused to look at the water making its way toward the rapids downstream. He skipped a rock along the gently flowing river, which hid a strong undercurrent. The sight of water usually calmed him but not today. Instead a sinister voice whispered to him, making a good case for why Maxwell shouldn't care about his world anymore.

"Why should you worry about my world's destruction?" Maxwell said, surprised by how threatening he sounded. "Didn't you once tell me that humankind and nearly every life on Earth was born because of space trash? That we were . . . How did you put it after a few Coca-Colas?" Maxwell made a show of trying to remember, when he recalled the man's words as clear as if he'd heard them minutes ago. "Ah, yes . . . 'organic material disposed in the vastness of space by a race residing in another part of the galaxy. This waste then took root on this planet like a fungus.'"

"Touché. But I also mentioned that this fungus has shown incredible possibilities, which is why my government had agreed to fund us to study and protect life on this planet." Gabriel tried to wipe the muck from his shoes on a sharp rock and failed.

Maxwell snorted. "If by possibilities, you mean finding infinite ways to torture each other and destroy the planet, then yes, we are indeed incredible."

His grip tightened on the improvised walking stick. The bark cut into his hands. "I will no longer let Earth be your testing grounds. Maybe it's time for the human race to die off and for a new one to take its place."

As soon as he said it, he sucked in a breath. These weren't his words or his voice. Or was it the truth from beliefs buried deep in his soul that this alien energy was forcing to the surface?

"That is not you talking." Gabriel reached inside his jacket for his revolver.

Maxwell's vision grayed out. The forest's vibrant greens faded to a sepia tone.

In with the good air, out with the bad.

His hands numbed. Not only his hands, but his arms, his shoulders, his chest. He couldn't feel his body. Couldn't make his limbs move even as Gabriel withdrew his gun.

His walking stick raised in defense. But it wasn't Maxwell lifting it. His knuckles had turned white as he fought against this force possessing him.

His body whipped around to gain momentum, and he slammed the branch into Gabriel's shoulder before he could shoot. The alien lost his balance and tumbled down the embankment, hitting his head against a jagged rock before slipping into the river. In seconds, the current carried his limp body downstream where it disappeared under the surface.

The haze cleared. Yellow sunlight filtered once again through the green leaves. Maxwell wagged his head.

"What have I done?" He dropped the branch. His body shook. Tears rolled down his cheeks, and he swiped them away.

He couldn't help Gabriel now, but there was still time to save the rest. "Get it together. You need to end this. Make it right."

He sprinted toward his cabin. Gabriel hadn't asked about the predictions Maxwell had written in his altered state, and now that alien would never know. He'd transcribed several predictions, which he thought important for his family's and humankind's future. No one, not even Gabriel or the Three, could read the text inside the Dark's diary unless they were possessed by the same corrupted spirit that Maxwell had channeled to pen it.

The aliens would never know the world's salvation had nothing to do with advanced computer technology or defense. Inside select humans lay a hidden potential to lead the world away from the darkness.

Maxwell only regretted that he wouldn't be there to ensure it happened. Because not only did these special humans hold the keys to salvation but also the keys to corruption. If this alien entity infected them or fed on their unique energy, it would be unstoppable.

The trail ended at a clearing where his log cabin stood. There he found two muscle-bound men and one Amazonian woman—the Three—standing on the porch. He never knew their true names. Doubted he could pronounce them anyway. Just like the title of their group, the Organization. The aliens used common human references for themselves and their establishments. Gabriel claimed it was to make it more relatable for the few humans who knew about them.

Maxwell believed they hid behind these simple names for protection. They didn't want people to know how powerful their band of aliens really were.

The Three held their hands folded in front of them. Sunglasses shaded their eyes. Perspiration glistened against their light brown foreheads. They wore black suits, white crisp linen shirts, and shiny wingtip loafers. The men had dark hair parted evenly on the side, cut within an inch of their collar. Even the woman, standing dead center, wore the garb of man. But her hair was red, the color of rotting carrots, and cut into a short pixie style.

"Afternoon," Maxwell called out in his most calm, pleasant voice.

"Where is Gabriel?" the woman asked, her face as devoid of emotion as her voice.

"He was a bit overheated. He needed to cool off." With long strides, Maxwell cut through the vegetable garden toward the wooden steps.

"What did you do to him?" Her neutral tone cracked. His heart raced at her underlying threat.

"I didn't do anything." He forced a smile.

The woman grabbed her spouses' hands. A warm wave of power ebbed past him. They were seeking out Gabriel.

Maxwell bounded up the creaky wooden steps to where the Three stood as sentinels.

"He's alive but unconscious," she reported then released her spouses' hands.

He let out a relieved breath at her news. He hadn't killed his old friend.

"But he told us what you've done." They sniffed the air in unison. Their lips curled in response to whatever foulness they detected.

He motioned between the woman and her husband standing at left. "If you'll let me pass, I'll give you want you came for."

"We searched. The Dark's journal is not inside." the woman replied without heeding his request to move. "Nor is its vessel."

Maxwell stared over her shoulder. Through the screen door behind them, he found the furniture tossed and turned. Floorboards were bent up. A hurricane would've left less damage.

The woman reached inside her jacket. Maxwell shuffled back with his eyes glued to the glimmering dagger she withdrew from a holster at her side. The blade was longer than a bowie knife with a tip that formed a spout similar to the pourers jammed into liquor bottles.

"What is that for?" he asked as a voice whispered from the far corners of his brain. *To bind us.*

"We need the vessel and the journal." She held up the blade either in a threat or to display its details so Maxwell would understand its full intent.

A crease appeared down the center of the blade, lined by alien lettering etched into the metal. Near the dagger's handle were two half circles large enough to wrap around a small bottle, like the one that held the Dark.

He got the picture.

"It's in my basement lab," he lied. "I'm hoping you haven't trashed that space like you did my living room."

"We have not searched there yet," she said.

"One bright spot in this day," he mumbled. "May I?" He nodded to the room over her shoulder.

She slid to the side as the two men stood back and let him pass.

"Care for a drink?" Maxwell pressed passed the Three and picked his way into his disheveled home.

"The journal and the vessel," she replied.

He watched where he stepped, careful not to land his bare feet on any glass. He vaulted over the couch and to the liquor cabinet bolted to the floor. "Are you certain I can't pour you a drink? It'll make this much easier."

"No," they said in unison.

"Suit yourself."

If Gabriel wasn't willing to take the chance, then Maxwell would. After experiencing what that darkness did to him with a small taste, he couldn't let it stay here to corrupt another and possibly destroy the world.

In with the good air, out with the bad.

The Dark's energy had waned since it had taken over, as if it had used up its strength to launch the attack on Gabriel. He hoped that would give him time to set his plan into motion.

He took another calming breath, calling forth his positive qi to keep the darkness at bay.

In with the good air, out with the bad.

Instinct told him that he had only one chance before the Dark realized what he was doing.

In with the good air, out with the bad.

Bending down, he opened the door to the liquor cabinet.

He didn't trust Gabriel or the Three to keep it safe from the Organization. Having experienced firsthand the possessive power of its contents, he wanted to remove this force far from his universe to save the next generation.

He reached past the tall vodka and rum bottles and pushed open a secret compartment that held a silver martini shaker. A static shock snapped against his fingertips. An icy sensation encased his hand, wrapping up his arm. Unfazed, he opened the shaker and a green bottle slid out.

"We don't have time for this. The longer it stays inside you, the worse this becomes for all of us," the woman said from behind him.

She moved near the dinette, clutching the handle of the blade. Along its silver surface, the alien letters glowed with a soft yellow.

"I want one last drink of my secret stash to lessen the pain." He ran his fingers along the unearthly hieroglyphics cut into the smoky green glass that kept the power contained and undetected. The ancient cork had an M wrapped in a Celtic design burned into the top. Once he uncorked it, he needed to drink it quickly before the Three sensed it or else his plan would be exposed.

He could do this. He *had* to do this to make his world safe.

Holding the bottle close to his body, he watched the woman's reflection in the window.

"What are you holding?" she demanded. The two men, larger than she by half a foot in width, flanked her sides, effectively blocking his exits.

Maxwell reached inside his pants where he had secured the journal to his waist by a linen cloth. Keeping the fabric wrapped around it, he held it over his shoulder.

"Give it to me." She started toward him.

Using his teeth, he pulled out the cork, spit it out, and shot down the cold, oily fluid.

"Stop!" she screamed.

He let the fabric slip. His bare fingers touched the leather binding for the first time since he'd ingested the alien oil a month ago.

The floorboards creaked behind him then . . . nothing. No sound, not even his own breath or heartbeat, which had been thudding in his chest when he shot down the swill. His eyes closed, but he could see everything. In front, behind, above, and even below his feet through the floor and into the dirt cellar, past the spiders spinning webs and the scurrying mice, and farther under the ground where worms crawled over long-buried animal bones, above the rooms making up his hidden lab and bunker. He shook his head, trying to bring his focus back to the cabin's room and onto the trio about to strike.

Time had stopped inside the cabin. The woman's long-fingered hands were wrapped around the handle of the knife ready to plunge it into his back. Her two meatheads had frozen with arms wide, hands pushing aside tables and lamps to tackle him. The furniture was suspended in mid-fall, the side table pitched on two legs, the lamp about to crash to the floor.

The bottle floated at chest level. A small amount of liquid remained inside. He hadn't consumed it all before his hand had released it and the world stopped.

The book vibrated against his palms, stirring to life.

In the window's reflection, he watched black oil bleed across his eyes. He wailed over the crushing darkness seeping into every pore. His body shook. Legs giving out, his knees hit the floor. He winced against the pain that didn't come.

Slowly he stood again. No, his body stood. He was no longer in control.

Outside the window, in the woods past the clearing, Stephen peered over the branches of a sapling. Maxwell's hand raised and the teen flew back, yanked by an invisible rope deep into the woods and out of sight.

No! He tried to scream.

The sound ricocheted inside his mind, never reaching his lips. His spirit shoved itself out to his limbs. He issued a strangled sound. The lamp fell, shattered. The table banged onto the floor. The tip of the woman's blade pushed into his back before the scene froze again.

He stepped forward, and the blade slid from his back. He pivoted to face the redhead. Using the book, he knocked the weapon from her hand. No sooner had the knife clattered to the floor than the book purred like a tiny engine under his palms. A black smoky funnel extended from the journal's leather binding. The mini-tornado remained small at first, no wider than his forearm, but with each ragged breath he took, the funnel grew. A pungent scent of incense overtook his nose, burning down his windpipe to his lungs.

The spirit possessing him cursed in an alien tongue and tried to release Maxwell's grip from the book, but it was too late. His palms were glued to it, unable to let go. Nothing could stop the book from opening the portal—not even the evil power inside him.

Maxwell should've been scared of what he was witnessing. The unfolding scene was from a horror film. It was nothing he'd ever seen before or wanted to see again. But he knew this was the only way to protect his people, and this notion of sacrifice allayed his fears.

The vortex grew larger than a basketball. Its mouth spiraled toward the woman. He watched in wide-eyed wonder as her fingers stretched to an unnatural length before the portal sucked her inside. The two men's heads and necks elongated into the expanding vortex like rubber bands. Their bodies appeared as an image on Silly Putty pulled to its limit.

The frenetic force tugged at Maxwell, first at his fingers then his arms, before his limbs bent unnaturally into the void. His body stretched until he didn't think it could stretch any farther without snapping apart. Then his surroundings dropped away and he was in another place.

Different but the same.

Chapter 2

Frederick, Maryland
January, Current Year

Kali Bordeaux considered herself to be part ostrich. She was certain of it. Her long legs, long neck, and tendency to bury her head during bad situations all pointed to her being related to the largest fowl.

Case in point: for the past three and a quarter weeks, she'd remained hidden inside DERST CEO Max Martin's not-so-humble abode, avoiding the paparazzi that multiplied outside his estate like bunnies with big, pointy cameras—horny for a story.

If she squinted through the living room window and peered between the evergreens, past branches weighed down with snow, she could make out the electric blue *Real Life Reality* media van. It hadn't moved since the night Max and Kali had disappeared when filming the web series' holiday special at her mom's house.

As far as Kali knew, no one had witnessed her popping them away, using her Quantum Transference ability (Q-T for short), and no one outside her work—even her family—knew about her ability to travel to an alternate universe (alt-jump). The cameras had caught them entering her mom's study but not exiting. Most viewers theorized they'd used a secret passage to escape.

Her mother, Deandra Bourdeaux, C-list reality web star, was staying mum on Kali's abilities, and she hoped it was because Deandra, her guests, and the production crew didn't recall what happened after she'd followed Max into the alternate universe and the world reset.

Of course, there were the rumors splashed over the tabloids, speculating she was a transhuman (human with special abilities) after an intrepid web entertainment reporter uncovered that she worked for UltraSecurity (U-Sec)—a security firm that partnered with law agencies to solve transhuman crimes. They hadn't yet pieced together that she was UltraAgent TimeTrap, which she found odd given the Internet gossip sites, but she didn't care to tempt fate by questioning why. She knew it was only a matter of time before they ousted her.

Fortunately, she'd only worked a handful of jobs for U-Sec since she'd developed her powers, and had Q-T'd in front of non-transhumans (N-Ts) only a few times. Those who had witnessed her ability had to sign an NDA per her boss Pax. Considering his intimidating appearance and take-no-prisoners personality, no one had ever refused or broken the NDA.

She ran her hand across the glass wall. It tinted gray, cutting her off from the world and the world from her.

"Snap out of it, Kali. You can't stay here forever," she said, as she'd told herself each day since the Evil Incident occurred and sent her burrowing under Max's high-thread-count cotton sheets.

She hugged herself to stop from shaking. The longer she stood facing the dull gray glass, the tighter she squeezed.

"You need to tell him about the inci—" she sputtered.

Clearing her throat, she tried again, "The inci—"

Alluding to it made her throat constrict as if she were allergic to the word, the idea. How could she give Max details of what she'd experienced in the other universe if she couldn't utter the nondescript word "incident" out loud?

"Just tell him what you saw," she whispered. "You can do it. For your own sanity, you need to."

Kali spun around in her plush *Star Wars* Chewbacca slippers and strutted with as much confidence as the comfy yet unwieldy slippers would afford her to the basement door leading to his lab.

After several deep breaths, she plunged down the stairs past his formal family portraits, past photos of Max shaking hands with politicians that segued into ones of his father posing with Ronald Reagan and finally into black and white pictures of his grandfather standing between the Kennedy brothers. The photos' eyes watched her descend, knowing her secret and judging—she was sure—her suitability for Max.

She reached the basement lab and paused. Her heart danced a jig when she saw him. Of course, it could be the fault of the Willie Nelson song he was playing that segued into a catchy fiddle-heavy tune by a band she didn't recognize, but which she was growing to like.

Am I starting to enjoy country music?

"You got it bad, babe." She shook her head and watched his fingers tapping across the keyboard of a laptop.

He sucked on his bottom lip, telling her that he was focused on the task. His light eyebrows were drawn down. Shoulders tense under his green hoodie, he hunched over his metal work table. He paused, cracked his knuckles then tilted his head from side to side, and cracked his neck.

He turned up the music, not noticing Kali standing there as she argued with herself whether to tell him about the Evil Incident or to make out with him. Because the latter would certainly relieve her tension. The former, not so much.

She took another fortifying breath then forced it out, blowing the bangs off her forehead. She would tell him. No matter what, she would force the words out. He had to understand why she was acting neurotic, clingy, agoraphobic. Why she refused to use her power for a quick pop to her condo to get toiletries and undies and clothes. Instead she wore his shirts and ordered personal items online. The one time they did leave his place, they used the underground tunnel from his garage that let out on the other side of his property to avoid the paparazzi, only to encounter them surrounding her building in downtown Baltimore.

If she would get over her dread and use her power, then she could transport herself anywhere in the world—or anytime in the past in a universe parallel to hers. No one had to know where she was. But she'd be alone because Max couldn't leave his job right now—something about a project deadline or meeting or whatever. And she'd rather be with someone she trusted than alone. Right now, being alone would be the second-worst-case scenario.

The first . . . well, that had already occurred.

Max was in the small group of those she could trust. In fact, he topped the list, since he had been kidnapped by the same alt-traveling douchebag that had taken her.

Kali squared her shoulders.

Ready or not. Here I go.

She made herself take that first step toward Max. The second wasn't as hard. Only fifty left to go.

Chapter 3

Same Place and Time, Different Perspective

Glen,
I'm the one who's deaf and you're the one who doesn't fucking listen.

Max began his reply to his best friend and DERST CFO, Glen Triman, before he deleted his words with hard tap, tap, taps. He could already picture Glen laughing when he read the message, amused that he had gotten his friend riled up enough to curse in an email. He always could agitate Max better than most, except for Glen's sister Mia, who had a particular talent for being annoying.

Glen,
I'm not interested in overseeing the Unicorn project. My priorities have changed.

Max paused and rubbed his temples. These words didn't sound right either. He needed a stronger reason if Glen were to accept Max bowing out of DERST's new multibillion-dollar bid. Glen had promised the client—and his board—that Max would be the project manager, and they wanted a better answer than he was too busy to helm it.

His friend wasn't stupid. He'd seen the web news. He knew what—or more precisely who—was keeping Max busy.

Glen,
I'm practicing tantric sex with my new girlfriend. We are constantly buck naked, in case the mood strikes. Your coming here would be awkward—

Of course, Glen would congratulate himself in finally getting Max out of his basement lab and laid.

Delete, delete, delete.

In his latest email, Glen had insisted on coming to Max's home to discuss his excuses and to meet his primary excuse in person. His flight would arrive tomorrow morning—from some defense industry conference or another—and he promised to drive straight to his friend's home for a conversation Max planned to skip, even it if meant hiding like a passive aggressive idiot in his basement.

Glen,
I know the BS Force is strong with you, but I won't fall for its odoriferous power this time.

Glen's father, Gabriel Triman, joked that his son wielded a silver tongue. Max called it Glen's Bullshit Force. He could never say "no" to Glen—a fact his friend had exploited since they were young, and which landed him in trouble more times than not. Although Glen's uncanny power had pushed Max to go in his place to the *Real Life* dinner where he met Kali.

So Glen could use the BS Force indirectly for good.

Max's eyes drifted from the screen to the ceiling as if he could see through it to his bedroom above where he'd left Kali sleeping. The past few days saw deeper cracks appearing in her perky veneer. When she thought he wasn't looking, her eyes would glaze over, her lips pressed tight as if trying not to get sick.

Whatever happened when she traveled to the alternate universe to save Max had frozen her ability. She danced around the specifics when he broached the subject and claimed she needed a vacation to reset her mojo. He didn't argue when she chose his home to rest, and he wasn't about to press her to explain why.

After the explosion at the DERST lab that damaged his eardrums, he hadn't wanted to discuss the traumatic event either. It took him months to confide in Glen, his oldest friend, how scared and impotent he'd felt after the accident. He'd awoken from his month-long coma to find the world had changed. However, it didn't take him long to realize that he was the one who had changed.

The world was the same selfish, violent place. His deafness reminded him of the fragility of life. How important it was to fund projects that could help people live life to the fullest instead of cutting it short. He wanted to create technology that could advance the human race.

And not abuse technology to hurt people and disrupt lives as that alt-traveler, who had ripped Max and others from this universe, had done. This man then locked them into cells for purposes still unknown to Max before the universe reset with Kali's help, righting their timeline and returning everyone safely home.

She'd done enough to save the world and earn this respite and earn the right to *not* relive the conflict if she didn't want to.

She hadn't been sleeping well this past week. He'd felt her toss and turn and woke to find her crying in her sleep. If her dreams distressed her, then talking about it would be worse, and he didn't want to cause her more pain.

Which is probably why he'd put off telling her the truth about what he'd been designing in this lab before they met.

Glen,
I need time. She needs to hear from me personally about what we've been working on.

Max deleted the sentence and hung his head in disgust.

He'd been waiting for the perfect time to tell her, but no time seemed perfect for what he had to say about DERST's recent deliverables. Max had led the team that built three Transhuman Protection Chambers (TPCs) for the DoD's Unicorn Project. Yesterday, he'd learned from the contractor grapevine that two of their units had housed Kali's best friend, UltraAgent Surefire, and her partner Raven in suspended animation before a rogue transhuman had released them.

After their in-house engineers had made a few modifications, the client had called for an expanded deliverable with multiple units for use in a secured facility being built at an undisclosed location.

From what Max could guess from their initial proposal, they were building a transhuman prison.

Glen,
I am recusing myself from the job. Conflict of interest—

He sucked on his bottom lip as he deleted *conflict of interest.* It wasn't as if he were making love to an extraordinary woman in need of being contained. She used her power for good. A prison wasn't a bad idea for some transhumans—like the dimensional traveler who'd kidnapped Max.

So why did he feel guilty?

He shook his head in disgust at his attempt to evade the truth. He knew why he felt guilty. He should just ask Kali if the rumors were true—if someone had captured Surefire and Raven and locked them in units like the ones he'd made.

Yet he clammed up every time he tried to ask her about it, and the longer he waited, the more she slipped into her current depressed state that she'd tried yet failed to hide from him.

He hadn't meant to hurt Kali's friends. He wasn't the one who'd flipped the switch on the TPC. Is the person who built the gun responsible if it's used for murder?

He rubbed the tense muscles at the base of his neck but he couldn't massage away his guilt. He'd taken the job for its big payoff. Mr. Triman, who in addition to being Glen's father was also a DERST board member, had landed this lucrative contract and allowed Max to earmark funds for non-defense projects if he took it on. It enabled him to green light personal projects that could help people live better lives.

Now he was experiencing a crisis of conscience like his grandfather had written about in his journals. Wanting to repent for the weapons he'd designed, Max's grandfather left DERST behind in the 1960s to travel the world looking for enlightenment. He then started a commune of which Max's father and grandmother never spoke about and ordered Max to keep secret. It was an embarrassing chapter for the family and DERST. The family patriarch seeking peace when he'd made millions from a company designed to support war.

Oddly enough, it was in the last pages of his grandfather's second journal, which contained New Age philosophies, where Max had found the plans for the dark energy reader that could pick up Kali's alt-jumps. He also applied these principles to the engineering plans, provided by the client for the tech used in the containment units that shipped out last year, including the prototype locked away in a secure room less than twenty feet from where he sat staring the computer screen.

Right under Kali's feet.

Despite this project being classified, he needed to tell her. No, he wanted to tell her. She deserved to know what he'd been working on. But first, he'd verify how the other units had been used, and if they were the ones her friends had been held in. Max wasn't sure if he'd be privy to this info, but it was worth a shot. Then he'd find out the rules for letting Kali know so DERST didn't get sued.

That was what he'd tell Glen. He needed more information and assurance that it wouldn't be used on law-abiding transhumans. If he didn't like the answers—he'd quit.

But would it be smart to quit? Someone else would take the contract and make that prison.

He let out a frustrated sigh as more pro and con arguments bounced around his brain.

Then again, maybe it was better that Max helmed this project. Then maybe he could ensure the end deliverable wasn't being used on the wrong transhumans.

Wrong transhumans? He groaned as this thought crossed his mind. Who was he to decide who were the wrong ones?

He cracked his fingers and popped his neck, relieving the tension and releasing the right words. He'd be honest with Glen—about his guilt, the moral dilemma of this job, and most of all, the woman who made him reconsider what he'd done and was about to do. He owed his friend that, even if Glen would worry about what Max was about to tell him.

Glen,
I'm falling hard. She's saved me literally and figuratively. And I can't in good conscience work this job until I have the specifics and assurance it won't be used for harm but protection as its name states. However, first she needs to know—

Max stopped typing. The hairs on his arms stood on end. A light tickle like a feather trailed over his neck. He slammed his laptop shut, cutting off the Dixie Chicks in mid-harmony, and jumped up to face Kali approaching him. She strutted past the large work table with the confidence of a model working the runway, wearing the slippers he bought her as a gag Christmas gift with as much love as if they were expensive Jimmy Choos. His vintage *Star Wars* shirt barely hung to her thigh. Blue leggings adorned with constellations hugged her long, lean legs.

She smiled at him, but it didn't reach her eyes. Something was wrong. His fingers fumbled to find his phone and turn up the volume on his hearing aids.

"Hello, you." He drew her close, hoping he could anticipate her problem. Maybe he could fix it. Save her as she'd saved him. "I thought you were still asleep."

He kissed her forehead. She was cool to the touch.

She pulled back. Her gazed dropped from his face to the middle of his sweatshirt. A fleeting smile crossed her lips at the drawing of a hammer on his sweatshirt with the words "This is not a drill" underneath.

"We need . . . " she paused to inhale a chest-expanding breath "to talk."

He studied her face for a sign that she knew what he'd been writing to Glen. "Are you okay?"

"Yes and no."

Maybe it wasn't that. Maybe it was something he'd done to upset her.

"If you're not happy here—"

"Oh, no, no. Here is happiness, trust me."

Her hands framed his face. A gesture he found both intimate and reassuring.

"But I need to tell you about the"—she inhaled another deep breath then pushed it out along with a word—"incident. What happened to me in the other universe."

Her palms trembled against his cheek. It pained him to see her that hurt, that afraid, a far cry from the feisty woman he'd met on the reality show set.

He turned his head to kiss her palm and encourage her to speak. "If you're ready, I'm here for you."

He lowered her hands. Keeping them wrapped in his, he perched on the table and waited for her to speak.

She sighed. "Why do you have to be this way?"

"What way?" he asked, worried he'd upset her, until the corner of her lips quirked up.

"So sweet." Her shoulders relaxed. She pressed her body against his and whispered, "And thoughtful." She kissed his cheek. "And sincere." She kissed the tip of his nose. "And handsome." She ran the tip of her tongue along his bottom lip. "And so sexy."

Max slid onto the table as she leaned into him. He pushed aside his laptop.

Not that he was complaining about her changing the topic, but he had to ask, despite his body telling him to shut up, "Thought you wanted to talk?"

"Later." Her lips crushed his in a desperate desire that melted away the world, leaving only the two of them.

Cool fingers slid under his hoodie as her tongue slid into his mouth. His hands ran over her soft cotton leggings and massaged her thighs before rising to hook his fingers into the waistband. Kali unbuttoned his jeans. He groaned into their kiss as she pulled down his underwear and wrapped her hands around him.

She broke from his lips to shed her shirt, revealing bare breasts. He took a nipple into his mouth and sucked harder when she gasped. He pushed down the waist of her leggings, and she wriggled out of them before kicking them aside. She shoved him onto his back as he scooted onto the table. His arm swiped aside wires, circuit boards, computer chips. She straddled him. He put his hands on her hips to hold her in place, guide her motions. But she knew how to satisfy him, make him cry out for more. How to make him burst with need until he couldn't hold back any longer.

After they were both spent, she gave him a long, satisfying kiss then rolled off him and slid his laptop farther away so she could lie next to him.

"I didn't mean for that to happen," she panted.

"I'd love to see it when you do."

She smacked his arm. "You know what I mean."

He retrieved his pants from the floor. "So, where were we?"

"Where were we, what?" She grabbed the shirt from the chair where she'd tossed it.

"You wanted to talk about what happened to you." He pulled up his pants.

The shirt covered her face as she slid it on. She replied through the fabric, "Later."

"It is later." He tugged on the shirt until her head popped through the hole.

"Later-er." Her forehead puckered as if trying to recall if that was a word. She slid her feet into the slippers.

"You're busy." She nodded to his laptop. "And I interrupted."

"Never an interruption if it's you." He grinned at the cheesiness of the line.

"Aren't you just a sweet daddy-o?" She gave him a peck on the cheek. "But seriously, babe. You got work. I got . . . well . . . work or whatever it is that Sean wants from me"—her hands flapped, emulating two fidgeting birds—"since I bailed on TransGen's last project for good reason."

"You're going home?"

"Can't stay here." She shrugged, avoiding his eyes.

"Why not?"

She laughed. Not the happy-go-lucky sound she made when she watched Monty Python with him. This laugh rung with a nervous uncertainty.

"Why not?" she repeated, more to herself as if to buy time to think of an answer.

"That's my question." Max hopped onto the table.

"And a good question for sure. But seriously, you know the answer." She crossed her arms as if to restrain her hands from more nervous flapping.

He waited, not because he liked to see her squirm, but because he hoped the longer she talked, the more likely she'd let it slip. While she was caught off guard, her defenses down, maybe he'd learn the truth.

She stared over his shoulder, and he jerked around to follow her gaze. For a second, he feared the door to the storage room, where he kept his prototypes and classified projects, had been left open.

But when she sighed and said, "It's way too early for a drink to help me say what I want to say," he knew she was looking at the bottles of liquor lined against the backsplash of the corner kitchenette.

"But oddly enough, I haven't been in the mood to drink anything stronger than tea, so there's that." She flopped into his desk chair and scooted closer until her arm rested on his knee.

"What's wrong?" he asked.

"I'll tell you, but it won't be pretty."

Max brushed soft strands of hair from her face. "I'm listening."

He waited, giving her time to compose her thoughts.

When a tear slid down her cheek, he touched her hand, hoping to comfort her.

"All right, here goes." She pulled away and scrubbed a palm down her face then continued, "I was fine at first, after going to the other universe to save you and experiencing the"—her lips quivered, as if having trouble forming the words—"Evil Incident."

"Evil Incident?" This was the first time Max had heard her say these words.

"It's what I've been calling it so I could keep it generic and not think too deeply about it." She lifted a shoulder.

"I don't know what to say." He ran his fingers through his hair, scratching his scalp. "I mean we made love in my grandfather's VW bus that night. I would never have done anything like that if I didn't think you weren't well."

"It's okay." She rubbed her hand along his chest, trying to calm him now.

"No, it's not." Had he been so blind desiring to be with her that he didn't notice she was dealing with something so traumatic? He felt like a complete ass. "It wasn't until a week later that I noticed something may be bothering you."

"I was hopped up on adrenaline right after. That kept me feeling peachy keen for a short time. As the week progressed, what I experienced sunk in. I couldn't un-see what I saw."

"And what did you see?" he prompted when she closed her eyes and went so still he couldn't see the rise and fall of her chest.

"Me." She swallowed.

He tried to process what she'd said, but his mind was stuck on this illogical statement.

"You saw you?" he clarified.

She nodded, her face turned from him, eyes shut, tears leaking down her cheeks.

She sniffed then added, "I was in a coffin."

"You were dead?"

"No, although I know that other Kali wished she was because she was me, and I know what I'd be thinking in that situation." She squeezed his leg as if it grounded her.

"It's confusing." Her bangs flipped across her brow as she shook her head. "There was another version of me—the second Kali, let's call her S-Kali for short—and another version of events that occurred previously in our universe. S-Kali went to that *Real Life* dinner, just like I did, but it was uneventful and afterward she alt-jumped to 1969 in the parallel universe I . . . she . . . whatever . . . sometimes visit. The man"—she paused, and Max got the impression she was rephrasing her word choice—"who is the Mack daddy of baddies then captured S-Kali in that universe and stuck her in a glass coffin with this disgusting oily slime—seriously, Slimer from *Ghostbusters* would've been grossed out—and siphoned off her mojo. Somehow he transferred S-Kali's power into a pack that his henchman, Stockwell, wore. It let him alt-jump like I do."

Her eyes moved from side to side, as if watching a scene play out in her mind before she said, "When Stockwell showed up to kidnap you at the *Real Life* dinner, he screwed up the timelines. I didn't make the jump after dinner because I was too busy rescuing you. And since I didn't make the jump, they never captured me and/or S-Kali, and Stockwell never stole my mojo to travel here. It caused a paradox. As soon as I encountered S-Kali, our universe reset as well as theirs.

"I only wished it reset my memories too. Because I still see S-Kali. Every time I close my eyes, she stares at me from behind that oily grossness."

If someone x-rayed Max's chest, they'd find his heart had split in two as he heard this news. He was at a loss for what to do and what to say. After Stockwell's failed kidnapping attempt at dinner, he then came to Max's house and took him. When they reached the other universe, the alt-traveler had thrown a sack over Max's head then locked him in a dark room. He hadn't heard any names or had time to register where he was before that room faded away, and he was sitting at the dining room table at the *Real Life* dinner with Kali at his side and no alt-traveler exploding the chandelier.

Max wanted to avenge Kali. He wanted to beat Stockwell to a pulp to find out why he did it, who he was working for. At the same time, he wanted to hold Kali and soothe her. But the way she maintained a distance between them, he sensed she didn't want to be touched. Not yet.

Needing to do something, he bolted to the kitchenette and grabbed a box of tissues. It was a lame gesture in the bigger horror-filled picture. Here she was describing a nightmarish experience, and all he could do was give her tissues.

"You saved her. She doesn't exist anymore," Max said as he handed her the box.

"Yeah, I saved her . . . myself . . ." She waved the box in the air. "But she still exists in my mind."

She took out a tissue then blew her nose. He stayed silent, waiting for her to finish, not wanting to interrupt her. Because he could hear in her voice that's what she needed right now. Not platitudes or ineffectual words of support but someone to listen, share the burden.

"I don't even know how long she was in that thing," she continued after blowing her nose a second time. "She said it'd been five years since she was captured. Then a week ago, random images started popping in my head. I thought I was making them up. Like I'd fallen asleep during a movie and could only recall pieces of dialogue and scenes. But they felt real, as real as anything that had happened to me, and these bits of memories showed me that they'd been experimenting on her for three years before they found a design that worked."

Max turned to the table behind him, pretending to sort through the items strewn on top. In reality, he didn't want her to sense his anger, his fear, and his guilt over what she'd revealed to him. If he thought long and hard enough— which he didn't want to do—he would see that the guilt came from wondering what experiments on transhumans had led to the tweaks the client had sent to his team for the TPCs in the Unicorn Project.

"Who did this to you? Who was Stockwell working for?" He looked at her again when he could keep his face neutral enough not to show the emotions tearing up his insides.

She dropped her gaze to the used tissues clutched in her hands. "I don't know. But he's still there, and I won't travel to the alternate universe as long as there's a chance that he's alive. S-Kali warned me never to go back."

"Then you know it was a man."

"Yeah, S-Kali mentioned it was the . . ." She wrung her hands. "Umm . . . a man. Didn't have time to get a name."

"He'll never hurt you again. I promise."

She offered him a sad smile as if she wanted to believe him but couldn't. "I know he won't because I'm not going there again. I made that promise to myself. I don't need you to protect me in this. What you did by listening to me at this moment, that's what I needed. I've never had a boyfriend do this for me before. Just listen. It's kind of weird, really. In a good way."

Slouching in the chair, she laughed.

"Surprisingly, I feel better. Not much, mind you." She rubbed the corners of her eyes then wiped her palms down both cheeks. "But a smallish anvil has been lifted . . ."

She trailed off and stood in front of Max, who was quick to don a hopeful, I'm-glad-you're-okay smile. At least that's what he assumed his smile conveyed, but when the edges of her lips drooped with worry, he knew his acting chops weren't good enough to cover up how he felt.

"Oh, I upset you, didn't I? Maybe I shouldn't have told you." She hugged him so hard his stiff back popped.

"Man, you're tense." She rubbed his shoulders.

Max's hands closed around hers to stop her. He wanted her to focus on what he was about to say.

"No, you needed to tell me. I wanted you to tell me. You shouldn't have to carry this burden alone." His words weren't as supportive as he wanted them to sound. His thoughts led him elsewhere. A voice in the back of his mind kept needling him about a question Kali had left unanswered.

"You mentioned S-Kali being held in a glass coffin. Was she in suspended animation?"

She shook her head.

"As I said, the thing was filled with a liquid that covered her body but she was awake." She flicked her fingers as if flicking off the goo. "A mask covered her face, allowing her to breathe. Tubes fed her and another one took her blood to synthesize her power. At least, that's what S-Kali told me before that version of the parallel universe collapsed."

"Would you describe it as a type of containment unit?" He held his breath, hoping against hope he was wrong. When her head bobbed in agreement, his heart sank into his gut.

"It was built using 1970s tech. Not as advanced as the units that held Surefire and Raven, which we originally thought were cryo chambers, but found they were something way more than that because the machines syphoned their blood to isolate their . . . Hey, that does sound like what happened to S-Kali!" She tapped a finger against her lip then tilted her head at him. "Did I tell you about what happened to my friends at Dama X's island? Because that's a whole other story and actually involves DERST and why Sean wanted so badly to meet with you at the *Real Life* dinner."

Max's mouth went dry. "Really?"

"Don't look so guilty. You didn't do anything wrong." She kissed the top of his head. "It's not like you're responsible for drugging Surefire and Raven and locking them inside those things. Let me get you some coffee. Strong coffee. Because this will take a while."

Chapter 4

The Morning After

"I don't deserve you," Kali whispered to the man sleeping next to her.

She flipped onto her side to fully face her dreamy love. His leg draped over hers as he slept on his stomach, his arm extended, his fingers grazing her forearm.

This was the first night since days after the Evil Incident that she'd slept straight through without bolting awake from a nightmare. One where she was S-Kali stuck in the oil-filled glass chamber unable to break free. Like a well-fed cow, she was kept juiced up on hormones to produce the maximum amount of milk. Except she wasn't producing milk, but blood containing special proteins from her DNA that made her a time-traveling transhuman.

Until she spoke about it, she hadn't made the connection to what happened to S-Kali to how they'd discovered Surefire and Raven hooked up to a similar blood-synthesizing device.

She shuddered and snuggled closer to Max and his warmth. Last night, it was a relief to talk about the EI—as she now referred to the Evil Incident. The abbreviation lessened its hold over her. But she didn't fool herself into thinking she had recovered. For sure, a weight had been lifted, but a satchel full of anxiety remained strapped across her shoulders.

And that stuff was heavy.

When she considered using her ability, even to travel through space within her own universe, an invisible vice would close around her neck. It would take several deep breaths, and swearing to herself that she wouldn't use her power, for the panic to subside.

Traveling to the alternate universe to see her long-gone family members was definitely right out. She'd do what non-alt-travelers did: reminisce with old videos and photos like the one propped against the lamp on the nightstand next to her side of the bed.

In the photo, her grandparents and father at fourteen stood in front of a small cabin on a commune, where they'd lived until it was disbanded not long after this photo was taken. She'd planned to alt-jump to see them in 1969 after the *Real Life* holiday dinner.

Well, not exactly those people standing in the photo, which was taken in this universe, her universe, but their dopplëgangers in the alternate one. Their appearances were the same. Their personalities were also similar. Enough that she felt a sense of peace and belonging when she visited with them. Something she hadn't felt with her mom since she was bitten with the reality web bug soon after Kali's father had died.

Alt-jumping there was the only way to see her father and grandparents again and enjoy her Pop-Pop's split pea soup, which his dopplëganger made perfectly and Kali could never get quite right. Twenty years ago, her grandparents had been killed in a car accident. A few years later, her father had suffered a heart attack. He'd had a bad ticker as her Pop-Pop would've said.

Kali had been monitored for heart issues since she'd developed her ability. One of the reasons it had taken several years for her to be released to work with U-Sec. They wanted to make sure her heart could handle it, and she didn't have a defect as her father had.

But none of that mattered now, since she was never using her power to go back to that universe, per S-Kali's warning about this mysterious "Man" waiting to capture her. And it wouldn't matter until she could get her anxiety in check so she could Q-T again.

She'd contact UltraAgent Oracle and ask what therapist her boss had seen, after her own EI landed her on a health leave for months. Of all the people at U-Sec, Oracle was the one who could offer her ways to cope.

But later.

She'd call Oracle later because now she enjoyed watching Max sleep, even though her stomach rumbled with hunger. She didn't want to get up and disturb him, disturb this perfect moment. Outside the floor-to-ceiling windows, snow continued to fall, coating the evergreens surrounding his home. Their limbs drooped with the heavy white stuff. Occasionally, big feathery flakes blew by, giving the impression they were inside a snow globe.

Max's crop of hair blended with the scene outside, his eyebrows and body hair and stubble all white. He'd gone white after the accident that took away his hearing.

He never elaborated on the details of his accident. Whenever she pressed him or, with a casual question, tried to trick him into talking about it, he shut down. Everyone had their own EIs. Considering that he'd given her space and never pressed about hers, she would do the same for him.

But it meant that she couldn't console him the same way he'd consoled her. She'd dumped a large pile of stressful pooh on him yesterday, confessing the reason for her not alt-jumping—she was afraid of getting captured again.

They'd talked into the night about her EI, and that story led into the Dama X tale. Kali figured he'd appreciate the details about that former cartel maven's high-tech island, since it had been built by Suarez Tech with help from DERST. Max's company eventually acquired Suarez Tech, long before he became CEO.

He was particularly interested in learning about UltraAgent Surefire and her boyfriend, Raven, and their powers. He'd heard the rumors that an Aztec goddess fueled their abilities. She'd confirmed the rumors but didn't reveal that Surefire's father, General Stephen St. John, was behind part of the operation to contain his daughter's power. She'd then have to disclose Surefire's real name, Synthia St. John, and it was up to her friend to decide who knew her identity.

Max had asked how this power couple's containment units looked and worked and what happened when they'd awoken Surefire and Raven. Questions she'd expected from someone who owned a defense and technology research company.

The more she talked, the more sullen he became.

"What's wrong?" She'd pressed him when he became so quiet that she'd believed his lips had been glued shut.

"It hurts to think how anyone could've done that to you or your friends. I'm sorry. Really, really sorry." He'd bowed his head while he shook it. Kali had been afraid he was going to cry. And she'd done enough crying for both of them.

"You're the sweetest." She'd kissed his forehead, her heart overflowing to see how much he cared for her, and how his feelings extended to her friends as well.

"Most wonderful, lovely person." She'd caressed his jaw to make him face her and laid a kiss on his mouth. "I'm so lucky to have you."

He'd jerked away and said, "I wish I was good enough for you."

"Don't say that." She hadn't known how else to respond. She'd assumed he somehow blamed himself for what had happened to her in the other universe. Like he'd gotten himself kidnapped on purpose.

She hadn't pressed him further, but instead had suggested a Netflix binge. But not even a round of *Mystery Science Theater 3000,* where they made fun of cheesy sci-fi films, could rouse Max from his gloomy mood.

He didn't get back to his work, which she'd interrupted that morning, until late. At midnight, she'd left him typing away on his laptop in his basement workshop. She never heard him come to bed. She assumed he'd stayed up playing video games to chill out.

Max's phone vibrated on the nightstand next to his Cybernetic Audio Implants (CAIs)—high-tech hearing aids that he would sync with his phone to hear. Usually, he'd sleep with them in. Kali assumed he'd removed them so he could rest. Considering the emotional day they'd had, she wouldn't begrudge him that pleasure.

She craned her neck to look at the phone. A photo lit up his screen of *Real Life Reality* star Mia Minx. Her lips were puckered into a duck face and . . . wait a minute . . . was she wearing a negligee?

Kali rolled her eyes. Throughout the *Real Life* holiday dinner, Mia been more interested in the Olympian sitting next to her than Max, who had escorted her there, but now that he was a pseudo celeb thanks to the mystery surrounding their disappearance from the show, she seemed eager to attach herself to him.

Underneath the photo appeared the text: *Don't you want to taste this cherry 3.13?*

Kali blinked and reread it.

Cherry 3.13? She pulled back from the phone in confusion. "What does that . . . ohhhh . . ." It took her a moment to decode what Mia was getting at. She meant pi, which would be 3.14 and some change.

Kali sighed. "Seriously, babe, stick to what you're good at."

Another text vibrated the phone. This one read, *Unlike Hon, I won't shoot first.*

She arched her brow. "I'm assuming you don't mean a Baltimore Hon but Han Solo. If you're going to win a geek's heart, do your research."

Mia was really laying it on thick. This was the first time she'd sent a sexy pic that Kali knew of. The texts over the past few weeks had been asking about Max's day or wanting to get together. He shrugged them off and either didn't respond or let Kali reply with a funny quip that became funnier when Mia didn't get the joke.

She thought about snapping a picture of her snuggling with Max, but that would be too obvious. So she grabbed his phone, snapped a photo of her armpit, with a slight growth of hair, and sent it with the caption, *Gggggaaaaaaaarrrrr. Arrrrhhhn.*

Let her figure out what that means.

As they say, don't piss off a Wookie . . . or a Kali.

She set Max's phone down and grabbed her own off the nightstand, trying not to disturb her man, who was incredibly cute in the way he insisted on touching her while he slept. After a few glasses of wine one night, he'd admitted that he didn't believe she was real. If he let her go, he was afraid she'd disappear. Her first instinct told her that he was full of it. But when he stared at her with his luscious gray-green eyes, so honest and raw, she couldn't chide him. Max didn't say what he didn't mean. She needed to get used to that.

Speaking of people who lied, Kali noticed her mom, Deandra, had left several messages. Just days after the EI, she'd wanted Kali at her house for Christmas because she "missed her."

Scratch that.

She'd wanted Kali at her house *with Max.*

Deandra had never requested that Kali bring her boyfriends before, but the *Real Life* channel would only record her Christmas day celebrations if Kali and Max were there.

She had lied to her mom and told her that she was sick, which wasn't far off since her stomach had grown increasingly queasy from her mounting anxiety with each passing day. Her mother then suggested Kali could send Max alone to her house for Christmas. When neither had shown up, Deandra then invited them for a New Year's Eve taping. Kali said Max was busy, and so he was. Busy cuddling her, making her breakfast, showing her his lab, and all the different ways they could make love in it.

Who knew a robot arm could be used for so many sexy things?

Carefully, she slid Max's leg from hers. She wriggled out from under the comforter and off the bed.

Her phone buzzed, startling her, causing her to fling it into the air. When she tried to catch it, the phone slipped from one hand to the other as if it were greased with butter. She caught it before it hit the floor and saw the number.

UltraSecurity. More specifically, Sean Vivas, one of U-Sec's owners.

She'd skipped out on helping his father, Victor Vivas, owner of TransGen—the company responsible for creating most transhumans including the accident that powered-up Kali—with a project between Christmas and New Year's.

But that wasn't why Sean was calling. Since he'd been nabbed by the alt-traveler as well, he remembered everything that had occurred, unlike those who had stayed put in this universe and time. He wanted to talk about what happened in the alternate universe to reset their timeline and land him back at the dinner in their universe, without any alt-traveler busting up the party again.

Considering that last night was the first time she'd discussed the EI with anyone, he couldn't complain that she hadn't shared the details with him yet—or written up a report to go with the overtime she'd charged U-Sec for saving Sean's butt and their universe.

An alt-traveling gal needed to make a living.

She also knew Sean wanted to talk with Max. Meeting the elusive DERST CEO was one of the reasons Sean had convinced her to attend the *Real Life—*ironically fake—holiday dinner in the first place. Of course, if she hadn't gone, she'd never be here now, snuggling with her geeky prince.

Technically, she owed Sean, but she'd never let him know that.

She sent his call to voicemail. It was a weekend. She was off the clock. Not that she was ever really on the clock. She was a freelancer, a contract employee. She made her own hours. And considering her year of battling Aztec gods, psychotic scientists, and manic magicians, a three-week holiday break was just what the doctor ordered.

Maybe longer. Could a blissful vacation be her life with Max? Could she continue avoiding the outside world and another EI by staying here with him?

He stretched, exposing his upper arm. The one with the tattoo. A logo, he'd joked, that belonged to "the Man," his grandfather's nickname, which was also the name of the evil villain who'd held S-Kali in the parallel universe in that coffin-sized tank from a Ridley Scott film.

She'd almost let slip that S-Kali had referred to her captor as the Man. It had been on the tip of her tongue, ready to tumble out. At the last second, she changed her wording. She didn't want Max to wonder if the Man in the other universe was a version of his grandfather, or if she believed his grandfather's doppelgänger could've done that to her.

She knew herself, and by default S-Kali's phrasings, well enough to know that referring to a big baddie in the '70s as "the Man" could apply to any power-hungry government or corporate tool. Besides, she'd never make an accusation that severe without evidence, especially if it would hurt someone she cared for.

She tugged on leggings then buttoned one of Max's plaid shirts over his *The Force Awakens* T-shirt, one not sold to the public but given to the movie crew. Max had connections all right, and enjoyed pop culture, which validated the argument that there was no way a sweet geek like him could have a grandfather—even in an alternate universe—who was evil.

She detoured into the bathroom to wash her face and brush her hair.

"You need to learn to trust people, babe." She pointed at her reflection in the mirror. Her skin was clearer and rosier than it had been in years. Her bedhead hair didn't look mousy anymore but glossy like a shampoo ad. Her brown eyes nearly glowed, not bloodshot and dull from the stress of peeking at the world hidden behind the curtain.

"Max is good for you. Don't screw it up." She wagged her finger at her reflection before stepping into the hall toward the kitchen.

Then she stopped and cocked her head. Max's phone vibrated against the nightstand with another incoming text. So Mia liked her armpit pic and Chewbacca quote?

Grinning, she hurried into the master suite and around the bed to the table. Then she scowled, her good mood dropping faster than acid at a Grateful Dead show.

Lighting up the phone's screen was an upshot of Mia's scantily clad body sprawled out—on Max's couch.

Kali glanced at Max and stopped herself from shaking him awake. He swore he'd never been involved with Mia. He joked about how he'd barely tolerated her since they were children.

She zoomed in on the photo, spying Max's new coffee table in the corner of it. The tabletop doubled as a computer screen that was hooked into a smart-system running the security cameras, lights, and appliances in his home. The timestamp on the table read 8:15 a.m. today.

According to Max's phone, it was 8:25 a.m.

Had Mia broken into Max's house? Was she lounging in the living room for Max to discover her?

"Oh, you messed with the wrong chick." Kali would get over her power anxiety real quick and drop Mia's lace-covered ass in the middle of the Jurassic Period. See if she could flirt her way out of that one.

Kali stormed into the hall. Lights embedded in the wood floor illuminated her warpath as she stomped to the living room.

"Are you effing . . . ?" Kali exclaimed then stopped, spun around.

The couch was empty. The glass walls were tinted gray, shading the room, unlike those in the photo, which let the light pour in. She glanced at the phone once more.

As she approached, the glass-top coffee table sprang to life with talking heads, videos of car accidents and war-torn cities, and *Real Life* celebrity updates.

"Mia!" Kali yelled.

She peeked in the closet and poked her head in the stairwell leading to Max's basement workshop. It was dark like the rest of the house. Although a pleasant scent, like floral perfume, lingered in the air. Then she remembered the security cameras.

She perched on the couch and entered the system's code into the console.

Besides the *Real Life* media people camped in the wooded lot across the street, no one was on his property. No footsteps led to the front porch in the knee-high snow. Kali found the feed for the living room that showed her in real-time sitting at the table and rewound the digital video to the timestamp on the text.

Mia wasn't there.

Kali flopped back on the couch in relief. Mia had manipulated the image. That crafty gal must've blended the two images together to make it seem like she was in Max's home.

The floral odor probably came from the house-wide deodorizing unit and not from Mia.

"This is war. But first, I need coffee." She marched into the kitchen.

The coffeemaker scanned and read her biometrics matched to those that Max had programmed into it, and began brewing her favorite coffee without her lifting a finger. This was yet another beta model Max was testing for eventual consumer release. His goal was to steer DERST out of the defense arena and into the consumer market by making technology affordable for everyone.

She wished him luck with that one. There was far more money in war than peaceful pursuits.

Kali groaned and shook her head. She needed to be careful. She was sounding like Synthia's father.

With each passing assignment, with each passing experience with whackjobs wanting to take over the world or destroy lives for their own twisted gains, she found herself becoming more jaded. Before working for U-Sec, she relegated power-hungry crazies to history or to Bond movies. Psychos who wanted to do harm existed, but they were few and far between. The media hyped events to sell airtime or web ads.

Oh, how wrong she was.

The coffeemaker's light flashed, indicating it was finished.

She took a sip. It was perfect. Just like this house. Just like Max. Which meant it was a matter of time before everything fell into crap-o-matic mode.

"Stop it, Kali," she muttered, checking her negative thoughts.

Every relationship she'd had before Max was for fun. She had never planned to marry. Either she'd end up with a narcissistic prick like her stepdad, or her spouse would be too good for this world and be taken early like her dad. She'd never wanted a family. The world was too crazy for innocents. Besides, she'd worked enough throughout her life, from being the TV perfect daughter her mother wanted to proving her science aptitude in college and grad school in a male-dominated field before her accident.

But now that she'd seen what life could be like with Max, she'd fight Mia and any alt-traveling villains to keep what they had.

Her phone dinged with a text from Synthia (aka, UltraAgent Surefire), her closest friend. Controlling parents were the glue that initially bound them together, but that bond was made even closer by their recent misadventures. Kali respected Synthia's toughness and hoped by being friends with her that some of that toughness might rub off on this peace-loving gal.

Last week, Synthia had called Kali to let her know she was in Utah with Raven. He had been getting pouty—Synthia's words, not Raven's—because he missed snowboarding. He had wanted to share his old love with his new love. And they both had wanted to act like a normal couple for a few days, which required Oscar-winning acting skills since Synthia was a conduit for an Aztec goddess—of whom Kali was not a fan—and Raven was only alive because that goddess's power had resurrected him.

And Kali thought her life was complicated.

She moved into the living room and ran her hand over the tinted picture window. The liquid crystals inside had dissipated to reveal the morning light reflecting off the snow-covered trees. The technology in the windows was similar, but not as high-end, as the ones lining Kali's temporary holding cell on Dama X's island, which had displayed videos of underwater scenes that looked so realistic, Kali worried they'd trapped her in an aquarium.

Last night, Max had admitted he'd learned about this man-made island from classified company files. It was a private, decades-old project, developed with Suarez Tech off the coast of Mexico in the Pacific Ocean. Dama X's uncle, the founder of Suarez Tech, had taken control of it before they could lease the island to technology and defense companies for private research away from the prying eyes of governments or competitors. Kali wondered how many hidden labs DERST (and other corporations) had where they could test the limits of not only weapon developments but also transhumans.

Geesh, give it a break. Kali bopped herself in the head to pry loose those pesky pessimistic thoughts.

She settled onto the sofa and read the rest of Synthia's text sent from a new number. She used burner phones to communicate with Kali, who would recognize her friend's messages by the matching greeting, "Hello, Double T."

Synthia was checking on her friend. She wasn't worried that Kali was diving in the couple pool too quickly—Synthia had no room to talk on that point. Kali was the only one she could trust with her whereabouts. Synthia's father wanted to protect her or potentially use her as a weapon. Hard to tell his motives when he'd lied more than a politician on deposition.

Her mother still didn't know the whole story about Synthia, just that she had run off with a former thief. But Synthia couldn't talk to her mother, because she was sure to tell the general. Her twin sister Heather had proven to be somewhat sympathetic after Synthia and other U-Sec agents had saved her from being an Aztec god's psychic meal, but she had her own problems.

Kali glanced at the news from around the world scrolling across the glass coffee table. The gossip channel flashed several photos of Synthia's sister and her former fiancé, who had taken issue when a woman the size of a fairy stole his betrothed from their bathroom. He had broken off the engagement, and Heather was off dating . . . wow . . . some prince from a European nation Kali had never heard of. That was quick.

She started to put down her coffee then stopped, her foot nearly kicked over a bottle of wine onto a leather-bound book under the table. After placing her coffee on a coaster, she picked up the wine and scanned the label of the vintage cabernet from the year Max had been born. A ribbon was wrapped around the neck holding a note that read, "Drink me." Embossed on the foil covering the cork was Max's tattoo.

The handwriting on the note wasn't Max's. It had a feminine flourish. Mia's, maybe? She set the wine down and turned to the book, which she noticed had the Martin family's logo on the cover just like the journals Max had shown her that had belonged to his grandfather, the man who had founded DERST and a man Max looked up to despite never having met him.

"What are you doing up here?" she asked it.

Max was careful to keep his grandfather's journals locked away in his super-secret safe. He'd let her look through only one of them (the other contained confidential DERST content) while he peered over her shoulder and pointed out nuances and phrases he liked that painted a picture of his grandfather. The journals showed a man ahead of his time, as if he could see into the future. Besides his journeys into New Age philosophies, he anticipated technological advancements that would occur thirty-plus years later—like the dark energy reader they used to track Stockwell, which could track Kali's jumps as well.

But this book wasn't like those other journals.

"Ow!" Static shock nipped at her finger.

Wincing, she extended her hand once more to the table and gave the glass top a quick tap. No shock. She eyed the book, attempting to understand how the leather and paper could channel enough electricity to shock her.

She placed her index finger on the book. It buzzed against her skin.

"Weird."

She rubbed her fingertip over the embossed logo—an M encircled by Celtic shield knots entwined. Initially, Max had said that the M stood for the Man, but later admitted he had been teasing her. It represented the surname Martin, the artwork inspired by his family's Irish heritage.

In the low light, the small knots were hard to discern on the leather, but she could trace their grooves with her nail. Max had explained that usually one shield knot would be used as a symbol of protection, but these knots were arranged in a circle around the M to grant an additional layer of protection.

When she'd asked what the Martins needed protection from, he had smiled and said, "I don't know. But it must be working. After all, you protected me."

Zap!

"Ow!" She shook out her hand against the low-voltage snap.

She looked under the table and ran her hands along the top and sides, expecting another static zing. She opened the control panel and found the grounding wire in place.

"You're losing it, babe."

She picked up the book and held it inches from her eyes. Other than the logo, it wasn't an exact replica of the journal she'd seen. The leather on this one was smoother with a silvery sheen. Its dimensions were odd—wider than a typical book. The edges of the pages looked like parchment, yellowed with age. It wouldn't surprise her to find a treasure map inside.

She glanced down the hall and held her breath. No sound came from the bedroom. Max was still asleep.

Carefully, she opened the cover. There was a dedication page, which she couldn't read since it was written in another language, but that handwriting looked different than other passages she'd seen written by his grandfather. Was that a French word? Spanish here . . . yes, that was Spanish. Oh, and an English word. A pounding grew behind her eyes as she strained to translate a simple sentence.

Kali flipped through the opening pages. The handwriting changed from chicken scratch to the smooth flowing letters of Max's grandfather.

Is that a drawing of a crystal skull?

She leaned closer.

"Lights to a hundred percent," she said.

Bulbs inside the walls illuminated the room in a warm golden glow.

Max had mentioned his grandfather went through a phase where he was into the occult—like many in the sixties—but last night he hadn't said he recognized the legend of the crystal skulls, even after she'd related how one of those skulls enabled a goddess to possess Surefire.

She turned the page to find a drawing of the skull circle. She scanned the text. Words were pieced together from multiple languages, including Greek with several Chinese figures. Letters and sentences appeared to change, slipping and transforming into something else whenever she tried to translate a character.

She turned the page and at the top were words she recognized. A name actually.

Stephen St. John.

Synthia's father, who Kali believed epitomized the definition of the Man. Officially a retired general and head of a DoD subcommittee that contracted U-Sec. Unofficially in charge of a black ops team trained to combat transhuman terrorist threats, something they learned on their last mission to Dama X's island.

Which, from the few words she could discern, appeared to be noted in this book as well.

"What the crap balls is this?" Kali's eyes crossed from the strain.

Her hand smoothed over a rough sketch. Were these the plans that inspired Dama X's island?

She turned the book sideways. The image was drawn horizontally on the page. She trailed her hand over drawing. Notes and schematics appeared in a legend at the bottom near the crease. Again, she picked out a few words. One of them was Suarez. Had his company been founded back in the 1960s? No, he would've been too young. In the briefing after the Dama X mission, the report chronicled Suarez's life up to his death five years ago from cancer untreatable by TransGen's gene therapy, which had eradicated almost all forms.

Kali scanned the text and more names popped out at her.

Synthia. Raven. Xochiquetzal.

What is this?

She flipped back to the front. The first entry in the scratchy hand was dated September 20, 1968. The entry for the man-made island was July 18, 1969.

Decades later, U-Sec agents would meet and partner with Dama X after they learned she was on their side. Gloria Vivas, another owner of U-Sec and a transgeneticist for TransGen, was still working with Dama X's doctors to determine the structure of the crystal skull's proteins and how it might relate to transhumanism. Lucinda Troy, the rat bastardess who nearly killed them all, remained in a cryo-state to stop her body from bubbling up and disintegrating after she accidentally pricked her finger with a transhuman viral protein that attacked her cells. For a person with a transhuman marker, the virus would've healed their wounds. In an N-T, it accelerated cell growth, or disintegration in her case.

This has to be a joke. There's no way Max's grandfather could've known about these people, places, and things. How could he predict the details down to the drawings and schematics and—?

What the ever-loving freak is this?

Kali shrieked before her heart plugged up her throat, making any sound impossible. She threw the open book on top of an image of her and Max at the *Real Life* dinner as it flickered across the gossip channel screen.

With much trepidation, as if expecting the page to bite her if she made any sudden movements, she bent forward over the book.

There it was, drawn in black ink. It wasn't her imagination. Underneath was a sketch of the glass coffin that S-Kali had been trapped inside in the other universe.

She scratched her nails down her forearm as if to yank out the various IVs she'd seen hooked into S-Kali's veins.

Max had never mentioned or hinted at this journal's existence. He hadn't batted an eye when she described this same device. Although he was interested in the details of S-Kali's prison along with Synthia's and Raven's units. Could this be why he was so upset last night?

If it wasn't for the fact that Max's handwriting was distinctly different from what was in this journal, and that the writing—except those pages in the beginning—*did* resemble his grandfather's, she'd be questioning whether Max was the one behind it. Even still, had he stayed up last night studying this book? Getting ideas for how he could use her? Why else would he keep something like this from her?

She sprung to her feet. Nabbing the book from the table, she held it between her fingers like a slimy, slithering snake. Once more, it vibrated with a current that by the laws of physics shouldn't be there.

She glared down the hallway toward the bedroom containing a blissfully sleeping Max. But not for long. With the book held aloft, she strode past the kitchen before her stocking feet slid to a stop. Cocking her head, she listened. From the coffee table, Max's phone announced another text. Kali hesitated, teetering between curiosity and fury.

A *Real Life* dragonfly camera flew in front of the window. She flipped it off before ordering the windows to frost, shading the room.

And that's when she noticed that the videos on the coffee table had been replaced. They no longer offered a series of boxes playing various news channels and talking heads and security footage. Now, a single image covered the surface that matched the image in the text lighting up Max's phone—from Mia.

Kali approached the table. Her eyes took a moment to focus. Her mind another moment to process what she was seeing.

It was a grainy photo taken in Max's basement lab, shot from his work table toward the secured room where he kept DERST's prototypes under cypher lock. Except the room was no longer locked. The door was wide open, displaying half-built robotic assistants and other equipment . . . and an item that looked all too familiar.

"No," she whispered.

This was a joke. A sick joke orchestrated by that soon-to-get-a-butt-whooping Mia, whose long, curvy shadow darkened the floor inside the room. Her face, partially obscured by the phone, was reflected in the glass of the evil device.

Kali grabbed the wine bottle from the table. She was going to show Mia what she thought of her gift when she pitched it across the room at her. She raced down the stairs, bottle raised over her head with one hand and the book zapping the fingers of the other. Lights flashed on in the lab as she jumped from the bottom step. The same floral scent that lingered in the living room intensified in the basement space and assaulted her nose. She sneezed.

"Where are you?" she yelled, blazing a hot trail to the open door of the previously secured room.

"Come out you—" An invisible noose tightened around her neck, rendering her mute.

It's real.

Mia hadn't manipulated the image displayed on the coffee table. Kali's eyes hadn't played tricks on her. No, someone else had been fooling her all along.

Someone she thought had cared for her.

In the middle of the storage room—with a spotlight over it, no less—was a version of Synthia's prison. This one consisted of half-glass sides with tubes trailing out like rubbery entrails.

She didn't think about her power anxiety. Didn't consider not popping out of there. She was an animal pushed into a corner, pushed to the limit. Fight or flight.

And she did what she'd always done best.

Her ability rose from her gut. A tingle rattled her bones. She pictured her condo in Fells Point in the city an hour away from this house. She'd get a few supplies like her ski jacket and toiletries. Then she'd go where she'd be safe— and to the only people she could trust.

Chapter 5

Later That Same Day

It was more comfortable than Max had assumed a prison would be.

He stretched out in the containment chamber. More than enough room for his six-foot frame. The padding underneath conformed to his body and contained massaging modules to stop bedsores from developing. This unit even included mechanisms for exercising limbs and rotating the body while it was in stasis to improve blood flow and stave off muscle degeneration. Air vents allowed oxygen to flow and kept the climate inside as comfortable as a spring day. This model could also be fitted to hold a transhuman in a cryo state.

Max flattened his hand against the thick glass. Despite these built-in comforts, this prototype was still a prison, cutting off the outside world's sounds and smells.

With a shove, Max could throw off the hatch and climb out and be free, unlike an unconscious Surefire or Raven or S-Kali in her old-school version of this TPC from the other universe.

No. Max shook his head. He needed to label it as Kali had: a coffin. Because once someone placed a transhuman into this TPC, they never intended to release them.

Despite the tech to keep them alive, these chambers were meant to hold transhumans whose power had grown out of control or who were out of control themselves. Particularly, the public and government officials were concerned about transhumans who had committed crimes using their powers. As far as he knew, there were only a handful of cases, but enough to frighten the public who feared a future epidemic. Although according to Kali, Surefire and Raven hadn't done anything to deserve being put into stasis. They'd kept their power in check and weren't a danger to society. In fact, they'd helped save the world on two recent occasions.

His computer tablet, which he'd set on his stomach, vibrated with an incoming message. His heart skipped as he glanced down at the screen. But instead of a reply to the many voicemails, texts, and emails he'd sent to Kali, he was greeted with a message from his dad.

His parents were back from their holiday whirlwind adventure and wanted to see Max before they took off again to Colorado to visit with his sister's family. They'd read the web news headlines and were keen to meet this new woman in Max's life. He detected an undercurrent of concern, given that Kali's mother was a low-level reality web star, as if they hoped her daughter had higher ambitions. Read: wouldn't embarrass their family by carving out a career as a web celebrity like Glen's sister Mia.

Then again, they didn't mention the super-powered elephant in the room that Kali worked for UltraSecurity. A fact that had been leaked on several gossip sites. Although his parents would've learned about Kali from their government contractor ties. His dad most likely called in a favor to his NSA pals to run a background check on her.

Man, he didn't need to deal with them now.

He closed his email app and brought up an outline of the United States on the small screen. The device projected a 3-D image above his chest, allowing him to lay back and study the map.

His software, used to track dark energy fluctuations, which they'd learned tracked Kali's movements as well, had picked up a burst at her place near the Inner Harbor about an hour ago and then a burst in Utah shortly after that. At least, he assumed she'd caused those, as well as the burst shown from his home.

At least Kali had overcome her anxiety to tap into her power again, even if it was to escape him. Max guessed she was visiting Surefire and Raven, who were vacationing at one of the many ski resorts there. She'd never revealed which one.

She was probably telling them what a devious prick he was, and he wouldn't blame her. When he'd woken to find her gone and the door to his prototype room open, he'd come to the same conclusion.

He was an abject prick.

Pop. Pop. Pop.

Three latches on the TPC locked into place. Max shoved his palms against the glass. It didn't budge. He craned his neck but couldn't see out the side to find who had locked him inside.

"Hey!" He banged on the lid. "Let me out." He punched the thick glass with the side of his hand, but he could scream all he wanted. Whoever did this to him couldn't hear him yell through its walls.

He ran his hands along the interior. It was an early prototype used for Max's team to take measurements and test the circuits and instruments. Maybe he could rewire a control panel to release the hatch.

"Shit!" He jumped when Glen pushed his face—contorted in a clown-like expression—against the glass above him.

Glen slapped the lid then said something between fits of laughter. Max slammed his fist on the glass to get his attention. He motioned to his ears to indicate that he couldn't hear what Glen was saying.

"Oh, right," he mouthed. He held up his finger for Max to wait.

The latches unlocked. He shoved the lid open.

"What the hell, man?" He grabbed the edge and hauled his body up and over the side. His legs swung down and he dropped to the floor.

"That was hilarious." Glen bent over, clutching his side to catch his breath. "I should've videoed it. Your face was priceless."

Without a word, Max stormed past Glen, out the door, and into his workshop.

"What's wrong? You got to admit that was funny." His friend trailed him across the room. He stopped behind Max when they reached the computer console at the base of a theater-sized glass screen.

"I told you not to come." Max sat and busied himself with waking up the mainframe.

"You did, and I disagreed, so here I am. Since when do I listen to you anyway?" he said.

Max snorted.

Glen took the chair next to him then made a show of looking around the room. "So, where's Kali—your excuse for wanting to ditch me and DERST's latest project?"

"She left." A tear seeped from Max's eye. He wiped it away before his friend could see it.

"When will she be back?" Glen rolled the chair closer until its arm bumped into Max's.

He stared at the computer console. The illuminated touchscreen blurred. "She won't be."

"I'm sorry, buddy." Glen rose and pulled a reluctant Max into a half-hug. He ended it with several hardy pats on the back. "You'll find another one."

Not like her.

"That's not the point." Max opened a location app. The glass monitor illuminated with a map of the United States, along with a blinking red dot outside Salt Lake City. The last place Kali had traveled.

"Yes, it is. You just met this girl. You spend two weeks—"

"Three weeks, two days and eight hours," Max interjected.

"Wow . . . let's back it up a sec." Glen grabbed his shoulders and forced Max to face him.

"Have you been crying?" his friend exclaimed with disgust.

He jerked away, averting his gaze to Glen's shiny loafers that, along with his tailored suit, appeared brand new. Even Glen's black hair and trimmed beard gleamed under the fluorescent lights in stark contrast to Max's rolled-out-of-bed style: flannel pajama bottoms, flip-flops, and his second-favorite *Star Wars* shirt. Kali had absconded with the first.

"This bitch raked you over the coals, didn't she?"

He shot him a side-eye. "Careful."

Glen lifted his arms in surrender. "Didn't mean any offense. I'm worried about you. I get angry when someone messes with family."

He nodded in understanding. They weren't blood brothers, but having been raised together since they were children, they considered themselves to be. Their parents were best friends and business partners. They celebrated holidays and milestones and took vacations together every summer.

"I'm trying to understand how this woman got under your skin so quickly, and why it matters that she's gone. You can have your pick of the litter. Women are lined up for you, literally outside your gate with that *Real Life* crew."

"Did anyone see you come in?"

"Come on, you know me better than that." He plunked back into his chair.

"Yeah." Max blew out a ragged breath. "I'm just on edge with the paparazzi camping outside my gate. I'm not used to all this."

On the large screen, Max brought up the security feed from the front of his property. "Finally got rid of those *Real Life* dragonfly drones after one crashed into my window this morning. It caused the alarm system to vibrate the house, which woke me up." *And I found Kali was gone.*

"How did you get rid of them?"

"Hacked into their system and sent the drone coordinates to the nearest army base."

Glen chuckled. "That'll teach them."

"Let's hope, because the paparazzi keep multiplying."

Max cracked his knuckles. Sure enough, the security feed showed more vehicles lining the narrow road across from his fenced-in property.

"This is more than a woman dumping you. You look like a quarterback sacked by the entire team."

"Feels like it."

"Just be glad you found out she was a flake before it got serious."

"She's not a flake." Max cut his friend a shut-up-now look, which, of course, didn't work.

"Whatever. You're lucky this happened before she got her claws in DERST and bled you dry."

And there goes Glen playing CFO, when Max needed a friend.

"Kali's not like that."

"Sure she's not. Haven't met a woman who wasn't."

"What about your mother?"

"That's different. She's my mom. Moms don't count as women. They're in the 'other' category. You've always had a soft heart for the ladies. You should've followed my advice: if it floats, flies, or fucks, rent it." He gave Max's shoulder a slap.

He knocked his hand away. For the first time since they were teens, he wanted to deck his friend.

Glen continued, seemingly unaware of or unconcerned with Max's growing temper. "You haven't dated since your accident. Don't fall for the first woman you meet that helped release your pent-up tension."

His job as a friend done, he crossed his legs and lounged in the chair.

Max touched the keypad. A video of his first-floor rooms replaced the outside footage. "Someone opened the door to the secured storage area and led Kali there."

"Who has access to it?"

"I thought only you, your father, and me. But it appears someone else does too."

Glen narrowed his eyes. "Who?"

He shoved his cell phone in Glen's face.

"Man." He averted his eyes and cringed. "Give some warning before you show a half-naked picture of someone's sis."

"Mia sent it this morning while I was sleeping."

"Didn't know you two were a thing."

"We're not. Kali saw this, and as you can see by the security video, she was looking for someone, presumably Mia, in my living room."

"Why?"

Max held up his phone again. This time Glen rolled the chair several feet back. "Just tell me."

"The timestamp is this morning. Mia is on my couch."

"So Kali stole Mia's spotlight from that *Real Life* dinner party, and to get revenge, my sister photoshopped herself onto your couch? It's not beyond Mia to do this."

"I doubt the image has been manipulated. Then there's another on my phone of the cypher-locked door having been opened with a light over the TPC. I can make out her face reflected in this glass case."

This went way beyond the narcissistic brat Mia could be. How could she know about the TPC in his storage room and how it related to Kali? She wasn't involved in the company or its contracts. Whenever she was asked by the media what DERST did, she'd respond by saying, "I'm too important to know what they do."

"Whatever Mia's reasons, she's not returning my calls. And she doesn't show up on the security footage. No one does. But there are a few weird time jumps, as if the video had been erased before Kali enters the living room."

Max brought up the video feed of Kali sitting on the couch and picking up a book and a bottle of wine, which she'd found under the coffee table. Next to that feed, he played the footage of her wandering downstairs to his workshop and discovering the TPC through the open door to the storage room. He looked down at the keyboard, refusing to re-watch the moment Kali discover that he'd betrayed her.

"I think Mia hacked into my security system. I'm running a program to figure out how."

"If she did, she didn't do it on her own. She can't install an app on her phone let alone hack into a system like yours." Glen pulled out his cell phone from an inside blazer pocket.

"What are you doing?"

"Calling her. If she doesn't answer, then I'll trace her phone. Ever since she ran off to host that underground conspiracy web show, I keep a lock on her."

"I don't remember her doing that."

"Exactly, I stopped her before she did or said anything stupid to compromise our family." Glen put the call on speaker. It rang and rang and rang a few more times before he hung up.

"What's that?" His friend swiped a hand at the screen where Max had paused the video of Kali discovering the storage room.

"You mean the book or the wine bottle?" Max asked.

"The book."

"Kali removed it from under the coffee table along with the bottle. I assumed it belonged to her." He figured it was her notebook where she kept track of her alt-jumps.

Glen stared at the screen with an intensity that made Max wonder what he was missing. "Zoom in on the book."

"Why?"

"Just do it."

He enlarged the picture to focus on the object, but the image was too grainy to discern any details. But that didn't stop Glen from swearing over whatever he saw in the pixelated feed.

Before he could ask what was wrong, Glen shot off, "What can Kali do? You wanted off the project because she's a transhuman, but you never said what her ability is. What is her codename?"

Max shook his head. "That's not for me to tell you."

"Someone powerful has been keeping her secret from the press, but I heard the rumors." Glen busied himself with his phone.

"What rumors?" He peered over his friend's shoulder and saw that he'd launched the software to trace Mia's phone.

"Haven't you been online at all?"

Max had but he wanted to know what Glen had heard.

"Some claim she can turn invisible. Others say that she can teleport. There's this professor of Mesoamerican studies who worked at the Smithsonian and last year he—" Glen's phone chimed. He glanced at the screen then did a double take. "She's here."

"Who?"

"Mia."

"No, she's not."

"Yes, she is." He held up his phone to show a bright dot with coordinates listed underneath.

"Over there." Glen jerked his head. "Through that wall."

"The garage?"

"Must be."

They ran up the stairs then down the hall to the door that led to his garage.

"Why would she be here?" Max led the way down another set of stairs.

"No clue. But it's Mia. I don't expect any of this to make sense." Glen's hard soles tapped against the risers behind Max.

Lights illuminated the garage lined with cars from models older than his father to LISA the Lamborghini in which he had driven Kali to his home that fateful night they'd met.

"What's that smell?" He covered his mouth against the offending odor.

"Cannibas mixed with Mia's favorite perfume." Glen stalked down the main aisle, passing Max.

When he finally registered the odor, he coughed. "We're going to get a contact high."

Once again, he looked over Glen's shoulder. The dot on his phone's screen transitioned from red to green the farther they walked into his garage and the stronger the scent of marijuana became.

The dot blinked a lime green. They skidded to a stop in front of his grandfather's restored Volkswagen bus.

"Please don't tell me . . ." Max yanked open the side door to find Mia—fortunately clothed in a snow white sweater dress and not a negligee—perched on the platform bed in the back of the bus. A cloud of pot smoke billowed from inside.

"What are you doing? I just had it restored," Max said, as if it would make a difference.

"A VW bus was made for smoking pot. I'm breaking it in." She offered him a half-hearted shrug as an apology. She snubbed out her joint in a glass tumbler lined with cigarette butts.

Max threw wide all the doors and vented the windshield in a vain attempt to suck out the offending odors before they permeated the polished new interior. Then he turned his attention back to Mia. But before he could climb inside and let loose the current of curses he had locked and loaded, Glen intercepted him.

"I got this." His friend angled himself in front of Max, effectively blocking out Mia.

He ducked to the left and Glen ducked to his right. "Out of my way."

"What are you going to do?" his friend asked.

"I'm going to . . ." He trailed off. *What am I going to do? Grab her? Toss her from the bus?* He wouldn't do any of that. Couldn't do any of that to her, let alone to anyone for that matter. And it's not like a strong reprimand from him would make a difference to Mia in her current state.

"That's what I thought," Glen said when Max didn't finish his declaration. "Let me talk to her. Get her feeling comfortable—"

"I think she already is." He glowered at Mia lounging on the platform bed like a stoner hippie queen.

"That she is. But I want her comfortable with *me* enough to tell us why she did what she did. And you playing bad cop won't work with her." Glen removed his jacket and hung it on the door. He rolled up his shirtsleeves like a farmer about to shovel into a waist-high load of manure.

"I need to know why she sent those texts and photos." Max propped his shoulder against the side of the opened bus so he could remain in semi-pot-free air and still hear their conversation.

Giving Max a reassuring smile, Glen climbed into the bus. He slid between the cushioned bench and the small linoleum table to the bed in the back where Mia sat propped against the wall. Her legs stretched over the length of the mattress, her ankles crossed. All she needed was a book to complete the I-have-no-care-in-the-world look.

"Are you all right?" Glen scooted to the edge of the bench.

"Why wouldn't I be?" She blinked at him.

Max hissed in disgust.

"For starters, you're high as a kite in Max's garage," Glen said.

"I like it in here. It's cozy. Safe."

"Safe?" Glen echoed. He shot a concerned look at Max, who nodded, noticing her word choice too.

"I did something even I may regret. Imagine that? Me, regret?" She snickered at her joke then let out a long, deflating breath. "But what are you doing here, brother dear? Weren't you out of town?"

Max cleared his throat to remind Glen to get back on track. He held up his phone with her sexy photo shoot lighting up the screen.

Her eyes narrowed on Max as if trying to figure out who he was or what he was about. "Oh, right. The texts. You're here about those."

"Among other things." He crossed his arms.

Glen batted his hand up and down like he was petting an invisible dog—a signal for Max to keep quiet.

When this was over, Glen better give him a medal for his restraint.

"Mia, I need you to focus. Why did you send those photos of yourself to Max?"

"It doesn't matter." She flicked a hand toward Max and his phone.

If he were a character in a cartoon, the animator would draw a nuclear cloud exploding from his head. And yet that explosive image couldn't touch the magnitude of anger steaming inside him.

"Just tell me why you did it. Why did you send those photos? Why did you open my secured room?" Max's voice rose with every word until it caused feedback on his hearing aids.

Mia set her jaw. Now he'd done it, sealed the vault. A petulant child could take pointers from her.

"Max," Glen spoke in an even tone meant to calm him, but it only added fuel to his fire because he was done with Mia's games.

"Do you hate me that much to ruin the best thing that's happened to me?" He continued to rant because, at this point, he didn't have anything to lose.

His gamble paid off. Whatever he'd said seemed to have flipped a switch in her brain. She swung her legs over the edge of the bed to face him.

"I did it to protect you," she said.

"From Kali?" Max balked.

"No, not Kali, you idiot."

He let the insult slide, an easy sacrifice when he finally had Mia speaking. He glanced at Glen, who appeared as confused as he was by her confession.

"Mia, Max is upset, and I'm sure you can understand why. Earlier you said that you were here because you needed to be safe. Help us to understand so we can help you."

"Me? You can't help me. Not anymore. And you can't help Kali either. Max is the one they want, and I should've let them take him. Would've been so much easier." She heaved a sigh. "Got anything to eat in here? I am starving." She hopped to her feet and proceeded to fling open the cabinet doors in the bus's mini-kitchen.

Max glared at Glen, who must've read his mind because he grabbed Mia's arm and asked, "Is Kali in trouble?"

"Ah, yeah, she took the journal, didn't she? And they need that, or else they can't do what they plan to do with Max."

Max walked away. He had to or else he was going to hit the bus and potentially dent it or break his hand or both, and that wouldn't do him any good. Once he cleared his head of both Mia's ramblings and the second-hand pot fuzzing his brain, he leaned back into the vehicle to find the siblings sitting together on the bed and whispering.

"What's going on? I'm starting to think I'm the one who's high here," Max interrupted them.

Mia's jaw worked back and forth as if she were fighting with herself whether to answer. "They're going to kill me for what I've done. That's why I hid down here."

"I still don't get it. Who did you piss off this time?" Max said.

"I made a mistake, okay? I wanted to do the right thing. They were after you, and I assumed if I could give Kali to the Organization then you would be safe. That's why I sent those texts. You let her respond to my texts before, so I assumed she'd see what I sent. We had been watching you. You were up late, so I knew you'd sleep in."

Max's head pounded, the lingering reefer smoke making it hard to concentrate, making him question his own sanity because Mia could not be admitting that she'd been spying on him. And worst of all, she couldn't be admitting that she purposefully put Kali in danger.

"Glen, please tell me she's having a bad trip. Or that I am, because if this is real . . ."

His friend hung his head as he tugged on his beard. A gesture Glen only did when he was worried.

Max waited for his friend to confirm this was a nightmare. That Mia's pot was laced with a narcotic that was making him hallucinate. But Glen kept stroking his beard as if the answer would magically appear and grant them three wishes.

"What is this Organization?" Max asked as he slowly processed Mia's confession.

"The man that the *Real Life* director partnered me with at the holiday dinner, he belonged to it. That guy—Robert—who won a gold medal for pitching poles or something or other."

"Javelin throwing," he corrected.

"Yes, what I said." She rolled her eyes. "Robert is part of it. He came on to me at the party to use me to get to our father." She rolled her eyes again. "I was onto him. He had too much interest in our family and business."

Max wanted to add, "and not you" but kept that comment to himself.

She continued, "Then he started spouting crazy things about other universes right before this guy crashes our dinner party, which I didn't remember until days later, when Robert showed me the video of what should've occurred before our timeline was supposedly reset. The cameras caught a bit of what happened before things went back to a semblance of normal. Our normal anyway."

His stomach dropped. He'd assumed the video feeds were overridden, along with the memories of those attending the dinner, when time rewound to before the dimensional traveler appeared.

"Who else knows about what happened?" he asked.

"The Organization, which Robert belongs to," she replied, eliciting an f-bomb from Glen. "They kept the video evidence hidden, even kept who Kali was from leaking out to the press."

It was Max's turn to drop a barrage of f-bombs. These people knew Kali's secret.

"I was protecting you from them," she went on, trying to convince Max of what, he had no clue. Her innocence? Her good intentions? "You're family, and Kali's not one of us. It's why I couldn't let them take you when I found out what they wanted to do.

"Besides, you couldn't handle that kind of power. Don't you agree, Glen? He shouldn't have it, right? It shouldn't be him." Mia looked to her brother for validation.

Again, Max was in the dark as to what all this meant. "Glen, please tell me that this is an elaborate joke, or maybe Mia has finally lost her shit and taken some heavy duty hallucinogen that even she can't handle."

He stopped pulling on his beard. "Remember the book that Kali took from under the table?"

"What about it?" Max replied.

"Mia stole it from our father. For a short period, it belonged to your grandfather."

"What are you—?"

Glen held up his hand for Max to hold his question. He addressed his sister when he asked, "I'm assuming that wine bottle was from dad's collection as well? And you added a something extra to it?"

"They meant for Max to drink it. That's what they thought I was doing here. That's why they helped me get into Max's home. But I couldn't let him take the bait, so I left it out for Kali. That woman drinks anything with alcohol. And once she drinks that wine it will open the journal and take that evil to the other universe where the Organization can't get it. And Max will be safe with no power as it should be." Under her breath she added, "Otherwise, it's not fair at all to me."

"What the hell are you talking about?" Max couldn't stop his voice from rising, filling the tight space with a frustration that rattled his bones. "And who is this 'they' that set this up . . . this Organization you keep talking about?"

"Our father worked for them decades ago until he broke free after a disagreement," Glen said. "All that time, he'd kept your grandfather's final writings hidden from them."

"You and your father kept one of my grandfather's journals from me? Why would you do that?"

"Because it's dangerous. It holds the essence of darkness—an experiment gone wrong."

Max was trying to keep everything straight. There were so many questions he had regarding this mysterious evil journal and who this shady Organization was and why they wanted him. But those questions didn't matter at this moment, because from all these vague responses, he determined one thing, which mattered more than anything else.

"Is Kali in danger?" Max asked Glen.

"Yes."

"Where is she?" He turned to Mia. "I lost her after Salt Lake City."

"I don't know." She stared down at her boots.

"Then we need to find her before they do."

Chapter 6

Later That Day
(but it seems earlier because of time zones)
in Utah

"Why couldn't you have vacationed in the Caribbean like normal, warm-blooded peeps?" Kali stepped onto the balcony where Synthia was lounging in the hot tub.

Scratch that.

She wasn't lounging anymore. Her friend and fellow UltraAgent was screeching and slipping under the water.

Synthia broke through the surface coughing and spitting up water. The lavender rock hanging around her neck softly glowed.

"You almost gave me a heart attack. Next time call first. Give a heads up." She slid a hand down her face swiping away the water.

"I couldn't. I left my phone at Max's."

"Why?" Synthia grabbed a fluffy towel off a nearby chair and scrubbed at her short do.

Instead of answering her friend's question, Kali removed the journal from her inside coat pocket and tossed it on a small wooden table. She then busied herself with setting the bottle of wine on the ground and settling herself into a teak patio chair.

"Do you mind if I vape?" Kali had brought her medicinal marijuana with her. When she'd first manifested her power, it calmed her jitters and gave her better focus over her ability. Today, she'd hoped it would calm jitters of a different sort.

"Are you having trouble with your power again?" Synthia stopped rubbing her hair to give Kali a once-over.

She shrugged and busied herself with prepping her vape pen. "I hadn't alt-jumped in a few weeks, ever since the EI in the other universe."

"EI?"

"Evil Incident." Kali peered over the railing of the condo complex in the upscale ski resort. She watched three snowboarders trudge along a snowy path three floors below.

"Is this about what happened in the other universe?" Synthia asked with a confused frown.

"I couldn't talk about it at all until last night when I finally told Max."

Water sloshed from the hot tub behind Kali, who kept her eyes focused on the snowboarders in their bright red and yellow jackets. She followed them until they walked between the buildings and passed by a tall man wearing a white ski ensemble and carrying a leather satchel the size and shape of a bowling ball bag.

"Did something bad happen when you told Max?"

Kali glanced behind her to find Synthia wrapping a robe around her bikini-clad body.

"Sort of." She puffed on the vape pen. Peering through the space between the buildings, she watched multicolored dots careen down the mountain. The tall man wearing white and possibly heading to or from a bowling alley was gone.

"Do you want a drink?" Synthia opened the sliding glass door. Her gaze landed on the wine at Kali's feet.

"Oh, this?" She sneered in the bottle's direction. "This is for you as a 'thank you' for letting me drop in. It's a pricey bottle, which I only know because one of my mom's boy toys gave it to her as a one-month sex-a-versary gift . . . or something like that. Anyhoo, Max's friend's sister, Mia, left it for him in his living room."

Synthia ventured, "Then you don't want any wine?"

"What time is it?"

"Eleven a.m."

"What about coffee?"

"Raven made a pot before he left to go snowboarding. Heavy on the vanilla creamer, right?"

"You got it, babe." Kali saluted her with the vape pen. "Oh, and check the front door. It was unlocked when I got here."

"You didn't pop inside?"

She squirmed under her friend's suspicious appraisal. "No, I alt-jumped to my condo first. Picked up a few things." Such as the winter clothes she was wearing, a duffel of essentials, and emergency cash. "Then I jumped to Salt Lake. I took a bus into town and hitched a ride on a Willie's Ski Shack truck to the old main street before trekking to your place."

During their last phone call, Synthia had given Kali her condo address in case she wanted to get away from the paparazzi. She'd probably never guessed Kali would seek her out to escape from Max.

"Why did you go through all that instead of doing your Q-T thing?" Synthia leaned on the frame of the open door.

"Max can track dark energy bursts when I travel." She blew out the smoke, and her nerves began to numb.

"Kali, how—?"

She put up her hand to stop Synthia. "On second thought, maybe not coffee, now that I'm chillaxing. How about water? Then we can talk."

"Be right back." Synthia slid the door closed behind her.

Kali shoved her hands into the pockets of her ski jacket. They had finally stopped shaking, thanks to the pot and being with her friend. She stretched out her legs, covered in her favorite jeans, which did nothing to minimize the cold. But she felt safer outside than in the warm condo. The crisp air made her feel more awake and aware. Plus, she didn't want to be confined in a room with that creeptastic book.

She'd dropped the statically charged, physics-defying journal on the small patio table, far enough away that she couldn't feel its effects. She was grateful to have it off her person. When she popped to Salt Lake City, she felt as if it were weighing her down, making it harder to trudge through the in-between— the shortcut she took when traveling through space. As if its gravitational force increased the longer Kali held it, which should not be possible. While any object with mass held a gravitational force, the force shouldn't increase but remain steady relative to its mass, and it wasn't as if this book was growing larger.

The patio door slid open and out stepped Synthia, dressed in leggings and a long wool sweater and snow boots. A lavender knit hat was pulled over her wet hair. She carried a tray with meats and cheeses and two glasses of water.

When Synthia hesitated, unsure where to place the food, Kali moved the book off the table and to the ground.

"Thanks for the kibbles. I should probably eat." Her stomach grumbled its appreciation as her friend set the tray on the compact table.

Synthia passed her a small plate, and Kali wasted no time cutting several slices of cheese and meat. She chewed on the scrumptious cheddar and salami and stared at the snow-covered mountain that loomed on the other side of the buildings, its peak covered by low gray clouds. She jumped when a flutter of wings passed by the balcony. A magpie swooped from the roof and into the tree below.

She took another puff on her vape before she realized it wasn't a dreaded dragonfly camera. *Real Life* hadn't found her yet.

Synthia touched her arm, and she jumped again. "Are you in trouble?"

Kali picked up the journal and winced at the snap of static electricity. She handed it to Synthia without a word about the book's weird vibe or the occasional shock it gave off. She didn't want to influence Synthia's reaction, which wasn't what she'd hoped for, because her friend eyed the book, shook her head, and then sipped her glass of water.

"What is this?" Synthia absently flipped through the pages.

"A journal, I believe, that belonged to Max's grandfather based on some of the handwriting in it. He died several decades ago." She stuck another cheddar-salami combo into her mouth.

"You stole this?" Synthia's two-colored eyes went wide.

Kali nodded.

"From a man who gave you the best two weeks of your life?"

"Three and a quarter weeks or so." Kali slunk down into her seat under the weight of Synthia's accusatory tone.

"A smart, hot, super-respectful man, who unlike the other men you've dated, has a decent job. No . . . wait . . . that's an understatement. He owns a billion-dollar company and isn't a control freak douche."

"Don't know if any of those attributes apply anymore," Kali muttered to herself.

"This is his property. It belonged to his deceased grandfather." Synthia's finger tapped the leather binding.

Kali studied her friend to gauge if she felt anything from that touch, but the only thing that Synthia's face showed was disappointment in her friend.

"Not to mention that you used your power to steal." Synthia leveled her with a look that spoke loud and clear what she was thinking.

The penalty was steep for transhumans who used their powers on N-Ts. Using powers to steal from the top one percent would most likely land them in a cryochamber—or a containment unit like the one in Max's basement—for the smallest crime.

"There are reasons for me breaking bad." Kali sat up. "Remember the boxes that Lucinda stuffed you and Raven in?"

Synthia froze in mid-reach for the salami. Her eyes locked with Kali's. She didn't have to respond to the question, because Kali knew she experienced bad dreams nearly every night after what had happened to them.

"I found a similar one in Max's house. In a locked room off his basement workshop. And there's a diagram of a similar chamber in that book."

Synthia pressed back into her chair. Her face puckered in disgust, which morphed to disbelief and then anger.

"It can't be." She clenched her fists. The light purple stone on her necklace glowed against her cream-colored sweater.

A flapping sound returned. Kali whipped her head toward the noise. Again, nothing but a bird. This one soared across and landed on the balcony of the building facing theirs.

She gave Synthia an overview of the morning's events along with a summary of the universe reset and finding S-Kali in the alternate universe.

"Now open the book. I want to use visuals for the next part," Kali finished.

Synthia rubbed her neck under her bobbed blonde hair. She turned around to stare through the sliding glass door into the living room.

"You're not feeling all prickly like when those crystal skulls are around?"

"I don't know." Synthia shook her head. "I had a sensation that Raven had returned. Probably just a reaction to your story after learning about another person who's betrayed us."

Kali rubbed her arms over her jacket as a chill crept along her skin, one that didn't come from the snowy air. Across from them, a magpie flew from a balcony. Drapes shifted as if someone had been looking out the glass doors at them.

Or as if they were checking out the bird that had landed on their balcony.

This paranoid feeling was . . . well . . . for the birds.

"I'm sick of being scared, Syn. If things get wonky, I can pop us out of here like that." Kali snapped her fingers. "And you can do that"—she twirled her fingers at the ground—"thing where vines appear from the ground and trap people. Not to mention, make use of your extreme powers when you goddess out."

"Goddess out?" Synthia's lips curled up into a smile.

"Trying out a new term. Thought you might like it. Kind of stole it from the Incredible Hulk, but I don't think he'd mind."

"That is the lamest . . . It's not even that funny . . . it's just . . ." Synthia laughed.

"Okay, okay, you don't have to be mean." Kali feigned hurt, but she was relieved her friend was amused. She hadn't seen Synthia smile like that since the Aztec goddess had claimed her as a vessel.

"When I alt-jumped to the other universe and saw myself trapped in that glass coffin"—Kali grimaced—"my other self said 'the Man' did it to her . . . me . . . whomever, whatever."

"And you said Max's grandfather's nickname was the Man. I'd say it was a total coincidence if it weren't for the fact that you found Max with a newer version of the device."

"Here's the dealio, babe. I've found that our alt-versions have similar personalities to us."

"You've met me?"

"Not you, I try to make sure I don't cross paths with anyone who may know my alternate universe self. It's one reason I stick to the past. But political figures and celebrities have the same rep. I mean Nixon was an asshat in both universes, but he got caught over there and resigned."

Synthia drummed her fingers on the journal and appeared to debate the issue. "How many people have been nicknamed the Man throughout history, especially in the '60s and '70s? Hippies labeled any guy over thirty that. You call my father the Man all the time. Maybe he's your villain in that other universe?"

"No, I have more colorful names for your father, and speaking of daddy dearest . . ." Kali wriggled her index finger at the book. "He's in there."

"Grandpa Martin knew my father?" Synthia opened the journal and turned past the beginning pages.

"Go to the middle," Kali said.

She flipped to the center. Her eyes narrowed then blinked before she refocused on the page. "I see Stephen St. John mentioned, but what language is this?"

"I don't know. I was hoping you could tell me. Some words look like Greek, some Chinese, some Spanish. Some might be Latin. I studied that in college, but I'm rusty. It's been ten years since I had to translate paragraphs of text like this."

"These pages contain a combination of languages, like French and Latin. And maybe German. I'm not a linguist."

"You're not, but another gal we know is." Kali pointed to Synthia's necklace.

"Are you kidding me? You want me to ask Xochi?"

Kali touched her friend's hand. "You know I wouldn't ask if I didn't think this was important. I don't call her the bitch goddess for nothing. But look at this."

She took the book from Synthia then opened to a page she'd marked. *"My father's name is in this book too. How is that possible? How did Max's grandfather know my father? My mother never mentioned this. I never found any Martins mentioned in my father's paperwork after he died. I need this mystery solved."*

"That is crazy." Synthia's eyes trekked over the page as her mouth hung open in disbelief.

"Ask Max," she stated with conviction.

Kali sensed that if she didn't agree to do so, her friend was more than willing to.

"You deserve an explanation for this," said Synthia. "You saved his life. The least he can do is tell you why he has this book and that *thing* in his basement."

"I can't see him now. I can't stand to think about being in his presence or looking at his two-faced face. It's just . . ." She threw back her head and groaned in frustration. "What if he was letting me stay with him because of what's in this book? Of what I can do? What if he wants to use me?"

Synthia sat back in her chair. "Like my father did to me? Wants to do with me?"

Kali hadn't planned to bring up that tidbit. She didn't want to discuss how Synthia's father saw her as a weapon akin to a nuclear bomb, owned by the United States, to be protected at all cost—even if it meant imprisoning her.

And he'd almost succeeded in locking her up with the help of Lucinda, which he denies.

"What happened to you made me more cautious about who knows about my ability. So far, Pax has kept your dad at bay. But St. John keeps bugging me to train in combat and get security clearances to contract with the secret services and black ops teams. You know I'm a peace-loving gal." Kali tipped her water glass to Synthia.

"People are scared of what we can do. My father is, especially after I—well, actually Xochi—turned him into a plant," Synthia said.

"He got better."

Synthia gave her a half-smile as she trailed her thumb along the rim her empty glass. "But it won't stop him from tracking me down, even if we didn't kill any of his men when they attacked us outside Dama X's island. You'd think that would count for something."

"He's afraid of someone using you."

"But *he* sees no problem in using me."

"The evil you know is better than the evil you don't. I think there's a bigger Big Bad. I've heard your dad allude to it. I know he's mentioned it to you."

"Monster stories to scare me into surrendering my freedom."

"It may not be fiction. And I think this book holds a clue. In fact, I think Max's grandfather might be behind the monster of the millennium."

"How do you figure?"

Kali opened the journal to another marked page and held it up to Synthia. "What does that look like?"

Her friend squinted at the sketch of a man-made island with layers of rooms built over an underwater caldera. "That's Dama X's island."

Kali bobbed her head. "Pax mentioned seeing the DERST name and logo on the interior structure when he broke out of his cell. Decades ago, Suarez Tech, the company owned by Dama X's uncle, had built this island as a private project with DERST. According to Dama X, after they were finished, her uncle didn't want to share the island with DERST anymore. So he kicked the DERST contractors off the island then hid its whereabouts from them and other investors."

She handed the journal back to Synthia, holding the book open to another page with a detailed drawing of the island with a cross section of various levels, containing housing to technology shops to medical labs to classrooms and dormitories circling down along a cone-shaped space into the caldera.

"When was this book written?" Synthia turned to the first page. In the center was a black printed M circled by the Celtic shield knots. Underneath, in scribbled handwriting, was a span of the years 1968–1969. Her light brows drew together.

"If these dates are correct, then he predicted the future. You need to tell Max about this"—she tapped the page hard with her finger—"about my father's name, your father, about everything."

It made sense to do what Synthia was suggesting. Talk to Max. So simple to say but painful to execute. Plus, how would she know he was telling the truth after keeping all these secrets from her?

No, it was easier to just avoid him and it and the entire situation. Move on with her life, whatever that looked like. Tell her bosses, Pax and Sean, and have them deal with it.

"There are two other journals he keeps locked up. I hadn't seen this one until this morning when I found it under his coffee table. I think he was hiding it from me and—"

"Why aren't you listening?" Synthia cut her off. "You need to confront Max. It's his book. If you don't want to do it alone, then we'll go with you. In fact, Raven and I should go with you, since we're affected by what this book has to say as well."

As comforting as it was to have her super-powered friends back her up, she was terrified at the idea of confronting Max. She shouldn't be afraid. He was an N-T. He had no superpowers that she was aware of, except the ability to rip her heart out and crush it to jelly.

Synthia laid a hand on Kali's arm and brought her back to the here and now. "What aren't you telling me?"

With a sigh, Kali straightened in her chair then said, "Go to the last entry."

She bounced her leg in nervous anticipation as Synthia thumbed through the parchment-like paper until she reached the drawing that made Kali's chest contract.

She inhaled on her vape and it didn't help.

"This is why I don't want to confront him right now. It's a similar chamber to what held you and Raven, but it's the exact device in which S-Kali was trapped. These tubes were hooked into her veins and siphoned her—my— power into a backpack-sized device that this soldier Stockwell used to travel into our world."

Synthia unfolded her arms. Color drained from her face as if she were about to be ill. "You . . . that other Kali was in this?"

"Figured you could relate."

"I wish I couldn't."

"At least Lucy won't do that to anyone again," Kali said.

Synthia shuttered and stared off in the distance, making Kali wish that she could take back her words. Lucinda, a transgeneticist who used to work with TransGen, had tricked Raven and Surefire, put them in stasis, and used their blood to increase the powers of other transhumans, as well as to enhance a weapon targeting men in the worse possible way.

"We'll go inside, open this." Surefire held up the bottle of wine. "And I'll call forth Xochi. But I'll need Raven's help. He should be down from the mountain for lunch soon."

Another fluttering caught their attention, different from the magpies' flapping. It was mechanical with gears clicking, wings buzzing, and it came from below the balcony.

Both women leaned over the railing to find a dragonfly camera soaring upward. It stopped and hovered a few feet away, the round lens, the size of a softball, aimed at them.

Chapter 7

Meanwhile, Back in Maryland

Is Kali in danger?
Yes.

Max didn't ask what kind of danger. He didn't ask why this organization had targeted him and what they'd planned to do with him. He didn't ask for details on this company or network or Legion of Doom-like gang that had Mia hiding in his garage like a runaway mob informant. Those explanations could come later. Once they found Kali. Once he knew she was no longer in danger.

It had been six hours since she had Q-T'd from his home this morning. Half of those hours Max had spent moping around, wallowing in his guilt, while this Organization set its sights on her. The more time that passed, the more likely they had gotten to Kali. So when he called in a favor from a friend at the NSA, and they'd found her through facial recognition software at a bus station in Salt Lake City, it meant that three hours ago she was alive and free and safe.

But they couldn't see which bus she'd boarded. At least ten buses had left that morning for various ski resorts and towns. His gut told him she was going to see Surefire, who was snowboarding with her boyfriend. That's what Max would do if he were in her situation—seek out his best friend, the only one he could trust.

And the one who would understand what it was like to be trapped in a high-tech coffin.

He unlocked Kali's phone, which she'd left behind. At least five numbers could be Surefire's. Of them, three were disconnected and two went into a generic voicemail. He hacked into the carrier's database looking for any numbers that matched those in her contacts list.

"I triangulated the cell tower signals and found a call to Kali's phone from a town in Utah a few days ago." Max brought up the United States on the large screen. He zoomed in on the bright red circle in the mountains outside Salt Lake City.

Glen scrolled through his search of Utah bus routes on Max's laptop. "Is that Willietown? I read in the *Post* that it's an up-and-coming boutique resort. Celebrities are flocking there instead of Park City to get away from the crowds and paparazzi."

Max ran his fingers along the smart-screen console, a semicircular glass-top computerized desk that served as the main interface for his computer system. He enlarged the area around the marker revealing Willietown in bright letters then selected the name. Photos popped up alongside the map showing a sleepy main street surrounded by luxury low-rise condos and high-end SUVs. At first glance, it appeared like an amateur had pasted two images together—one of an idyllic, bygone era and another of a glitzy, over-developed wonderland.

"I got it! A bus left this morning from the Salt Lake terminal bound for Willietown." Glen clapped Max's shoulder. "That took less than two hours to do. The CIA has nothing on us."

Max gave his friend a weak smile. Glen was staying positive for them both, a true feat considering the negative emotions weighing him down with a heavy boulder of guilt hanging around his neck. The reason why Kali hadn't used her power to pop directly to Surefire wasn't lost on Max. She didn't trust him not to use his dark energy detector to seek her out.

"DERST has a facility near Willietown?" Max pointed at the screen where a blue star appeared close to the town. The map software automatically displayed the company's remote offices and headquarters.

"About two hours west of there. But it was only temporary, to support a military testing ground a decade back," Glen said.

"Ugh . . . that name. Willietown," Mia slurred. "Sounds like a last stand in a gay Western." She'd spent the last hour passed out on a cot in his basement. Based on her speech pattern, the nap hadn't helped.

Glen rolled his eyes at her. "Go back to sleep."

"But I want to help."

Max would suggest that she shower and drink a pot of coffee. But both he and Glen agreed it best to keep an eye on Mia in his basement workshop.

"You've helped enough already," he said under his breath.

"If you let me have my phone—" she began.

"No," Max and Glen replied in unison. They kept their eyes trained on the large computer screen with their backs to her.

"I'm not the bad person here."

"And neither is Kali, yet you set her up," Max countered.

"Seriously, have you met her mother? I assumed she would be the same kind of opportunistic wench," she said.

"She saved my life!" Max whirled on her.

"Exactly."

"And what is that supposed to mean?"

"She saved you so you'd trust her. Why else would she save you? She didn't know you then."

"I don't have time for this." His focus returned to the screen.

"Mia, go get something to eat at the kitchenette, as far away from us as possible without leaving this room." Glen's good brotherly vibe had soured.

"Why won't you let me help?"

"Okay then, what else can you tell us?" Glen spun on her.

"I told you what I know."

Which was that she didn't know where Robert was. His contact information proved to be a dead end. She had nothing to add about the Organization. Glen was in the dark as well. Over the years, his father had shared the barest of facts with him, merely referring to the Organization in the same terms one would use to describe the bogeyman.

"Let me at least call our father," she pleaded.

"I can't get through to him. But when we do, I recommend that I do the talking first. It would be best to have him hear from me what happened," Glen said.

"Then I will raid your kitchen." She turned on her heel then stomped across the room.

"Don't touch the alcohol," Max called after her. She flipped a manicured middle finger over her shoulder.

"When this is over and we find Kali, I need you to tell me exactly what happened when you were kidnapped," Glen said.

Max hadn't had time to give him details about his kidnapping to the alternate universe and certainly said nothing to him about Kali's Evil Incident. He only mentioned that there was an attempted kidnapping and Kali risked her life to save him. Glen had voiced concern that the Organization and his kidnapper were linked.

"Later," Max repeated. "I don't want to be distracted more than I've already been."

He shot a look toward the kitchen where Mia guzzled down a can of Coke.

"Can you talk to Sean again? Let him know that we think Kali's in Willietown. Maybe he's gotten in touch with her or Surefire," Max asked, so he could concentrate on other efforts like calling back his NSA contact about hacking into any surveillance cameras in Willietown.

Of course, neither were the main reason he'd avoided calling Sean. He didn't want to explain that Kali had run away because of him.

"No problem." Glen pulled out his phone.

Max smiled at his friend, grateful that he could rely on his help. How Glen's older sister had turned out so different was an unsolvable mystery.

From the direction of the kitchenette, a plastic bag crinkled. At first, Max checked his hearing aids for static interference. Then he glanced around to find Mia toting a bag of potato chips and chomping on several at a time. She set the large opened bag on top of his tools and mechanical components and leaned over the worktable. Her soft sweater gaped in the front, showing off a glittery white tank top underneath. While she picked through the assorted electronics and wires and circuit boards, Max shifted his attention back to his screen and his mission and tried to pretend she wasn't there.

A difficult feat when she started batting a prototype pulse taser back and forth between her hands. He considered letting her continue. Maybe it would go off and give her a shock, enough to make her act like a normal person in this abnormal situation.

"Stop," Max ordered after he heard the metal weapon sliding along the table for the twentieth time. The noise grated against his hearing aids and nerves.

Glen glanced at them from the other side of the room where'd he'd propped himself against the kitchen counter while he spoke to Sean.

"Does it work?" She held up the weapon.

"Yes and no." Max snatched it from her before she shot herself or him. "I'm working out the kinks."

After the kidnapping, he'd taken the pulse taser out of storage but found it needed some modifications. The finished version was kept at his Shenandoah cabin where his father had set up a small arms testing range. Since his accident, he'd shut down the range as he shifted his team's focus from weapons to creating socially minded tech.

He set the pulse taser on the computerized desktop out of Mia's reach.

"I need my phone." She pouted.

"Why?"

"I need to brand, talk to fans. It's hard work being a celebrity and maintaining that status. I need to be constantly connected. Coincidentally, my fans want to know why I'm not in Willietown. *Real Life's* filming a series there with mostly C-listers, which might be why I wasn't asked, since I'm on their B-plus-list. But maybe that's why Kali went there? She wanted to get screen time. Her mom must've told her."

"She hasn't spoken to her mom in weeks, and she hates anything to do with that show," Max said, then he paused to consider what this information meant, his brain working out an answer before he knew the question. "The *Real Life* crew is in Willietown?"

"What about it?"

He spun around to his computer console. The keyboard lit up on the desk's shiny black surface.

"What are you doing?" Mia sidled next to him.

"Hacking into the *Real Life* dragonfly server. I logged into their network earlier and was able to control a camera outside my house. If their cameras in Willietown are online, hooked to the same network, I may be able to control one from across the country."

"This should be fun." Mia flopped in Glen's vacant seat.

After searching through the *Real Life's* servers, Max found the files and apps controlling the dragonfly cameras. He scrolled through the lines of code for any signals coming from Utah.

"Got it." He loaded his own code into the device, possessing it like a high-tech demon.

"Sean is getting UltraAgent Oracle's help," Glen announced as he approached them. "Now that we're fairly sure about the location, it may make it easier for her to track Kali down."

"How?" Mia asked, skeptical.

"Telepathically. Oracle's abilities have grown over the last few months, and she can search out certain brain patterns. Sean didn't go into specifics, just said that she's still having trouble controlling it, so not to hold our breath." Glen took in the image of snowy streets and renovated turn-of-the-century buildings that filled the screen. "What are you doing?"

"I took over a dragonfly camera from the *Real Life* crew filming in Willietown. It's a long shot, but it may give us a visual on Kali."

"Unfortunately, Surefire didn't tell any of her bosses at U-Sec where she was staying. They only knew she was in Utah," Glen said.

"Then cross your fingers this will work." Buildings, cars, and skiers' bright snow jackets and hats blurred across the screen as the camera broke from filming a scene on the pavement outside a historic hotel (where two women were having a disagreement about bowling averages of all things) to soar above the town.

"I don't blame Surefire for not telling anyone. I wouldn't want the bosses to know my business either," Mia said as if she knew what it was like having a job like Surefire's.

Max maneuvered the camera up a two-lane road that cut through rows of dirt-colored condo buildings to a ski resort base camp. It zipped above the heads of returning skiers and those sitting outside a bar. A group of kids threw snowballs at the camera, and Max had to quickly swing it around to avoid being hit.

His facial recognition software sorted through the video feed onscreen and didn't pick up Kali in crowds gathered around the fire pit or in the outdoor bars or walking along the ski shops.

"You're not going to find her." Mia opened Max's laptop, which Glen had discarded on the table, and pulled up a browser. "She could be anywhere."

"You're not helping," Glen said.

"Only managing Max's expectations, brother dear."

The camera left the base camp and passed through a narrow space between two buildings, where a group of snowboarders were walking past a tall man in white. Max flew the camera around a tree then back and forth and up and down the buildings to the left. Two men splashed water at the camera from their balcony hot tub. An older woman regarded the camera from atop her book as she lounged in full ski attire in a chair with a bottle of vodka by her side.

Maybe Mia was right. This was a fool's errand.

He raised the camera high above the buildings. That's when he noticed another man wearing a white jacket and ski pants, and then two more people in the same type jacket exiting the building facing the base camp. They trudged along a snowy path crisscrossing a tree-lined area toward the condos behind theirs.

"Was there a sale on white ski outfits?" Glen swiped his hand at screen.

Mia flicked a look at the screen then back to the laptop.

"I don't know. Let's get closer." Max lowered the camera as a group of four similarly attired people gathered under a tree to stare up at the building. Zooming in, Max followed their gaze and saw movement on an upper balcony. The dragonfly device drifted up the three floors and stopped to find Surefire and Kali standing at the railing.

"It's them. It's Kali." And she was okay. She was alive.

"Who's that in the living room?" Glen pointed.

Max refocused the lens toward the glass door behind the two women. A large man in a white jacket stood inside with a glowing orb-like thing in his hand and a gun in the other.

Something hit the dragonfly camera. A snowball? A rock? A bullet? One second the camera caught the ominous man in Surefire's living room, and the next, the screen filled with a white and gray blur as the camera spun out of control and crashed into a snowdrift.

Chapter 8

Where Last We Left Our Heroes in Utah

Kali gaped at the dragonfly camera that floated in front of her at eye level. She tore her gaze from it to glance at Synthia, whose face mirrored her own horror.

"They found us," she murmured.

A spray of snow hit her face from a snowball striking the camera, which sputtered and fell.

Kali.

"Did you say something?" She whipped her head back and forth to find the source. It didn't sound like Synthia's voice. It was too deep.

Kali, you're in danger. Call Sean. Tell us where you are.

Synthia leaned over the balcony.

"Oracle?" Kali whispered, although the UltraAgent's voice came from inside her head.

"Something's wrong. A group of people all dressed in white are gathering in the courtyard." Synthia staggered from the railing and knocked over the chair where she'd been sitting.

Oracle's presence flickered like the fleeting warmth of a dying flame. It wasn't suffocating, as it had been when she'd possessed Kali months ago on Dama X's island, and the other agent had taken control of her body. It was a quiet voice that made Kali wonder if her mind was playing tricks.

"I think Oracle's reaching out to me. She's saying that I'm in danger." Kali watched her friend lean against the chair she had just righted.

She peeked over the railing to find three men standing directly below, dressed in white jackets. They watched a woman scramble up the snowdrift to retrieve the fallen camera.

Get out of there. They want the book. Oracle's tone turned desperate. *Max said—*

"Ugh!" Kali grabbed her head. A sharp pain shot through her skull and cut off Oracle.

"Kali, do you feel it too?" Synthia gripped the wooden chair so hard the back splintered in her hand. "I think someone has a crystal skull."

Synthia's kryptonite. The goddess whose power resided in Synthia had a crystal skull that provided a battery boost for her conduit. There were thirteen skulls in total. If Synthia came in contact with the other skulls, when their energy was activated, then their power fed off hers and drained her.

Static nipped at the air. But it wasn't overwhelming like when she came into contact with an entire skull group, which would hose up Kali's power too.

"We need to go." Synthia reached for the sliding glass door as it slid open to reveal a man in a white ski outfit. The same man Kali had seen cutting across the courtyard.

His left hand gripped a gun. On a table next to the balcony door, a blue crystal skull had been set.

Synthia gaped at the skull. Her knees wobbled in response. The large man snaked an arm around her neck, stopping her fall. In the other hand, he brought the gun up to her temple. He dragged her into the living room.

Kali stood stunned. Fear screamed for her to pop away. Instinct told her that man would kill her friend if she did.

"Grab the book," he barked.

Kali picked up the journal and held it close to her side. It hummed against her jacket like a small engine revving to life. She grabbed the bottle of wine, the only weapon nearby.

"I know you." She stepped inside but didn't close the door. "You're that guy who hooked up with Mia at the *Real Life* dinner. Robert the Olympian."

"You're smarter than you look."

"And you're more of a dick than I remembered."

Synthia let out a cry as he tightened his grip on her neck. Her friend's face flushed red as she wheezed to catch her breath. The rock around Synthia's neck paled, turning a grayish purple.

"Please, stop. You're going to kill her." Kali tried a different tactic, as hard as it was to do. She gripped the wine bottle's neck, wanting to smash it across his square jock head.

His grip loosened and Synthia gulped at the air. Her eyes landed on the crystal skull. Kali knew what she needed to do. She had to get the skull out of the room, far from her friend.

"I want you to take that book and bring him back," Robert ordered.

"Who?" Kali shot back.

Synthia flailed her arms in an effort to dislodge him. But the skull was weakening her powers and her strength. He ground the barrel of the gun into her temple. "Don't move again. You're too weak to survive a bullet to the head."

He was taller than Kali recalled. And Synthia was petite. She looked like a first grader struggling against a high school bully.

"Take the journal to the other universe. He needs it to return."

"Who?" Kali asked again and stepped closer.

"The Dark. The Man."

"The Man?" Kali's stomach retched. He couldn't be talking about the same one who held her captive.

"Maxwell Martin's grandfather," Robert clarified. "The grandfather of the guy you've been screwing."

Kali was going to pass out or scream or run away or break this damn wine bottle over Robert's head. She couldn't decide. This was all too much, too confusing.

"You know who I mean," he said.

"Did Max send you?" She finally got the words out.

"He was supposed to be the one, but you'll do."

She frowned. "You're not making any sense."

"Take the book and meet the Man. The date is in the journal. The last page." His finger rested on the trigger.

Kali inched closer to the table where Robert had set the skull.

He bellowed, "Don't even think about it."

"I can't exactly open the book with this wine bottle in my other hand, can I?" He nodded for her to go ahead, and she set the bottle in front of the skull. As instructed, Kali flipped to the last blank page. July 20, 1979. "And *where* am I going?"

"The universe next to ours. The only one you travel to, UltraAgent TimeTrap."

She tried to act cool, as if Robert saying her codename hadn't shocked her.

"He'll meet you in this town at the base of the mountain. Go. Now," Robert said.

"Then what?" Kali asked.

"You bring him back here at this time and moment, and I don't kill Surefire. We both know she can't fight back. Not with that skull sucking her power."

How did he know all this? Had Max told him? Was Robert working for him? Kali didn't have time to rack her brain for every detail on what she'd told Max about Synthia. She didn't have time to chastise herself for jumping to conclusions, assuming Max was behind this.

She only had time to agree to this psycho's demands. "I'll do it."

Giving Synthia the barest of nods, Kali's fingers skimmed the skull as she pretended to reach for the wine bottle. The set of her jaw told Kali that her friend knew what she was about to do, and she was ready to fight when Kali did it. A tingling sensation danced along the flesh of Kali's arm. Without the others in the group, the skull didn't emit enough energy to block hers, which meant her plan might work.

Might.

"What are you doing?" Robert yelled. "Leave the wine here. You don't need it."

He was so concerned about the wine that he hadn't noticed Kali's hand coming in contact with the skull.

In that moment, Kali summoned her power. It spread like wildfire to her limbs. Then she popped into the in-between.

She tossed the skull aside. It stretched into a blob before floating away into the gray swirling space between the dimensional planes. Gripping the wine bottle and the book, she started forward into the other universe. She was going to a different time than Robert had demanded, far in the past to hide this book. By the time she returned, Synthia would have Robert beaten down, wrapped up in vines, and wishing he'd never stepped a toe in Willietown.

Kali pressed and pushed, but the dimensional plane didn't budge. When she tried to picture a faraway date and a place in the alternate world, she couldn't move. The journal became heavier, going from a one-pound weight to a twenty-pound dumbbell.

What are you?

She double backed to her universe and hoped that Synthia had time to disable Robert.

Picturing the condo, she focused on the configuration of the room and on appearing behind them.

The tile floor of the hallway materialized first. The kitchen to her right. A wall to her left where a large mirror hung. The living room in front of her, where Synthia slid out from under Robert's arm, which she twisted, causing him to pitch forward. She planted a palm in the center of his chest and sent him flying into the wall and cracking the mirror.

"Seven years bad luck, asshole." Kali swung the bottle. She missed—she never claimed to have good aim like her friend—and the bottle broke against the wall next to his head. A piece of glass sliced his cheek. He collapsed to the floor, grabbing his face.

Shouts came from outside with a familiar male voice slinging insults above the rest.

"Raven," they said in unison.

Across from the apartment, people appeared on various balconies, pointing at whatever was unfolding on the ground below. Two dragonfly cameras flew past the windows. An older woman in the other building tossed a liquor bottle from her balcony then raised her arms in victory. Kali hoped she was on their side.

Synthia glanced from Robert, moaning on the floor, to the balcony.

"Go!" Kali shooed her friend. "Help Raven. I've got this guy. If he tries anything, I'll drop his butt between the universal planes with that skull."

"Yell if you need anything." Synthia's eyes glowed a soft purple, reflecting the stone around her neck. She sprinted from the room and onto the balcony. She leaped over the railing and dropped out of sight.

"What the fuck did you do?" Robert bent over, rocking back and forth.

He looked up at her. His eyes were unfocused. An oily black film slithered across them.

"I didn't do anything." Kali picked up the neck of the broken bottle. She lifted it to her face. Droplets coagulated on the jagged glass and moved upward, which was impossible. She tossed it to the tile floor where is shattered. A black inky blob separated from the red wine.

"No." Robert backed away. His hands shoved against broken shards of glass, slicing his skin.

The quarter-sized ink stain slid into a wound on his right hand.

All she could do was stare at Robert, who reached for the journal, which she clutched to her chest. The book revved in her arms. She eased it from her body. Her chest constricted, heart raced. A sour taste coated her throat. She needed to let go of it—wanted to let go—but she couldn't.

Robert's hand swiped across the leather binding. It disappeared inside the book, followed by his forearm then the rest of his arm.

"No!" he screamed.

The book tugged on Kali's fingertips as a whirling fan turned on inside it, creating a funnel that protruded from the book. The dark cloud covered Robert's shoulder and head. His one free arm waved wildly, trying to grab onto anything to keep him tethered.

Kali struggled to pry her fingers from the book, but they were stuck like glue. The whirlpool's force pulled on her scalp. Smoky tentacles shot from the leather binding and traveled up her arms to her shoulders. Her neck bowed. Her body bent forward, stretching into the funnel. Robert's flailing hand caught in Kali's hair and held on.

He hauled her headfirst into the swirling black pit of a rabbit hole.

Chapter 9

Watching from Maryland

"No!" Max kicked the desk chair behind him and sent it rolling with a crash into the wall.

"We'll sort this out." Glen held up his hands in a gesture meant to placate but only agitated him more, because his friend looked as if he had no clue how to handle the situation.

He took a breath and focused again on finding a solution.

"I'll get another camera." He searched the *Real Life* servers for a different dragonfly to hijack. Then he stopped because he forgot the obvious, simple next step.

"Call the cops in Willietown," Max ordered Glen.

"I'll find their number." He nabbed the computer from his sister's lap.

"I was using that," she screeched.

"Yes, I see that. On helpful research, like watching the *Real Life* channel." Glen took himself and the laptop to the other side of the room.

Max scanned the server files and found another active camera in the Willietown vicinity. Before he could overwrite its system, Mia spoke up, "You don't need to do that. The other cameras are already filming them. It's all over the web, which I would've showed you had Glen given me a chance."

He switched gears and brought up the *Real Life* web channel on the big screen.

"Who is that hottie getting jumped?" Mia propped her elbows on the desk.

"That's Raven," Max said.

Mia gazed up at the screen where Raven was throwing off a stocky man who had lunged onto his back. A glass bottle landed out of nowhere, smashed against the assailant's head, and knocked him out.

While Raven waved his thanks at whoever had thrown the bottle, another sucker punched him in the stomach. Raven grabbed this attacker by his snow jacket and pitched him into the building's brick wall.

"Where's Kali?" Max asked.

The cameras surrounded the fight in the open area between the two condo complexes. The video streams were split between three cameras catching different angles. Residents gathered on the balconies to watch. A few brave onlookers stood in the shoveled walkways between the buildings leading to the base camp.

"Is that Heather St. John?" Mia gasped.

A camera caught a woman running onto her condo's balcony and vaulting over the railing.

Surefire.

A woman screamed as Surefire landed in the snowbank three floors below. She disappeared into a snowdrift. Over the video, a *Real Life* commentator echoed Mia's question about the woman being Olympic gold-medalist Heather St. John. But what she did next was nothing the commentator thought Heather capable of.

The snow bank exploded as if a bomb had gone off, sending a man and woman in white careening into a nearby tree. Out of the debris, Surefire floated above the waist-high snow. A purple halo coated her body.

The commentator called off screen for his producer to get information on Heather's twin sister, Synthia.

"The police are on their way. Someone already notified—" Glen looked up from his phone. He pointed a shaky finger at Surefire. "What is she?"

"An UltraAgent with the power of a goddess," Mia said. "I heard the gossip but assumed it was from a fake news site. Talk about ratings gold. I wouldn't be surprised if they offer her a contract for her own series after this display."

"Where's Kali?" Max asked again, not expecting an answer. More like speaking a wish out loud to give it more power in the hope that it would come true.

Surefire whipped out her arms and rotated her hands. Branches dipped from the evergreens and wrapped around the man and woman, struggling to stand in the snow at the base of the trees where they'd been tossed by Surefire's energy bomb. An assailant detoured from ambushing Raven and faced her, a knife raised in his hand. He sprinted forward. She threw out her hand and without touching him knocked the weapon away. Raven yanked him around and slammed his fist into his jaw, knocking out teeth and staining his white jacket with spots of blood. The last of the attackers ran away, shoving into the crowd that had gathered between the buildings. Raven started to follow, but Surefire grabbed his arm and pulled him to a stop.

The voiceovers reported the police were en route. As the commentators chattered on, a whirling noise deafened the speakers. The couple looked up at the third-floor balcony. One of the *Real Life* cameras flew toward the sound.

"Is that where Kali was?" Glen asked.

"I think so," Max said.

As it entered the room, the dragonfly camera halted feet from the funnel. The video cut out then appeared again. Jagged lines and static interrupted the feed. Objects in the posh living room hung suspended as if by wires. The feed cleared enough for Max to see past the pixelated image to a mind-bending scene.

"No!" He reached out as if he could grab Kali's hand through the screen and keep her from going into . . .

"Is she getting sucked into that book?" Max was surprised at how calm his question sounded.

"Yes," Glen said softly.

"Did you know about—?"

"In theory, not in practice," Glen replied before he could finish his question.

"This can't be real," Max uttered.

"It is on the *Real Life* channel," Mia said.

Max refused to dignify her reply with even a side-eyed glance, because he couldn't stop staring at the sight of Kali's body bending forward and stretching like Play-Doh.

The panel streaming the outside camera feed caught Surefire and Raven disappearing then reappearing onto the balcony, as the interior camera recorded Kali's head, then torso, then legs and feet disappearing into the book along with the smoky funnel. The camera crashed to the tile floor along with plants and knickknacks and picture frames. It landed on its side next to a broken wine bottle.

"She went into that book and I think that guy did too," Surefire said to Raven. The camera's microphone picked up their conversation.

Small boots passed in front of the camera tipped on its side. Black snowboarding boots paused in front of the camera. One foot lifted and stomped on the lens. The feed went dark.

The remaining cameras swooped in. A bright lavender light flashed inside the condo.

"I thought Heather's twin sister—Synthia is it?—went crazy. Had to be put away," Mia said.

The lights in Max's workshop glowed purple. Or maybe his eyes were tired, and he was seeing things. He squeezed them shut and when he opened them the room still held a purple hue.

"Oh, I was put away, but not for what you think." Surefire appeared in the room next to Raven, who cradled a glowing skull.

Glen dropped his phone to the floor, but he didn't seem to care. He was too busy staring at Surefire as she stormed toward him.

"You aren't Max." Her wet boots squeaked to a stop in front of him. She held the Man's journal out from her side as if she didn't want to touch it more than necessary.

"I am." Max stepped from the console into her line of sight.

She marched from Glen, who continued to stare at her with his mouth opening and closing like a fish out of water. She stepped up to Max to stand toe-to-toe with him. He had to look down to meet her eyes, an odd shade of violet. She held the journal up to his face. The black leather was worn at the edges. In the light, the binding had a golden sheen. The logo embossed on its cover was the same as his grandfather's journals.

"What happened to Kali?" Max asked.

"I was hoping you could tell us. Because this thing"—she tapped it with her finger—"opened a portal, and we have no idea where it led."

Max checked his hearing aids, hoping he'd misheard her, because he didn't want to believe what had unfolded in front of the cameras was true.

Surefire flipped open the book to an image straight from Kali's nightmares.

Then Max understood what had initially spooked Kali when the surveillance feed had shown her reading this book in his living room, and why she ran, after discovering the TPC in his basement.

Diagrams were scrawled across the pages depicting the object that Kali had described to him in detail. It was the same device that had trapped S-Kali in the alternate universe and a rudimentary version of the TPC he'd helped create.

His mouth went dry. The other journals weren't magical. Well, as far as he could tell. He hadn't attempted to open a portal with them. That idea had never crossed his mind, nor had the idea that his grandfather could possess extrasensory abilities that allowed him to predict a TPC decades ago. As far as Max knew, no transhuman living today had the ability to predict the future.

"How is this possible?" he said.

"You figure it out. It's your grandfather's handwriting." She slapped it against his chest.

Chapter 10

Similar But Different

After being pulled and tugged like dough through a spaghetti machine, Kali found herself staring at a blue sky while lying on her back on soft grass. The first thing she realized was that it was hot—summer sticky hot—and thankfully, there was no snow. Kali hated snow almost as much as she hated being unexpectedly sucked through dimensional portals.

She pushed off her hood. With slow, deliberate movements, she rose to a seated position and tested her equilibrium. The world wasn't spinning like a gyroscope, so she had that going for her, even if she was a bit disoriented. She shielded her eyes against the bright sun.

"Screw off," Kali said to the pounding that started at the base of her neck and marched forward with the intensity of a drum major. She closed her eyes and pressed her palms over them.

A bee buzzed her ear. She swatted at it then slipped out of her puffy winter coat.

Squinting, she looked around to find herself at the bottom of hibernating ski slopes. In the distance, hikers traversed a path on their way to the summit. Ski lifts rose quiet and empty. The buildings opposite the mountain comprised a simple, no-nonsense base camp next to a gravel-covered parking lot.

Inhaling as if she were about to dive into freezing cold water, she tapped into her power.

It puttered, fizzled, then nothing.

"Let's try this again." She focused on home and waited for the familiar hum.

A slight static blip tickled her core then retreated. Whatever had shot them through the portal had also drained her power. No wonder she had a headache. Her body was weak, her mojo tapped out.

Out of the corner of her vision, she noticed a white ski jacket. From the marshmallow mound, a moan emanated, then a "what the fuck?" that grew into another expletive-laden sentence.

Rising to her feet, she shed her thermal shirt to reveal a tank top. Fortunately, she wore jeans and not ski pants. Although what to do with her wool-lined snow boats was another question.

"You!" the Olympian—Robert was it?—yelled. "What did you do?"

And here it came. This freaking guy blaming her for what happened. He held a gun to her best friend's head and threatened to blow a hole in it but thought this situation was her fault.

Kali sprinted in the opposite direction, toward a plain concrete structure. As she ran, she shouted between huffs, "It was that journal. It opened up a portal."

"Bullshit. You opened it and took me with you."

She hazarded a glance in her rearview as he ripped off his jacket. His face was blow-a-gasket red. Sweat streamed along his brow. His drenched thermal shirt stuck to his torso. He barreled in her direction, easily gaining ground on her. He looked meatier and meaner than he had in the condo. Or maybe it was the I'm-going-to-tear-you-apart look he gave her that made him appear more menacing.

Cardio wasn't her strong suit. Her pace slowed. She huffed and puffed then petered out. He closed in on her. She spun around and back stepped with her hands held up, palms out.

"Easy, there."

He grabbed her arm and twisted. She fell to the ground, her only option if she didn't want her shoulder to dislocate or arm to break.

"Can't . . . talk . . . pain."

He let go but didn't move far. She rubbed her shoulder and knelt on the ground.

"Looks like we're in the mid-to-late seventies. And if that portal follows my power's time-traveling rules, then we're in another universe," she said.

Robert—although Kali was apt to call him a few other choice names— glanced around then back at her. "I can't believe you took me here."

"I didn't do jack. It was the Man's journal. I will replay the scene in terms that you can understand. When you touched it, it went all . . ." Kali whirled her hands in the air and made a buzzing noise with her lips. "And a portal opened then we went through the in-between, and it spit us out like pureed broccoli from a sick baby's mouth."

He stared at her. Blinked. Then he pivoted in a circle, arms waving violently. "Where's the journal?"

She scooted back from him. He had no weapon that she could see besides his strength, which he'd proved was greater than hers. Even if she used her self-defense training, she doubted she could take him down or disable him for long.

Keeping herself out of grabbing distance, Kali rose and retraced her steps to the spot where she'd awoken. The grass blades were bent, forming an outline of her body.

"That's freaky. There's no book. Must've stayed back in the condo. Hold on." She spied a groundskeeper walking from the ski lodge. He toted a rake over his shoulder.

Kali jogged over to him.

"Hey, where are you going?" Robert tagged along, close on her heels.

She ignored the jackass jock and said to the older man, "Excuse me."

"Yep?" Groundskeeper Grizzly Adams took in her boots and ski jacket wrapped around her waist but didn't offer any comment.

"I'm about to ask you two odd questions. I don't want you to think that I'm crazy but here goes."

"Shoot." He swung his rake off his shoulder to lean on it.

"What year is it?" she asked

The groundskeeper flicked a look at the glowering jock glued to her side then back to her. He had the best poker face she'd ever seen. If he was fazed by how they were dressed and what she was asking, he didn't show it.

"1979. What's your second question?"

"Did the Titanic sink?"

"What are you talking about?" Robert was about to suffer a heat stroke if he didn't take off his thermal shirt and calm down.

"She's talking about the Titanic. You never heard of it? It's all my grandpap talked about. Been plays and movies made about it sinking." The groundskeeper scratched his chin through his gray beard.

Robert shrugged. "Not much of a theater person."

"Suit yourself. Is that all, miss?" He slung the rake back over his shoulder.

"Public restrooms and a pay phone?"

"Around the back. May want to get yourself a drink, too, at the diner across the street. It can get awful hot in Utah in July, especially if you've been dipping into the peyote."

"We're not on drugs," Robert said as the groundskeeper headed on his merry way.

"If you say so." He let out a wheezy laugh.

Kali made a beeline to the bathrooms. Robert grabbed her wrist and yanked her around.

"What was that about?" he demanded.

She broke free of his grip. "We've been sucked back in time, but not in our universe. We're in a parallel one—the one where I'm supposed to meet the Man."

"Shit. You're right. We're in the month and year written in the journal."

"Normally, I could pop us out of here and back into our universe, but my power is tapped out."

"Is this where you took the skull?"

"It's long gone. Sandwiched between the worlds."

His large hand smacked her across the face, sending her to the ground, her head missing a softball-sized rock by inches. Blood pooled in her mouth where her teeth cut into her cheek with the force of his blow. She spit out the blood then felt herself go very still. That stillness scared her more than anger or fear would have, because it signaled her fight or flight response was about to take over.

And with her power AWOL, flight wasn't an option.

"Something's wrong. My veins are on fire. I can't cool down." He paced frantically at her side.

Kali reached for the rock that she'd nearly smashed her head on. She hazarded a glance at the agitated man and then remembered the wine bottle.

"There was black stuff in the wine. It went into your cuts." The fingers of her right hand wiggled the rock from the soil while she held his eyes; their hazel color appeared to darken.

"Then that's why—" He screwed his eyes shut and bent over as if he were about to vomit.

"That wasn't meant for me." Robert kicked the ground. "It was meant for Max."

"Max?" Kali exclaimed then wished she would've kept quiet when he reeled on her. His face was so flushed with anger, she worried lava would spew from the top of his head.

"Or you." He shoved a thick finger in her face. "After that bitch screwed up our plans, I was going to force you to drink it and activate the portal, if you refused to go on your own, or your power couldn't bring back the Man." He was crying now. Big sloppy tears mixed with perspiration that dripped from his forehead. "That's why the journal opened, because it infected me. It's inside me. Oh, shit, it's inside me."

"I don't understand a word that's coming out of your mouth." Kali eased into a sitting position. Her empty left hand rested in her lap, while her right hand gripped the primitive weapon behind her back.

He squatted in front of her, rapped his knuckles on the top of her head. "You were supposed to drink it. Not me. It could kill me."

"Then what would it have done to me?"

"It doesn't matter." His face was inches from hers. Typical square jaw, deep-set eyes, and a bully-like sneer. "Because you don't matter."

Her left hand shot out and wrapped around his throat, catching him off guard, and shoving him onto his butt. He snickered at her attempt to hurt him, so distracted in his amusement that he didn't see her right hand swing down and hit the rock into this temple.

"Fuck!" His hands swiped at her.

She dodged them and used her momentum to land another blow. He flopped onto his back. She scrambled to her feet and stared at the bloodied rock in her hand then at his temple, where a stream of red coated his brown, shaggy hair. He was breathing. Part of her felt relieved and another part, a deep, dark part, wished he hadn't been.

She dropped the rock and scurried toward the bathrooms.

Then she heard a sound that quickened her heart and her pace.

A helicopter.

Without turning around, she knew it was cresting the mountain.

The Man.

She didn't waste any time confirming her suspicions. She sprinted the several yards to the building where the groundskeeper said the bathrooms were. Her jacket fell from around her waist but she kept going. She rounded a corner and slammed into the first door she came to. It wasn't the bathroom but an office. No one was there. She continued through to a supply room with racks of ski equipment—a dead end. She grabbed a ski pole. The end was pointy enough for her to get a good poke in.

Who was she kidding? They had rifles and handguns—and that glass coffin.

She climbed a metal rack to peer out the windows lining the top of the supply room. The helicopter landed in the field where they had awoken. She couldn't see Robert.

Sliding to the floor, she pictured her condo in Baltimore in her universe, in her time. Her power churned, sputtered, then died. If she was a car, smoke would be billowing from the hood.

I'm not going to panic.

She took a breath and tried to calm herself. Why hadn't she taken yoga with Pax and Oracle? Her breath hitched.

"Are they after you?" the groundskeeper asked as he entered the room. His breath was heavy, uneven, as if he'd run a great distance to get there.

She nodded and held the ski pole in front of her.

His beefy hand swatted it away. "Did you do something bad?"

She shook her head then opted for the truth, well, the part of the truth that wouldn't make him think she'd lost her mind. "They want to use me. They were doing experiments on me and they want me back."

She held his foggy brown eyes and didn't flinch, didn't blink, didn't look away. She wanted him to understand she wasn't lying.

"Goddamn government," he muttered. "Ever since Tricky Dick was president, things have gotten worse. Not that they were perfect before, mind you. 'Cause I can tell you some stories."

He disappeared behind a rack next to her. Through the ski boots lining the shelves, she watched as he squatted on the other side. Outside the walls, men's voices drifted closer. They'd found Robert.

"Let's go then." A hatch opened in the floor and he motioned for her to climb inside.

She scuttled to the hole. Dipping her head down the shaft, she was greeted with blackness.

When she hesitated, he said, "It's an underground passage between the buildings. Mostly it's used in the tourist season to make deliveries. It'll take you to the hotel across the way. Tell them Willie sent you. They won't bother ya."

She climbed down a wooden ladder and he closed the hatch. A metal lock screeched into place seconds before she heard the office door fly open, followed by a cadre of boots stampeding across the wooden floorboards. Dust drifted onto Kali's head. She fought the urge to sneeze. She covered her mouth and slid backward until she bumped against the concrete foundation.

"Did a woman run in here?" a gruff voice asked Willie.

Kali held her breath and went completely still. If she could stop her heart from thudding, she would have.

"No . . . No one working today but me," Willie responded then added as if in an afterthought, "You know, I did see a young lady as I was making my way here. Tall and skinny like a beanpole, running to the parking lot. She jumped in the back of a pickup truck. They headed east."

"Thanks for your time, sir," the soldier replied.

"Anything to help out the Man," Willie said with a chuckle.

Chapter 11

In Max's Basement Lab

Max caressed the book's smooth leather. This mysterious journal had belonged to his grandfather, and it had also ripped the woman he loved from his world.

"Don't do what's she's asking. Don't even touch it." Mia tried to snatch it from him, but Max angled away.

Surefire scowled at Mia, who slumped back into the chair and propped her feet on the computer console.

"Who's she?" the UltraAgent asked.

"My sister," Glen replied.

"Oh . . . her." Surefire rolled her eyes. Mia's reputation preceded her.

She nodded at the journal that Max continued to clutch to his chest. "Where did this book take my friend?"

"And the man who held a gun to my girlfriend's head." Raven stood behind Surefire.

"What man?" Max asked, then he recalled the figure the dragonfly camera had picked up standing inside the condo.

"Kali said his name was Robert. I think he was the guy Mia hooked up with at the *Real Life* holiday dinner." Surefire looked pointedly at Glen's sister.

Mia lifted a shoulder. "He had his chance."

"For what?" Glen asked.

"To do the right thing," she replied.

"And what would that be?" Glen said.

Mia offered another nonchalant shrug.

"Moving on from Miss Not Helpful over there," Raven said. "We watched the bottom of Kali's boot disappear into the leather binding."

"Robert was already gone. The book was laying where I'd left him, and his gun was still there," Surefire added.

"Ergo, he probably got sucked in too." Raven crossed his arms.

"Did anyone drink the wine?" Glen asked.

"No," Surefire replied. "But Kali smashed the bottle against the wall when she tried to hit Robert with it."

"Then he may have been—" Glen retrieved his phone from the floor without finishing his thought.

"May have been what?" Max asked.

"I need to talk to my father." Phone clutched in his hand, Glen scurried to the far end of the room.

Raven and Surefire looked to Max, their eyebrows raised, arms crossed.

"Mia's and Glen's father was the one who kept the journal. I didn't know about it until Glen saw Kali holding the book in my security footage." Max filled them in on Robert's role and what he knew about the Organization.

"Mia stole it from her father for this group. They were after me and wanted me to have the journal and, I guess, open this portal by drinking whatever the wine was laced with. But Mia double-crossed them and set it up for Kali to find."

"Oh, really?" Surefire cocked her head at Mia.

"Really." She lounged back in the chair as calm, cool, and composed as before.

"You set up my friend?"

When Mia merely met Surefire's glower with one of her own, Max explained, "She did it to protect me."

"From what?" Surefire demanded.

"You saw what happened," Mia said.

Surefire's necklace glowed. The hairs on Max's arm stood on end as if from a static charge of an impending lightning storm.

"And you didn't care that it would happen to Kali?" Surefire said.

"She's not family," Mia stated.

"But she's our family." The UltraAgent's voice dropped an octave.

Max winced from a sudden ringing in his hearing aids.

"Take a beat." Raven wedged himself in front of Surefire.

"Step aside," she ordered, and again Max recoiled at the deep pitch that made his hearing aids screech.

Raven exhaled a long, ragged breath and moved next to Max. "We don't have time for this."

"I'll make it quick." She slid to the side to get around them.

Pop!

The taser went off.

Raven arched his back, his face contorted in pain. Max lunged forward and caught the guy before he fell. He tried to hold him up, but his weight was too awkward. Instead, he eased him onto his stomach. The back of Raven's jacket smoked from the blast that tore up his back. The smell of singed cotton and flesh filled Max's nose.

"Hmmm." Mia held the taser up, puckered her lips, and blew across the barrel. "It does work. Trigger is a bit loose though. Might want to fix that."

She swung the weapon at Surefire.

Chapter 12

Kali Is Where We Left Her

Kali remained in the nook under the floorboards of the ski rental shack. She huddled in the far corner on the damp dirt of the dugout basement, her legs pulled up to her chest, her face buried in her knees to muffle any cries that leaked from her mouth.

According to her watch, she'd been there for an hour. Her joints and muscles ached from holding the same position for so long. But Kali was afraid to move, to blink, fearful she'd make a sound that would give her away to the soldiers while they did one last sweep through the office and supply room overhead.

She stared into the pitch-black corridor in front of her that Willie had said led to the hotel across the road. She didn't know what she'd find there, who would help her, and how she would get away undetected. With her stretchy jeans, tank top and snow boots, she didn't blend with late '70s summer fashion.

The floor above rattled as the helicopter's engine revved to life. It took off, leaving a heavy silence in its wake. Kali released a ragged breath and stared into the weak light filtering through the floorboards, illuminating dust motes floating in the air. Thirty minutes had passed since she'd last heard Willie's voice from the office.

For the third time, but what felt like a hundredth, she took inventory. Her burner phone, which wouldn't work in this time anyway, was in the coat that fell from her waist when she was running like a mad woman. Her U-Sec issued watch that her bosses used to track her work-related Q-Ts was in a desk drawer at her office. Her passport (she'd left her license at Max's) was in her back pocket along with a credit card from her world. She had five dollars stuffed in her front pocket, but like her other money, it would be slightly off in this universe. The smaller bills might pass a cursory inspection as long as they didn't check the dates. At her office and home, she kept a safe with currencies and denominations from this universe—assuming this was the alternate universe she usually visited. Based on the Titanic sinking here, according to Willie, then her assumption seemed legit.

She took a chance and stretched out her left leg then her right. She rotated her shoulders and flinched when her back popped as loud as a firecracker in this tight space. She couldn't stay here all day. She needed food, water, and a bathroom.

Yep, she stood and felt the pressure in her lower abdomen. A bathroom would be a good thing. That's what she got for drinking a glass of water before alt-jumping. Not that she'd done it on purpose. It was that damn book, and now she couldn't alt-jump. Her power would build and then go "poof!" leaving her frustrated and spent. She'd had a similar problem with a different type of climaxing, but that was another thing altogether.

The idea of climaxing made her thoughts go to Max—a place she didn't want to go—because she wasn't sure how she could be both angry and aroused with the same person. Men who deceived you shouldn't be that hot or that good in bed or that thoughtful in buying her warm, comfy Chewbacca slippers.

They shouldn't come wrapped in the man of your dreams.

Kali had been right for once. The perfect dream wouldn't last.

She frowned as she replayed the events from the beginning and tried to piece together what she knew from what had happened, but nothing seemed to fit. What was Mia's motive? To break them up?

No, that didn't seem it.

Why had Mia left the book for her to find? Why had she led Kali to the secured room? Did she want to scare Kali away, warn her about Max?

No. She shook her head hard. *That woman doesn't give a hoot about me.*

She recalled Robert's comment about Kali not mattering. A sentiment that hurt her even though she knew better than to allow that jock's cruel words to affect her. He would've forced her to drink the wine if she refused to get the Man, and then she would've been infected with whatever it was that had infected him.

So, did that mean that he and Mia were working together?

That scenario felt right in her gut . . . but not quite . . . because where did Max fit into these nefarious plans?

More questions flooded her brain. Enough to drown her in this dry, dank cellar.

During his tear-filled tirade, Robert mentioned Max was supposed to drink the wine and open the portal, but some "bitch" screwed it up. Kali? Mia? Who knew?

Nothing makes sense. She lightly banged the back of her head against the concrete wall. Maybe the jolt would shake loose the missing pieces to this insanely complicated puzzle. But the only thing the banging shook loose was another question.

Robert went off the rails in the crazy train when he learned about the black oil seeping into his cuts. What was that stuff? And how could it enable someone to open a dimensional portal?

She shuddered and scrubbed her hands down her arms as if the vile substance was crawling inside her as it had crawled into Robert's cuts.

He'd planned for Max to drink it and open the portal, so did that mean Max wasn't working with them? So "them" must be part of the white jacket brigade that had jumped Raven outside the condo.

Then again, why did Max have a journal that detailed Kali's worst nightmare? The handwriting on some of the pages matched Max's other two journals. Besides the size and the leather binding being slightly different, there was no doubt it had belonged to his grandfather at some point.

Why hadn't he told her about it when she described what happened in the alternate universe? And why had he kept the containment unit a secret?

Maybe he couldn't tell you, the sensible, logical, unemotional part of her brain argued. *He was trying to protect you. He didn't want to scare you away. The containment unit was a proprietary project for a client. He could've been sued for showing it to you.*

It still didn't make it right. At any time during their talk, he could've admitted what was in the book. They could've discussed it, and after she freaked out, she might've listened. Because deep in her broken heart was a pocket of hope that this was all a big misunderstanding.

But then again, he could've been playing her, gaining her trust until . . .

Enough! Her subconscious yelled because she was too afraid to yell it out loud.

She took in a centering breath. Cowering under a ski shack wouldn't find her answers. It wasn't going to get her out of this situation and back home.

Or get her to a bathroom.

Kali brushed the dirt from her pants and forced herself to step into the corridor. She blanked her mind so it wouldn't play every scary scenario of what might be waiting for her inside that dark hall. Otherwise, she'd stay rooted in place until she withered away—after peeing on herself, which seemed more comforting than trying her luck in the unknown. But she had to try. She owed it to Surefire and Raven, who were probably worried sick and would spring into action to get her back. An action that would lead them to confronting Max and that bitch goddess doing her sexual whammy thing on Max—which Kali shouldn't care about but did. And what if Max tricked them and trapped both Synthia and Raven in another prison?

Ugh! She wanted to scream and couldn't, so she settled for gnashing her teeth, which she'd read people did in biblical times to vent frustration, but it didn't provide the relief a well-bellowed swear word would've given her.

Food was the answer to getting her power back. Or maybe it was the journal, which obviously wielded an energy field strong enough to form a portal. But where was the book? Had she missed it along the grassy slope?

Had the soldiers found it? Or had it been left behind at the ski resort in her universe?

She trailed her hand along the rough concrete walls of the tunnel. Slow and deliberate steps carried her forward over the uneven dirt floor. The corridor turned to the right. For a few paces, she was in complete darkness. The meager light from her hideout gone. She willed herself ahead.

Something tickled her fingers. She jerked her hand back from a spider web.

"Argh!" she cried then clamped a hand over her mouth. She scampered though the dark, flinging her arm wildly in the air trying to dislodge the sticky web. She ran her hands over her short hair and neck then down her body, feeling for any hitchhiking insects. She didn't have the fear of bugs that Raven did, but she wasn't a fan of them hanging on her either.

The corridor curved again to reveal a dim light shining between floor-to-ceiling stacks of boxes. Wedging her fingers between them, she found they were empty and began unstacking them until she created an opening into a small storage room. She picked her way around cartons of booze toward a neon orange and green flowered curtain.

Parting the fabric, she discovered a long aisle cutting through tall metal shelves. Tentatively, she stepped into the aisle, entering a basement so wide and deep that Kali couldn't see the other side from where she stood. Racks held boxes of toilet paper, cleansers, and laundry supplies. Farther down the aisle, the supplies became food-related: cans of tuna fish, bags of chips, bottles of soda, loaves of bread, boxes of pasta, and jars of various sauces and peanut butter.

"Score," Kali whispered. She nabbed the peanut butter, a loaf of Wonder bread, and a bottle of Coke—not exactly a meal of champion UltraAgents, but it would do.

An opening in the cinder block wall revealed a toilet and a utility sink with a dingy mop and bucket pushed into the corner.

Kali was relieved to relieve herself. That important to-do item off her list, she took stock of her surroundings. To the right of the bathroom was a door. Opening it an inch, she discovered that it led to stairs to the floor above. She put her ear to the crack and listened to find a few muffled, faraway voices. Shoes plopped across the first floor, leading in the opposite direction. From what she could discern, maybe two, possibly three people were above. Carefully, she closed the door.

With snacks in hand, she walked in the opposite direction from the stairs and turned down the last aisle, the top of which was lined with rectangular windows to her left. Sunlight filtered through the panes, which were in serious need of a cleaning. But at least she could see as she picked her way to the back corner, as far from the stairs as possible. Using a cardboard box containing napkins as a table, she sat on the floor and opened the bread then used her fingers to spread the peanut butter. She washed it down with the soda, which tasted richer and more syrupy than what she was used to in her time and universe.

And because she couldn't cut a break, what sounded like a small Dutch army in wooden clogs clopped down the steps as she stuck a finger covered in peanut butter into her mouth. The basement door creaked open. Two women discussed theories about the soldiers' visit as they entered the basement.

"Gross. Who didn't flush?" A teen squealed, as girls that age are prone to do, taking dramatic offense to everything.

Pulling her finger from her mouth, Kali tried to see past the metal racks and boxes but was too far to spot anything but bare legs. She wiped her peanut-buttery hand along her jeans.

"Probably Willie. He was down here showing the soldiers around. Not sure what any of them were looking for," the other woman said. She sounded older—definitely more mature—but not by much. "Geez, Willie left the light on in the back room again."

The woman's tennis shoes squeaked against the floor two aisles away from Kali, who held her breath and froze with peanut butter and her tongue stuck to the rough of her mouth. Her eyes tracked back and forth and up the aisle, looking for a place to hide.

The toilet flushed. Kali used the sound to mask her shoving the bread, peanut butter, and the empty Coke bottle behind the makeshift table box. She swallowed the peanut butter and prayed that it would provide enough fuel to resurge her power. Closing her eyes, she took a deep breath and concentrated on pulling the energy from inside her chest and letting it float to her—

"And who do we have here?"

Kali jumped up from her cross-legged position. A woman who appeared a few years younger than Kali, wearing tiny jean shorts and a plaid shirt, stood at the end of the aisle with her hands on her hips. Her straw-colored hair was pulled back in a tight braid, making her sharp features more severe.

Kali opened her mouth to talk, but the woman spoke for her.

"Meditating?"

Kali nodded.

"Dressed a bit warm, aren't you?"

Kali nodded again, and because she wasn't quick enough to think of anything better, she said, "Um, Willie was supposed to meet me here."

"He was, was he?" She grinned as if she knew Kali's secret—a naughty one, based on the way she wriggled her brows.

The toilet flushed again and the girl called, "Hey, Teri, where did you go?"

"Down the last aisle. We have a trespasser."

"A trespasser?" The person belonging to the girlish voice click-clacked in her heavy clogs to stand behind the woman she called Teri. She looked to be a teenager, possibly related to the braided gal. She had the same light hair and skin, but hers was peppered with freckles and less sun damage. She wore tight bellbottom jeans and a yellow peasant blouse.

"Should I call the cops?" she asked between rapid chews on her gum.

"She's skinny enough, I think we could take her." Teri grinned.

Kali wouldn't argue with that assessment. This woman was broad-shouldered, her legs thick with muscle built—she guessed—from years on the ski slope.

Teri laughed when Kali's worry must've shown on her face.

"Nah, I'm messing with you. Willie's taken women down here before. He's a Casanova, that one."

"Yuck." The teen stuck out her tongue and made a face that Kali wished she could've. Instead she bowed her head, pretending to be embarrassed.

"You didn't see those photos of Willie from twenty years ago winning all those ski competitions. He was the bee's knees, according to our mom before the Korean War made him lose a few screws. Of course, I've heard rumors that he has other attributes that women love." Teri winked at Kali, who tried to give her the most convincing "oh, yeah, he's well-endowed" smile.

"I'm not even going to ask." The teen spun on her clogged heel, almost falling down.

"Kathy, you're going to break your neck in those," Teri admonished.

The girl saluted her with the middle finger.

"I'm telling Mom," she yelled at her back.

"No, you won't." Kathy nabbed a box of crackers from the far end of the aisle and took off upstairs.

Teri rolled her eyes. "That girl is so spoiled. Come on, I'll take you to Willie."

"Thanks," Kali said truly grateful for her help.

And more grateful that her luck appeared to be turning around, until they started up the stairs and Teri asked, "What's with the boots? It's hot as hell out there."

"It was chilly this morning when I went for a hike. My roommate stole my hiking shoes, so I had to wear these."

Terri nodded, as if she bought the explanation, but Kali sensed she wasn't out of the interrogation woods yet.

Once upstairs, they entered a lobby with brown paneling and wooden furniture topped with floral-printed velvet cushions. Antlers served as lamp bases. On the far end of the room was a stone fireplace with a giant moose head overseeing two guests reading newspapers. To her left came the smell of home cooking from the hotel's restaurant set with oak tables and checkered tablecloths.

Teri strutted pass the front desk, which was lined with so much wood paneling it would've blended with the walls if it weren't for the green rotary phone and another antler lamp topped with an orange lampshade. The woman ducked into a back office then came out and scanned an adjacent hallway then went into the restaurant. She asked a waitress named Flo if she'd seen Willie. The waitress hadn't but offered a laundry list of suggestions for where he could be.

"I can call him on the intercom." She pointed to a large silver device behind the front desk.

"That won't be necessary. I'll go outside and see if I can find him." Kali peeped through the windows. No sign of soldiers, but she needed to be sure.

"What was the deal with the military? Were they doing some kind of exercise? Is there a base close by?" Kali did her best to appear nonchalant as she looked at the black and white photos of local skiers on the wall and came to a stop at one name, William Nolan, written on a photo of a young man hoisting a trophy over his head. Something about that image and his background in the Korean War sounded familiar.

"I don't know what those soldiers were doing here. You think they'd tell us anything?" Teri took a seat behind the receptionist desk. "You like that picture of Willie there?" She jerked her chin at the photograph Kali was staring at. "See, I told you he was a cutie."

She wiggled her brows in response. "Yeah, buddy. A real hot dog."

"See any more of those men out there?" She inclined her head toward the window by Kali.

"Not a one," she replied.

Teri busied herself with shuffling papers on her desk. "They took a man into custody. Not sure who he was. Never saw him before. I guess he had an accomplice because they searched the buildings for somebody else. Willie said he saw them take off in a truck. Seemed like they may have gone AWOL from the base a few miles away."

She studied Teri's face to determine if she suspected Kali of being the accomplice. Before she could guess what the woman thought, Teri's eyes narrowed and she jumped up from behind the desk, making a beeline for Kali who braced herself for an attack.

She swatted at Kali's breast. Then stamped her foot on the floor. "Spider. Not the dangerous kind, don't worry. We have an infestation of them in the underground passage."

Teri paused at her statement, and Kali could almost see the woman's brain processing what this meant.

The door opened and Willie barreled inside toward the basement stairs.

"Caught your girlfriend sneaking about in the storage room," Teri said to him.

"What?" He skidded to a stop.

She pursed her lips and waved a hand in Kali's direction, where she stood behind the open door that almost slammed into her when Willie barged in.

"You kept me waiting and waiting." Kali snaked an arm around his shoulders. Years of being on reality television taught her a thing or two about faking it.

Willie's mouth opened but no sound came out. His forehead crinkled, deepening the already deep creases.

"Remember, the basement?" Kali jabbed her elbow into his ribs. "You told me to meet you there?"

"Right, right." He wagged his head. "I was a bit distracted by those men acting like they owned the place."

"They find what they came for?" Teri glanced from Willie to Kali, expecting it seemed, to catch one or both in a lie.

"I think so." Willie shuffled his work boots along the wide floorboards.

"Hmmm," Teri responded.

Kali grabbed Willie's hand. He stiffened then relaxed and gave her fingers as squeeze. She took it as a sign he would play along and tugged him out the door.

"So, where did you two lovebirds meet?" Teri leaned on the desk.

"Here and there. I just got in town. I'm an old friend." She stepped onto the porch.

"Not that old." Teri grunted.

"Daughter of an old friend," Willie clarified and seemed pleased with his lie until Teri pulled a look of disgust.

"It's not like it sounds." Kali propped the door open with her foot. "You said you were going to give me a tour then get some grub. Nice meeting you, Teri."

She yanked Willie onto the covered porch that overlooked the two-lane street in front of the ski shack where she'd been hiding. The road was a typical small town main street, lined with houses and shops still standing from the turn of the century. Green mountains rose around them. She wished she could enjoy the scenery. If this universe followed the history of hers, then in a few decades the ski shack would be demolished for condos. High-end ski shops, boutiques, and restaurants would possess the century-old buildings.

Kali glanced up and down the street. An old black Lincoln sedan drove by.

No, not an old Lincoln, she corrected herself, a new one for this time period.

"Come on." She led Willie down the two steps from the porch onto the sidewalk.

"Where are we going?" he asked.

Kali dropped his hand.

"I don't know. Just away from there. Teri was asking too many questions. I had to make up the story about us hooking up."

"No problem." He puffed up like he enjoyed the idea.

Kali eyed the nearby buildings and residences. "We need to talk in private."

They passed a couple who greeted Willie before eyeballing Kali's attire. In this small town, it was impossible for her to blend.

"I live around the next block over the bowling alley. Let's go there." After the couple was out of earshot, he added, "They took your friend."

"He wasn't my friend, but that doesn't matter because I still need to save him. I can't leave him, as much as I want to."

"He's gone. You can't get back inside that base. Security is tight, and the buildings take up a few acres. But you know that already."

It took Kali a second to understand why Willie thought she'd know about the base. Then she recalled she'd mentioned how they'd experimented on her and decided to give him a portion of the truth.

"It was dark when I . . . um . . . Robert and I . . . escaped. They kept me in a metal room with no windows inside a glass and steel coffin. I didn't even know what state I was in, let alone city." Besides her blood pumping a tad harder, she didn't feel the stomach-souring anxiety she'd felt before when mentioning the EI. Maybe it was a sign that she was making a small progress in coming to terms with it.

"Those sons of bitches," he spoke in a voice so low Kali had to lean into him to hear his words. "I knew they were up to no good."

He continued in his gravelly voice, "That base sprung up a few years ago. Suddenly a herd of DERST contractors took over the town while they built it. Not one of those gents would talk about the project. Maxwell Martin had them all under a gag order."

"Did you say DERST? Maxwell Martin?" Kali skidded to an abrupt stop. Until Willie said those names, she hadn't realized that a microscopic part of her believed Robert had been lying when he'd said Max's grandfather would meet her in this universe.

Willie paused a few paces ahead when he noticed she was no longer at his side.

"Then you didn't know who was keeping you either?" He squinted against the sun.

"Something like that," she said.

Willie stared at her for a heartbeat as she held her breath, afraid he was going to ask why they'd done that to her. Instead he said, "Some of the townspeople think it's UFO-related, on account of Roswell."

"Isn't that in Arizona?"

"Yep, but there've been weird things going on here in Utah as well. Unexplained things ever since that base was constructed. And those men were private security. I know my military uniforms, and those aren't any of ours."

Kali suddenly recalled a poster at the bus terminal in Salt Lake City in her universe. It was the way Willie stood there with his hands on his hips and searching the street as if peering into the vast horizon, looking at an improbable future.

"What's the name of this town?" she asked.

"Springhill, because of the hot springs over that hill."

"You'll own this town someday."

"Come again?"

The poster at the terminal advertised Willietown and showed a statue of a burly man holding a rake. It also told his story. He'd won a settlement from the government and a contractor—DERST?—for chemical weapons used in the Korean War, along with unauthorized medical trials done on his troop. He bought this town with the funds and helped rebuild the community.

"It won't happen until later, after you get that settlement."

"Settlement? For what?"

"You were right. The government did tests on you and your men. Make them pay."

"How do you—?"

Angry footsteps closed in on them, interrupting Willie's question. He shoved Kali behind him with a quickness she didn't think he was capable of.

"What the heck?" she croaked when she leaned around Willie's thick frame to find Teri aiming a shotgun at them.

"Move aside, Willie," Teri said.

"What is this about?" He raised his hands.

"She was with that man those soldiers took. They were looking for another person, a female. Now I won't tell anyone what you did because I know you're a sucker for a pretty face."

"I offered to help her. She hasn't done anything wrong," he argued.

"Then why were they after her? Why send in those troops and drag off her accomplice," Teri went on, the gun lowering a fraction with every word. "The government wouldn't do that to a citizen if they weren't a threat."

Kali and Willie both let out the same bitter chuckle.

"Oh, honey." She shook her head, which only made Teri tighten her grip and straighten the shotgun so it pointed at Kali's forehead.

She ducked behind Willie again.

"You've no idea what goes on and what they've done to innocent civilians. A few years ago, government scientists gave bar patrons acid to test its effects without telling them. When I was in the military, they did experiments on me too. It wasn't the Korean War that screwed with my head and my health. It was what they did. I've told you that, and you still don't believe me. But I know the truth. Besides, those guys weren't soldiers. They're hired guns for DERST. If they work for our government, I've never seen their branch." Willie lifted his hands higher, trying to placate Teri.

Kali spied a van parked across the road and wondered if she could use it as a shield before Teri got off a shot. Considering how steady the woman held the gun, she figured she was a pro who would take the shot without question. She looked to her right, hoping to find a store to run into, but a few feet away was a barber shop, closed on Sundays.

And since it was closed, that meant today was Sunday.

"I called the authorities. They're on their way," Teri said.

Kali's heart sunk.

"Why did you go and do that?" Willie took a step forward.

"Back off, Willie. That girl is dangerous."

"Did they tell you that? Because they lie, just like they lied about my discharge." He took another step toward Teri.

With as nervous as the woman was becoming, Kali feared the gun would go off and kill Willie. She couldn't let that happen.

Taking a fortifying breath, she stepped around the large man. "It's fine, Willie. Let them take me. I don't want anyone to get hurt."

"And neither do we." From behind Teri, a woman with flaming red hair stalked toward them, flanked by two men in mirrored sunglasses and electric blue leisure suits. The woman's breasts barely stayed in her very deep V-neck flowing pantsuit as she dragged Kathy alongside her. They stopped a few paces away, and one of the disco-party men pointed a gun at Kathy, who stumbled in her clogs to stay standing, her quivering face drenched in tears.

Teri lowered her weapon. "Let go of my sister."

"Place the rifle on the ground and we will," the woman replied in a cool-as-snow way that matched what Kali expected a woman who dressed as her to sound like.

Teri asked, "Who are you?"

"No one, as is she." The woman tilted her head in Kali's direction.

Chapter 13

The Goddess Is Out at Max's House

"Stop!" Surefire threw out her hand.

A charged breeze blasted past Max like a cool wind from an A/C vent and snapped against his arm. Mia screamed. The pulse taser flew from her grasp and onto the floor.

Glen moved to help his sister, but Surefire stepped between them. Her hand lifted like a crossing guard stopping traffic, and he froze in mid-sprint.

"I can't move my legs." His face strained as his upper body bucked against the unseen force holding him in place.

Mia cursed. Her skin flushed. Muscles tensed in her neck as she tried to move.

"What's happening to us?" Glen cried out to Surefire.

Instead of replying, she sashayed closer to Mia, her head held high, back straight. She was a queen inspecting her court. A gauzy halo of violet coated her from head to toe.

"What should I do with them?" she asked in a voice different than Surefire's. It held an accent Max couldn't place, an underlying sultry purr that wasn't her style.

Raven craned his neck to look at her from where he lay, sprawled on his stomach. Through the charred hole in the jacket, Max saw his skin shredded, muscles exposed.

"Holy hell, Raven." Max tore off his own shirt and pressed it over the wound to sop up the man's blood. How he was still alive and able to move was beyond Max.

"It's . . . only a . . . flesh wound." Raven chuckled then wheezed.

"You need a hospital." Max looked to Glen, who was staring at him, pleading for help. Considering that Raven had a hole in his back, he took priority.

"Don't hurt them, Xochi. We're in enough trouble already," Raven said between shallow breaths.

"Xochi?" Max exclaimed.

Surefire's attention whipped from the two playing a supernatural game of freeze-frame to Max. The way her eyes traveled from his feet over his pajama bottoms to his bare chest made him want to cover up, put on a long coat. She swayed close to him. Clamoring to his feet, Max shuffled back and bumped into the chair behind him.

"Xochi," Raven warned.

"What?" Surefire's lips pouted. "I can't have any fun?"

She placed a hand on Max's chest and ground her body against him. He tried to shift his hips back, embarrassed by his reaction to her, especially in front of her boyfriend.

"Max meet Xochiquetzal . . . ugh," Raven groaned, pausing for another breath, "the Aztec goddess who uses Surefire as a conduit."

It was different seeing her possession in person than it was having Kali explain it to him. Also, scarier and freakier and many other adjectives that came to his mind.

Surefire's toasty fingers danced across his chest.

"Goddess of love, so don't be too concerned about what you're feeling. It's normal," Raven explained when Max cupped his hands over the front of his pants.

Kali never mentioned the side effects of meeting the goddess.

"Mmm . . . I like this one. He's handsome, smart, rich," she said.

"You taking inventory?" Raven coughed.

She stared into Max's eyes, and he found it hard to look away. A violet light covered her two-toned irises, which swirled, forming purple pinwheels. He felt dizzy and scared yet warm and comfortable at once. Then Kali came to mind and how she should be here and how much he needed her here.

He edged back from Surefire-Xochi.

"You are in love with Kali, aren't you? The one who calls me the bitch goddess?" She nodded, answering her own questions. "I like her. But this one," she tossed a scathing look at Mia, "not so much."

Surefire-Xochi did a double take. Mia had broken free from the invisible bindings. She had thrown herself to the floor and grabbed the pulse taser. Showing more spunk than he'd ever seen from her, Mia flipped onto her back, aimed the taser, and let loose another blast. Max ducked. Surefire-Xochi slid to the slide. The pulse hit the concrete wall causing a floor-to-ceiling crack.

"Enough!" Surefire-Xochi roared.

The taser flew from Mia's hand into Surefire's. Her fingers squeezed the weapon, crumbling it into a wad of plastic, metal, and circuits as if it were papier-mâché.

"Stay," Surefire-Xochi ordered in that deep purr that made Max uncomfortable. His body continued to react to her every word and movement, leaving him feeling like a hormonal teen unable to control his body.

The concrete floor vibrated under Max's feet.

"Xochi, no," Raven pleaded.

Cracks snaked under Mia's feet. She cried out in terror but didn't move—couldn't move, based on her grunts of frustration as she gripped a thigh and struggled to lift it. She finally pried first one foot loose then the other one. Her upper body leaned forward like she was pushing against strong waves.

Max watched the scene unfold. Glen was still stuck, but Mia was fighting back and making headway. Max couldn't move either, but not for the same reason as the brother and sister. He wasn't sure what he should do. He didn't know what he could do against someone as powerful as this goddess.

Surefire-Xochi tilted her head and her gaze swept over Mia. "You're something else. More than human."

She twisted her hand. The concrete under Mia's feet cracked. Roots shot up from them. Their dirt-caked skeletal fingers crawled up Mia's legs, weaving around her calves.

"You bitch," Mia seethed.

"Only one person can call me that." A root wrapped around Mia's mouth. The more she clawed at it, the tighter it became.

"Don't!" Max finally said, or maybe he yelled it. Everything was surreal. His brain was having a hard time processing what was happening. But what he could discern was that this possessed woman was about to kill Mia.

Glen must've had the same fear, because he bucked against his invisible restraints with more force and pleaded for the goddess to stop.

"I won't kill her. This vessel won't allow me," Surefire-Xochi told him. "Even though it would give me pleasure to shred the supple flesh from her bones." The goddess grinned at him as if she'd been discussing how much she'd like to build a snowman instead of ripping a woman apart.

"Now let us mend him." She clapped her hands and dropped to her knees at Raven's side.

Max moved his shirt from where he had placed it over Raven's back. The blood had started to clot.

"Impossible," he murmured.

Surefire-Xochi rubbed her hands together. Fuzzy balls of purple light grew from her palms into melon-sized masses. She placed them over Raven's wound, and the torn skin knitted together. His tattoos formed vibrant pictures again, without a scar or scratch marring the swirling, colorful lines and fills.

Max could only stare at what he saw. He couldn't utter a noise. It was inconceivable.

"Much better." Raven rolled onto his side then sat up. He shed his jacket and shirt, both shredded as his skin had been.

"Oh, man, my jacket is hosed." He threw it down and shook his head.

"Mia will buy you a new one," Max stated.

"I will?" came her muffled reply.

"I don't even know where to begin." He continued to stare at the healed man.

"Can you let us go?" Glen asked, pulling Max from his daze.

"If you damage my vessel or my lover, I will hurt you." She motioned to Raven.

"I'm not yours, Xochi," Raven replied.

"So you say." She shrugged.

"Glen won't harm you," Max said, refusing to vouch for Mia. In his opinion, she needed to remain tied up.

Surefire-Xochi inclined her head. Glen teetered forward then caught himself on the table before he fell. He moved toward his sister, struggling against the roots digging into her skin.

"Don't." Surefire-Xochi held up a finger.

Glen looked from her to Mia then back to the goddess.

"Oh, but you . . ." She sauntered up to Glen. Her hand pressed against his chest over his dress shirt. "Now your heart is ripe for the taking."

She raised onto tiptoes to bring herself to his eye level, while Glen stared at her as though transfixed. Her fingers played with his beard.

"Glen," Max said when his friend leaned down to kiss her.

Raven jumped up and pushed them apart. "That's enough, Xochi. He's not why we're here."

Glen lurched back and banged into the table. He shook his head and blinked like he was waking from a dream. "What just happened?"

"The Aztec goddess of love," Raven explained. "You must've missed her introduction earlier when she was examining your buddy over there. But you aren't in love, so her power can be overwhelming."

Surefire-Xochi squinted at Glen. "Like your sister, there is more to you too. Who is your father?"

"I—" he swallowed, then asked, "Why?"

"Xochi, listen, we can get to know . . . who are you again?" Raven turned to him.

"Glen. I'm Max's friend. DERST CFO." His eyes tracked Surefire's every movement as if she were the most fascinating thing he'd ever seen.

And most likely she was, because Max found himself transfixed too, and was trying not to insult Surefire or Raven by gaping at her.

"We can get to know Glen later, after we bring back Kali from inside the journal," Raven said.

"The book." Surefire-Xochi looked from side to side as if it would materialize in her presence by mentioning it. "Kali wanted me to translate it."

Kali. Max's heart ached at the mention of her name. He picked up the book from the floor where he'd dropped it when Mia shot Raven.

"This is it." He placed it on the metal table in front of her.

"My vessel didn't feel it, but I can." Surefire-Xochi laid her palm on the center of the book. She closed her eyes and frowned.

"What is it?" Max asked.

Surefire-Xochi started to shake, a slight muscle twitch that expanded to a full body convulsion.

"Surefire, no!" Raven wrapped his arm around her in an effort to peel her from the book, but her hand was stuck to it and the book stuck to the table as if its weight had increased to that of an anvil. Her eyes rolled back in her head. Max feared she was having a seizure.

A loud ringing stung his ears. He dug out his hearing aids, but he could still hear it.

An explosion rocked the room, but not from a bomb.

From a burst of energy—like the one that had destroyed his lab five years ago, put Max and three employees in a coma, and destroyed his hearing.

Chapter 14

Standoff on Main Street

Kali shifted on her feet and scanned the area for a way out.

"Are you from the government?" Willie addressed the redhead.

"No, we're not," the woman said, neutral and cold as Kali suspected her eyes would appear under her dark sunglasses.

"What about DERST?" Willie asked.

She shook her head.

The UltraAgent debated her options. Go with Ms. Strange and her two Electric Boogaloo bodyguards or face the Man, who would be arriving any minute. The known evil versus a potential unknown evil, who could also be lying about not working with DERST.

What to do? What to do? Kali nervously tapped her foot.

An unfinished master's in physics didn't train her for this, except to figure out the amount of force she needed to exert to take out the woman and two men.

A lot.

They were at a standstill, on the pavement in this town that Kali bet had seen many standoffs during the Old West days.

Willie took her arm, and Teri, with a surprisingly stronger grip, seized the other.

"You can have her. Let Kathy go," Willie said. From the side of his mouth he whispered to Kali, "Sorry, but they're like family."

"It's okay," she whispered back.

The man lowered the gun from Kathy, who went limp in a melodramatic heap—a tactic that probably worked with her folks when she was five and would've worked with anyone else to make them let go. But the redhead was strong. She propped Kathy up with one hand as if the teen were a Raggedy Ann doll. The woman's feet didn't wobble in her slingback heels.

When her captor didn't release her, Kathy pulled and kicked with her heavy clogs, one of which flew off and hit the Leisure Suit to the right in his shin. The redhead appeared unfazed by the hitting and kicking. The teen's efforts were as effective as a fly banging into a horse's rump as far as this woman was concerned.

Kali swallowed the lump in her throat as Willie and Teri forced her toward the odd trio.

"Let my sister go." Teri released Kali and Willie followed suit.

Teri set the shotgun on the ground by her feet and raised her hands in surrender. The redhead set Kathy free. Teri opened her arms to her sister, who limped on one clog then tumbled into her embrace.

Kali stood in the center of the imposing trio, toe-to-toe with the woman whom she decided to refer to as Red and the two similarly dressed men as the Double Mint twins (humor helped diffuse her fear a little). She considered sprinting across the street, but she doubted she could get far. As if reading her thoughts, the Double Mints closed in along her sides.

The woman's wide, shiny red lips stretched into a broad smile, displaying a perfect row of pearly whites. "We've been waiting for you, Kali Bordeaux."

She didn't know how to respond to that statement so she didn't.

Red nodded toward Willie and the two women. "Take care of them."

"We had a deal." Willie went for Teri's shotgun.

"What are you doing? They gave me to you." Kali moved between them and Willie, hoping to give him time to pick up the weapon.

When Red placed a hand on her forearm, a trickle of energy pricked at her skin—a warning not to get in her way. A small display of power to show what she could do, but it wasn't without cost. The woman's hand trembled, as if the effort had been too much for her.

The shotgun in his grasp, Willie used his bulk to form a barrier between the odd three and the young women. The weapon didn't deter the men who took two long strides toward them. They halted with their backs to Kali, so she couldn't see what Willie and the two women saw. The Double Mints removed their sunglasses. Without uttering a sound, Willie, Kathy, and Teri collapsed to the ground.

"What did you do?" Kali craned her neck to see around the men's shoulders.

"Letting them rest," Red said. "Don't worry. No harm will come to them. This universe has been altered enough."

The men donned their sunglasses again.

"What will happen to them?" Kali asked.

"They'll have a story to tell their friends and the—" The woman lifted her face to the sky. A helicopter was approaching. "We must go. Come."

Another charge of power zapped Kali's forearm.

"Who and what are you people?" She rubbed at the singed hair on her arm.

"We're the Three." Red wrapped a hand around Kali's bicep and pulled her into a jog, which seemed impossible given the woman's high-heeled sandals.

"The three what?"

"Just the Three. Your human mind cannot process our true names so we simplify things for you."

"Okay," she replied because what else do you say to that kind of insult?

She gave Kali a side-eye and trudged ahead. "You may refer to us individually if that makes it easier."

"Red and the Double Mint twins?" She let slip because that's how her mouth worked—or didn't work—in anxiety-laden situations.

One of the men chuckled behind her. At least someone thought she was funny and got the reference.

Based on Red's annoyed frown, she didn't. "You may refer to me as Dara. They are Tomas and Gilroy."

Kali couldn't tell which of the men were named what and decided it was easier to go along as if she had. Dara guided her around the corner. Their two-man entourage brought up the rear.

"Where are we going?" Kali glanced around, wondering if someone had seen them, but the main street and the side street were both as empty as a ghost town.

"Somewhere safe," Dara stated.

"Just to be clear, you're not taking me to DERST's base and to the Man?" Kali struggled to keep up with the woman's accelerating steps.

"No." Dara tugged her around another corner into an alleyway where a car had been parked—the Lincoln she'd seen earlier.

Emboldened by Dara's response, Kali said, "So you're not working for the Man, but based on your abilities, I'm assuming you're not from here."

They stopped at the car. One of the men—Tomas or Gilroy?—opened the passenger door for Kali.

"We're from the District," Dara responded.

"Indeed, D.C. is a foreign place," Kali quipped.

"Not Washington, D.C., but the District. Another planet located in our universe from where you've traveled," Dara said then took the driver's seat.

Chapter 15

Having a Blast with Max

The blast sent Max careening into a robotic arm across the room. Pain ripped through his shoulder and back. His head slammed into the metal rivets. He dropped to the floor onto his side.

The ringing in his ears stopped, consumed by the dead silence he loathed. He rolled onto his back and his vision blurred. Energy rippled across the ceiling, refracting the light into waves. Were these ripples real or caused by his pounding head? He rubbed his eyes, and when he opened them again the distortion was gone.

Just like the last explosion.

But not quite the same as the one that took his hearing, Max reconsidered. He was still conscious so he had that going for him. His hearing was already gone; the explosion couldn't take that again. This one wasn't as forceful as before, but the oppressive energy exploding from the journal felt the same.

With slow, deliberate moves, he sat up and assessed the damage. He felt along his scalp where he'd banged into the rivets and came away with blood on his fingers. His shoulder throbbed but wasn't broken. A nasty welt appeared along his triceps. He was certain there were more lacerations and bruising on his back that he couldn't see but could feel.

He searched out Mia, no longer tied up in the spot where he'd last seen her. Past overturned equipment and chairs, he found her trying to pick an object off his table. Glen came up behind her and gripped her arm to stop her. She shook him off then ran.

Max hauled his aching body from the floor. Pain shot up his leg to his hip. He limped to Glen, who jogged to meet him halfway. His lips formed words Max couldn't make out. Glen pointed to the stairs that Mia was climbing two at a time, then he put out his palm indicating for Max to stay.

He concentrated on his friend's lips, trying to read them. Glen must've noticed Max struggling to understand because he accentuated, "I will get her."

He pressed a scrap of paper into Max's hand then sprinted after his sister.

Scrawled on the crinkle paper was the message, "Father will meet you."

"Where?" he asked as he twisted around to find his friend gone.

Turning his attention back to the wrecked room, he skimmed over the busted furniture and equipment and scattered circuitry for Surefire and Raven.

Before the blast, they stood where he was currently standing in front of the journal, which now was set inside an indentation on the steel work table. Not a scratch marred its glossy leather binding.

A dark blur caught the corner of his eye. He spun, tripping over various bits, to find Raven's dark head poking above the console that had sat beneath the large screen, which had shattered in the explosion. Shards hung from the ceiling where the screen had been, like jagged gray teeth. Glass crumbled under his shoes when he rounded the cracked computer console to find Surefire on her back and Raven holding her hand. She nodded as Raven spoke words Max couldn't hear.

He was relieved to see that she was alive. Based on her lying under the screen's remains, he assumed she had smashed into the glass monitor, flying nearly twenty feet from where she'd been standing. Her eyes were no longer purple. The hairs on Max's arms didn't stand on end. No static energy lingered in the room.

Raven waved his arms at Max to get his attention. He was asking him a question. Max focused on his mouth.

Bandages. He was asking where they were. Max pointed upstairs. The medicine chest was in the master bathroom. He started toward the steps to get them when Raven pulled him back. He said something about the journal.

"What?" Max asked.

Raven held up his index finger for Max to wait a minute. Bending down, he scooped up Surefire and cradled her in his arms. He brushed the glass out of her hair as she leaned her head on his shoulder. After Surefire was situated in his arms, Raven jerked his head toward the stairs and Max led the way. As they passed the book, he tapped Max on the shoulder and pointed to it, motioning for him to pick it up.

Max hesitated at first before sliding his fingertips over the leather binding and embossed M. It didn't feel different. Didn't explode with energy, knocking him across the room. Holding his breath, he wedged his fingers between the spine and the metal table until it came free. He flinched, expecting retaliation, but nothing happened. With a small, triumphant smile, he held it up for Raven to see that the situation was diffused.

He gave Max a smile that a parent would give a child who had used the light switch for the first time. He started speaking again, but Max held up his hand to stop him.

He said, "Can't hear. Not good at reading lips."

Raven gave him the thumbs-up.

As he climbed up the steps, Max's leg throbbed in protest, but he clenched his teeth and pushed past the pain. A blast of cold air greeted him at the landing. The front door hung wide open. No one was outside. Not even a dragonfly camera or lights from vehicles. For the first time in weeks, the street outside his property was empty. A brisk wind blew across the snow, covering footprints leading from the porch down the steep stairs to the walkway.

He pulled the door shut and bolted it. Then he showed the couple into his bedroom. While Raven placed Surefire on the bed, Max went into the bathroom to dig out the first aid kit from the vanity. He found his spare CAIs and synced them to his phone's app (fortunately, that hadn't been damaged) and adjusted the volume.

Surefire opened her eyes when her boyfriend dabbed at the cuts along her forehead. Max figured she'd be out for hours after taking that kind of hit. He wanted to call for an ambulance but decided to follow their lead. Considering they were transhumans and powered by an otherworldly force, he doubted a traditional hospital could help them.

"How are you?" Max perched on the edge of a chair opposite the bed.

"I'll live. Barely." With a groan, Surefire bent forward to stretch her upper body over her legs.

"Come on now. It's not like you busted through a hundred-thousand-dollar glass monitor." Raven dabbed the back of Surefire's neck with a cotton ball soaked in alcohol.

"Can I help?" Max asked, feeling helpless as he watched Raven clean her wounds.

"Her jacket and shirt took the brunt of the hit. We need to get them off since they're caked with blood. Got anything she could wear?"

The back of her coat was torn to pieces, riddled with holes as if shot with a swarm of pellets. Through the rips, her skin was raw with scrapes and scratches.

Happy for something to do, Max hobbled into his walk-in closet to the drawers, forming a short corridor leading to a room half the size of his expansive bedroom lined with wooded shelves and racks and more drawers. Kali had joked how his "closet" housed a better clothing display than a boutique.

He sorted through the drawers for something warm for all three of them. His jacket and shirt shredded by the taser, Raven's torso was bare as well as Max's since he'd used his shirt to plug up the man's wounds.

Max shrugged on a henley. Clutching a large sweater and sweatshirt, he stepped into the room to find Raven taking Surefire's shirt off.

"Uh, sorry." He ducked back into the closet and turned around. Limping backward to the bed, he tossed the sweatshirt and wool sweater over his shoulder.

"The sweater will be big on her. Sweatshirt should fit you fine," he said with his back to them for their privacy.

"You can turn around, Max," Surefire replied. "I have on my sports bra. It's about the same as a bathing suit."

"No, I'm good." He crossed his arms and stared into the closet.

"He's more of a gentleman than I am," Raven said.

"That's for sure." Surefire snorted.

"And what is this?" Raven exclaimed. Max twisted around then stopped himself when he wasn't sure if it was safe.

"What's what?" he asked.

"A Steelers sweatshirt?" Raven said.

"Not a Steelers fan? Oh, that's right, your name is Raven," Max said.

"Watch it, buddy. Don't assume. You know what they say about people who do."

"He's a huge Steelers fan. I'm starting to think it's a cult thing, really. All right, Max, you're safe to look." Surefire's small frame was indeed swimming in his sweater, which hung down to her thighs over her leggings.

"Love this sweatshirt, man. Superbowl XL. One of the best games when Parker ran seventy-five yards for the touchdown. Bam!" Raven held up his hand for a high-five, and Max slapped it because he couldn't leave a guy hanging.

"I was at that game." He had almost added that he'd been there with his father, but that wouldn't have been true. Glen's father, Mr. Triman, had taken him when his own dad bailed at the last minute to spend time on some celebrity's yacht.

"I'm jealous." Raven touched the shirt's decal with reverence.

"How are you two not freaking out?" Max asked, dumbfounded at this conversation.

"When you've seen what we've seen, you learn to roll with it." Raven pulled on the shirt

"Max, sit. You're bleeding." Surefire scooted against the headboard and patted the space next to her where Kali used to sleep.

Used to sleep.

Raven nudged him to the bed and gently forced him down.

"It's nothing." He tried to wave the guy off, but he wasn't having it.

Raven parted Max's hair to inspect his scalp and whistled. "It might need stitches."

He flinched as his fingers prodded the wound.

"Anything broken?" Raven asked.

"I don't think so." He rotated his left shoulder then flexed his muscles. Both were tight with bruising but neither felt broken. The side of his thigh was tender. Under his pajama bottoms he felt a nasty welt forming. His ankle was sore, possibly sprained. Considering the blast was strong enough to toss him over ten feet, he was lucky.

"Give me the first aid kit." The bed bounced as Surefire moved behind him.

She touched an alcohol-soaked cotton ball against his cut. Max sucked in a breath against the sharp pain.

Raven shined a light from his phone into his eyes. "Doesn't look like a concussion."

"I'd use Xochi's power to heal you, but I'm tapped out," Surefire said. He heard her rummaging through the box. "Superglue. This will work. My gymnastics coach used it on us when we cracked our faces on the balance beam. Man, that would smart."

"What happened in my basement?" Max held his breath as she squeezed the glue into his cut while pinching it together.

"The energy in that book knocked Xochi from me. That's never happened before. A crystal skull containing another deity's power will weaken her or make her to retreat, but not yank her away."

"Like the skull you brought with you?"

"That one contains Xochi's essence so it strengthens her and, as her conduit, me too." She finished patching his cut then sat back. "Here's the short and sweet of it. There are thirteen crystal skulls. Each one connected to an Old One, who was worshipped by the Aztecs and other civilizations and called by many different names over the millennium. Xochi is an Old One. Her power resides in my cells and Raven's too."

"To a lesser extent," her boyfriend chimed in. "I'm not her vessel, but her energy keeps me alive."

"Usually, I can sense her lurking in the back of my mind, constantly eavesdropping like a nosey neighbor," Surefire said. "But it's radio silence inside my head."

"You're not healing as well as you usually do," Raven noted.

"My power's drained. Until I reach Xochi again, I won't know what happened. Unless the journal can tell us," Surefire said.

"We can't stay here," Raven said.

As if on cue, a helicopter flew over the house, followed by the wail of sirens approaching in the distance.

"Get the skull," she said

Raven raced from the room in a blur. Seconds later, he returned with it.

Surefire hugged it to her chest and screwed her eyes shut. Her face pinched in concentration. She reached out her hand, and Raven took it.

A light flickered inside the skull then faded. A flashlight losing its charge.

"It's not working." She threw back her head in frustration. "I can't reach Xochi to give us a power boost and transport us like she did from Utah to here."

"Where are we exactly?" Raven asked. "We just told her to take us to you."

"Outside of Frederick, Maryland," Max replied.

"Crap," they said in unison.

"My family lives in Owings Mills. Then there's an army base where my dad . . ." Surefire took in a nervous breath and appeared more shaken than she had after the explosion.

"There's a back exit to my garage. It leads to a farm I own and will get us to the main road undetected." As long as Glen stopped Mia before she told anyone about it. Although if the Organization was helping Mia spy on Max then they already knew about it.

Even more reason why they couldn't stay at his house.

"Where will we go?" Surefire asked. They both looked to Max, who had no idea what to do next.

"Give me a moment while I put on actual pants and shoes." Max shuffled back to his closet and into the changing room. One side held his suits and formal wear. The other three walls contained his collection of vintage and prized t-shirts, along with his preferred style—jeans and sweatshirts. Within this section, he'd cleared an area for Kali. Several drawers held her underwear and socks. He ran his hand over a shelf stuffed with her sweaters, pants, and leggings. A few vintage dresses she'd bought online to keep at Max's hung on a rack, including the Halston she'd worn the night they'd met at the *Real Life* dinner.

In the bedroom, Raven and Surefire tossed around ideas for where to hide out but discarded each one as not secure enough.

Max slid off his pajama bottoms then grabbed jeans from a middle shelf. His phone dinged with an incoming text. Quickly, he tugged on his jeans and retrieved his phone inside his discarded pants.

Expecting a text from Glen, he was shocked instead to find an audio file sent from Mr. Triman of John Denver singing about country roads taking him home. As the song played, its meaning combined with Glen's odd note dawned on him.

Max's father and Mr. Triman used to sing this song to him and Glen on the way to the cabin in Shenandoah. Since their cabin wasn't in West Virginia, their dads would change the words to "my Virginia."

Grabbing a coat, he plodded back into the bedroom as fast as his stiff leg would let him.

"I have a plan," he announced.

"Good because we don't." Raven tried to scoop up his girlfriend, but Surefire batted him back.

"I can walk. I'm getting stronger." She hopped off the bed as if to demonstrate she was telling the truth.

"Lead the way," she said to Max.

The stabbing pain increased, but Max didn't let it slow him down. He lurched through the living room. Blue and red lights reflected against the snow. The explosion would've triggered the house's security to notify the police and fire departments. Emergency vehicles were parked outside his wrought iron gate, which was locked. The snowdrift at the base of the gate would make it hard to open. That would buy them some time.

He led the couple past the basement stairs to another set at the end of the narrow hall. Holding onto the railing, Max hopped down the steps on his good leg.

"I am in love," Raven said when the lights beamed down on the collection of vehicles. Raven trailed his fingers along the hood of a 1968 Mercedes. "I totally want to marry you right now."

"Fickle, thy name is Raven," Surefire uttered. "Steelers and sports cars will make you forgive anything."

"I have my standards." He pulled her into a hug.

"Besides, I didn't say anything about forgiving just yet. It doesn't erase the fact that you have a transhuman containment unit in your house," he said to Max. "You're not completely in our trust circle yet."

"I won't let you down."

"You better not." Raven kissed Surefire's head, but his eyes bored into Max's as if to hammer home the point of what was at stake.

Max searched through the keys hung on a rack near the stairs, deciding on the Ford Bronco. He'd reconfigured it for better gas mileage, making it into a hybrid. One of his pet projects was retrofitting older vehicles to be fuel-efficient. The Bronco should get them where they needed to be on less than a full tank. It had more than enough room in the back for Surefire to rest. Plus, it handled like a beast in the snow, along with bonus features that could aid in their escape.

"Where are we going?" Surefire asked.

"Good question." Raven raised his dark brows at Max.

The doorbell rang. The security monitors over the key rack revealed men in black uniforms, not police as he'd originally seen outside.

"Where did they come from?" Max asked.

"They're my father's people. He knows we're here," Surefire said.

"We've got to go. I don't care where as long as it's not here," Raven said.

The third monitor displayed the back exit from the underground tunnel that would deposit them on a farm road about a mile from the house. So far, no one was there, waiting to ambush them.

"We're going to my family's cabin in the Shenandoah. It's secure, and someone should be there with answers."

Chapter 16

The Fourth Wheel on the Road

Kali squeezed her hands together on her lap, so Dara wouldn't see her shaking as she processed the woman's—scratch that—*alien's* unexpected answer.

"The District is another planet? So you're like . . . aliens?" Kali cut a glance to Tomas and Gilroy, who took up a good portion of the wide back seat. Both faced forward with their matching sunglasses covering their eyes. Both rested their hands on their knees.

"We prefer to be called Custodians." Dara steered the car onto a road leading out of town.

"I'm totally confused. What do you want with me? How did you know I was here? Why are you even in our world or *this* world?" Just when she thought she couldn't be shocked anymore, she meets aliens.

The car made another turn. This time onto a two-lane highway that cut through a valley peppered with ranches and farms. They accelerated toward a mountain range. Snow covered a few of its tallest peaks.

"I'll begin from your beginning. Our race owns your planet and allows humans to occupy it. We bought it at the birth of Homo sapiens. We maintain it. Keep you safe. You have no idea how many close calls you've had. One time over the Netherlands, we had a battle with—"

"Lady, I think you've been tuning in and dropping out with Timothy Leary. Or else I've been and don't know it." Kali blinked rapidly. "Which is a bit of a bummer because this is not a good trip."

"You are not having an LSD experience with Dr. Leary. I assure you this is real, and you are in real danger." She shot a look in her rearview mirror, which made Kali do a half-turn in the seat to see if anyone was following. Gilroy—at least she thought it was Gilroy, he kind of looked more like a Gilroy than the other—rolled down his window and leaned his head out to scan the sky.

"Is the Man following us?" she asked Dara, who kept her sunglass-covered gaze glued to the road.

"What do you know about the Man?" She accelerated the car.

"What do *you* know about him?" There went Kali's smart mouth kicking into high gear whenever she was nervous. And being driven into the mountains by supposed aliens upped the nervous factor by a thousand. "I'd like answers first, because I am totally freaked out and questioning my sanity—which has always been in question, but still—what do *you* know about the Man, and how do *you* know about me, and where are we going, and—"

"She talks a lot," Gilroy or Tomas said from the back seat.

"We should put her to sleep until we get there," the same or the other added.

"Uh-uh, you keep those shades on. I don't want to see what's in your creepy eye sockets." Kali crossed her arms snug across her chest.

Maybe this was a dream. It had to be, because nothing made sense.

"That is enough." Dara flicked a glance from the road to the two men in the back seat, as if they were siblings teasing their sister during a car ride to granny's.

"Kali is our guest," she continued in a calm, motherly tone that made Kali more uncomfortable than if she were screaming obscenities. "She is our way back home."

"I am?" Kali croaked. "You want me to pop you back to your home planet . . . this District or whatever?"

"Only back to our collective universe. We will find a transfer to the District, if we so desire, after we contain the Dark." The engine strained as Dara gunned the car up a steepening slope.

Kali's brain took a minute to catch up with Dara's last words: the Dark. She'd added it with a casual flair as if Kali should know what it was.

Which she didn't. At all.

"What the ever-loving freak is the Dark?" Kali said.

"An energy from this universe that became sentient after it corrupted a Custodian in ours. Maxwell Martin ingested this essence to unlock the journal, which is why we're here," Dara said with the patience of a parent explaining why the sky was blue for the hundredth time.

"Whoa, whoa, whoa . . . what?" Kali shoved her palms outward with each exclamation as if she could physically back Dara up to the part where she dropped the mad Maxwell bombshell.

"We told you this the last time," Gilroy said.

"When we tried and failed to save you," Tomas said.

Kali wrapped her hands around both sides of her skull to keep it from exploding. Because what they were saying didn't make sense—yet, did. In the recesses of her mind, this Dark reference sounded familiar, like a conversation she'd overheard between two strangers sitting behind her on a long plane ride.

"Pull the car over." Kali lowered her hands as the world whirled around her.

"I can't do that." Instead, Dara rolled down the window on Kali's side as if this would be an acceptable alternative.

The cool, pine-scented air streamed across Kali's face, blowing back her bangs. But it wasn't enough to straighten her spinning head.

"Pull over . . . please." She gripped the door handle.

"No time," Dara said. "We need to get to our lodge and regroup. Where did you stow the dagger and the bottle?"

Kali blinked again as she registered the question. Dara was talking as if Kali being here had been planned, as if she knew what the hell this alien was speaking about.

"I need you to stop." Kali covered her face with her hands. *Stop the car. Stop talking. Stop expecting me to understand.*

"Not until we—"

Dara's words faded out as Kali's power kicked in, and she popped from the car and landed with an "ugh!" on her bottom on the shoulder of the road.

The car skidded to a stop. The alien sitting behind Kali—Tomas, perhaps?—flung open the door, jumped out, and tore down the road after her.

Kali focused on her power, trying to get it started again, but her engine was dead.

"No!" She crab crawled away from the towering-inferno of a man closing in on her. Pebbles and sticks dug into her palms.

"We're not going to hurt you." It was Tomas. His nose was straighter, thinner than Gilroy's whose nose flared at the nostrils and angled up at the tips. His black feathered hair had so much hair spray not a strand moved as he ran.

Gilroy slowed to a jog behind him. His black hair was also feathered, but a few of the layers stuck out from the breeze blowing through it. Dara stomped awkwardly in her sling backs down the slope. The two men parted to let her pass.

"Why did you do that?" she said not nearly as angry as her body language conveyed.

Kali set her bum on the ground covered with soft, brittle pine needles. "I didn't mean to pop out of the car. It just happened. My power's not working right. I don't have control over it. I can only Q-T a few feet, so alt-jumping home is right out until I regroup, which I can't do in the car with you blowing my mind with stuff about how you met me before and how you tried to help me and couldn't." Kali shook her head. Based on their neutral, mannequin-like expressions, they didn't understand where she was going with this.

"I don't remember you," she continued. "I did meet my other self locked in this glass container filled with slime. Then the universe reset. Every now and then I get one of previous Kali's vague memories, but that's all." She raised her palms showing she had nothing to offer except pebbles stuck into her skin.

The two men drifted back from Dara. Tomas positioned himself like a sentinel staring down the road. Gilroy moved in front of the car, keeping a lookout in that direction.

Dara remained with her heeled-feet firmly planted. A gust of wind blew strands of her rusty red hair across her golden brown skin. She looked like a model in one of those incongruent photographs found in fashion magazines.

Where they'd show a glamorously dressed woman standing on a side of a mountainous road as if her car had broken down on the way to a Hollywood party via the Rockies.

"I don't know what this Dark is. I definitely don't have this bottle or dagger thingy that you're talking about," Kali went on.

Birds chirped in the trees next to the road. She took comfort in their soft, familiar songs until Dara broke from her reverie to squat in front of Kali.

"How did you get here?" she asked.

"A portal opened and sucked me inside. I think it was created by this journal," Kali said.

"Go on." Dara placed her long, elegant fingers decorated with two plain gold bands on Kali's thigh.

"This guy Robert attacked my friend and I at her condo. He wanted me to meet the Man in this universe and return him to ours. Instead, we fought back. During the fight, I smashed this bottle of wine and then . . ." She thought about the dark oil inside the bottle. "This black stuff slithered inside his cuts before the portal opened."

Dara's warm fingers touched Kali's chin, forcing her to lift up her head.

"What are you doing?"

"Making sure you're clean." She withdrew her hand.

"Of what?"

"The Dark." Dara rose and trudged up the steep road to the car.

"The stuff that leaked into Robert is the Dark?" Kali said to Dara's retreating back. She scampered onto her feet.

"Yes," Tomas replied as he walked up alongside Kali and clutched her hand.

She tried to break free but he kept walking, pulling her along with him. If they'd met her before, then they knew how her power worked. By touching his skin to hers, he ensured she didn't leave again without taking him too.

She tripped in her clunky snow boots to keep up. Gilroy opened the passenger door then slammed it shut after she sat inside.

She could cut the tension with a jackhammer. Learning that she came through the portal instead of on her own volition must've put a Grand Canyon-sized kink in their plans.

Dara revved the Lincoln's engine and jerked the car into drive.

"I'm sorry," Kali said to ease the thick air of frustration in the car. Whatever had upset them appeared to be her fault.

"Do not apologize." Dara's words were no longer measured and calm but weighed down with disappointment.

And Kali couldn't help believing she was the main cause of it.

"We should have stayed to see Willie Nelson," Gilroy said with a dejected sigh.

Kali had to look at his face to make sure she'd heard him correctly. "What?"

"Willie Nelson, the country singer," Gilroy said, and Kali was relieved that she hadn't been pushed off the crazy cliff yet. She had understood him.

"What does he have to do with anything?" she asked.

"While we were on vacation, our inside source at DERST informed us you'd arrived," Dara replied.

"We were in Las Vegas," Tomas added with a wistful smile.

"We saw June Carter and Johnny Cash. Willie Nelson was supposed to play tonight," Gilroy said.

"We like country music. It soothes us," Dara said as the car descended a winding road.

Then that explained their designer duds. Dara's she now recognized as a Valentino pantsuit, which would fit in with 1970s Las Vegas or even Studio 54, not so much the mountains of Utah.

One mystery solved. Five hundred more to go.

"You're upset that I came through this portal," Kali stated.

"It's not as we had planned. We assumed you'd be better prepared. As it is, you are not equipped to face the Man."

There was another meaning hidden under Dara's statement. She wasn't equipped with this bottle or the dagger, as the woman had referenced earlier, and also wasn't equipped to fight against the Man in another way.

"Once my power returns, I can get us back home," said Kali.

"That's out of the question. We can't leave without Maxwell Martin. He is of our universe and doesn't belong here. The Dark inside him doesn't belong here." Dara slowed the car as they approached a wire pole topped with a red reflector stuck next to the road. "And you can't travel with the Dark through universal planes without it being contained."

"Inside this bottle you mentioned?" Kali offered thinking that she may finally be following this conversation.

"Yes, or within the host's body with the blade embedded in the solar plexus," Dara said. "That was our secondary plan. But we prefer not to travel with an impaled host. More opportunities for things to go wrong."

This idea of impaling the Man, while somewhat comforting on a revenge level, was growing more discomforting as the full impact of what Dara had revealed hit Kali like a boatload of slime that S-Kali had been pickled in.

"You said the Man is from our universe?" Kali processed another tidbit they'd casually thrown at her.

"Yes," Dara replied.

The knuckles on her right hand turned white as she gripped the door rest. The Man who S-Kali had warned her about, who had syphoned her power and locked her up in that slime was Max's actual grandfather.

Not the version of his grandfather born in this universe. The blood relative of the man she'd been living with, sleeping with, falling in love with.

"Son of a rat bastard," she said.

Like grandfather, like grandson. Explained why Max had a similar device in his basement and why he had the journal with the designs inside.

Although, did he know the book was also a means to this universe?

"How did the journal activate the portal?" Kali braced her shoulder against the door as Dara took a sharp turn onto a gravel drive past the red reflector.

"Its binding came from a Custodian. When Robert touched the journal's skin, it interacted with the Dark inside him, acting as a key."

"The journal is of alien origin?" Did that mean Max is . . .? Kali shook her head, unable to finish the question and afraid that would indeed push her over the crazy cliff and into the pit of insanity.

Focus on one head-pounding mystery at a time.

"The outer skin was created by us as a failsafe for the Dark. One of ours took it upon themselves to use it to bind it into the journal. This Custodian had an innate ability to see the future. They believed they could use the Dark to enhance this ability," Dara said.

"It worked," Tomas added.

"But not as they planned," Gilroy finished.

The car rocked along the rough road that cut through a copse of trees. Low limbs brushed against the windows. The rocking made Kali's stomach queasy.

Or it could be the words coming out of these aliens' mouths. A Dark-infested, future-telling Custodian wrote the journal and predicted the schematics of Dama X's island and the names of her and her friends.

But this didn't explain how this journal was in Max's possession.

"There were two sets of handwriting inside that journal," said Kali.

"One was the Custodian. The other was Maxwell Martin," Dara replied.

"It worked for him also," Tomas added.

"But not as planned," Gilroy said.

"Hold on a minute," Kali said as they entered a clearing. "That journal didn't originally belong to Maxwell Martin?"

Dara parked the car outside a rustic log cabin, replete with a tin-roof porch and rockers. An overgrown vegetable garden was set off to the side. Pink flamingos stood guard amongst rose bushes in front of the porch.

"My brother trusted Maxwell to hide the journal and the Dark contained inside the bottle. But Maxwell became tempted by the Dark and ingested it. While under its influence, he transcribed predictions that might occur about transhumans." Dara cut off the engine.

"Transhumans like me?" Kali prodded.

"My brother couldn't read the full predictions. Only a few words and images. But from what was garnered, someone of your ability would be born."

"Then how did you know my name?" Kali asked as Dara opened the car door.

"As we said, we met when you were here last, before the universe reset." She got out and shut the door on Kali's next question.

"You mentioned that but what happened?"

"You were being kept at the Man's home," Tomas said, opening his door and getting out.

"And we couldn't save you," Gilroy slid out and shut his door.

"But I saved myself," Kali whispered to the empty car. She slumped forward and wondered at how she could save herself from this predicament. Last time was an accident. No way that would happen twice.

Gilroy opened her door and swept out his arm in an invitation for her to exit.

But she had the Three—People? Aliens?—to help her. She wasn't alone, because this time, they had saved her before the Man caught her. The idea didn't give her much comfort. Maybe because the Three seemed less confident since they'd learned her power hadn't transported her here.

She pivoted in her seat to get out. The air was crisper with less humidity. Critters rustled the trees above. Sunlight shown down on the cabin like a spotlight on her salvation or damnation. Hard to tell by the way her luck was going today.

"Where did you take me?"

"One of our homes. I'm hoping our brother has left us a new message." Dara walked toward the porch. Her sling back heels sunk into the grass, impeding the long strides she took to the house. She kicked them off, stepped into a flowerbed on the other side of the stairs, and paused between the two plastic pink flamingos.

"And we need to get supplies from here." Gilroy drummed his fingers on the car door.

"Like the dagger?" Kali asked.

The dagger that impales the host's body. Kali started to stand then fell back on the seat when the ground dipped forward and back.

Tomas came up to Gilroy's side. "No, that dagger was dropped in the cabin."

"Left behind when we crossed over." Gilroy held out his hand to help her up.

"Give me sec for my head to go straight." She folded her long torso over her knees. "Not that it was ever straight to begin with."

"This disoriented feeling is to be expected," Gilroy said.

"We experienced it too. The journal's portal feeds on your energy," Tomas said.

In the distance, gears ground to life. A loud squeak like rusty nails cutting across a chalkboard stung Kali's ears, cutting a shiver down her spine. She stood up in time to see the steps leading to the porch slide to the side and reveal an entrance below the cabin.

Her quick popup made the blood rush too quickly to her head. The world teetered and tottered and the peanut butter rose in her throat. She gripped the top of the door to steady herself.

"Help her," Dara told the men.

They stared at one another, seeming to have a silent debate about who was going to do it.

"No help needed." She flapped her hand. "I'm fine. Geesh. My mojo is just off."

After several quick breaths, her impromptu lunch stayed in her stomach.

"What's a mojo?" Tomas asked.

"If you have to ask, you don't have it." Her head spun again, causing Kali to stagger, and not walk as she'd planned, in the direction of Dara. She paused and took another breath then tried walking again, this time with success. Eyes on the ground, she willed her feet to pick an even path forward.

"So you were sucked through the journal as well?" she asked to focus on anything other than her unsettled stomach.

"In 1969, when Maxwell Martin opened a portal into *this* world and into the same year, we were caught in its wake," said Gilroy, who must've drawn the short straw because he took her elbow to steady her and, she was certain, to make sure she didn't pop away again.

"You've been here for ten years?" she said, recalling what year Willie had told her.

Kali didn't have the travel log to reference where she kept track of her alt-jumps, but she was sure she'd never alt-jumped to 1979.

"Not by choice." Tomas paused at the stairs leading under the porch.

Gilroy guided Kali to the hidden basement.

"What are we doing down there?" She stared at Dara's back as she descended the steps that ended at a metal door usually found on naval vessels, not under a cabin in the Utah woods.

"For the last ten years, we've been gathering supplies, hoping to create a portal back to our universe. But we've been unsuccessful. This world's technology is not advanced enough, and if our kind visited this Earth, they never stayed." Dara beckoned Kali to follow.

Gilroy held onto Kali as they descended, and she was grateful because her head was all air. Bobbing on her neck like a balloon. The steps were uneven, having been carved from the bedrock below the cabin.

Dara wrenched open the latch and the metal door issued a cringe-worthy noise. After everyone entered the pitch-black basement, Dara flicked on the lights and shut the door. Once more gears churned, and Kali assumed this noise indicated the porch steps were covering the bunker's entrance.

And the room did remind Kali of a military bunker. Fluorescent lights hung suspended from the ceiling by metal chains and cast a yellow-green light over the concrete floor and walls. The room was damp like a tomb. Opposite the door was a slender refrigerator and sink. A linoleum table graced the center. Lining the two long walls of the rectangular room were folding tables and a lopsided oak desk with a dilapidated chair propped against it.

"I can see why you've had no luck." The equipment spread across the tables was rudimentary, and it included several items she'd seen at a Smithsonian museum exhibit on computing history. An Apple II was set on the rickety desk against the wall along with a plotter and an HP computer. Metal pieces, screws, and circuitry were scattered alongside gutted machines.

"But you won't need any of this stuff. Once I'm juiced up again, then I can take us back home like that." Kali punctuated the statement with a snap of her fingers.

"Juiced up?" Gilroy echoed.

She spied a refrigerator in the corner. "A drink and food, if you have it. I need to convert sustenance into energy to fuel my power. Whenever I try to get home, I'm blocked. I'm assuming it's because I'm low on alt-jumping juice. Maybe from the energy sucking portal as you suggested."

Dara removed her sunglasses and the men followed suit.

Kali screwed her eyes closed and put up her hands to block them.

"Why are you doing that?" Dara asked.

"I saw what you did to Willie and the sisters. The twins took off their sunglasses and hypnotized them." Kali cracked an eye to find all three with the same amused grins.

"We can't control you by looking at you. We wear those glasses because of how our eyes appear. We don't have contacts to cover them as we do back in your—our—universe." Dara and the men tossed their sunglasses onto the table.

Kali was transfixed by what she saw. Their irises were golden, appearing to sparkle in the dim room.

"Trippy," she murmured.

"Gilroy get the Cokes," Dara jerked her head to the refrigerator. "Tomas see if Gabriel has left a new message."

Tomas jogged over to the wall next to the refrigerator as Gilroy opened its door and retrieved four bottles of soda. Kali tried to make out what appeared to be foreign letters carved onto the wall where Tomas had positioned himself. But Dara moved in front of her, blocking both the male alien and the wall as she pulled out a red vinyl seat at the square table.

"Sit," she said.

After putting down the drinks, Gilroy took a chair and Dara followed suit.

Kali remained standing. "After this day, I may need something stronger than soda."

"Alcohol, you mean? I'm afraid we don't have any of that. Doesn't do anything for us. Caffeine, on the other hand, that's the elixir of the goddess."

Kali stared at the brown fizzy liquid, wondering what she was missing.

"It's our metabolism. Caffeine affects us like wine affects you. It calms us." She took a long drink followed by an "ah" right out of a commercial.

Kali glanced at Tomas, who had yet to join them. "What is he looking at?"

"My brother found a way to communicate with us from our home universe." Dara watched as Tomas placed his hand on the wall.

A golden light like rays of sun shot from under his palm. Under the carvings, more symbols appeared, but these weren't etched into the wall. Golden holograms projected onto the surface.

He shoved off the wall. The gold light in his hand disappeared along with the symbols.

"No new message," he announced.

"Maybe he is at the other cabin." Dara patted the chair next to her. "Have a drink, Kali. We all earned it today."

With them sitting there and enjoying their drinks, Kali stood frozen, dumbfounded at what Tomas had done and at finding herself in this basement bunker, drinking sodas with aliens like they were old friends enjoying a poker night.

You'd think nothing would confound her given the past year. Her best friend had become a conduit for an Aztec goddess who could make vines grow out of nowhere. Then there was Dama X, taking a page from Wonder Woman and creating her own Themyscira.

A trio of aliens shouldn't bother her.

"Screw it." She sat.

Gilroy opened the remaining bottle and slid it across the table to her.

The Three drank their sodas in silence.

Kali wrapped her hands around the cool bottle and racked her brain for what she wanted answers to most. She felt like she'd been playing a game of twenty questions with these aliens, with one question leading to another intense discovery and then leading to a I-wish-I-had-never-asked conclusion.

Like how were they communicating with Dara's brother? Could they get a message to U-Sec and her friends? And what did they mean about the Man being corrupted by the Dark? And how exactly does this Dark work?

"How did the universe reset?" Dara asked before Kali could fire off her own questions.

She took a sip of soda, wishing for something stronger. However, when she started to tell her tale of the Evil Incident and Stockwell using her power and meeting S-Kali and the warning about the Man, she found the words no longer burned up her throat and caused her head to throb. It was if in retelling the tale yet again gave it less power than holding it inside.

"After S-Kali told me what happened to her, I was shot back to my universe to just before everything went down at the dinner. That means Stockwell, the Man's henchman, never kidnapped my ex-boyfriend, who shall not be named."

Because he had a transhuman prison in his basement and merely thinking his name had the power to make the bile creep up her throat.

She took another sip.

"Stockwell used your power to travel to the future in our universe from his time. Can you travel to the future of this one from your time?" Dara asked.

Kali rolled this idea over. "I tried once but I was blocked. I can only travel into the past and present, as related to my present, of this universe and not a minute into the future."

"You must be tied to your time," Dara said.

Kali had assumed the same. They'd started tests to understand why, but Kali became sick of TransGen's scientists monitoring her. She didn't believe that knowing the future of the other world was important.

"When I travel into the past of this universe, I'm gone for the same amount of time when I alt-jump back. If I spend a week here, then I'm gone a week back home. But the reset was different. S-Kali was gone for several years. Unless the time in my world progressed that many years into the future before Stockwell traveled into my past and . . ." She chugged on her soda. "The paradoxes of time travel can be overwhelming when you're not dealing in mathematical theories but with what really has, is, or will happen to you personally."

Kali sighed. "I wish I could be more help to you."

"What was the latest year you've traveled?" Dara propped her elbows on the table.

"January 1998. I visited Washington, D.C. That's when I learned about one major difference between our universes. I saw these billboards for the *Titanic* movie, which was a huge hit in this universe but was never released in ours because, well, the Titanic never sank."

Dara perked up. She grinned at Tomas then Gilroy.

"What did I say?" Kali found herself smiling too. At what, she had no clue. But Dara's excited expression made her hope that all wasn't lost.

"This universe goes on. It doesn't die out with us and the Dark." Dara took the men's hands.

"Why would this universe die?" Kali's hope busted like an old tire.

"Because when the Dark dies here, its energy will implode, and it will take this universe with it," she said.

"That's why we can't leave the Man behind here," Tomas said.

"And why we were seeing Willie Nelson before he was sucked into the black hole along with us," Gilroy said.

"But now he goes on making music with his friends." Tomas beamed.

Chapter 17

Max and Friends Hit the Road

"Don't do it, Raven." Surefire leaned between the front bucket seats.

"What don't you want him to do?" Max tightened his grip on the steering wheel of the Bronco as the truck accelerated farther into the tunnel leading to the back exit. Lights above them turned on then off after they passed.

"We can't take the risk that they'll see us." Raven braced himself against the dashboard.

"I don't have much power left. And the skull's preternatural battery is drained."

"They're not taking us again, Syn," Raven said with a franticness that made Max wonder whether he should be more anxious than he was.

"Listen to me, you've never made a car disappear before and not one with three people in it," Surefire argued.

"Disappear?" Max exclaimed.

"Fine." Surefire threw up her hands when Raven screwed his eyes closed. "But if you pass out, I'm not waking you up, and I can't be responsible for what I do to you."

"Is that a promise?" He grinned.

"You wish."

"Are we almost there?" Raven asked Max.

"The exit is in fifty yards. Why?" He straightened the wheel as the truck bounced over a speed bump.

"Because I don't know how long I can hold it." Raven's face tensed like he was shoving a great weight.

"Raven—" Surefire ventured.

He shushed her.

"You'll pay for that later," she said.

"Promise?"

"Shut it, and prove me wrong." Surefire grabbed the back of Raven's neck.

"What are you—?" Max jerked to the side as her fingers formed a vice around his neck as well. He accelerated up an incline and the exit came into view. As they approached, a garage door slid open to reveal a rickety barn filled with hay and empty stalls. The barn doors opened with a loud creak when the truck hit a sensor in the floor. The vehicle bounced into a field and disappeared.

What the—?

The steering wheel, the truck, Max's hands and arms—all gone. He floated above the dirt road between dried-out rows of corn coated in snow.

"How?" Max said but didn't, because he no longer had lips. The sensation gave new meaning to being lightheaded.

Not sure, just can. Need to concentrate, so I don't mix us up, came Raven's voice from . . . where did it come from?

Mix us up? Max blurted. Again, not aloud, his words vibrated the air.

A helicopter flew into view. A spotlight trailed over the dead fields.

See? Raven's voice echoed around Max's being, whatever was left of it.

You're right, she replied from behind or above Max, he wasn't sure, because the helicopter circled the road before disappearing behind the trees.

Can't hold it much longer, Raven said or thought or whatever.

Max couldn't analyze it too closely because he was overwhelmed by seeing and feeling and hearing his surroundings at once. His essence—or whatever he was now—floated from the snow-covered field above the plowed road cutting through evergreens and leafless trees. Branches dipped, heavy with snow. The night sky was clear enough to see the Milky Way's thick starry blanket stretching across the sky. Maybe he could touch it? Become a part of it, if he was closer.

Stop. You could float away and we couldn't gather you back. Surefire's voice vibrated around him, tugging him down like he was a balloon on the end of a string.

Max banged into . . . or his cluster of atoms banged into . . . the solid journal. It hadn't become invisible like the rest of them but floated along the road as if carried by a specter.

Raven. Stop now. You're going too long, Surefire pleaded.

That's . . . what . . . she . . . said, Raven grunted.

Really?

Max's lungs inflated. He found himself gasping for air as if breaking the surface after a deep dive. The truck's seat formed underneath him. The windshield appeared next then the steering wheel under his trembling hands. He slammed on the brakes, causing the truck to fishtail to a stop at a crossroads.

His entire body vibrated as if he'd shot down five espressos. He took several breaths to ground himself before asking, "What just happened?"

Raven slumped in the passenger seat. His head rested on the window.

"Magic," he slurred.

If Max didn't know better, he'd think the guy was drunk.

"It sucks a lot of our energy to do that. We've never made a truck disappear before." Surefire yawned. From the rearview mirror, Max watched her stretch across the back seat.

"Got any food in here?" Raven's words came out garbled as if it was a chore for him to speak.

"I might have a bag of nuts. Could be stale though." Max rummaged through the center console. He found an unopened bag of almonds from when he and Glen had taken the truck to go hiking near his cabin.

Max turned on the wipers to clear off the window wet from snow falling off the trees. He squinted past the watery streaks to read the road sign. They were about two miles north of his property. A left turn would lead them to the interstate south toward Virginia, but there would be police patrolling the highway with speed traps, leaving them exposed. He opted to take the back roads. It would add an hour or so, but the chance of them being detected was slimmer.

Raven tried and failed to open the bag of nuts.

"Here." Max tore it open and handed it back to him.

"Thanks." Raven dumped the nuts into his mouth.

Max's eyes flicked to the rearview mirror once more. The road behind them was empty. No sign of the spotlight or helicopter or military vehicles.

He touched three buttons on the 1980s tape deck and it dropped down to reveal a small screen.

"Are you James Bond?" Raven said between crunches.

"No, but I watched enough movies as a kid to get inspired." The screen lit up and he entered a passcode.

The vehicle's exterior shimmered as the nanoparticles in the metal, glass, and rubber of the truck reflected the environment, rendering them invisible.

"Your car can turn invisible?" Raven's mouth fell open. From the back seat, Surefire emitted a soft snore.

"Yep." Max made a left onto the road.

"Why didn't you tell me?"

"I would've had I known what you were going to do. At least you proved Surefire wrong."

"That alone was worth it." He leaned on the console and looked back at his sleeping girlfriend.

"I still don't understand what I experienced or how it happened. I can't stop shaking." Max held up his quivering hand to prove the point.

"You did good. You didn't freak out as much as I thought you would." Raven dug out a nut from the bag.

"I've alt-jumped with Kali and was kidnapped and held captive in another universe. I guess not much surprises me anymore."

"I felt the same way, until I saw this book"—Raven pointed to the journal set on the wide dashboard—"floating between us. I couldn't turn it invisible. There was a force field around it. That's never happened before."

"Then how did you get it to my house?" Max checked his odometer then his mirrors once more. He hoped to remain invisible for several more miles, as long as other cars didn't appear on the road.

"That's the strange part. We didn't have any trouble traveling to you. Almost like it pulled us to your house." He gave Max a side-eyed appraisal as if waiting for him to reveal a hand he'd been hiding.

"I'm as much in the dark about this journal as you are."

Raven nodded but he didn't appear to fully buy Max's claim. "You said someone's meeting us at your cabin."

"Glen's father. He knows about this journal, which is why he never told me about it."

"To keep you safe?" Raven suggested.

"That's the theory, and I plan to find out for sure." Max touched the control screen. With a shimmer, the invisibility cloak fell away, revealing the beige Bronco. He depressed another series of buttons and the vehicle's color changed to blue.

"This is insane—and a thief's wet dream. No offense. I'm reformed," he cut a quick look at the sleeping Surefire, "but APS could've used this back in my day."

"APS?"

"Artifact Procurement Specialists. A fancy name for grave robbers. It's how I made my money before the goddess put my skills to better use."

"I envisioned it as a way to protect our soldiers. Eventually, I'll patent a version for personal use. Maybe sell it to the upscale car market to fund other projects. If you can't make up your mind between red and black, you can have both. Never thought about it from a criminal perspective."

"When you grow up in that world, it's hard to think otherwise. You look for the angles. How to get yours, to take what you're owed because no one's going to give it to you. In fact, they'll try to take from you, so take from them first. That was my dad's philosophy, the legacy he left me." Once more Raven glanced over the edge of his seat at Surefire. He stared at her for a few seconds before turning back to Max with an unreadable expression. "It helps when you meet someone who gives you a different perspective."

Max vaguely remembered stories in the news about an UltraAgent turning rogue and teaming with a thief. At the time, he thought the story was exaggerated to make, well, news.

"How did you meet? If you don't mind me asking."

Raven chuckled. "How long is this ride?"

"Four hours."

"Then we got time. Plus, it'll keep me awake. Talking about it gets my heart going in a good way."

Raven gave him the details about working for APS before he died, raiding Xochi's temple during an archeological dig in Mexico. He explained how she resurrected him for a job that would redeem him—returning sacred objects to their rightful owners and rebalancing the world's energies. Unfortunately, the non-rightful owners were oftentimes museums or influential private collectors. These thefts put him on U-Sec's radar, and Surefire was assigned his case. She cornered him at a warehouse where they were both captured by Raven's cousin, who was trying to raise an Aztec god. They ended up partnering to defeat this ancient god and his cousin to save the world.

Midway through Raven's story, they came across a rest stop. Pulling his hood over his head, Max ran to the vending machines and bought a bounty of snacks. Raven tore into them like he hadn't eaten in days.

Through bites and sips, Raven described how Xochi had tricked them, and Surefire ended up as a conduit for the goddess. Then how they were tricked again, but this time by a doctor they'd trusted, who was synthesizing proteins in their blood to create super drugs, enhancing transhumans in powerful and gender bending ways.

The story that took place on Dama X's island, what Kali had related to him.

"Then that's how you ended up in the TPC," Max said.

"TPC?"

"Transhuman Protection Chamber. Or glass coffin, as Kali calls it."

"The device Kali found in your basement?"

"A similar model."

"A *protection* unit, huh?" Raven whistled.

Max wanted to explain that it was easier to sell to the government and the public when they attached euphemistic words like protection instead of prison to a product's name.

But this man didn't need to hear an explanation. He needed to hear an apology. He deserved an apology and even more.

"I'm sorry," Max said.

Raven gave him a half-shrug. He balled up an empty chip bag. "Guess the government sees it as protecting the public from us. They're afraid of Surefire—and me to a lesser extent—falling into the wrong hands and being used against the country. Oh, yeah, and the man leading this *procurement* effort is Surefire's father. Needless to say, we don't get along."

"Surefire's father is trying to kidnap her?"

"He wants to make sure she's 'protected.'" Raven put air quotes around the word. "We think he was behind the push to synthesize her power, but he swears the scientist who put us on ice was acting alone, and that she'd lied to him as well. He could be telling the truth, but it's hard to believe when the man bleeds bullshit."

"Who's her father?" Max asked.

Raven eyed him as if assessing whether he should say. Then he shrugged, bit into a granola bar, and said, "Stephen St. John."

Max wracked his brain. Why did that name sound familiar?

Then he remembered.

"Kali spoke about him." Like one would speak about the bogeyman, in hushed words, as if saying his name too loud or too often could conjure him. But she didn't say he was Surefire's father.

"Kali was avoiding him. What does he want with her?" asked Max.

"To use her powers for black ops missions. Train her to be a soldier, since no one else has her ability. But that's not who she is."

"Not at all."

Right then, Max swore to himself that he'd protect Kali from St. John, Aztec gods, whatever and whomever wanted to use her, even if she no longer wanted a relationship with him. With his connections, he could keep St. John from her, so he couldn't make her into something she wasn't.

He squeezed the steering wheel. "Could Surefire's father have ties to this Organization?"

"Doubt it. Those people in white who attacked us weren't working with St. John's black ops army. We fought his peeps with Dama X. They are experienced soldiers. The ones in Utah weren't. And I'm grateful, because if they had been, we may not be in your car now." The granola bar gone, Raven tore open a bag of Tastykakes.

He offered Max a cupcake. How this guy could eat that amount of processed food at a time like this was beyond him.

"Thanks." He took the cake when he got a whiff of the sweet scent, making his mouth water. Oddly enough, the chocolaty cake elevated his mood a smidgen.

"One thing I've learned is that supernatural beings don't make things easy. The more complicated, the better. When you're old enough to have literally seen everything, you need to create your own entertainment," said Raven.

"Then you believe supernatural beings are behind this journal?"

Before this evening, he had never considered theories of the preternatural as anything more than fairy tales. And he never believed in the rumors of what some UltraAgents could do before he met Kali and her friends and seen the goddess Xochi using Surefire.

"Do you have a scientific explanation for that portal?" Raven said with a mouthful of cake.

"No." Max turned the truck onto the road leading onto his grandfather's property.

The Bronco bounced over a foot of snow covering the driveway. The truck's lift kept the drive train above the snow. "No Trespassing" signs were posted along the tree-lined route. They arrived at the gate, which was chained shut.

Offering to unlock it, Raven unbuckled his seat belt.

"I got this." Max pressed a button hidden under the steering wheel. The gate lifted straight up, allowing the truck to pass underneath.

"Forget Bond. You're Q." Raven buckled up again.

He allowed himself a smile at this reference. The guy hadn't seen anything yet, because Max wasn't taking chances. If that Organization could find Kali in Utah so quickly, then they might not have much time before that group found them here, and he wouldn't make it easy.

"You do know you're driving directly into three big trees?" Raven braced himself against the seats. A plastic bag of trash fell from his lap.

"What trees?" The pines parted on cue as the truck zipped past a sensor. Jets blew air from under the bumper to cover their tracks.

"This is insane," Raven muttered.

"*This* is insane?" Max laughed.

"Point taken."

The truck bounded along the snow-covered route. Fortunately, Max had driven this road so many times he could do it blindfolded. They hit a slippery patch, and the truck pitched to the left. Surefire squealed.

"You okay?" Raven called back to her.

"What the—?" They hit another big bump and she seemed to swallow her next words.

"Sorry." Max turned the wheel. The tires spun for purchase.

"Not to be a back seat driver, but we're about to crash into a frozen waterfall," she said.

"He's got this." Raven pushed back against his seat as the truck lurched forward. "You do have this, don't you?"

The ice wasn't moving. The sensor could be frozen over or the snow could have coated it. Max slowed the truck, but not too much, because the snow was deeper and this stretch was steeper. He didn't want to get stuck.

"Come on," he whispered to the controls. He pulled out the headlight switch and turned it counterclockwise ninety degrees. A laser shot out. Max focused it on the area where the sensors resided.

"Whoa," Raven and Surefire both uttered.

He held his breath. They were coming in too fast. He eased his foot off the gas. The truck slowed but kept sliding toward the ice.

When they were a mere foot away, the frozen door loosened and lifted but not fast enough. The bottom of the ice door scraped the roof of the truck. Lights came on as they drove into the tunnel that his grandfather had blasted out more than fifty years ago for this private underground bunker. In the rearview mirror, Max made sure the door shut behind them.

"My father and I added extra security features," he explained.

"Extra security features is an understatement," said Raven.

"I would ask how you can afford this, but you're a billionaire," said Surefire.

Max shifted in his seat. He never realized how different he was from the majority of people until he spoke with those who didn't grow up in his world.

"Dude, don't be embarrassed." Raven nudged him.

"I didn't mean to offend. I'm in awe of what you've accomplished," she said.

"I didn't create this. It was built by my grandfather. Then my father and his business partners added to it. I only made these upgrades so I could work in peace. Plus, it's a real-world demo of the security measures we can design for our clients. I needed to justify these expenses to the board somehow."

They reached the end of the tunnel, and he parked the truck in the widest of the three empty spaces. He was disappointed that Mr. Triman hadn't arrived yet.

Max tucked his grandfather's journal into a wide pocket inside his coat and headed to a steel-reinforced door. He laid his hand against the small rectangular screen next to it then positioned his eye over the retinal scanner.

A hiss of air released and the door opened.

"Because we're underground, the temperature will be a constant sixty-five degrees," he said.

"That's better than ten degrees outside." Raven handed a bag of chips and bottled water to Surefire.

He led them up the stairs that had been chiseled into the bedrock and to another door that led to a circular room—the lounge, as his father and his friends had referred to it. An orange shag rug left from his grandfather's heydays—now considered vintage by most, tacky by Max—appeared as the sun in the middle of the floor. Living room furniture from a 1960s Sears catalog was set over it. The interior had been well-preserved, having not seen much use except for the few times a year they vacationed here when he was young, and when he came to escape his home lab, too easily accessible to Glen and other board members who liked to drop in unannounced.

In the corner was a bar, because every living room had a bar back in the day, even one that was an offshoot of a private technology research center.

"It's like we've stepped into a time capsule. I can see why TimeTrap liked you." Surefire spun around, taking in the room.

"I've replaced some of the furniture in the other rooms, but I concentrated mostly on upgrading the electronics." Max retrieved the book from the inside pocket of his jacket, which he then shed and tossed on a chair.

Raven made a beeline for the refrigerator behind the *Mad Men*-era bar. "Any food? Maybe protein-based? I just ate my allotment of cakes and chips for the year."

"Through here." Max waved them down another corridor leading to a galley kitchen lined with stainless steel cabinets and appliances.

"A few frozen meals are in the freezer. Can't guarantee they're not freezer burned. It's been awhile since I was last here. There's beef jerky in the pantry in the back. I take it on my hikes," he said.

"Awesome." Raven opened the freezer and tossed a few meat-filled frozen dinners on the counter. Surefire sidled next to Raven and yawned. He kissed the top of her head.

"No rest for an UltraAgent," Raven said.

"And no rest for Kali. I've got the power of a goddess at my disposal, and I've never felt so helpless," she said.

"Hope's not lost yet." Max held up the journal.

Surefire eyed the book with disdain. Her face paled enough for Max to notice. "After I eat, I'll contact Xochi again. See if we can figure this out."

"What about your friend?" Raven popped a chicken dinner in the microwave.

Max checked his phone. No messages from Mr. Triman or Glen. "I don't know. He isn't here yet. His SUV wasn't in the garage, and I would've been notified if he'd entered the bunker."

"Then we hang tight." Raven set the timer on the microwave before opening another boxed meal.

"Go ahead and eat. I'll join you after I do one thing," said Max.

"Promise me you'll eat something. You'll be no good to Kali if you're too weak to think." Surefire opened a drawer and took out utensils.

"I promise."

He left them to heat up their food and went through a door at the far end of the narrow kitchen. Cool light illuminated a small office with a glass-top computer desk in the center. A few servers lined the right wall. To his left, stairs led to the old cabin above. At his back was the door to a tech lab, similar to the one underneath his home but a quarter of the size and not as well equipped. He used this area as a retreat to generate ideas. He would then take those ideas and build the devices at home with a small team or at DERST if he needed more resources.

He took out his phone. One missed call from his father. None from Mr. Triman. He tried calling him. The line rang and rang never going into his voicemail. He tried Glen. The call immediately entered his voicemail, which was too full to save another message.

Max tossed his phone on the desk. Four hours spent on the road to meet with Mr. Triman. Now he couldn't get it touch with him or his son. Every minute with Kali trapped inside some book or portal or other dimension was another minute that she could be hurt or killed.

Mr. Triman's cryptic audio text made Max believe he was in trouble. He couldn't text plainly but had to rely on a riddle to tell him where to go. It made sense to meet in this underground bunker, which was secure and contained tech and resources. Although how his tech could be used to open a supernatural portal and find Kali was something he was relying on Mr. Triman knowing.

The screen on his phone flashed with a reminder of another missed call. Max's father.

He sighed. The last thing he wanted to hear was his father berating him for not responding to his earlier message. When they finally took a break from jet setting, his parents wanted—no, expected—their children to drop everything to see them.

This time they'd have to wait. Until Max found Kali, nothing else mattered. Work, family, everything else in his life was on hold.

He drummed his fingers. Stared at the alert. But he was the one on hold now. Waiting for Mr. Triman, for Glen, for the power couple to eat before they took their next steps. This might be the only time he'd have to listen to his father's voicemail.

He braced himself for a guilt trip. What he got was the reason why he couldn't get a hold of Mr. Triman.

"Maxwell, call us as soon as you get this. Gabriel is missing, and Glenna can't get a hold of their children. She came home tonight to find Gabriel's office ransacked and a man in white fleeing the scene. She traced his phone and it's offline. According to phone records, the last message he sent was to you. Call us now."

His heart thundered in his chest. Blood pumped so fast he became dizzy.

Either Max had been set up to come to the cabin and this was a trap, or Mr. Triman had fled the scene before the break in and was in hiding. Had Glen known? Was that why he gave Max the note before he left?

He placed his palm on the edge of the desk to start the computer. The screen displayed his desktop apps and a corner grid showcased web news channels. One video streamed an aerial view of his home in Maryland, with police and unmarked trucks in his driveway and along the road. People trudged through the snow with flashlights. Others entered and exited his home, some with boxes, some empty handed. An imposing man stood on the porch in a dark wool coat directing the operations. Max couldn't see his face to identify him.

He couldn't do anything about the authorities at his home. He shut down the video and brought up feeds from the surveillance cameras inside and around the property where he currently hunkered down.

No signs of life. Not even animal footprints disturbed the snow outside. Inside the underground structure, the cameras showed empty, dark rooms. No movement triggered the motion-detector lights.

He let out a relieved breath that no one had found them. But he wouldn't allow himself to fully let down his guard until Mr. Triman arrived.

If he ever arrived.

Sensors lined the property and buildings. They would pick up anyone approaching—either Mr. Triman or the police or FBI or someone wearing white, which seemed to be the standard uniform for those working with the Organization.

If and when a trespasser arrived, he hoped Surefire's ability would be back online for them to disappear from here.

Although disappear to where was a problem for later. There was a family vacation home in the Turkes and Caicos, but that wouldn't provide the security or resources they needed. That is if Mr. Triman was indeed missing, and if that text was sent by this Organization to get Max alone and set him up.

In the meantime, Max would do what he could with what he had in case Mr. Triman never came.

He opened the journal to the pages describing the TPC and Kali. He placed it face down on the desktop and scanned them, repeating the process until half the text was scanned. He uploaded the digital files to his decryption software. It ran in the background while he finished scanning the rest of the journal.

An error message popped up before the software could decode the first page. He ran it again. Another error message. This time the screen blinked and his hard drive shut down. A tendril of smoke drifted from under the desk. Dropping to his knees, he pried open the circuit board.

Fried.

This was a top-of-the-line processor. He'd used it to generate thousands of lines of code over the summer without a glitch.

He popped back over the desk and stared at the journal with a new level of wonder and fear.

"What is different about you and why?" Max murmured.

The leather was marred by ashy gray marks and a bronze sheen. It wasn't as smooth as the other journals he'd left in his home safe. But it had the same embossed logo. His grandfather began using the emblem after he'd traced their family history and found tapestries and other ancestral items that employed this design.

His father had related this story to him after Max's accident while he was recovering in the hospital. So he'd chosen to have the crest tattooed on his arm to inspire him to be more like his grandfather and push his limits in ways that didn't align with his father's beliefs or DERST.

Now he truly needed to test his limits. This book held the secret to finding Kali. She'd risked everything to go after Stockwell to save him in the other universe. He owed this to her.

He owed so much more to her.

He scrutinized the book, willing the information to come to him. He scoured the pages until his head pounded and his eyes watered from the shifting text, which had been written in two different hands. The second set of entries was in his grandfather's fluid cursive. However, the first few entries were in a writing style Max didn't recognize. He wondered if this book had first belonged to another.

With its appearance and content being different from the other journals in Max's possession, he considered it had to be different on an atomic level, especially to cause that explosion. He needed to switch gears and discover the type of energy it stored. Then maybe he'd uncover answers the elusive text wouldn't give him.

He hustled through the door into his mini-lab. In the far corner was a rectangular glass case, the size of a home aquarium. Above and below were sensors that could detect and decode items on a cellular level. If this journal contained an energy force, the machine would find it.

Max sealed the glass shut over the book. The sensors churned on. Two long metal arms proceeded to scan the journal, first the top then the bottom, then they swooped around the edges.

A monitor lit with rows of numbers showing the cellular structure and creating a 3-D model. A red line flashed. It detected an anomaly that should not exist within the book's elements. Dark energy was present along with an unknown force. This dark energy was similar to what Kali expressed when she alt-jumped but not exact. Something was off about it.

"I contacted Xochi," Surefire spoke from the doorway.

Max started at her voice. Engrossed in what he'd found, he hadn't heard her approach. Raven stood behind her, sucking down a bottle of water.

"She won't come back with that thing around," she continued.

"Did she give you any indication of what it was?"

Surefire nodded with eyes wide with worry—a worry that bled into Max.

"She said it's the power that imprisoned her and the other Old Ones in the Garden. And the same power that destroyed the world the last time."

Chapter 18

Kali Shares a Drink with New Allies

"You're talking about a cosmological collapse." Kali's fingers ached from where she'd gripped the metal edge of the table.

"If we don't neutralize it, then this energy will expand rapidly in this universe. But I believe we succeed since you experienced this universe in the 1990s."

"But that was before the reset." Kali instinctively went for her phone in her back pocket to research theories behind a collapse of this magnitude. But she'd left it at Max's. Not that it would work in this year (or universe) decades before the Internet and cell towers in every county.

"I need to understand what I'm going up against. We're talking about something a bazillion—and I'm not using scientifically backed numbers here—times stronger than an atomic bomb. There are theories about universe expansion but—"

"Kali, stop. The physics behind this energy field is beyond your current comprehension. It will take too long to educate you about this subject. For a millennia, we have studied it, eventually designing tools that can contain and neutralize it," Dara said.

"Unfortunately, those tools are in the other universe," Tomas added.

Dara glared at him and Tomas lowered his eyes. When she addressed Kali again, it was with an encouraging smile. "Focus on getting your power back online to transport us home after neutralization."

Right. She could do that. Focus on what she understood—her power.

Although she didn't understand it as well as she should, considering it was her body, and neither did the TransGen doctors who oversaw her. It had hurt when she first got her powers, like a giant palm smacking into her. The small particle accelerator her professor had designed accidentally discharged with Kali in the room, and she was in the hospital for two weeks in a coma. When she woke up, she felt different. It wasn't until she popped into another universe and time that she learned how different.

"I could help her." Gilroy rubbed his palms together and a golden light appeared. The same as what Tomas's hand emitted when he read the wall.

Dara touched his wrist and shook her head.

"How can he help?" Kali stared at his palms as the gold light faded from them.

"Gilroy has the ability to heal. He thinks that he may be able to use his power to fuel yours but it's too dangerous at this time."

"Too dangerous?" Kali looked from one to the other.

"We need all his strength to confront and contain the Man. If he uses his ability on you—"

"Then he will be as useless as me," Kali sighed.

"Exactly," Tomas said.

Until Kali returned to full operating capacity, she was dead in this alt-universe's water, hanging out with the Three as they brooded into their Coke bottles because this portal kick-started by an alien energy may have negated Kali's powers. The same portal that had brought them here with . . .

"Wait a minute," Kali said. "Why were you with Grandpa Martin when he opened the portal?"

"We were attempting to stop him from ending the world."

"So he's even a bigger douche than I previously thought."

Dara looked to Tomas and frowned. They appeared to confer although no words emanated from their lips. Tomas made a squeezing then spraying motion in the air as if accentuating his silent explanation.

She turned back to Kali. "Ah, a douche. Vulgar, but I understand."

"You can read minds?" Kali blanked out her thoughts. UltraAgent Oracle could read minds. In fact, she could do more than read minds; she could control a person if she forced her full consciousness inside them.

"Only one another's. The three of us are connected. It is what happens on our wedding day."

"You three are . . ." Kali shifted her gaze from one to the other.

Gilroy's black eyebrows rose, his expression bemused.

When no one finished the statement for her, she said to Dara, "You have two spouses?"

Kali couldn't handle one lover. The idea of two made her head—and other areas—spin.

"Both sexes on our world sometimes take two mates. It makes life easier."

"I don't see how that's possible," she replied.

"Our society is more evolved than yours. Females have always been equal to males. We're valued for our contributions and share power with them. As for our relationships, we are free to make our own choices, and some of us find polygamy to be desirable."

"But you're their leader, aren't you?" From what she'd seen, Dara was the alpha in this trio with the men heeding her beck and call.

"Each of us is born with particular gifts. Each stronger in different areas," she replied.

"We take turns," Tomas added in a way that hinted he wasn't only referring to their social dynamic but their behind-closed-doors one too.

Kale's cheeks grew hot.

"Does that make you uncomfortable?" Gilroy's lips twitched as if trying to suppress a smile.

"Whatever floats your three-person boat," she said, wishing her cheeks would cool down.

Dara's body began shaking with laughter. She fell against Tomas, who grinned in response. Gilroy tossed his head and chuckled. Kali found herself joining in, despite not knowing what was funny—her comment or a mental joke shared amongst themselves.

"Put a fork in me, I'm done. You've truly broken this gal." Kali hitched a thumb at her chest. "First you tell me that you bought my Earth in some kind of cosmic real estate deal. Then you lay on me that you're humankind's protectors—"

"Custodians," Gilroy corrected.

"Yeah, that." She tipped her bottle at him. "Then my ability was negated by an evil alien energy in that portal."

"I mean . . ." She choked on a chuckle or maybe it wasn't a chuckle. Maybe she was starting to cry. "I don't even know who or what I am anymore. You mention in passing that you couldn't save me before and that—"

Yep, she was crying. She'd gone from hysterical laughter to ugly sobbing in two sniffs. She grabbed a paper napkin from a metal spiral holder in the center of the table.

The Three stopped laughing. They sat up in their chairs and leaned forward with their elbows on the table.

Kali blew her nose in the rough napkin.

Dara spoke, "In time, all will be revealed. For now, I want you to focus on the main task at hand."

She touched Kali's hand, stopping her in mid-reach for another napkin. "There is a reason you came to us on this day."

She recalled the date written in the journal. Robert had ordered her to travel to that specific time. "Because that's when the Man knew I would arrive? Someone, somehow communicated to him that I'd be there at that time."

"The Organization. They are former colleagues, and we believe they employed this Robert who came through the portal with you."

"An organization of what?"

"No, the Organization. It's a group of beings whose purpose changes as leadership changes," Dara said.

"We were aligned with them," Gilroy said.

"At one time," Tomas said.

"But when new management took over and attempted to use the Dark against our warnings, my brother and I broke ties with them," Dara said.

Kali was somehow following all of this. Maybe her mind wasn't shot after all. "The Custodian who wrote the first pages in the journal. Was he with this Organization?"

They nodded.

"Who are these beings?" Kali asked.

"Those who value life on Earth differently than we do. Those who see the weaponized potential of the power that's inside the Man as a means to an end," Dara replied.

It finally dawned on Kali that the Man, if these aliens' account was correct, was no longer an ordinary human. He was super human.

She took a breath, trying to fill her lungs but couldn't. Her leg bounced under the table. Her hand shook as she grasped her soda bottle. She was frightened at this sudden clarity of thought, of the pieces clicking together to reveal the demon hiding in the background of the picture.

S-Kali had never stood a chance against him.

Would she this time?

"It has fully possessed Maxwell Martin," Dara continued, seemingly unaware of the fear gripping Kali's body. "The Organization planned to approach the Dark while it was in a weaker state, hoping they could better control it when they bring it home."

Weaker state. At least there was some silver sheen in this.

Swallowing the increasingly large lump in her throat, Kali said, "Let me see if I'm following you. The energy in this world can't support you or the Dark. The Man's body and yours are slowly dying."

"Close to dying," Dara said.

"Which is why we saw Johnny Cash," Tomas said.

"And were going to see Willie Nelson." Gilroy crossed his arms and Kali worried he was going to cry. Either over the lost Willie Nelson concert or dying, it was hard to tell.

"Let me explain in terms you can understand," Dara said.

Tomas leapt to his feet and jogged to the refrigerator. He took out an apple and placed it on the table in front of Kali. She concluded that Dara had ordered him to do so through their alien mind connection.

That could come in handy if Kali ever dated again. Would interspecies dating be possible? If the wonder twins, despite their bad taste in leisure suits, were any indication of what their men were like, then maybe she could give them a go.

Who was she kidding? They weren't her type. She only had one type, and he was back home and he wanted to shove her in a box and—

Kali was crying and didn't even realize it until Tomas exclaimed, "It's only an apple. You said you wanted something to eat. I'd forgotten to bring it with the sodas."

"Thank you. It's perfect." Just as she thought her relationship with Max was.

She sobbed as she picked up the apple and took a bite. It was sweet and mealy and she'd never tasted anything so good.

The men appeared uncomfortable with her second crying bout of the day. Tomas excused himself to presumably to go to the bathroom, if these aliens relieved themselves like humans. Gilroy stared down at his hands folded in his lap and probably wished he had thought of Tomas's idea first.

When Kali had finished her apple and her sobs had subsided to sniffles, Dara said, "Better?"

She nodded and wrapped the core in one of her discarded napkins.

"You mentioned that you needed to eat to fuel your power."

Kali nodded again.

"Imagine if the calories in this apple didn't convert into energy. You could eat as many as you wanted, but it wouldn't be enough. Eventually you would wither away, die of starvation. Well, that is what is happening to us. The energy residing in our universe that feeds and sustains us is not found in this one."

"Because the Dark used to be a Custodian like you with the same physiology, then that's why it's weak too?" Kali offered.

"Yes and no. Unlike us, it feeds off human life. But the humans in this world do not emit the same energy that it needs to survive. Their essences cannot sustain it."

"And Maxwell Martin is the Dark?"

"The black matter you saw entering Robert has multiplied inside Maxwell Martin, snuffing out his entire consciousness. He consumed a large quantity, nearly all we had. It is what makes him, for lack of a better descriptor, evil."

"Maxwell Martin wasn't responsible for your imprisonment," Dara continued. "It was the Dark controlling him. The person we knew was well-intentioned and assumed he was doing right by removing this substance from our universe."

Then Max's assessment of his grandfather was correct: he'd been a good man. Had been a good man until this thing possessed him. But what was Max's excuse for owning a containment unit?

"Does his grandson have this Dark thing inside him?" she asked.

"No, it wasn't part of him when he conceived his son so it wouldn't have been passed to his grandson."

Kali wrung her hands. "Can the Dark—" It sounded so weird to ask this. "Eat you?"

"It can infect us. But since our bodies have weakened as well, it won't make sense for it to possess us."

"Is the journal here? I couldn't find it after we came through the portal." Kali glanced around, certain she'd spy it on a table.

"No, it can't travel through—" Dara started when Tomas and Gilroy lurched up from the table.

Their hands fisted. They tilted their heads in unison.

"Not good," Tomas uttered.

"What isn't good? What was that?" Their alarm made Kali alarmed. Anything that could scare these three beings was enough to put her on high alert.

"They're here," Gilroy announced.

"Took less time than we assumed," Tomas added.

The ceiling vibrated. *Whomp-whomp-whomp* of helicopter blades signaled its approach.

The Three hurried into the center of the room. Kali remained sitting, her hands wrapped around the now warm bottle. Her heart thumped in time with the chopper blades.

"We need to leave. We're not prepared." Dara stared at the ceiling.

"How?" Kali asked, still not moving. There were no windows in the basement to confirm who it was, but the boots stomping across the floorboards justified Kali's paralyzing fear.

A man's voice rose above the patter of combat boots. "There's a basement."

Stockwell. Kali would know that ass's voice anywhere. She'd first heard it over three weeks ago and nearly every day since in her nightmares.

Kali was unable to feel or move a muscle like a deer caught in an array of headlights, thinking that if she became like a statue, then no one would notice her.

The Three bent their heads back. Their eyes followed the boots stomping across the floor like angry drum beats. Dust from the ceiling fell onto Dara's face. She didn't wipe it away. Instead she lifted her hands and the men walked to her.

"Kali," she said.

Dara wanted her to enter the circle they had made. But fear continued to paralyze her. The men were on the porch. Voices barking orders were now outside the hidden entrance to the basement. A hard object slammed into the wooden steps outside.

Kali jumped with each hit. Gilroy left the circle. He bent over and hugged Kali around the waist. He didn't complain when Kali spilled the remains of her soda down his back and the bottle dropped to the floor.

He slung her over his shoulder as if she were a bag of mulch.

The banging and slamming became louder. With a crack, the steps splintered. They were outside the metal door to the basement.

Bang! Bang! Bang! Kali glanced up to find dents in the door. It shook on its hinges. Another forceful hit and the door would cave in. What they were using to crash through that thick door, Kali didn't want to find out.

Hanging upside down against Gilroy's back, Kali couldn't see the trio's faces. She did see his hand clasp Dara's. Against her chest and stomach, Gilroy's muscles hummed with an *om* sound like what a Buddhist monk would make during meditation. The sound and vibrations increased, spreading into her body until her bones rattled with it. Her ears filled with the *om* until she no longer heard the hits on the door. Then a gold light, the same color that Tomas emitted when he touched the wall, rose from their feet to cover their bodies.

An explosion rocked the room. The door crashed open. Stockwell marched inside ahead of his men. He raised his gun. Kali screwed her eyes shut.

Chapter 19

Max and Gang in His Virginia Geekcave

"Wait . . . what?" Max sputtered. Did Surefire say the world had been destroyed once before? And the energy contained in this book played a role in that?

"Breathe, buddy. It's just Xochi being, well, Xochi." Raven followed Surefire into the room.

"You know it's more than that, Raven," she said.

He shook his head. "I'm trying not to scare the guy too much. Look at him. If he turned any whiter, I'd mistake him for Casper."

Max rubbed the back of his neck. "Tell me what the goddess meant, because I scanned this book and found traces of an energy similar to what is emitted when Kali alt-jumps. How is this possible? And how could this be related to the world ending?"

"You may want to sit for this." She beckoned Max into his office.

He retrieved the book from the machine. Surefire perched on one of the three green leather chairs forming a semicircle in front of his desk. Raven lounged in another.

"According to Aztec mythology, the world has been destroyed and reborn several times. You can find similar beliefs in other cultures too. Xochi was once human, elevated to goddess stature along with the other Old Ones. But an imbalance occurred on Earth, when the Old Ones abused their power, triggering a force that locked them away in the Garden, a place that's not quite part of any universe."

"A supernatural penalty box," Raven said.

"But what does this have to do with my grandfather's journal?" he asked.

"She didn't say." Surefire clasped her hands.

"Which means she doesn't know." Raven crumpled the empty plastic bottle in his hand.

"And she doesn't know how to find Kali?" Max searched Surefire's eyes for a hint of hope.

She looked down to her hands, knuckles cracking as she wrung them.

"Then we're on our own to figure this out." *At least until Mr. Triman gets here, if he ever does.*

Max's phone buzzed in his jean pocket. He slid it out and glanced at the screen. "It's a text from your boss Sean."

"You should call him. He may be able to help with this journal." Surefire rested her hand on Max's forearm.

"How?"

"He's enhanced," she said.

"Like a cyborg, but not the kick-ass Van Damme kind," Raven added.

Max was too stressed to smile at the movie reference. "I saw what he did at the *Real Life* dinner. He fried the alt-traveler's pack, but how can that ability help us now?"

"Sean has a rare neurological disease in which signals can't travel from his brain through his nervous system to regulate breathing, heart rate, and body movement. But that doesn't matter," Surefire said with a wag of her head. "What does is that TransGen, his father's company, rewired his neurological system using the same principles as a computer. His brain contains biocircuits—a biological-based circuit board—that allows him to live. But this enhancement also gave him an ability to interface with computers. He's been practicing and getting better."

"He totally schooled me in Call of Duty. I owe him for that." Raven tipped his crumbled bottle in a mock salute.

She continued, "On the Dama X case, he created a software program for his sister Gloria to isolate the genes being manipulated by a potent drug."

"Penises shriveling up. Men becoming women. Really scary stuff," said Raven.

Surefire glared at her boyfriend.

"Shutting up now." He raised his hands in surrender.

"The point is that Sean could help translate this book. For experienced programmers, the software needed for the Dama X case would've taken weeks to create. He did it in hours. Call him." She pointed to his phone.

Until he heard from Mr. Triman, he was out of options. The longer it took to find answers, the greater the possibility that Kali could be hurt or worse, a subject he didn't care to think too deeply on.

He closed his eyes, willing away the vision of Kali's body floating in a slime-filled TPC.

When he opened them, he said, "I'll call."

He strode over to an older model computing desk, the one that hadn't been fried trying to process the journal. The surface lit up with a keyboard. He removed his phone from its case and set it directly on the glass. Circuits lit up under the phone, connecting it to the hard drive. A projection of a computer screen formed in front of them. Across the image, Sean's number and name appeared.

The line rang once before he answered.

"Did you find Kali?" Sean's eyes darted from Surefire to Raven standing on either side of Max.

He could almost see Sean's biocircuits processing the scene.

"She went into a portal created by a book." Surefire leaned against the desk in front of the screen.

"Then the video on the web news is real?" Sean fiddled with a Pop Art tie lying against his wrinkled gray shirt. From what they could see of his electronic desktop, the glass monitor was cluttered with images from the web. "I've been at the office since this evening answering calls about her. I told the media it wasn't true."

"What isn't true?" A woman with straight dark hair popped over Sean's shoulder. He jumped to the side, his chair rolling back.

"Hey, Gloria." Surefire waved.

"Where did you come from?" Sean admonished. "My door is locked."

"That's Sean's sister and business partner," Surefire whispered to Max.

He nodded, having recognized her from magazine and web news articles on TransGen and U-Sec.

"You can't keep me out of your office. Surefire, what's going on? What did Max do to Kali?" Gloria demanded.

"I didn't—" Max started.

"She spends the holidays with you and doesn't call or show up for work, and you're not to blame?" Gloria countered.

"Who are you blaming for what?" A broad-shouldered man with a mop of blonde hair appeared over Sean's other shoulder.

"Why are you here?" Sean frowned at him.

"Gloria texted me that you were talking to Surefire. I'm afraid that I might've broken the door handle to get in."

Sean's jaw ground back and forth as if working out a good comeback.

"Hi, Pax." Surefire smiled at him.

"What's going on? Is that Max Martin? Where's Kali?" came the rapid-fire questions from her other boss.

"We're with Max, but we don't know where Kali is. She disappeared into one of his grandfather's journals." She gave them a synopsis of the day's events so far.

"Where are you? I'm coming to help," Pax said.

"We don't need you here. We're safe for now," Surefire replied.

Pax bobbed his head, although his scowling face communicated loud and clear that he wasn't happy to do so.

"Keep my father off our scent, if you can. That's what you can do for us. We need Sean for this one," she said.

Sean straightened in his chair. "You hear that? They need me. So you two can get out of—"

"No," Gloria and Pax cut him off.

Sean threw his head back, as if pleading with a higher power for strength. When he lowered his eyes to the screen, he asked, "How can I help?"

"Max is going to send you pages from the journal that created the portal," Surefire said.

"I'm giving you access to a folder on my personal server that contains the scanned pages. It also contains the software I tried to use to break the code. Surefire said you have a knack with computers."

Gloria snorted. "He likes them better than people."

"Right now, yes," Sean shot back.

Max set up a secured login account and sent the information to Sean. "If we can break the code used to write this journal, we might be able to save Kali. You get her back, and DERST will give U-Sec whatever you need."

"Nice of you to say, but saving our agent is our only incentive," Pax said.

"But we'll discuss your offer after we find her," Sean added quickly.

"I have to warn you. The circuits overloaded on my newest computer when it tried to decode these pages."

"But you haven't used anything like me before," Sean said.

Pax and Gloria groaned.

"What?" He looked from one to the other.

"I'm staying with you," Gloria said.

He ignored his sister and turned his attention to the desktop screen. His fingertips glowed electric blue. Lines lit up along the veins in the backs of his hands. "I received the files. I'll call you when I have something."

The screen went blank. The ball handed off. Now all Max could do was wait. Wait for Sean, wait for Mr. Triman, wait for Kali.

And Max hated waiting.

As if sensing his frustration, Surefire said, "Why don't you get some rest until we hear back from Sean? Clear your mind so you'll be able to help Kali. And eat something, for goddess's sake."

Max stretched, his back and neck popping. "There's a bedroom on the other side of my office, if you two want to nap."

Raven yawned. "I think we'll take you up on the offer."

"I'll head upstairs to my grandfather's cabin. There's a couch." *If I'm able to sleep at all.* "I can heat up some canned soup." Which sounded simple and light, since his nervous stomach wasn't strong enough to handle a heavier meal.

With a promise to wake them as soon as Sean called, he trudged up the steep stairs to the cabin above.

He stepped inside to the smell of mothballs, wood, old furniture, and the remnants of a spicy cologne.

Then he heard a woman's voice.

Kali.

Chapter 20

Max Hears Voices

Max scanned the dark living room of the log cabin. It was empty, but he swore he'd heard Kali's voice. There was no mistaking the quippy way she spoke.

"Kali," he called out, even if his gut told him she wasn't there. He was grasping at brittle straws, trying to hold onto this disintegrating hope.

He flipped on the light illuminating the sofa, chairs, and knickknacks—but no Kali.

He checked his phone. Checked the app that synced to his hearing aids. They both were working. He turned down the background noise, turned up the sensitivity. A feature he rarely used, rarely had a need for. He tuned into a thump, thump, thumping sound. A heartbeat? Most likely a mouse creeping along the rafters.

With measured steps, he made his way to the kitchen, set off from the living room under the loft that served as the only bedroom. He paused when he got another whiff of the same spicy cologne.

While he stood there, trying to determine where the scent originated, a woman dropped the f-bomb next to his ear.

Max whipped his head from side to side. That time her voice was unmistakable, and she was joined by others. They were having a conversation. Deep bass-like voices and two lower-pitched ones crisscrossed another like music layered with various beats. He tried to tune into the dialogue but couldn't pick out specific words, like listening to an argument from the other side of a wall. Based on the tones, none of them were Surefire or Raven.

He hobbled to the back windows then the side and front ones. Only untouched snow and trees surrounded the cabin, no signs of people.

Beneath the floorboards was twenty feet of rock reinforced with steel. No way sound was traveling through that. He reset his hearing app to its normal settings.

"I'm losing it. I'm hearing ghosts."

His stomach grumbled. Surefire was right. He should eat. The dessert cake provided a quick sugar rush but no sustainable fuel. Coffee and whatever canned soup he'd stashed here might help him think clearly—and dispel the ghostly voices.

He plugged in the coffee maker and opened the top cabinet for the filters. The pleasant cologne drifted past his nose again, stronger this time. It triggered a childhood memory of playing with his toy cars, while Mr. Triman rolled up the rug under the coffee table to scrub a spill off the floor. Max sniffed at his shirt then inside the cabinets to find the source.

"I'll take a cup. I would've made my own, but this machine is more complicated than quantum computing."

Max jerked around and dropped the opened bag of coffee. Grounds spilled over the countertop.

"Mr. Triman?" Max sputtered, attempting to decide whether Glen's father was real or a hallucination like the voices.

"It is." He appeared amused by Max's confusion. "I apologize for my delay in getting here. I'd arrived earlier to stash some special items then needed to leave again to meet with an old friend who is securing things for me while I'm gone."

"How . . .?" Max's mouth stopped working, his circuits overloaded at finding Glen's father materializing from the shadows on the other side of the kitchen counter. Despite the rustic location and deep snow outside, Mr. Triman wore a pinstriped suit, maroon bow tie, and wingtip shoes—the same outfit he'd wear to a board meeting at DERST.

"How did I get here?" Mr. Triman finished Max's question.

He nodded when he was unable to find his voice. There were no tire tracks leading to the bunker or footprints in the snow leading to the cabin, and unless Mr. Triman had stowed galoshes somewhere, he couldn't—and wouldn't—have trudged across the knee-high snow in $500 dress shoes.

"I'll tell you everything that I should have told you years ago," Mr. Triman said.

"About the Organization?"

"About them, too. Glen said he briefed you."

"He gave me an overview but no details." Max was relieved to hear Glen's name mentioned. It signaled to him that he was safe. St. John's team hadn't taken him, thinking that he had helped harbor Surefire and Raven, which is why Max assumed they showed up at his home.

"By the way, my father left a message an hour ago. Your wife and my parents are really worried. They don't know where any of you are."

"That's for the best until we resolve this situation. Did you call your father?"

"I only listened to his message. But I did try calling Glen and you. Then I spoke with Sean Vivas at U-Sec."

"Don't call your father back. His phone doesn't have the security that we and, I'm assuming, Mr. Vivas has."

That was true. Max's phone had been retrofitted with Sat-phone capabilities to render it harder to trace.

"I only ask as a precaution," Mr. Triman said when Max had grown quiet as he retraced his steps since leaving home, worried that he'd left clues as to their whereabouts.

"The friend I mentioned who is helping me has military connections and has eyes on the Organization while we're here," Mr. Triman continued. "He's also working with Glen to solve our other problems."

It made sense that Mr. Triman had called in a favor from one of DERST's military contacts, and it gave Max a measure of relief that they had armed backup.

"What about Mia?" he asked.

"She's under Glen's watch. By the way, she is grounded. Don't believe that being an adult will get you out of groundings." Mr. Triman graced Max with his trademark fatherly smile. "We have much to talk about, regarding this predicament. But first, let me help. I hate wasting food."

He moved around the counter and into the cramped galley kitchen. He nudged Max aside to position himself over the spilled coffee. Arms outstretched, a gold light emanated from his palms facing down. The grounds slid across the counter and back into the bag like a film playing in reverse.

Yet again, Max was rendered speechless. His mouth opened then closed then opened again like a dummy that had lost its ventriloquist. Mr. Triman held out the once-again-filled coffee bag for Max to take. He stared at the bag then at Mr. Triman's hand—brown as he always remembered, no longer emitting a dark yellow hue. His gaze rose to the man's face, the same face he'd known since he was a child.

Max even experienced the same sense of calm when looking at his deep brown, nearly black eyes, which always regarded Max with kindness, not pity, while bandaging his cuts and scrapes as a boy when his own parents were too busy to notice. His bald head gleamed in the kitchen lights. His regal confidence and intense features made a young Max imagine this man could've been an ancient Babylonian or Egyptian king or maybe a cosmic superhero from one of the comic books he'd devoured. A man quick with a smile or sage advice, Mr. Triman was different, but in a way that attracted not repelled.

But now—

"I'll set it here." He placed the bag on the counter next to the coffee maker.

"I took the liberty of stocking your refrigerator." He edged past Max to open its door. "I thought you could use some sustenance with the day you've had."

He removed butter, cheese, yogurt, and eggs and set them next to the stove. Then he stepped around a still-stunned Max to remove a frying pan inside the oven where it had been stored.

Questions bounced around Max's brain, but he still couldn't make his mouth utter any of them because he couldn't get past that a gold light appeared under Mr. Triman's hands and the coffee grounds moved on their own accord. He kept searching for a logical explanation and instead was left literally dumbstruck.

Mr. Triman proceeded to heat the pan, adding a pad of butter. "Coffee? Can you make it? I could use caffeine for this conversation."

Maybe it was the normal way Mr. Triman spoke the request, but Max woke from his daze enough to pour the grounds into the filter and start the machine.

"So that's how you operate it. I prefer the Mr. Coffee products myself. One button. Nice and simple. Life is complicated enough." Mr. Triman winked at him as he cracked the eggs with flair on the side of the pan.

"How did you . . .?" Max finally found his voice yet wasn't sure what he should start with. "What are you?"

"Food first. That's an order from your elder." He gave him a playful slap on the back.

The familiar way Mr. Triman acted kept Max off-balance. In thirty-plus years, he'd never seen this man do what he just did. He never saw him as anything other than a family friend, Glen's father. Now, he didn't know how to view him, what to feel about him.

He trailed Mr. Triman to the small oak dining table, the same table that had graced this space since he was a boy. This was one of the few pieces—like the burnt orange recliner and wagon-wheel coffee table—he hadn't switched out for modern furniture when the rest had deteriorated with age.

Mr. Triman took a paper napkin from the holder in the center of the table. He fanned it out and placed it on his lap as if it were linen and they were dining at a fine restaurant.

"You have questions." He blew on his coffee.

Max blinked at his eggs, unable to bring himself to eat.

"Please eat. I hate eating by myself while another picks at their food." Mr. Triman cut up his eggs in small, bite-sized triangles.

Max forked a few bits of scrambled eggs, which Mr. Triman had made special for him with milk and yogurt. The same breakfast he'd cooked for Max whenever they stayed at the cabin or at Mr. Triman's lodge in Utah to go skiing. The same breakfast he'd loved since he was five. Now it appeared off, tainted, like even this food wasn't what it seemed.

"What are you?" he asked again.

Mr. Triman dabbed the corners of his mouth with the thin napkin. "I am not from France as I told you."

"No shit," he said.

"Tsk-tsk," Mr. Triman exclaimed. He disliked profanity, thought it degraded human language, which he deemed as sacred.

"I am from—to put it in terms with which you are comfortable—a galaxy far away. I must admit that although George Lucas came close with the politics, the space flights and battles were not accurately depicted."

"You're an alien?" Max swallowed a mouthful of eggs. Instantly they crept back up his throat.

"Don't talk with your mouth full, and, yes, I was not born here. But we do not like the term alien." His top lip curled as he said the word. "We prefer foreigner or visitor, or even more appropriate, Custodian. Alien always sounded vulgar to me."

"We?"

"There have been many Custodians of Earth over the millennia. My sister and I were part of the last crop."

"Where is she?"

"The same place your mate is."

"My mate?"

"Sorry. Forgive me. Your girlfriend." He chuckled. "Never liked that term either. She's your lover, your counterpart, your partner. I quite approve of her. Very resourceful in saving you once."

His statement took Max aback. Had Glen told him about the alt-traveler?

"Is Glen like you too?" Max didn't want to offend Mr. Triman by saying alien again.

"Mia and Glen are my biological children. They are, to use earthling terminology, mixed race, both human and Custodian. Although *mixed race* is another vulgar term earthlings use to describe a child, for example, of a black woman and a white man. You are all of the human race."

So many thoughts filled Max's brain that his head became heavy under the weight. He rested his elbows on the table and rested his head on his hands. Did Glen and Mia know who their father is? Does the Organization contain aliens—Custodians—as well? What is their purpose on Earth? Why did Mr. Triman hide his grandfather's journal?

Yet none of those questions mattered. At this moment, he didn't care if he never got any answers as long as Mr. Triman told him one thing.

"Do you know how to get Kali out of the journal?"

"She's not trapped inside the book. She's in a parallel universe. Where you were taken and where she can travel." Mr. Triman dabbed his mouth again then placed his fork and knife at an angle on his empty plate.

"How do you know what she can do?"

"Let's say that I wish I'd known sooner," he replied before adding as an aside, "And had a more affable recruiter to request her help."

Max didn't have a chance to inquire what Mr. Triman meant, because in one fluid motion the alien was standing, gathering their plates and saying, "Shall we retire to the living room to discuss this? These chairs are a bear on my back. I told your grandfather they were uncomfortable, but he insisted on this style. Wanted to keep it simple or whatever.”

He took their plates and cutlery into the kitchen, making Max feel as if he were the guest in his cabin.

“You knew my grandfather?” Max remembered that his dad and Mr. Triman had met at college after his grandfather had passed.

“Of course.” Gliding into the living room, he gestured with an elegant flick of his wrist for Max to sit on the recliner.

He retrieved the journal where he’d left it on the counter. “How’s that possible? You’re not that much older than my father. You would’ve been in your twenties when my grandfather died.” Max plopped into the lumpy recliner and rested his hand on the journal in an attempt to ground himself and convince himself that this conversation wasn’t a dream.

“I’m a lot older than your father and even your grandfather, but that’s not what we’re here to discuss.” Mr. Triman sat on the sofa and crossed his legs. “So far, the Organization doesn’t know where we are, although I’m not holding my breath that they won’t find us—and soon. That said, we need to be the ones to reopen the portal, which is why I wanted us to eat. You may not get another chance for some time.”

Max rubbed his thumb over the journal’s leather binding. “Then you know how to open it?”

“One way. But it’s a last resort.”

“I’ll take a last resort. Does this mean you can read it?”

Mr. Triman massaged his hand over his thigh. “There is only one method to read the text. Unless you’ve discovered another?”

“I ran the pages through several decrypting applications and in the process I burned up the hard drive on my new system. I enlisted Sean Vivas to help decode them.”

“The cyborg who owns U-Sec?”

Max arched his brows. “According to Surefire, he interfaces with computers and is a whiz at programming with a biocircuit implanted in his brain.”

“Let’s hope he doesn’t burn up too.”

“I warned him, but he seemed confident he wouldn’t get hurt.” Max took out his phone and found no missed calls or messages from Sean. He set it on the other cushioned arm. “I’ll check in with him soon. I just sent him the files. I didn’t know if or when you were going to show up. At the time, he was all I had.”

“I will always be here for you, especially when I say I will.” Mr. Triman leveled him with a look that said there was only one answer he’d accept from Max.

He nodded. “I know.”

"After all, we are family," he said.

Max wondered at his word choice in referring to him as family like Mia had, using that as her excuse for putting Kali in harm's way. Ever since the lab accident that claimed his hearing, Mr. Triman had been more attentive to him, even helping him build his home-based workshop and earmarking company funds to work on his own projects like his cybernetic hearing aids.

"You said you had a way to get Kali back. We're running out of time. She could be hurt—"

"Or dead or soon-to-be perfectly safe at home," Mr. Triman said in a casual way as if he were stating options on a menu.

"Dead?" Max leapt from the chair. "That's impossible."

Max didn't know whether to cry or punch or scream. He wanted to do everything at once.

"Sit down. Calm down. In with the good air, out with the bad." Mr. Triman expanded his chest with a deep breath and released it as he would when a young Max would throw a tantrum.

But this wasn't a broken toy or a taunt by Mia. This was the life of the woman he loved.

"How can I be calm when I failed her? She saved me, and I couldn't do the same for her."

"Because it's no use speculating on where she is at this moment. She's alive in the past. And I will explain all this, but please take a seat. You are making me nervous."

"She's alive." He threw up his hands and towered over Mr. Triman. "She's *not* alive. What are you saying?"

"In the alternate universe, in our current year, she is either no longer living or no longer there. I've tried to get a sense of what had or is occurring but can't with the tools at my disposal. But I do know she exists in 1979 where the portal sent her. Which means when you travel to that universe, you will be arriving when she is alive before anything ill befalls her."

"What happens to her?"

"Pardon?"

"If she was alive in 1979, what happened to her that she didn't live to her senior years?"

Mr. Triman motioned to the chair, indicating for him to sit.

Max didn't want to sit. He wanted to move. Forward preferably. With a frustrated groan, he sat, because Mr. Triman wouldn't speak until he did what was asked.

Satisfied that Max heeded his request, Mr. Triman began, "For many years, I have been using a crystal skull powered by the ancients, along with that journal, to bend the two universes closer together to where they barely touch." He held out his hands, one over the other to demonstrate his point.

"The journal's dark energy can be amplified by the power contained inside each of the thirteen crystal skulls. This home, along with my cabin in Utah, exists on the parallel plane as well. When the journal and skull are next to one another in a structure that exists in both worlds, then I can clearly communicate with my sister and have been doing so for many years, until my skull was stolen last year by a so-called magician to raise a god. It was then recovered by UltraSecurity. However, before they could return it to me, the Organization took it, presumably to attempt contact with the other side. Although this time they used it as a weapon to weaken Surefire.

"But now it is truly lost." he continued. "From the video feed inside the condo, I believe Kali dropped it between the planes to help Surefire. That's why we can hear echoes of conversations from the other universe while in this cabin. The energy from the trapped skull is bending the planes closer."

"I thought I was going crazy."

"You heard them because you were holding the book. It amplifies their voices."

"Did your sister say anything about Kali?"

"I lost the ability to contact them after the timeline reset, since the Organization had stolen my crystal skull. But before the reset, their last message concerned an alt-traveler, they didn't know her name, who'd been kidnapped by your grandfather. They'd planned to save her."

Max touched his hearing aids to make sure they were there and he wasn't mishearing Mr. Triman. If he could, he'd touch his brain to make sure its synapses were firing.

"Did you say *my* grandfather?"

"The man who sent the alt-traveler after you and kidnapped Kali to use her power is your grandfather."

"How is that possible? He's dead."

Mr. Triman downed the rest of his coffee. Without any indication that he heard Max's words, he rose, wandered into the kitchen, and poured himself another cup before settling back onto the couch.

Annoyed with this silent treatment, he was about to repeat his question when Mr. Triman pointed to the wall between two windows that overlooked the woods. His eyes tracked over a black stain on the logs. Max had assumed the dark blob was from an electrical fire. No amount of scrubbing could remove it.

"Your grandfather opened the journal's portal in this room," Mr. Triman said.

A creeping chill danced up Max's spine as if Mr. Triman claimed the devil had once appeared there.

"The last time I saw him, my sister and her spouses were near that stain. I was standing right there." Mr. Triman flicked a glance at the front door. "Your grandfather had shoved me into the river. After I fished myself out, I transported here. I opened the door in time to see their bodies disappearing into the gray void, like in the video of Kali. Minutes later, I awoke on the front porch. I must've been thrown by its outer current and blacked out. I searched the cabin for them and found the journal on the floor next to the window."

"You're wrong. My grandfather died from a stroke. He's buried in a cemetery near his house in McLean."

"That's what your grandmother wanted people to believe. He needed to be dead so she could move on, claim the insurance money, settle his affairs. I didn't meet her until after Maxwell disappeared and I'd befriended your father. Even so, I pulled a few strings and made this happen for her. I owed it to your grandfather for not being there sooner for him."

Max wagged his head. Mr. Triman was wrong. His grandmother wouldn't have lied about her husband's death, the father of her son.

He slid from the couch to squat in front of Max. He took his hands in his. The gesture was meant to be comforting, but with the amount of lies he'd been fed all his life, he wondered how much of Mr. Triman's comfort was an act. How much all the care he'd lavished on Max had been too.

For what end result, he had no clue.

"I took your father under my protection as he was finishing his last year of college and starting grad school. I came to him under the guise of friendship and that of a mentor. I couldn't protect your grandfather, so I sought to keep his son safe from the supernatural aspect of this business, which had corrupted his father. Unfortunately, I coddled him too much. He was a partier, a spoiled man, opposite his father, as many trust fund children can be, turning out so different than their industrious parents. He had and has no vision, unlike you." He beamed at Max as proud as if he'd been Mr. Triman's son.

Releasing his hands, Max pressed back in the chair wanting to phase through it, disappear from this liar's presence. His emotions were a blur, his mind doubly so. He wanted to leave this cabin, no longer the soothing place of his childhood but a home haunted by spirits that should be dead but weren't.

But he couldn't leave. Not without answers that this man could give him, answers that led him closer to the truth and closer to getting Kali back.

"My grandfather is still alive?" Max whispered.

"Yes and no."

He covered his face with his hands. Every nerve in his body was pulled to the limit, about to snap.

"No more cryptic responses, I need answers I can use," Max demanded.

Mr. Triman reeled as if slapped. He had never raised his voice to him, and he regretted it immediately, but he needed this man—or whatever he was—to tell him the truth, the truth about everything, and a calm tone wasn't doing the trick.

"I wished I'd known sooner the range of Kali's ability and had approached her myself. Maybe this mess wouldn't have happened. I had no idea what she was capable of until recent events. I'd assumed her power kept her tethered to our universe."

Max bent forward and planted his elbows on his knees. "What do you know about Kali?"

Mr. Triman picked at fuzz on his pant leg and appeared to make an effort to avoid Max's eyes. "She was interning on a project co-funded by a DERST subcontractor, part of an R&D effort I took interest in. There was an . . . incident. The lead physicist wasn't injured, but Kali ended up in the hospital. I thought that was it. TransGen took over her care and sealed her files. I only heard about her ability after she worked on the Surefire case, through a close contact who then confirmed her power after the incident at Dama X's island—another story that made its rounds with our fellow contractors. Then she followed you through the portal when you were kidnapped. I assumed she could trace dark energy or maybe her ability helped unlock the portal—"

"How did you know all this about her?" No wonder Kali was paranoid. Mr. Triman and this Organization were probably a drop in a large bucket full of secret agencies and creeps keeping tabs on her.

When Mr. Triman wouldn't look at him, Max bolted to his feet and winced at the shooting pain that sliced up his thigh. "Was it your military contact who spilled her secret?"

"Some of the information came from him," he replied and Max was glad that he showed some remorse.

"Can you get Kali back home or not?" Max propped himself against the chair's arm.

"I've been trying to retrieve my sister for over forty years."

"That's not an answer." Max grabbed the journal from the recliner's arm. He flipped it open to the page with the drawings of the TPC with tubes slithering from it like octopus arms. "That's one reason she left and took the journal. She thought I was planning to do that to her."

He shoved the open book in front of Mr. Triman. His dark eyes tracked over the page.

"That's similar to what your client had my team build to contain rogue transhumans. But they didn't say it was to imprison Kali and her fellow agents."

He peered up at Max. "Why would she think that?"

"Because UltraAgent Surefire and Raven were held in a similar TPC—one that syphoned their powers."

"I heard."

"Did your friend tell you that Kali followed me through the portal?" When he nodded, Max went on, "But what I bet he didn't know is that she met an earlier version of herself, who had previously traveled to that universe."

"The reset," Mr. Triman muttered to himself.

Max continued wanting him to understand the weight of what Kali had experienced, "This version of her was locked in this machine"—he tapped the image with his finger—"hooked to these tubes, these very ones which were drawn by my grandfather decades ago, and are surprisingly similar to the plan your client gave to my team. These tubes drained her power and transferred it to the man who kidnapped me and the others."

"Its intent was not for Kali," Mr. Triman said more to himself than to Max.

"Then who was it for?" He snapped the book closed.

Mr. Triman repeated more loudly in his deep baritone, "Not Kali."

The older man rubbed his hands together. "Let's go back to what you said about this mercenary using Kali's power. This may mean her ability can't transport your grandfather from the other universe. Or else the Dark would've used her to return here during the previous timeline, and all this would be over."

"The Dark?" Max spat. "Is this some kind of *alien* force that you can't explain?"

Mr. Triman flinched at the word *alien.* "Don't get smart."

"What aren't you telling me about this book? I analyzed its molecular structure and found it contained traces of dark energy, similar to yet different to what we have here. It nearly destroyed Surefire when she tried to read it. The goddess, Xochi, said the energy contained in the book is the same one—"

"Xochiquetzal?"

"She's the supernatural force using Surefire as a vessel."

"Is she well?" He gazed up at Max with concern.

"I guess." He raised an eyebrow at this question. "She's refusing to come back to our world with this book anywhere near her. She claims the energy stored in it is the same kind that locked her and the Old Ones away."

As if summoned, the door of the underground bunker opened. A soft violet glow shone across the living room. Surefire stepped into the cabin. She held the crystal skull, pulsating with a purple light that covered her body. Scratching his chest and suppressing a yawn, Raven trailed her into the room.

"I guess you know there's an intruder in the house. A well-dressed intruder." Raven pulled a face then shook his head. "This one woke up, braving the evil journal for a public service announcement." He motioned to his girlfriend.

"Xochiquetzal," Gabriel whispered in reverence.

"You two know each other?" Raven pointed from one to the other.

"He is a Custodian." She held out her hand to Mr. Triman, who raised it to his lips.

"What the hell is a Custodian?" Raven crossed his arms.

"Mr. Triman is an old family friend and Glen's and Mia's father. He's an alien . . . I mean not from this world," Max said by way of introduction.

"Xochi, I didn't know you hung with aliens." Raven cocked his head, staring at Surefire as she held Mr. Triman's hands and gazed into his eyes like he was her long lost lover.

"We were intimate at one time." Surefire-Xochi graced Gabriel with a smile that hinted at the special times they'd shared.

Raven rubbed a hand over his face. "This is awkward."

Mr. Triman addressed him. "I apologize. I'm taken aback at seeing her again. It's been at least six hundred years."

"Six hundred and fifty-two to be exact," Surefire-Xochi replied.

"And neither of you kids look a day over a thousand," Raven said.

"He's a child. Don't mind him." She batted her hand in his direction.

"You're using the woman I love as a puppet again. I don't want you to do anything that either of us will regret," Raven said.

Surefire-Xochi placed her palm on Mr. Triman's chest over the handkerchief sticking out of his breast pocket. "You're in love, Gabriel. Why are the good ones always taken?"

Raven tossed up his hands.

"Because they can't wait around forever, my hummingbird." Gabriel's fingers caressed her cheek.

Surefire-Xochi's lips slid across Mr. Triman's palm. Max was uncomfortable watching this intimate display but not as much as Raven. He touched the man's shoulder when it looked like he was about to intervene. His hands clenched for a fight.

"I'm good." Raven crossed his arms again. "It's hard to separate the two. I'm seeing the person I love more than anything snuggle up with an alien ex-lover. But it's not really her."

"I don't know how you handle it."

"Not very well most of the time," Raven replied before saying to Mr. Triman, "We can take you to the actual Xochi, if you want. But right now, can we hold off on this reunion? We have a friend missing."

"I know. That's why I'm here. I was explaining to Max about the Dark." Mr. Triman released Surefire-Xochi's hand.

"It used to be a Custodian," Surefire-Xochi said. "The Organization used her to rid the world of us. We'd become too strong for them to control, and the Custodians decided to reset the world."

"It was a mistake," Mr. Triman stated. "I am truly sorry."

"And yet another level in this complicated story." Max stepped toward Surefire-Xochi, who floated backward, her glowing purple eyes glued on the journal he held.

"Keep it away from me." She bumped into a counter stool. It teetered and banged to the floor.

Mr. Triman positioned his lean body to block the journal Max held from Surefire-Xochi. As soon as he moved, his head lifted then tilted, honing into a sound Max couldn't hear. "They're here."

"Who?" Max glanced at the front windows, expecting to find the Organization's white clad soldiers on the porch.

"Kali and my family," Mr. Triman said. "They're trying to communicate."

Max held his breath and listened in vain for the inter-dimensional voices that Mr. Triman claimed to hear.

"I got nothing." Raven looked to Max, who shook his head.

Although when he adjusted his hearing aids, turned up their sensitivity, he did hear a murmur like the background noise of a group conversing on the lawn outside.

Angling his head from side to side, like one would adjust an old TV antenna for better reception, Mr. Triman crisscrossed the room twice. He paused and gaped at the area that recently had been re-sanded and covered with an Oriental rug belonging to Max's grandmother, under which Max had found his grandfather's other two non-supernatural journals stashed in a secret compartment under her dining room table.

"Help me move this." Mr. Triman pointed to the wagon-wheel coffee table.

Max and Raven slid it off the rug. Then Mr. Triman flipped up an edge exposing the wood below.

"Please place your skull on the floor, Xochiquetzal," he said.

With a flourish, she set the glowing skull where Mr. Triman indicated. As soon as she released it, the purple halo surrounding Surefire's body went out. She stumbled, and Raven caught her before she fell, as the goddess left the building and her vessel.

"Max, the journal." Mr. Triman beckoned him.

"What are you trying to do?" He hesitated, concerned about getting the book too close to the skull and causing a reaction like when Surefire-Xochi touched the journal in his lab.

"When I walked across this area, I felt a tremor, like a wave breaking against the shore. This floor is original. In the past, my sister and I have written on spaces like this to communicate. Placing the book and the skull on the surface allows me to glimpse into the other world. Most times I can hear them speaking. The voices are faint but discernible. I fear they are writing a message to ensure there is no miscommunication."

He placed the book on the floor.

"A knife." Mr. Triman snapped his fingers.

Max retrieved a paring knife from the kitchen. As he handed it to Mr. Triman, the floorboards shimmered. An image came into focus. Crude etchings, glowing with the skull's purple light, appeared on the floor in front of Max's eyes. They formed words in no language he'd seen before.

Mr. Triman ran his long fingers over the surface.

"What does it say?" Max asked.

"Kali can't access her power," Mr. Triman said and began cutting his reply into the wood.

"Why is that?" Surefire hovered several feet behind them, keeping a safe distance from the journal.

"They believe the portal's energy syphoned off her power. They're worried they won't be able to return in time." Mr. Triman carved with more gusto, as if lives depended on what he was writing.

"Right here is Kali's name. She's with them. I'm assuring them that we're working with her friends to find a solution." Mr. Triman swiped his hand across the carvings to clean away the shavings.

Max pressed his fingertips along the symbols Mr. Triman had indicated referred to Kali. He hoped to feel her touch or smell her sandalwood perfume or hear her laugh again. But he only experienced the same emptiness in his gut that had plagued him since she left.

"Do you think she'll see a message from me?" Max looked to Mr. Triman.

"Certainly." He held the knife handle out to him.

His injured thigh protesting as he lowered himself to the floor, Max considered what he was going to say and how he was going to say it. He longed to pour out his heart. Carve a sonnet that Shakespeare would be proud of. Grovel to let her know how sorry he was. But that would take time he didn't feel they had. So he carved a heart with their initials. Elementary, he knew, but it was simple and pure, like what he felt for her.

He waited for a reply as the kitchen clock ticked the seconds away.

Then a glowing purple slash appeared in the center of the heart. He dropped the knife.

"What happened?"

"I don't know." Mr. Triman shifted and his heel kicked into the rug, exposing another cluster of alien text. His eyes widened at the words etched in a different hand than his sister's.

"What are they saying now?" Max asked.

"Not they, this message is from your grandfather."

Chapter 21

Kali Wakes in Another Cabin

The *om* chant segued into a ticking clock. Far in the background, crows called out to one another. Kali inhaled and drew in a mildewed scent. Yawning, she stretched her limbs. Her cheek scraped against scratchy woven fabric. Eyelids fluttering open, she rubbed away sleep and tried to process why she was staring up at the A-framed ceiling of a log cabin.

She pushed up onto her elbows and craned her neck to peep over the back cushion, past a brass floor lamp to a picture window, overlooking a wide porch with a low-pitched awning. The foliage was greener, denser than she remembered seeing in Utah.

She flipped around.

"Geeze-o-whiz!" She clutched her chest to stop her heart from bursting through it in fright.

The Three towered over the sofa like creepy siblings in a horror film. They stared down at her with eyes not as sparkly as before. The gold had lost its luster, leaving their irises to resemble copper pennies.

After her heart slowed to a less-panicked rhythm, she asked, "This is a different cabin in a different place. How?"

"We can disassemble and reassemble atoms to move them through space," Dara explained.

"What Surefire can do. At least, that's one theory." Kali swung her legs around to a seated position. Covering her mouth, she yawned again and rotated her stiff shoulders. Why did she feel so sleepy? It's not like she'd used her power to Q-T here, unless this was a side effect of passing through the journal's portal.

"Yes, what Synthia St. John can do," Dara agreed.

It took a moment for the sleepy haze to lift and for Kali to process that Dara had spoken Surefire's real name. "You know her?"

"She's with my brother."

"What? Where?" Kali leaped to her feet. Her eyes swept across the room in search of her friend.

"Not here. She's in our universe."

"Oh." Kali's excitement disintegrated, leaving an ashy taste on her tongue.

Then she recalled the Three mentioning another cabin, where they could communicate with Dara's brother. She wondered if this was it.

"Where are we?" She took in the rustic interior. It felt familiar, not as though she'd been here but had been to someplace similar.

"We're in the Shenandoah Valley. The place where we first arrived in this universe, where it all began," Dara said.

"You took me across the country?"

"Yes."

"I thought your power was dying."

"That is why we used a car to travel from the town to our lodge. We needed to reset our mojo—as you would say—after transporting ourselves from Las Vegas to Springhill to save you."

"You cut it close, didn't you? If I hadn't escaped the first time then . . ." Kali shuddered.

"I apologize for our delay," said Dara.

"Our contact had to track us down," Tomas added.

"We got the message in the casino, while waiting for Willie Nelson's rehearsal to start," Gilroy said, and then added in a conspiratorial note, "We were going to sneak in."

"I get it. Geesh, I ruined your night." Kali tossed up her hands.

"Only if your power doesn't return and we die," Tomas said.

She rolled her eyes, tired of this Willie Nelson guilt-trip.

Dara shooed the men away from Kali, and she wondered if her face reflected her thoughts about what she'd like to do to them and their passive aggressive comments.

"As I explained before, what life force remains in us, we use sparingly," Dara said, circling back to the conversation before Gilroy derailed it with his Willie Nelson woes. "For emergencies only."

"Like popping out of the basement before the Man could nab us. I totally get that." Kali bobbed her head. "And why Gilroy can't give me a potential power boost with his healing mojo. So he can keep his strength for when we confront the Man or the Dark or whatever."

So much to keep track of. Which brought Kali around to Dara mentioning Synthia's name.

"How did your brother meet up with Synthia?" Not that she wanted to look a gift alien messenger in the mouth, but it seemed odd that her friend would suddenly be helping Dara's brother.

In response to her question, Dara stepped aside to reveal a braided rug, folded back. A wagon-wheel coffee table had been set on top of it. On the exposed floorboards were etchings in a language Kali didn't recognize, part hieroglyphic with what appeared to be Latin letters mixed in.

She slid off the couch to run her hands over the carvings. Tomas knelt across from her and placed his glowing palm on the floor as he had on the wall in the other cabin. Between the lines of etched alien letters, gold ones shimmered into view.

"Are you telling me that your brother in our universe scratched out these words?"

"Synthia lent my brother her crystal skull. His was stolen. When the journal is in the presence of a skull, it creates a bend in the universes and causes an overlap. He's been using his skull and journal to speak with us on occasion. At times, we can hear his voice."

"Then it's like a black hole? The journal and the skull are creating a strong gravitational field that distorts time and space," Kali suggested, trying to put it into terms she could grasp.

"Similar, yes," Dara replied.

"But I can't feel anything. Shouldn't we, along with everything in this room, be pulled toward it?"

"Again, it's a similar principle but not the same force."

She shook her head at Dara's cryptic response but let it go. Because an explanation for the "how" wasn't important right now.

Kali ran her fingers over the last marks. "What does this say?"

"We are to employ the contingency plan."

"And what is that?" Kali asked.

"Has your ability returned?" she rejoined.

"It won't return in time." Gilroy sulked.

Dara shushed him. "We do not know that."

With all eyes on her, Kali couldn't shake this guilty feeling gnawing at her gut. Yes, guilty for not having the power to get them home. Her ruby slippers had lost their gleam. They'd tied their hopes to her and she'd failed. Not that she'd done it on purpose.

The Three stared at her in silence, as if she were a pot full of water they were waiting to boil.

Unnerved, she slunk past them to the wide front window. The pink sky turned a soft yellow, becoming brighter with each passing minute. A sparrow flew in and out of the overgrown azalea bushes below the porch railing. A wasp buzzed past the window. Remnants of a small vegetable garden choked by weeds remained in the yard overgrown by knee-high grass.

"What time is it? Because it looks like early morning, and it was the late afternoon when we left Utah."

"You've been asleep for more than twelve hours. We were waiting for you to wake, hoping the rest would restart your ability," Dara said.

With a deep breath, Kali sent her feelers down, down, down, and deep into her center where the warm fuzzies of her power resided.

There it was—a lukewarm purr. Vibrations in her gut sent a tingle to her chest that danced its way to her fingers. She flashed into the in-between—that no-man's land between universes—and then she stood outside on the porch. A wasp dive-bombed her head. Batting at it, she squealed and ran inside.

"So it's sort of working. I can go, oh, about four or five feet. Unfortunately, that means alt-jumping back home is right out. I'm not at full strength yet," she said.

"It's a start." Dara smiled.

Gilroy's stony expression softened. He and Tomas shared a hopeful look.

She was starting to feel normal again—her version of normal. "Any food here?"

Judging by the layer of dust coating the tables, the cabin was either a bachelor's pad or a vacation home that hadn't been used for months.

Dara jerked her head toward the kitchen in the back of the living room, tucked underneath a loft. Gilroy and Tomas hastened to the task, opening cupboards and drawers and the refrigerator.

"Sour milk. Rotten apples. And"—a loud sniff then a grunt of disgust—"a moldy onion."

Tomas set the stash on the counter separating the kitchen from the living room and small dining area. Two oak bar stools were pushed under the tiled counter.

"If vomiting is the goal, then bon appétit." Kali strode across the creaky floorboards to help with the search.

"Crackers. Blackberry jelly. Both unopened." Gilroy placed the jar and box of crackers on the counter.

She pulled out a spindle-back stool and hopped onto it. "Now we're talking."

The two men continued to hunt through the cabinets. The final cache consisted of canned beans and jars of homemade pickles, strawberry jam, and beets.

She eyed the array of food. "We'll start with the crackers and jelly and maybe do the beans later."

She dipped the saltines into the jelly jar. "Not bad, a little stale, but the jelly is yummy in my tummy."

Gilroy filled a glass with water for her.

"Thanks," she said between bites.

The two men stood in the center of the narrow galley kitchen with their arms crossed and watched her eat. She tried to ignore the feeling of Dara's eyes focused on her back. Once, she glanced down at her chest to make sure the woman's heated gaze hadn't bored a hole through her body. The sound of her cracker chewing competed with the kitchen clock ticking to her right. It read 8:30 a.m.

"Did you always live in Utah?" she asked to break the silence and distract them from watching her munch.

"We live there part-time. We bought a cabin that mirrors the one my brother has in our universe and to be closer to the Man's base and track his movements."

"You said you tried to save me before the reset." Kali found this revelation comforting. Her other self, S-Kali, had guardian angels who had been trying to rescue her. She hadn't been alone.

"We were caught, but it is unclear what happened after." Dara pulled out the stool next to Kali and perched on its edge.

She wondered if their alien abilities had allowed them to remember what occurred before this universe changed. The only ones beside Kali who retrained their memory in her universe were those who had been taken by Stockwell. Two were security guards working for the *Real Life* crew. Both received new job offers at TransGen and a hefty raise to ensure their discretion.

"Our memory is fractured like recalling a movie's plot we'd watched years ago," Dara said.

"One that we starred in," Tomas said.

"And now we're in a new one," Gilroy finished.

"We won't make the same mistake again," Dara said.

Kali's stomach churned at the alien's ominous inference. Or maybe it was the stale crackers and questionable jam, which was labeled blackberry and tasted like sour grapes.

"How do we avoid another mistake?" she asked.

"We made a deal with someone who is willing to help this time." Dara sat back in the chair.

Walking from the kitchen, Gilroy huffed, giving the impression that he didn't agree this "someone" could aid them.

After he passed behind Dara, Kali's eyes locked on a series of photos over the woman's shoulder. They were aligned on the wall under the clock. A familiar face was prominent in each one. That face set every nerve in her body to high alert.

Nailed to the wooden logs were framed black and white portraits. Several larger versions of these images were displayed in the stairwell of Max's home. The first showed a young Maxwell Martin Sr. and his wife cradling their infant son. Below that photograph were others of Maxwell shaking hands with President Kennedy and leaders from that era. In the middle of these photos was a colorized one of the same man in flowing garments taken in front of a cabin. If Kali were to guess, he was at this cabin.

"What the doppelgänger is this? Why are there photos of the Man in here?" Kali lifted a shaky finger at the framed images.

"This lodge belonged to the Maxwell Martin in this universe until our version appropriated it," Dara explained.

"Appropriated it?" Kali coughed. A jam-covered cracker stuck in her throat.

"Took over his identity."

"Then where is the Maxwell of this world?" She took a long drink of water.

"Dead, we believe."

The water stung the back of her throat. "Why are we at his house?"

"Because this cabin is nearly identical to his in the other universe. We have used this one along with our Utah abode for years to communicate with our brother."

Kali hadn't considered she'd awoken in the Man's cabin when Dara said they'd traveled to the place where it all began.

"The Man hasn't been here in a year. Only his associates use this cabin on occasion to hunt. This is where we sometimes pass messages to our mole."

A cold settled in her bones as another puzzle piece snapped into place. If they were communicating with Dara's brother in the other universe, at a cabin belonging to Max's grandfather, and Synthia was with them at said cabin, then . . .

"Is the Man's grandson with Synthia in our universe? Is he working with your brother as well?"

The Three glanced at each other doing the psychic conference thingy. "Yes."

Synthia had seen the images in the journal. She'd heard Kali's own testimony about what Max had in his home. Yet she was with Max, a situation that led to other questions about his connection to these aliens and their goals. Had Max, along with Dara's brother, planned to use Kali to save the Three once he understood her power? Had he planned to use that containment unit as the Man had to drain her power if she didn't comply?

And was her friend safe or was she locked away in that techno chamber in Max's basement, so Dara's brother could use her crystal skull to communicate with his family?

She wished to every single force in the universe that she had Oracle's power to read minds, so she could rip the truth from Dara and her men and not get drips of information that barely covered the canvas let alone painted an image.

Maybe the person with whom they had made a deal was the Man himself. But that didn't make sense given what they'd told her. Unless this deal was their backup plan. If they sacrifice Kali to him they may gain his trust, capture the Dark, and somehow open the portal back home by draining her power as Stockwell had.

As if sensing her anxiety, Dara rose and touched her hand. Flesh against flesh, so if she Q-T'd now, Dara would be coming with her.

"Get off." Kali jumped from the stool. It fell to the floor with a thud, creating a barrier between Dara and her.

The two men watched as Dara stepped over the downed stool.

Kali backed up until she bumped into the banister leading to the loft. She needed space to think, sort out her thoughts without any alien interference.

"Don't. Just don't. You're working with his grandson. Our trust level has dipped into negative digits."

"That TPC in Max's lab wasn't meant for you."

Kali was certain she'd get whiplash with how quickly this woman yanked conversations into different directions.

"How do you know about that thing in Max's home?" She'd only told them about the Man's version in this universe where S-Kali had been trapped. She flicked a nervous glance at the mystery message on the floor then back to the alien inching closer.

"Our brother and a partner commissioned DERST to create the chamber to entrap the Dark when it returns to our universe." Dara held her hands up in a placating gesture. Her careful steps reminded Kali of a zookeeper approaching a pacing tiger.

"My best friend and her boyfriend were trapped in a thing like that. And I can't stop seeing myself—S-Kali—locked inside a similar device before the reset. None of us have anything to do with the Dark, yet it was used on us."

"The technology was misappropriated. It was not originally meant for transhumans."

She snorted at this woman's word choice. Dara sounded like Stephen St. John, issuing excuses and not taking any of the blame for what happened to his own daughter.

"It was misused." Dara's rephrasing didn't help.

Kali glowered at her. Misused, misappropriated, it didn't matter what term this alien applied to it. That containment coffin was a danger to her and to her friends and to every transhuman society deemed a monster.

"Those with whom Gabriel partnered to fund this project were concerned by the powers transhumans were beginning to wield. So my brother made concessions with them," Dara continued.

"And Max knew of these concessions?"

"His grandfather, possessed by the Dark, built the device which held you in this universe. Max had nothing to do with that."

"That's not my point and that wasn't my question." This female alien failed to understand that it wasn't that Max had built this transhuman prison, but that he'd never told Kali. It was under her feet as they cuddled in the living room watching movies. It was under the floor of his bed where they made love. It was behind a wall in the room where she'd finally mustered the strength to confide her EI to him.

In order to have built it, he had to have known its purpose even if he hadn't intended for the device to be used on Kali, her friends, or other UltraAgents. By not admitting what he had helped create, he'd lied to her. He'd listened to her tearful, anxiety-ridden tale, and he didn't say a word about what he knew. He'd ripped the trust out from under their relationship and set fire to it.

Looking back, it made sense why he'd been concerned when she told him what happened to Surefire and Raven and what had happened to S-Kali in the other universe. Probably afraid she'd leave after she learned the truth.

And if Max's sullenness meant he was remorseful, it didn't change what he didn't do. He had opportunities to ask for Kali's understanding and forgiveness.

"He didn't tell me." She had had enough of lies from her mother all her life. She wouldn't excuse that trait in her lover.

"Did you consider that maybe he couldn't?" Dara suggested.

"Are you saying that maybe this project was classified and he could get in trouble?"

"Yes."

"There is always a way." When you love someone, you figure it out. You get permission. Max is the CEO of his company; he had the power to influence the rules if he wanted to.

But he hadn't.

"Max is sorry. He made a mistake," Dara said.

"How do you know?"

The alien pointed to the floor. "Our brother told us. Max isn't your enemy. He's working with your friends to bring us back."

Kali rubbed her temples. Even if Synthia was safe with Max, which Kali wouldn't believe until she personally saw her friend, it also didn't erase what he had built. It didn't erase the distrust he'd sown that grew like vines over her heart until they threatened to crush it.

"He loves you." Dara beckoned her to the floor. "See what he drew."

"If you love someone, you don't keep secrets from them. Secrets that could hurt them."

Wiping away tears, Kali took the long way round the living room to keep as much space as she could between them. Gilroy stayed behind the dining table. Tomas came up behind Dara to stand on the opposite end of the message. He knelt and placed his glowing palm on the floor once more.

Kali paused a foot from the carvings and peered at the shimmering letters.

At the end of their message was a heart with K + M carved inside. Kali hadn't seen it before because it had been under her butt when she'd squatted on the floor. A perfect place for it, if you asked her.

"Bastard," she uttered.

She spied a sharp knife in short reach of the etching. She picked it up and stabbed it into the center of the heart.

Doing her best *I Dream of Jeanie* impression, Kali crossed her arms and again tried to access her power to alt-jump or even Q-T to the porch, but again, was left with fumes.

"He is our contingency. Our way home if your power doesn't work. Show respect for the sacrifice he's about to make," Gilroy said.

Now they were playing on her sympathies, and they'd already toyed with her enough. "If I can't take you back, then he's going to do it? And how is that? I'm not buying what you're selling. Max can't alt-jump."

In unison, Gilroy and Tomas lifted their chins. Their eyes closed, faces clenched in concentration, as if zoning into a sound. At first, Kali didn't hear anything except the ticking clock. Then the unmistakable whirring blades of a helicopter filled the room. Judging by the loudness of the engine and the blades slicing the air, it was swooping in for a landing.

"It's too late." Gilroy sighed.

"We couldn't change the outcome," Tomas said.

They hurried from the kitchen to help Dara flip the carpet over the floorboards.

Men's shouts came from outside. Boots hit the porch.

Someone yelled for the key.

"Guys. Threesome." Kali's shoulders twitched in time to the shoes shuffling on the porch.

Someone called out that he had the key.

"I think it's Martin . . . the Man." Kali turned from one alien poker face to another.

"Hey!" She snapped her fingers. They were mind conversing again and leaving her out.

They broke from their daze and joined hands. The *om* chant started up. A gold light flashed like a camera bulb, momentarily blinding her. When her eyes adjusted, she found herself alone in the cabin.

A key turned in the lock of the front door.

Chapter 22

Max Gets the Message in His Cabin

An icy puff of air hit the back of Max's neck. Goosebumps spread along his arms. He glanced over his shoulder, expecting to find his grandfather or maybe Frosty the Snowman—considering this day, nothing was impossible. But everyone who was in the room had gathered at its core around Mr. Triman, as he knelt next to the message Max's grandfather had supposedly carved from the other side.

He studied Mr. Triman as he read over the mixture of human and alien letters. Max hoped to discern a sign of frustration—or of hope, as far-fetched as that seemed—in his expression. But his face displayed as much emotion as the knitted owl hanging on the wall by the front window.

After what felt like hours but was only five minutes, according to Max's watch that he checked every other second, Mr. Triman rolled back on his heels and sighed.

"What did he say?" Max asked.

Fixing him with a weary look, he replied, "He wants you in exchange for Kali."

Part of Max expected the message to say just that. Because despite the dread that settled in his gut like a chunk of ice, he'd believed in his heart the only way to save her would be to go himself.

He tried to take in the good air to alleviate the mounting stress.

But there wasn't any good air left in the room, only a raw chill that stung his lungs as he announced, "Then I'm going."

"That's a bad idea." Surefire shook her head.

"I second that," Raven said. "Besides, you don't have the power to travel there. How is he supposed to do this exchange?" Raven directed the question to Mr. Triman, who rapped his knuckles against the floorboards as if calling on woodland spirits for luck.

Without acknowledging Raven's question, he stood and swiped his palms across his pants.

"You're turning two shades of gray. What aren't you telling us?" Raven stepped aside to let Mr. Triman pass.

Max's family friend paced to the dining table then to the antique corner liquor cabinet and back again. His slender fingers tapped a beat on his lips. A gesture Max recognized to mean that he was considering options—all unacceptable.

"What do I need to do?" He put himself in front of Mr. Triman, halting him in his tracks before he could do another nervous loop.

"I came prepared for the worst and hoped other options would avail themselves. But we may not get another chance at this," he replied with a heavy sigh.

"You're not asking me to do this. I'm volunteering."

As his brown eyes bored into Max's, a golden light flickered behind his tinted contacts. He'd never noticed before that they were tinted.

"You need to ingest the Dark to open the portal," said Mr. Triman.

"This same Dark that Xochi, a goddess, is afraid of?" Surefire asked.

"Does anyone else think the Dark sounds like a death metal band?" Raven interjected.

"Really, Raven?" Surefire whirled on him.

He shrugged. "I'm trying to lighten the mood and show how messed up this situation is. Because I don't think that Max should let anything that sounds like a B movie demon near him, let alone inside his body. Dude, take it from us. Supernatural entities will screw with your life, and once they're inside you, they're a part of you forever."

Raven punctuated the word "forever" with an exaggerated shudder. Surefire wrapped an arm around his waist.

"At least we're in this together." She kissed his shoulder, and he squeezed her closer.

"I wish we weren't, for your sake," Raven said.

Max's phone rang. He darted to the chair where he'd left it.

"Sean?" he answered.

"I have a raging headache but some answers."

"I'll put you on v-comm." Max placed the phone in the center of the dinette. An image of Sean with an ice pack on his head projected above the screen.

"Can you see us?" Max and company gathered around the table.

"Yes." He squinted into the lens. "Is that Gabriel Triman?"

"Mr. Vivas." He inclined his head at the projection.

"Why is he there?" Gloria pushed Sean aside.

"Give me space." He nudged his sister away.

"Those pages almost killed you—"

"Didn't kill me, just overloaded a few circuits."

"Smoke came out of your ears." She wiggled a finger in his ear.

He swatted her away. "You're exaggerating."

"It would have, if we hadn't cooled it—"

"Did you translate the journal?" Max interrupted, afraid their bickering could go on for hours.

"A few pages," Sean said.

"Before his brain nearly had a seizure." Gloria huffed.

Shaking his head, Sean lifted his eyes to the ceiling then said, "I can send you what I could translate."

"Give us a summary," said Max.

"We're all fudged," said Gloria.

"Anything more specific?" He frowned.

"There's no way this was written decades ago." Gloria butted in before her brother could reply. "It contains a history of transhumans. How to genetically create them, and how to uncreate them."

Sean slid his chair closer to the camera, effectively bumping his sister out of frame. "Besides TimeTrap, it mentions Pax, Oracle and me, plus others who work for U-Sec, and some who don't—to our knowledge—exist yet. How is this possible?"

"And St. John." Pax loomed over Sean's shoulder.

"What did it say about my father?" Surefire bent down and rested her elbows on the table in front of the projection.

"That he'd try to unite transhumans to stop foreign entities from destroying Earth. Not very specific on who these foreigners are and the type of destruction."

Surefire stepped away from the video feed, as did Mr. Triman.

"We're talking about the man who allegedly," Raven used air quotes to highlight the adverb, "worked with Looney Lucy to kidnap his own daughter?"

"Appears so. We haven't asked him about the journal. Didn't want to give away the fact that we've been talking to you. Last we heard, his team was at Max's house," Pax said.

"They're the ones I saw on the video feed." Max turned to Mr. Triman for confirmation, assuming he knew these people were stationed at his home, but he kept his attention fixed on the projected images.

"Does he have any clue where we are?" Raven asked.

"We spoke to Glen. He's been in contact with St. John and said that his team won't be coming for Surefire and Raven. They're standing down."

Max sent up a prayer of gratitude to his friend—and his BS Force, which he assumed was the reason St. John wasn't going after his new friends.

"If these predictions are real, then what my father said about a larger evil was true." Surefire propped herself against the counter separating the kitchen and dining nook. She gripped its edge as if it was the only thing keeping her upright.

"Even so, it doesn't make it right, what he's done to us . . . to you," said Raven.

She gave him a half-hearted nod.

"What did the pages read?" Mr. Triman asked.

Sean slid the ice pack from his head. "First, regarding Kali, the journal details how to recreate her powers as well as how to siphon them off."

"No one else can have access to this book," Surefire said.

"Fortunately, it seems I'm the only one who can translate it, and I'll keep those translations safe." He tapped his forehead.

"You're storing them inside your brain?" Max asked.

He beamed. "No safer place."

"Did it provide instructions for retrieving those stranded in the other universe?" Mr. Triman moved to stand next to the stained wall.

"Sort of, but that's where things get weird," said Sean.

"*Get* weird? Have you been listening to this conversation?" Raven blew out a breath.

"I have to qualify what I'm about to disclose. I could be way off in my translation," continued Sean.

"Say it anyway." Max leaned closer to the projection.

"A person needs to become one with the book to open the portal."

"What else?" Max asked, because the way Sean dropped his gaze made him wonder what information he was leaving out.

"It's you." Gloria's sharp features filled the video feed. "The book lists your name as the one to open the portal, although it could be referring to your father or grandfather or maybe your son. Do you have a kid?"

He shook his head.

"It's Max." Mr. Triman rested his hand with reverence on the spot where the portal had once opened. "It has to be him since his father . . ." He paused and for a moment seemed to struggle for the right phrasing. "He doesn't have the proper genetic makeup to handle it. Max's body can hold its power, just like his grandfather's could and has done."

"How do you know this?" Gloria asked.

"After Max was hospitalized from the accident in his lab, I reviewed his medical records. With permission from your father, of course," Mr. Triman said as an aside to Max.

But it didn't matter that his father had given their family friend permission. What mattered was why Mr. Triman wanted to see his medical records in the first place. Gloria looked as perplexed with Mr. Triman's answer as Max was. But before she could interrogate him, Max felt he needed to answer a more pressing question.

"Did you know my name was in this book?" he asked.

"I can't read the pages. Only someone who has consumed the Dark can translate them, unless they're a transhuman computer." He flicked a finger at Sean's projection. "The Dark could quickly and fully possess me with merely a drop. A human could last longer, but it can cause adverse effects like an aggressive cancer. But there are some, like you, who are made to handle it."

"Then Max has a transhuman marker," Gloria said.

"In a way," Mr. Triman replied.

Kali had explained to Max how transhumans had a special port in their genes, allowing them to develop their abilities, where others exposed to the same situations or experiments either died, became ill, or went on to live normal lives without any genetic changes.

Max had assumed he was an N-T, non-transhuman. A person without any special talents. But this changed everything he believed about himself and his history. Who was he? What was he? Did Mr. Triman know how Max had inherited this trait? Would he tell him if he asked?

So many questions upon questions bobbed through his mind. But he needed to stay focused for what he alone could do.

"More proof that it's on me to save Kali," he said.

"Max, we'll find another way. If we have to create another Kali—" Gloria began.

"Which we won't," Pax interjected.

"We'd need to find the right person with a similar transhuman marker as Kali," Gloria continued. "And it could take over a month, if not a year, before they have enough control to travel to the other universe."

"I won't wait," Max said.

"Technically, we do have time." Sean nudged Gloria aside. "Whatever's happened to Kali, has happened."

"Been there, discussed that." He crossed his arms. "Besides, I get the impression we are under the gun." One belonging to the Organization, which Max didn't want to take the time to discuss with Sean when he didn't understand the full details himself.

"Months from now, we can send someone back in time to retrieve her," Gloria said.

"That is if you can find a person with the transhuman marker who can develop Kali's *specific* ability. And you haven't found another since she got her powers," Max argued.

Sean plunked the ice bag back on his head. Gloria pulled her lips into a tight line.

"The decision is made." And Max had never been so sure of a choice in his life.

"What are you saying?" Pax leaned across Sean's shoulder. His scowling, square-jawed face filled the screen, as if he knew what Max meant, as he if wanted to reach through the video feed to stop him.

"He's going with the kamikaze option," Raven said.

"Don't. We can—" Max hung up on Gloria, not in the mood to hear more reasons why he should wait. He powered down his phone.

He turned to Mr. Triman. "Where is the Dark?"

He walked past the stained wall to the antique liquor cabinet in the corner. "I hid it here. That's why I was at the cabin the first time before you arrived. I needed it out of my house before they attempted to steal it, after they realized Mia had tricked them. There's a small amount left. Your grandfather drank most of it, and another drop was stolen by my daughter and used to open the portal Kali went through."

"Just a drop?" Surefire exclaimed.

"A single raindrop containing this parasite could infect you if it entered an orifice or wound." Mr. Triman bent down and opened the creaky cabinet doors.

"How did it get into the wine bottle Mia left for Kali?" Max watched Mr. Triman slide his arm past a vodka bottle to open a hidden compartment he'd never known was there.

"Mia used a needle to inject it through the cork, which had the shield knot imprinted on top." He removed a bottle, moss green and the size and shape of a half-sized wine bottle with no label. A crumbling cork plugged the mouth.

"It was a vintage wine from a case given to clients for DERST's silver anniversary. She passed it off as where I'd been hiding the remaining Dark." Mr. Triman held up the bottle.

"You keep the Dark inside that?" Raven said. "I can think of other, more appropriate liquors. Jägermeister comes to mind."

"This glass contains a neutralizing energy field, along with a shield knot ward for additional protection against the spirit inside." He jiggled it. The liquid sloshed inside.

"I'm assuming the bottle Mia used didn't offer the same fail safes," Max said.

"Mia didn't understand the principles behind this containment device. Fortunately, the wine she used had the shield knot on the cork, even if it had been put there for marketing purposes. It kept it secure for the short time it was inside," he said.

"Until it busted." Surefire glared at the bottle.

"It will take a bullet to crack this one." Mr. Triman shut the cabinet. "Mia was clever enough to use the wine as a decoy. She did have your best interests in mind, Max. In doing what she did, she disrupted the Organization's plans for you."

"And led them to Kali," Max said.

"That was most unfortunate, indeed, and I'm truly sorry for that." Mr. Triman set the bottle on the dining table.

"You're sorry," Surefire seethed. "Your daughter needs to pay for what she's done."

"She was trying to stop the Organization. She chose the wrong way to do it," Mr. Triman argued.

"That means nothing," Raven said. "And what is this Organization that attacked us in Utah?"

"A group of beings from my planetary system that includes a branch of the Custodians who helped study and contain the Dark."

"Did they also give it that stupid name?" Raven said.

"It was the best translation from our language. We tend to keep things simple for humans to comprehend," he replied.

Raven rolled his eyes at this insult.

"Our word for it roughly translates to *light of nothing.* We shortened it to the *Dark.* Custodians' abilities come from a type of light energy abundant in our sector of the universe. It's a force undiscovered by your current technology. Earth contains trace amounts. When a Custodian's power is corrupted by this opposing energy, it snuffs out their light, leaving nothing," Mr. Triman said.

"Nothing?" Surefire and Raven said in unison.

"What does that mean for me?" Max asked.

"You are special, with the right mix of DNA to retain who you are. You have the potential to fight it," Mr. Triman said.

"What is in that bottle exactly?" Max motioned to it.

"As Xochiquetzal revealed, the Dark corrupted a relation of mine. She was a Custodian with the rare ability to alt-travel. In fact, she discovered this dark energy force responsible for the creation of the parallel universe."

Mr. Triman stooped in front of the sofa to retrieve the journal. "She was the only one in a thousand years who had developed the ability to travel inter-dimensionally by rendering her light energy neutral to pass through dimensions."

"Like Kali," Surefire said.

"Kali isn't as powerful because she was born on Earth." As soon as he lifted the book from the floor, the glowing alien letters faded, leaving behind the scratches Mr. Triman had made.

He caressed the leather cover then replied, "When this Custodian had been studying the neighboring universe—where Kali and my sister are now—she'd tapped into this dark energy. It's the same force that is expelled in trace amounts when Kali travels to the other universe or the plane between our worlds. The Custodian thought she could convert it into a weapon to protect humans in our world."

"You said this energy was used to lock the Old Ones away."

"Indeed." He carried the journal to the table, holding it as reverently as one would hold an urn. "She wielded this alternate energy to form the gap between worlds and entrap them there."

"The Garden," Surefire murmured.

Mr. Triman inclined his head at her in agreement. "In doing so, she became possessed by the Dark, and it melded with her life force and became sentient. Through her, the Dark spread by feeding and infecting humans and Custodians. It took us centuries to stop her and drain the Dark into this bottle."

He set the journal next to the alien flask on the table.

"Hold up." Raven grimaced. "That bottle contains alien essence? Dude, that's definitely worse than Jägger."

Max clutched his stomach at this revelation. Downing pureed alien had to be the worst of the worst.

Mr. Triman didn't appear to notice Max's disgust, because he continued his lecture on Dark history as if relating a twisted fairy tale.

"After becoming infected," he went on, "she couldn't neutralize her energy to travel between planes. After she died and the Dark was drained, her residual cells regained the ability to neutralize energy again, but only Dark energy. None of us could use her remains to create a portal unless we were infected. That is the reason why we saved her husk, hoping we could someday isolate what was left of her power to send one of us to the other universe to study this energy more." He trailed a finger over the embossed leather. "It's also the reason why a rogue Custodian, who infected himself with the Dark and wrote in the journal, tanned her skin to bind it as a failsafe, in case he needed to send himself away."

"It's a Necronomicon?" said Raven.

"Explains why it's slightly different than the other journals." Max found his voice despite being sickened by the idea that he'd been toting around a book made from tanned alien skin.

"And that explains how it can open a portal to the other universe." Surefire put a few more feet between her and it.

"How did you drain the Dark into the bottle?" Max asked, hoping to take the conversation away from flesh-bound books.

"With this dagger." Mr. Triman reached under his jacket and pulled out a long blade. The sides of the tip were curved inward, forming a sharp-pointed spout.

He held the handle out for Max to take.

"Go ahead," Mr. Triman said when he hesitated. "You'll use this to neutralize the Dark and return home."

Max wrapped his hands around the handle lined with ridges, made from an animal horn, possibly a ram. It was lighter than he anticipated and purred against his palm as if it contained a tiny motor.

"Many daggers were created over the years by different civilizations. This one was forged by my sister and her husbands when they fought a Dark outbreak alongside the Celts. They called it the Triskele Dagger. It contains silver mixed with a metal alloy found on my home planet, the District. You'll insert the blade into the solar plexus. Right here." He poked two fingers at the center of Max's torso. "You'll then attach the bottle to the knife like so."

Mr. Triman twisted the handle and a silver half circle extended from either side. He demonstrated how these circular brackets would hold the bottle in place, fitting its mouth against the spout to collect the liquid.

"Then this is how I drain the Dark from my grandfather and Robert. Will it kill them?" asked Max.

"Unless his mind can fight the Dark's hold, then it will snuff out Robert in days. Regarding your grandfather, the Dark has taken full possession, he is already gone."

"I need to impale them," Max said to himself, wondering if he spoke this statement aloud it would make it less gruesome.

But it became more so. The idea of stabbing a stranger, even one who had assaulted Kali and Surefire, turned his stomach all shades of sour. Then to harm his grandfather—the man whom Max had grown to idolize—with this magical dagger upped the nightmarish scenario. Mr. Triman was asking him to kill his hero.

Could he do it? He'd never faced having to kill another. He'd only gotten into a handful of fights as a child, and even then he'd been defending himself or Glen or Mia, who'd had a propensity for stomping on the wrong people's toes. In most of those cases, he'd talked his way out of the fight with Glen's help. He prided himself on being the diplomat, never the soldier.

"Can you do this?" Mr. Triman asked.

"Yes," he replied, because that was what this man needed to hear. That's what Max needed to say to make those standing around him feel better about him going.

"Once I neutralize the Dark, how do we return?" he asked.

"Since the Dark contains the essence of the first Custodian, it should also retain the alt-traveling properties that will be reactivated once the host is drained. Although, I conjecture that your grandfather's body will be the stronger generator with the Dark having years to embed itself into his DNA. The portal should reopen by using your grandfather's or Robert's body like we can with the journal."

"It *should* open the portal?" Surefire put her hands on her hips like a mom who'd reached her limits with a child skirting the truth.

"I've never done this before. I had hoped Mr. Vivas would've uncovered more clues in the journal. Alas, all I have are theories based on my studies of the Dark," Mr. Triman replied.

"Which are?" Surefire rotated her wrist like she was reeling a fishing rod.

Mr. Triman removed the bottle from the knife and put them both on the table.

He addressed Max when he said, "By draining the Dark from your grandfather, you will seal it within this vessel"—he touched the bottle—"stopping it from entering another host after you return it to our world. The Dark can only pass between universes within a sealed vessel such as this bottle or inside a host's body, neutralized by the dagger."

"Is that why the Dark didn't travel with Stockwell? Because it wasn't neutralized?" Max said, trying to follow.

"That is one guess. Since Kali's energy is light-based as well, having originated in our universe, she has to make her energy neutral to travel between planes. She can't make the Dark neutral, only herself and any non-infected persons traveling with her."

"What will happen to my grandfather's body if we use it to open the portal? The journal didn't pass through the planes with Kali. Will his body stay there?" asked Max.

"It may pass through the portal too. Again, I've never done this before. It's all conjecture." He laid a hand on Max's shoulder. "What I do know is that the Dark cannot be allowed to return to our world unbound, you need to drain it into the bottle. And then—"

"Turn the blade on himself, because Max will need to be neutralized as well," Surefire finished.

"My sister will do it," Mr. Triman said.

"Oh man, this isn't right. It's one thing to drink that shit, another to be impaled," Raven said.

"If it's not bound inside Max, the Dark's power will increase when it arrives in our universe, because the energy that nourishes it resides here."

"What will happen to me?" Max asked.

"Even with the blade piercing your body, you will survive. The Dark will keep its vessel alive, so you should survive until we can remove it from you."

"Will Max be aware of what's happening to him?" Raven asked and Max understood what he meant. Would he experience the pain of having an alien knife stuck inside him?

"I don't know. The Dark may take over his consciousness, and he'll have no idea of what is happening," Mr. Triman replied.

"Or he could be aware of everything," Raven said.

"This idea is getting worse and worse," Surefire said.

"If we bring the Dark to our world unbound within Max, it will be harder to stop and contain. It will gain strength by draining life forces from transhumans and those—like you and Raven—powered by a higher entity before feasting on the rest."

"It wants us for a meal?" Raven scrubbed a hand down his face. "And I thought we'd heard it all."

"The Dark will attack you to not only increase its power but to protect itself. Transhumans pose a threat. The stronger transhumans become and the more mankind unlocks transhuman potential, the more resistance the Dark has to its plans."

"Plans?" Max asked.

"Power over Earth. Over the universe," said Mr. Triman.

"Then the Dark imprisoned Xochi and the others in the Garden to save itself as well," Surefire said.

Mr. Triman nodded. "At the time, we thought it was the best course of action to protect humans from the Old Ones' powers, but the Dark had manipulated us. It put those ideas in our minds."

Max sucked on his bottom lip as another thought came to mind. "Stockwell was kidnapping transgeneticists from the past in our world. Was it because the Dark doesn't want transhumans to exist?"

"Stockwell did what now?" Raven asked.

"Kali told me about what she'd experienced, but I didn't have time to relate it to you. I almost feel it would be better that way. Except the part of not having you." She took Raven's hand.

"It wouldn't be, trust me," Mr. Triman said.

"Is this what Xochi has been talking about? She keeps making all these doom and gloom references but doesn't elaborate because, you know, that would be helpful," said Raven.

"One of them, yes." Mr. Triman didn't give more details. A habit, Max was learning, of ancient beings. Reveal enough to motivate but not enough to disclose their full intent.

"But you are right, Max. Transhumans do pose a threat to the Dark. Besides Custodians, they are the only ones who stand a chance against it," Mr. Triman said.

"Where are the rest of the Custodians? Those from your planet? Can't they help us?" Surefire asked.

"Yeah," Raven chimed in. "Since they created this mess."

"The bottle and the dagger are the best defense we've created thus far. Most Custodians left Earth after the war with the Dark took many of our lives. A handful joined the Organization. I'm afraid that the new powers elected to rule the District don't see the value in Earth anymore. They've cut resources for the Custodians. We're on our own." Mr. Triman lifted his hands in apology. "But that doesn't diminish what we can accomplish. We have each other and U-Sec, along with my sister and her spouses when they return, to keep the Dark from wreaking havoc again."

"Will Max become evil?" Surefire looked at him with so much worry that Max felt the need to comfort her and ensure her that he would be fine even if he was anxious as well.

"Only if he embraces it. A strong-willed person with the genetic makeup to thwart the Dark can hold it back. However, it will forever be a part of him even when we remove it." Mr. Triman turned to Max and said, "You will need to recognize it and understand how it affects you."

"He shouldn't put himself in jeopardy like this. Kali wouldn't want it," Surefire pleaded.

"I can't leave her to face the Dark alone. If this is the only way to save her, then I'm willing to make the sacrifice," Max said.

"Let's go back to what you just said. You'll remove the Dark from Max, but it will always be a part of him? Which is it, buddy?" Raven asked.

"It will leave its mark but not enough to possess him," Mr. Triman explained.

He touched the handle. Golden rays shot from his fingers. Alien letters, etched into the blade's gleaming surface, glowed in response. "Each day the Dark is inside Max, it will grow. That's why it's important he returns quickly before it progresses, and he can no longer control it. When he returns, we will immediately drain the Dark from him. I won't lie. It will be painful. And there are no guarantees that he will survive."

"You're not going it alone. We're coming too," Surefire announced.

"Huh?" Raven's mouth gaped open. "Fine. I'm game. What do we need to do?"

"You will lose your power if you travel there," Mr. Triman said. "Dara's energy has faded over the years, but she retains her core abilities—although a weaker version. For you, it will be instantaneous. You'll no longer be connected to the goddess. She holds no sway in that universe."

"I'd be free?" Surefire glanced at the crystal skull on the floor.

"You would be free of the goddess, but how much life you'd have left is another question. Having her energy ripped from your body could cause you to go into shock," he said. "But Raven would certainly die. The goddess's power keeps him alive, and her energy doesn't exist there."

"I'm glad we never took up Kali's offer to see the other universe," Raven said.

"No kidding," Surefire replied as she picked up the skull and cradled it in the nook of her arm.

Raven scrubbed a hand down his face. Then he paused before he whirled around to Mr. Triman as if an idea dawned on him. Judging by his scowl, it wasn't a good one.

"You said this Organization originally wanted Max to open the portal, but Mia set up Kali instead." He jabbed a finger at Mr. Triman's chest. "And yet here we are giving them what they wanted in the first place."

The older man raised his hands to show that there was nothing up his sleeves. Raven wasn't buying it.

"Max, can you vouch for your family-slash-alien friend here?" He lifted a brow at him.

Max considered the question. Throughout his life, he'd felt closer to Mr. Triman than his own father. But now, his whole world had been turned upside down by what this man had kept from him.

"He's lied to me all my life," Max replied.

"So that's a no?" Raven ventured.

"I don't know anymore. My whole life is in question, but I don't have the time for the truth or his version of it," Max said.

Surefire wrung her hands. "Don't do this. I'm begging you. Trust me, it never goes as planned."

"I can't leave Kali. She didn't leave me."

She gave him a sad smile. "I get it. I do."

Before he could consider that he was about to drink what remained of an alien, and be forever changed, Max gripped the neck of the bottle. He expected it to be cold, but it was warm like a carafe of coffee. He twisted the cork. It came out with a pop. A licorice smell filled the air.

"Argh." Surefire covered her nose.

"Smells like evil's gym socks." Raven coughed so hard he gagged.

"What's wrong with it?" Max sniffed the mouth of the bottle. It smelled of black licorice and reminded him of ouzo, nothing stomach churning.

Max held it up to the light and slowly tipped the bottle side to side. A viscous liquid oozed around the interior, reminding him of engine oil, which was better than reminding him of what it really was.

Removing a pen from his inside breast pocket, Mr. Triman opened the journal to an empty page then scrawled a time, location, and date on it. He flipped to a previous page and scratched out a different date.

"This is how the journal knows when to deposit you. You'll arrive hours before Kali and my sister. Do not contact them, or you will change what has already happened and that universe may not survive another reset. Keep yourself hidden away until your grandfather arrives. When he seeks you out, get close enough so you can isolate him and do what you need to do."

Max stared at the bottle. He should feel nervous or scared to ingest this thing called the Dark. But both those feelings had passed, leaving behind a certainty that this was the right thing to do, the only thing to do to save Kali and the others.

"What about a weapon? The dagger will work up close, but you may need something to subdue him," Raven suggested.

"You're right. I didn't think of that." Pain resurged in his bruised leg as he hobbled downstairs through his office and into his workshop where he kept prototype weapons.

Max chose a taser similar to the one Mia had used. It was fully charged, no chance of running out of bullets. If it was powerful enough to disable Raven, odds were good that it could take down a human possessed by an alien entity.

He strapped on the holster and grabbed a lightweight jacket to cover it. His leg and joints protesting the effort, he limped upstairs to the cabin. Mr. Triman, Surefire, and Raven huddled in front of the basement door and parted to let Max pass.

"Here we go." Bronze streaks flashed and slithered in the droplet as he tilted the bottle to his mouth.

"Be careful." Surefire's hand reached out as if to stop him then dropped it back to her side.

He met her eyes and nodded that he understood there was no turning back.

"When the portal opens, we'll retreat downstairs," Mr. Triman said.

As he moved to the stained wall away from the group, Max slid the dagger into an inside pocket of his jacket. He set the book on top of the corner liquor cabinet. His eyes strayed to the stain on the wall next to him.

Mr. Triman took a deep breath, bringing in the good air or at least trying to. "You only need a small drop on your tongue."

"Bottoms up," There was a sadness in Raven's words, as if he were saying goodbye for the final time.

"Yeah, bottoms up," Max echoed.

"Stop!" Mr. Triman hurried from the doorway. "Only a drop. That's all."

He snatched the bottle from Max, as if he were a toddler who'd picked up a carving knife from the table. Taking Max's hand, he raised it palm up, keeping his underneath to ensure it stayed still. He lifted the bottle. With a slow, careful tilt of his wrist Mr. Triman laid the bottle's lip on Max's index finger. Eyes trained on it, they waited.

"Mr. Triman," Max began when his arm got tired from holding his hand aloft.

Then a drop, no larger than a pinprick of blood oozed onto his fingertip. Quickly, Mr. Triman righted the bottle and re-corked it.

"A drop," he reiterated as if Max had never heard the concept before, so he needed to be extra clear.

Max stared at the oily decimal point against his pinkish flesh.

"Put it on your tongue." Mr. Triman watched as Max did what he was told.

Once Max licked the drop from his finger, Mr. Triman ducked inside the doorway of the basement stairs. "Now put your hand on the journal."

Max complied and closed his eyes. His tongue tingled. A bitter licorice taste coated his mouth, spreading from the tip to the back of his throat. This sensation reminded him of going to the dentist to get a cavity filled after they stuck him with the anesthesia. He moved his tongue around his teeth. If felt thick and heavy. The numbing agent stopped mid-way down his throat.

Swallowing, he cracked open his eyes and stared at the journal. A static shock hit against his palm but nothing more.

"It's not working," he said, words coming out slurred.

"Wait. It might take time," Mr. Triman called out from the stairwell on the other side of the now closed door.

"Maybe I need more of it? Because of my genetic makeup, you said I was more capable of handling the Dark. It could need the rest for it to work. There's not much left." Max shook the bottle to make his point.

"Absolutely not!" The door opened a crack, and Mr. Triman's bald head appeared over the edge, followed by the top half of his face. Brows lowered over his dark eyes to accentuate his point. "Patience."

Max gave it a few more minutes. The clock across the room taunted him with every tick of the second hand. He drummed his fingers against the cover.

The room grew colder. He shivered under his jacket and looked to the front door, assuming it had opened and swearing he heard the hinges creak. Then he heard a voice. No, multiple voices. Men shouting. Furniture being overturned. Under Max's feet, the floor vibrated from a struggle taking place that he couldn't see but could certainly feel and hear.

The sounds of the fight faded, replaced by a woman . . . no, not any woman, it was Kali . . . crying out.

The terror in her voice pricked him like a hundred needles to his heart.

Max put his lips around the bottle's mouth and downed all of the Dark.

Chapter 23

Kali Left Behind

"Oh, fu—"

The doorknob turned with a screech, but the door didn't budge.

"Forgot about the deadbolt," a man said, followed by keys jingling.

Kali tore up the stairs to the loft. Her long legs took several steps at once. She vaulted over the bed toward the opposite wall and ducked as the bolt slid open along with the door.

Lifting the bedspread, she saw the frame was high enough for her to wriggle under. Dust bunnies the size of pet hamsters blew about and tickled her nose. She held her breath and continued to slide until she banged into a storage chest.

I'm not going to sneeze. I'm not going to—

"Check upstairs," the same man ordered.

Thump. Thump. Thump. The steps to the loft creaked under the weight of heavy boots treading closer to the top.

"What you got there, chief?" Stockwell's Aussie accent sent shivers up Kali's spine.

"Food left on the kitchen counter. And someone moved the furniture. Lift the rug."

Fabric shifted. Something soft flopped to the floor. Kali assumed they were rolling back the rug.

"Maybe those freeloaders from the commune broke in, ate your food, and made this graffiti. They were pissed when you evicted them."

"There aren't many of them left, and those who remain nearby are too scared to return. No, this is the work of the Three."

"Right, I see," Stockwell replied.

The Man's guard reached the loft. As he stomped alongside the bed, floorboards vibrated under Kali's torso. She took in as little breath as possible, willing her heart to slow its incessant beating.

"We lost the Three again," Stockwell said.

"That's okay, son. We'll get them soon. They'll be back around."

She couldn't see what they were doing, her vision blocked by the bottom of the railing running along the footboard of the bed.

"What's with the heart and K and M?" Stockwell asked.

"We'll see soon enough, I'm sure," said the Man.

Kali covered her mouth, inhaling through her fingers when she dared to take a breath. The chifforobe door creaked open. Clothes shifted, hangers banged against the interior. The door slammed closed.

"Was she the one with the Three, like those two birds told us back in Utah?" said Stockwell.

"You got it, champ," the Man replied. "Bring the dude inside."

Stockwell whistled then called out two names. "Hey! Bring in the bloke."

To her right, she heard the bedskirt shift and the floor creak. The soldier must've lifted it to check underneath. He kicked the chest and it banged against Kali's right side. Her eyes watered as dust balls rolled by her face when the chest shifted.

Polished combat boots marched across the foot of the bed. They paused. Kali sucked in her lips, held her breath, and waited for him to lift the bed skirt on her side.

"Nothing up here, sir," the guard announced before he bounded down the stairs.

Taking a much-needed breath, Kali allowed herself to blink. Her nose started to run. Postnasal drip tickled along the back of her throat.

A multitude of people trudged into the cabin. Various voices—all male—mingled with rubber soles scuffing and squeaking against the floor.

Robert's panicked cries rose over the bustle of bodies. "You can't do this to me. I'm here to help the Dark get home. I'm with the Organization."

The Man chuckled. "Oh, man, that's a good one. *The Organization.* They're still around, huh? I assumed the council would've imploded under the pressure of their egos. Intergalactic beings don't play well together, and they certainly never played well with humans. Which makes me wonder what you're doing with them."

"They've opened up their ranks to humans who have potential," Robert said.

"And they chose you?" Stockwell punctuated his sarcastic question with a whistle. "They must really be desperate."

"I was an Olympic athlete!"

"That means nothing to me," the Man retorted.

"The Organization has grown stronger since aligning with humans," Robert continued unabated. "They've expanded their reach and have been recruiting transhumans as well. With your help, the time has come for their plans to—"

"I won't help you or this damnable Organization," the Man interjected. "The Dark doesn't need them. We don't need them."

The first floor creaked under the weight of bodies moving around. Kali got the impression the Man was walking to the center of the living room trailed by a few others, one of whom was being dragged.

"Now that you've awoken from that nasty head bash this brings me to my first question. What do you know about the woman who did that to you?"

"I don't . . . argh." Robert grunted. Kali could picture him grinding his teeth against the pain from whatever they were doing to him.

"You want to reconsider your answer?" Stockwell said.

From her vantage, Kali could see the beams of the ceiling where brownish light reflected against the wood as if they'd opened a treasure chest filled with bronze. She couldn't take a chance to move closer to find the light's source. Her eyes watered again from the dust. A stream of tears soaked her cheeks.

"Do you know what this means?" The Man's voice was calm, scholarly, a professor teaching a class.

Robert groaned again.

"The letters K and M with a heart around them. This text mentions a misunderstanding between them, which could be why there's a slash over the heart," said the Man.

It finally dawned on Kali that the Man was reading the text sent from the other universe. She could only see the message when Tomas touched the floor and lit it up. Did the Man have this same power?

"I'll tell you who she is, but I want a deal," Robert said.

Kali's heart thudded. Any louder, she feared it would give her away.

"You aren't in a position to make one," Stockwell said.

"Now let's hear what he has to say," the Man said.

"When you find her, I want to go back home," Robert said.

"And how will we do that? We don't have the means to travel there. Otherwise, I would've been back years ago."

"As I told you, she can help you," Robert went on. "That's what she does. She's a transhuman. An UltraAgent. Her name is Kali, but her alias is TimeTrap. She travels between universes."

Kali's stomach grew sicker and sicker. If they found her and expected her to do this, she couldn't deliver. And without this mysterious dagger neutralizing him—per the Three's history lesson—then she risked endangering her friends, her world, if she did.

"If she is TimeTrap, as you claim she is, then maybe she has already returned to her home and left you here."

"She lost her power. That's why she ran. But I think it might be temporary. She came through the journal's portal instead of jumping here herself. It may have messed her up."

"You think, think, think, yet give no facts that I can use. Only reiterating what was written here," said the Man. "The one thing I know for certain is that you can't handle the Dark. It's gobbling you up."

The Man's observations must've been the truth because Robert pleaded, "Put me in stasis if you will. I can help you once you get to our universe. I'm begging you to show mercy to a loyal member of the Organization."

When no one replied, Robert went on, sounding more desperate. "The letters on the floor. That's M and K for Max Martin and Kali Bordeaux."

"Max Martin?" Stockwell snorted. "This is Maxwell Martin. Why would they draw a heart to represent this woman and the Man here?"

"Hold on, Stockwell." Kali pictured Grandpa Martin placing a hand on the soldier's shoulder like a master would tug a dog's collar to keep it in check. "From what year did you travel?"

"Do we have a deal?" Robert asked.

"What year?" the Man asked again, his voice not wavering from his therapist-like tone.

Robert hesitated—a bad decision because he issued another pain-filled cry before he gave them the year.

"Sir?" Stockwell asked before repeating himself, making Kali wonder why his boss had gone quiet.

"Give us a moment," the Man said softly.

"Then we're done with him?" Stockwell asked.

"Yes."

"What do you mean?" Robert said, frantic.

Stockwell whistled. A herd of shoes scraped and shuffled across the room. The door opened and closed. A breeze blew up and agitated the dust.

Oh, no. Kali fought the urge to sniffle against the tumbleweed of dirt and hair dancing under her nose.

"Shhh . . . don't worry. This will only hurt a bit. Then it will all be over."

"What are you going to do to me? I'm on your side. I can . . . help . . . I will . . ." Robert's words faded, replaced by a gurgling sound.

"You have something I need. A bit of me is inside you, and if you don't mind, I'd like to have it back."

Is he talking about the Dark? Kali wiggled her body forward a few inches until the bedskirt settled over her forehead. She lifted the lacy edge but still couldn't make out the scene below.

A heavy object tipped over and banged into the floor. A table, maybe? A thump then a crack of possibly a lamp hitting the floor. Grunts and curses echoed in the room. Rubber soles squeaked against the floor. All these sounds painted a picture of Robert fighting and losing against a much stronger person. But as far as Kali could tell, Stockwell and the others had left the room, leaving just the Man and Robert, which meant this athlete was no match for this person nearing his sixties.

Kali's scalp prickled. Static electricity, the same sensation when she'd touched the journal, charged the room like the precursor of a lightning strike.

A dull thud reached her ears like the sound of a large body collapsing to the ground. Screwing her eyes shut, Kali quieted her breath and listened. Only one pair of feet walked below her and the steps weren't Robert's.

A deep sigh came from the living room. The sound was followed by the scraping of a knife cutting into the floor. Was he sending a message to Dara's brother?

The scraping continued for a few more minutes. Then she heard the sweep of fabric wiping off a surface, and she pictured him using his sleeve to clean away the shavings. His feet—was he wearing flip-flops?—shuffled across the room. The door creaked open. Another breeze blew into the room. Dust bunnies once again bounded around Kali's nose as she took a quick breath.

Then she coughed.

And to add insult to injury, she sneezed.

Chapter 24

Max Leaves His World Behind

"No! Don't—" Mr. Triman's panicked cry dropped into silence. He froze in mid-action of running into the room. His mouth wide open yet not a sound emerged from it.

"Mr. Triman?" Max ventured in the eerie silence of the room. The clock no longer ticked. No snowy wind blew against the windows. Raven and Surefire didn't make a peep from the stairwell behind Mr. Triman. He wondered if they had been frozen in time too.

The dull light of the room faded into a sepia tone then to black and white. The bottle slipped from his hand. He caught it before it hit the table.

Max wagged his head and coughed. The oily liquid slid down his throat, leaving a smoldering trail of fluid in its wake. A searing burn spread across his chest and down his torso. The sensation threw out tendrils down his arms to his fingertips, which rested on the book. The black cover embossed with the Martin seal wavered.

With his free hand, he shoved the cork into the bottle and then placed it into his jacket's zippered pocket. Max staggered as if drunk as his hand passed through the leather binding and disappeared into a cold void up to his wrist. He tugged but couldn't yank free. The smell of burnt incense assailed his nose. He watched in horror as his forearm stretched like Plastic Man from the comics. His arm flattened into a noodle shape before his shoulder followed inside and his head bent back at an angle that should've snapped it in two.

Blackness encased him. This cold vacuum pulled his body in every direction. He had no idea where he ended or began, because he couldn't feel anything and couldn't see anything. Unhinged from a physical form, he was merely a consciousness floating in space.

The blackness parted like heavy drapes across a stage, revealing a moon-like glow. It grew slowly at first and then it flashed, leaving him in darkness again, but now it was the darkness of night and there were floorboards underneath him. He smelled the mildew scent of an old water leak. On his back, he stared at the wood beams forming the A-frame ceiling of his grandfather's log cabin. The blackness faded to gray, revealing recessed ceiling lights, a dining table and chairs to his left, and the floral patterned cushions on the wooden living room furniture.

He propped himself onto his elbows and waited for the room to come into focus. It was almost what he remembered as a child. Furniture was slightly off. The pattern was different, larger flowers with vines, not a small, dainty pattern on the couch cushions. The braided rug was wider, allowing all the furniture to fit neatly on it, whereas his cabin had the Oriental rug from his grandmother's house. She'd offered it to him when the old braided rug had fallen apart.

Max hauled himself to his feet without any discomfort.

"That's weird." He kicked out his leg and rotated his ankle. Rubbing his hand down his hip and thigh, he felt no pain. The aches and stiffness were gone.

As much as he wanted to savor this wonderful side effect, Max had a job to do. He pulled up a corner of the rug then ran his hand over the smooth surface. They hadn't been here yet.

When Mr. Triman's sister and Kali arrived, he couldn't let them know he was here. He recalled what happened when Stockwell arrived in their world to kidnap Max. It stopped Kali from going back in time and getting abducted by the Man, thereby changing the entire timeline so Stockwell no longer had the ability to travel to their universe. If the Three and Kali found Max in the cabin, then they wouldn't leave the etchings telling him to travel here . . .

Classic alt-jumper mistake, as Kali would say.

The Triskele Dagger lay at his side, having fallen from his jacket when he appeared. He snatched it from the floor and held it close. He prayed he could do what needed to be done when the time came. He was thankful Glen wasn't there. He'd remind Max how he had trouble breaking the claws whenever they ate steamed crabs. Of course, Glen's BS Force might be handy to subdue his grandfather. Considering that Glen was part alien, Max didn't doubt this BS Force, which they'd joked about all these years, was a real power.

Glancing up at the loft, he decided to hide there until everyone—including his grandfather—arrived. He climbed the steep ladder steps. Set against the left wall was a chifforobe, but that would be too obvious a hiding place. His foot kicked against an object under the sweeping bedskirt of the four-poster bed. With a grunt, he tugged on the leather handles and slid out the heavy box. It was nearly the length of the bed. He opened it and stumbled back into the chifforobe, which thudded into the wall.

Moonlight filtered in through the dirty windows above the headboard. It landed on the opened chest across the white naked breast of a withered man.

I have to be seeing things.

Max fumbled to turn on the light set on the nightstand. He lowered the lamp over the chest and what it held. He tried to convince himself it was a trick and that this was a Halloween prop, someone's deluded joke, but his mind wouldn't buy it.

He placed his fingers on the neck. The paper-thin skin collapsed under his light touch, forming a small hole. He jerked his hand away. The dead man's eyelids were sunken as if there were no longer eyes in the sockets. He moved the light over the chest until it unplugged from the wall, putting him in the dark again. He scampered to plug it back in. He'd seen too many horror movies not to be freaked out kneeling next to a mummified man in the dark.

The yellow light illuminated the room once more, sending away the imaginary monsters and leaving Max to confront the real-life terror. He forced himself to study the body again. The chest and stomach were shriveled. It looked as if he'd been excavated from an Egyptian tomb.

A troubling thought occurred to Max, one that he tried hard not to consider, but once the idea formed, he had to face it.

The shape of the corpses' eyes. The rise of the cheekbones. The size of the forehead.

"No, it couldn't be," he whispered, because he didn't want to fathom how this could be real. He sat back against the chifforobe, his head resting against the carved vine on the door.

What if he was the Maxwell Martin from this universe? And what if his grandfather had done this?

But how? Could the Dark suck the life force from a human body and dehydrate it? And why keep it stored under the bed like old letters or souvenirs?

Max closed the lid and locked the brass latches. With reverence, he pushed the chest back under the bed.

He rose to his feet as a pain seized his heart. He doubled over. His hands clutched the bedspread. A low growl rose in his throat, and a cold burn spread down his torso. Seething rage like he'd never experienced before flooded his emotions in seemingly unending waves. He pushed against the current. Struggled to control his hands that curled into fists itching to punch, rip, destroy.

In with the good breath, out with the bad.

He exhaled then inhaled again and again, until he made a puffing noise like the train in a popular children's story he used to love. *I think I can. I think I can.*

He had thought he was above the Dark. He thought that he could handle it. He wasn't a hothead. He wasn't a man who sought out fights. He'd made weapons for alpha soldier types, but he never used them. He'd been foolish enough to believe the Dark wouldn't affect him as it would someone who wanted to embrace it.

Then again, could this be his true self? Did it reveal a person's true dark side?

Outside, the sky grew brighter. The cabin glowed with a soft, welcoming light. His insides twisted. The walls were closing in on him. He needed to get out. He couldn't stay a minute longer with the dried-up husk in the loft. Finding the body of his grandfather, or alternate-world grandfather, had been the catalyst. The spark that sent his rage ablaze.

He pictured his favorite path that led from the cabin to a tiered waterfall ending at a small stream emptying into the Shenandoah. He pictured Kali there, barefoot and splashing him as they waded in the stream. He never had a chance to show her his cabin in the summer, and he longed to share it with her. Share everything with her.

His hands uncurled. His muscles relaxed. He let out one last ragged breath and felt nearly normal—not quite his calm self, but not ready to rip the room apart either.

Careful not to disturb anything else, he righted the lamp on the nightstand and wiped the dust away with his shirt so it didn't look like it had been moved. He descended the stairs and spied the liquor cabinet in the far corner. He stashed the bottle and blade inside, not wanting his grandfather to find them on his person, until he was ready to deal the final blow to the Dark. Under the recliner, he hid the pulse taser. His grandfather was certain to check him for weapons when he gave himself up for Kali. He didn't want to hamper that exchange.

With a last glance around the room, he walked out the door. The tears came as he hit the second porch step. Anxiety over what he'd seen, over this whole day, hit him with the force of a brick to the head. He doubled over and vomited into the overgrown shrubs.

Wiping the back of his mouth with his hand, he looked around until he spied the same yet different path that cut into the woods up the mountain to the waterfall. The sunlight breaking through the trees warmed his face. With a parting glance at the cabin, he hiked up the trail to clear his mind and plan how he was going to save Kali from that vampiric monster that sucked the life from the Maxwell Martin of this universe.

Chapter 25

Kali Hides from the Man

Oh, crap. Oh, crap. Please say he didn't hear me sneeze.

Kali pressed against the chest under the four-poster bed and wished she could phase into it. She tried to tap into her ability. Her power's heat reached her fingertips then petered out. It puffed and fell like a deflated soufflé.

The front door slammed shut. Kali screwed up her eyes and listened for a step, a breath, a fart, anything.

A throat cleared. One heavy, self-assured step after another drew closer to the loft stairs.

"I know you're in here. Come out, come out, wherever you are," the Man said, singsong.

Really? He was going with that clichéd phrase? It might've worked on a five-year-old Kali, but it wasn't going to work on this almost thirty-year-old. She held her breath and stilled her body. She pretended she was dead. But that was a morbid thought, and it just served to upset her further, so she decided to focus on being alive but not making noise, breathing but not inhaling dust . . . oh, no . . . she was about to—

She sneezed.

The door swished open and Stockwell announced, "Sir, we have a situation."

"Handle it," the Man said dismissively.

"I think you should see him first."

"Who?" Quick flip-flopping steps retreated across the room.

"Says he's your grandson," the Aussie replied.

Kali's head popped up and hit the bed boards with a loud bang.

"What was that?" Stockwell asked.

"A mouse whose piece of cheese just arrived," the Man said.

"All right then."

Their voices faded as they stepped outside, and the porch creaked under both men's weight. The door closed, cutting off the rest of the conversation.

Heart racing, Kali slid from under the bed.

Was it really Max? Or was it the Max from this universe? But wait . . . no, it was 1979, it couldn't be.

She sprang onto the mattress. Pressing her cheek against the windowpane, she craned her neck to see past the corner of the cabin, but the only view was of a large tree with a wasp's nest on the far side.

Maybe I could open the window.

A wasp zipped past the glass.

And get stung to death in the process.

She jumped to the floor then bent over the loft's railing as far as she dared. Her upper body dangled over the edge to sneak a peek outside the closest window.

She didn't see Max, but she could see a guard's back with a rifle slung across it.

She pulled herself over the railing then stopped when her eye caught an object in the living room that hadn't been part of the decor earlier. Her fingers tightened on the railing to keep from fainting.

"Robert?" Kali croaked.

Propped in the corner under a hanging crocheted owl lay a human raisin wearing white ski pants and snow boots.

"No, no, no." She shuffled from the edge until the backs of her legs hit the bed. She fell with a squeak onto the lumpy mattress.

She couldn't stay in this cabin, not with what remained of Robert under the same roof. She rubbed her palms against her eyes to erase the image, but her mind had other plans and her body too. Whatever was in her stomach threatened to make a hasty exit if she didn't do something.

How to get out of here . . . how to get out of here . . . Kali rocked in time to her thoughts.

"Let's try this again," she whispered.

Her power was there. It only needed coaxing and maybe a dose of adrenaline mixed with fear, which was good because she had fear in spades.

She visualized where she could materialize that would give her a good view of the outdoor scene and not draw attention to herself.

Her power rose then cut out.

"Ugh!" She slammed her palms on the bed.

What is blocking it?

"Only one other way."

She crawled toward the headboard. She balanced on the springy mattress.

"Here goes everything." She opened the window and lifted her leg through the opening. With an anxious eye on the wasp's nest, she stretched until her foot touched the closest and thickest branch.

"You can do this." Straddling the sill, she lifted her other leg through and lowered her weight into the tree.

"Reach up and balance on the branch above," she coached herself. "You've done the ropes course before, even if it was only three feet off the ground and with a harness." She looked down then snapped her eyes shut against the vertigo. "Okay, don't look down, and don't think about how the grass appears to be sliding further away."

A bug dive-bombed her head. "And don't think about the wasps and their big, pointy stingers."

She planted one foot in front of the other. The leaves rustled. A wasp buzzed past. Bending at her side, she peered around the corner to the front lawn. The backend of a helicopter came into view. She craned her neck and edged a foot closer to the trunk.

She caught sight of Max. Her Max.

No, she shook her head and sniffed. Not her Max anymore. Her eyes watered and not from dust or pollen.

She couldn't tell if he was hurt. As he knelt to the ground, his legs appeared stiff. He struggled to bend his knees.

Why was he kneeling?

She scooted a few inches over and stretched her neck until she saw the ends of two rifles pointed at him.

Chapter 26

While Kali Hides, Max Reveals Himself

Kill them all.

The voice started as soon as the helicopter soared over the tree line and over the spot where Max had been meditating on a boulder by the waterfall. He hadn't meditated for years, he was ashamed to admit, and the peaceful act kept the Dark at bay.

Until he heard the telltale sound of blades slicing the air, then all hell broke loose inside him.

The Dark awoke with a start. Immediately, it sought out Max's anxiety, his fear, his hate—all the negative feelings he'd neatly buried thanks to hours of solitude and meditative calm. But when the Dark rose again, it ripped through Max's hard-earned peace, seeking out then sinking its teeth into the raw, painful emotions. It was as if the Dark sensed who and what had arrived and wanted Max primed to fight and primed to join with the remaining Dark residing in his grandfather.

Enlivened by this rage-filled caffeinated cocktail, the Dark sent out a blast of nervous energy that Max couldn't ignore. His hands and arms shot out from their folded position as his heart revved up. He launched to his feet. The adrenaline hummed inside his muscles, which twitched with the need to run, the need to go, the need to confront his grandfather.

Now.

With ease, he sprinted along the path to the house. No pain hindered his leg or seized up his back or shoulder. The bruising was gone. Over the past few hours, the cut on his scalp had healed. The scab flaked off. He felt stronger and healthier than he had in his college days. The evil oil proved to be a medicinal tonic, although with demon-level side effects.

His moist henley shirt stuck to his body under his coat. The summer humidity became more oppressive the faster he ran. With the sleeve of his jacket, he wiped away sweat before it stung his eyes. The day was heating up. With the dagger and taser stowed in the cabin, he no longer needed his lightweight jacket. He tore it off and tossed it onto a branch when he reached the edge of the clearing.

He ducked behind a tree and watched the soldiers—no, not soldiers, they were private security—exiting the chopper onto the overgrown lawn in front of the cabin.

A blonde man emerged. He wore a military-style haircut and had a swagger stolen from a 1970s action villain.

Stockwell.

Seeing this man again, the one who'd kidnapped Max and who'd used Kali's power, sent Max's anger erupting into volcanic levels. Echoing his darkest desires, the Dark cursed and plotted Stockwell's demise, whispering about all the torturous things they should do to him. Max wagged his head to dislodge its hold on his thoughts. But what frightened him the most was how the Dark used a deeper, sinister version of his voice. If it took form, Max suspected it would look like him but with a Van Dyke. Because evil loved facial hair, according to the movies.

Max chuckled at this ludicrous thought. How he could be thinking of bearded baddies at a time like this made him question his sanity, made him wonder if maybe this was his way of downplaying the seriousness of the situation. Because he didn't want to think too hard about what was fighting to take hold of him. If he could picture it as a ridiculous movie stereotype, then maybe he could control it.

The laughing did help. He felt more in control of his body and his emotions as if the silly feeling sent the Dark away, maybe even annoyed it. Unfortunately, it didn't last long.

He's here, the voice forced its way into Max's mind again.

A man who looked to be in his early sixties stepped from the helicopter. Max gripped the tree trunk to keep himself from bolting toward him.

At first glance, Max would've pegged him as a religious guru, with his loose-fitting linen pants and a ratty cardigan over a V-neck shirt along with sandals. However, the longer he studied the man, the more he recognized the same long strides as his father, the same way of walking with his chest puffed, arms back, head up. It was the same way Max strutted into the office to meet with the board to show them that he was competent to run the latest project or request funding on personal ventures.

This man was his grandfather.

And all Max felt was what the Dark wanted him to feel. The desire to drain the alien oil from his body, not into the bottle, but inside Max. It would join with the rest of the Dark, and Max would be unstoppable.

No! He shook his head hard.

His nails dug into the bark. He didn't want to be unstoppable, and he certainly didn't want the Dark to be that powerful. Already this thing was trying to corrupt his mind and heart, ruining this moment that he'd dreamed of. At times, he'd wished his grandfather had been his father, because he would've gone on adventures with him across the country, searching for answers to life. He had poured over his journals until the picture he created of his grandfather resembled the characters in his favorite comics—a sage, aging hippie advising the heroes on how to save the day.

When Max met him in his fantasies, he would embrace him. Tell him how much he'd inspired him. They'd share a beer and Max would share his deepest passions, and his grandfather would share his wisdom.

And now he didn't care if he never spoke to this man or saw him again. He might as well have been looking at a stranger, a dispensable background character in Max's story.

And he hated the Dark for that.

His grandfather lumbered up the porch steps. From the cabin's side window, a gold light flashed, the same color that Mr. Triman emitted when he cleaned up the coffee grounds and when he revealed the writing on the floorboards.

"Let's do this." Max started forward then stopped when two guards dragged a tall, athletic man from the helicopter. He was struggling to stand. His head lulled from side to side as if drunk.

He wasn't sure why, but he sniffed at the air like a wolf catching the scent of prey. In doing so, he discovered a faint smell of licorice. His mouth watered. This man also contained the Dark, but a trace amount. He was Robert. The one who went through the portal with Kali. Max now had both Dark-infected men in one place. He could drain them at the same time, but he needed to move.

His muscles hummed in response, as the Dark agreed with his decision to act now. It tugged on his chest, using an invisible chord that led him from the woods and across the lawn. He held up his hands while he approached. The Dark implored him to go straight to his grandfather, but Max forced his steps to take him to the guards, knowing that they would shoot him if he ran into the cabin.

He struggled to keep his arms lifted. His hands had increased in weight like they held heavy dumbbells. The Dark hated to show any weakness, least of all appearing to surrender.

Two guards—one short with slick black hair and the other tall with curly brown hair—stood in the center of the lawn away from the chopper. The shorter man noticed Max approaching them. He swung his rifle off his back. His partner followed suit.

"Halt!" the tall one shouted.

"This is private property. You're trespassing," the other said.

"No, I'm not. This is my property. I'm Maxwell Martin's grandson," he replied as if it didn't sound ridiculous that Martin's nearly thirty-year-old son could have a child who was thirty-two.

The two men shared an incredulous look. "Do you mean his son?"

"Grandson," Max stated again.

"On your knees," the nearest one ordered.

Max strained to lower himself to the ground. He was sure the guard thought he had an injury, seeing how stiff and hard his knees were to bend. The Dark ranted and rage. It didn't want to kneel in submission.

The shorter, stubbier guard felt along his torso and waist for weapons. He found Max's cell phone in his back pocket and held it up. "What's this?"

"A phone," Max replied.

Holding it up to the sunlight, they both squinted at it before tapping the screen. It lit up before fading to black.

"It's no phone I've ever seen," the dark-haired man said. "Could be a bomb."

"Who are you, and what is your purpose here?" The brunette kept his rifle level with Max's face but far enough away that he couldn't reach it.

"I'm Max Martin, your boss's grandson, and I'm here to meet with him. He's expecting me." Max laced his hands behind his neck. The Dark began whispering obscenities, urging Max to rip the rifle from the closest man's hands. Shoot the surrounding guards. Go on a rampage.

"Would it hurt if you ask? If he says I'm crazy, then you can arrest me or escort me from the property." Max managed to smile at them.

"He does resemble our boss a bit. Has his eyes," said the taller guard.

"You think everyone looks like someone. You said I looked like Squiggy from *Laverne and Shirley.*"

Max wanted to add that the guy did resemble the character, but based on his tone, he didn't appear happy with the comparison.

The Squiggy-looking guard strutted away and called over his shoulder to his friend, "Stay here. I'll check with Stockwell."

Max's blood pumped harder when he heard that name Stockwell.

Kill him.

Max forced out the bad breath, the bad thought. It whistled through his gritted teeth. But it only helped for a moment. Because when the guard reached the porch and Stockwell turned his attention to him, Max's mind replayed in cinematic detail this alt-traveler ripping him from his world and tossing him into a dark cell. Then came the conclusion that set every nerve on edge: Stockwell was responsible for trapping Kali and using her power. He was the reason Kali had left Max. He'd hurt her, locked her up, made her distrust—

"Stop it." Max gave his head a shake.

"What did you say?" The man's rifle lifted higher.

"You can stop pointing that weapon at me. I'm not going to do anything," Max said.

"That's right, you're not doing a thing."

Max twitched as the guard edged closer. So he wouldn't lunge at the man, Max laced his hands together so tightly his fingers had lost all feeling.

"Williams, put the gun down," Stockwell bellowed.

"Sir?" He lowered his weapon as Stockwell and Max's grandfather approached.

"Leave. Go stand over there. Guard the tree. Go take a piss. I don't care. Just go somewhere else." Stockwell swiped his hand toward the back of the house where a sprawling oak tree stood.

The guard trotted off.

His grandfather extended his hand to Max, hauled him up to his feet, and into a bear hug so tight Max's back cracked.

"So good to finally meet you," he whispered against his ear.

He sounded like Max's father but with a deeper, grainier tone, one that would be good for telling stories around the campfire. He'd heard his voice in old family movies and interviews and newsreels from his heyday. It was a comforting voice. That is, it used to be comforting to Max.

"You too." He patted his back.

For a moment, he meant it, because without warning, the dark tide receded, leaving him to indulge in a small piece of happiness at meeting his grandfather. The man who'd built the family business then turned his back on everything to pursue another life—a peaceful, meaningful life—before he left and ended up here with a not-so-peaceful one.

Where he killed a man, his doppelgänger, and stored the body in a box under a mattress. A mattress covered with a quilt most likely sewn by the dead man's mother like the ones stacked in the closet in Max's cabin.

"Let me look at you." Grandpa Martin stepped back and placed his hands on either side of Max's face.

"You have my eyes. Same color." He turned his face toward the sky. Max squinted against the bright sun.

He blinked when he noticed Max's ears. His fingers touched the hearing aids inside.

"You won't need these anymore." He removed them and tossed them to the ground.

His hands dropped to Max's arms. His eyes tracked over his grandson as if he were taking inventory and liked what he saw.

He broke out in a smile that somehow managed to appear both hungry and cheery. "You are a breath of fresh air. Just what the doctor ordered for this old soul."

Every word his grandfather spoke, every breath he took was crystal clear to Max's ears. The birds singing and the insects buzzing behind the house, the creak of the giant oak's branches from critters climbing across them. He'd never heard with such clarity without his hearing aids even before the accident.

He tried not to think too hard about what this could mean. Having his wounds heal from the journal's blast was one thing. Having his permanent hearing loss healed, took it to another level—a more frightening one.

He'd rejected transgenetic treatments for his hearing loss. The ear's functions were so delicate and intricate that doctors hadn't found a successful treatment that worked for all. Genetic remedies could alter him forever with adverse side effects, some tolerable and others that left damage worse than the malady.

His final drink from the bottle must've sealed his fate. With every passing hour, the Dark burrowed further into his cells, repairing his body, forging bonds with his chromosomes—merging with him.

Surefire was right. There was no going back from this.

"Come. Let's go inside." His grandfather slung a lean yet strong arm over Max's shoulder. "We have much to talk about. Plus, I have a groovy gift for you."

Chapter 27

Kali Left Hanging

Don't you dare feel sorry for him.

Kali chided her sentimental self when Max knelt in front of the two armed guards.

"Come on, move," Kali whispered as the men flanked Max, blocking him from her view.

She shimmied more to the right. One of the guards, who reminded her of a 1970s television character—Squiddy, was it?—walked out of sight to the front of the house.

Moments later, the slimy bastard Stockwell sauntered into view and shouted to the remaining man guarding Max. He waved his arm and pointed toward the back of the cabin.

Readjusting the rifle onto his back, the guard trotted toward the tree then changed course to the woods.

Kali let out the breath she'd been holding. That was too close. She shuffled her feet along the branch back to the window then stopped when a flash of off-white caught her eye. The Man was approaching Max in flowing linen pants and an old sweater. He pulled him to his feet and into a hug—and Max let him, returning the embrace with several pats on the back like they were old chums.

Her heart sunk. She was going to be ill or fall out of the tree.

Yep, the second one.

Her foot slipped. Her snow boots were not made for climbing.

"Whoa." Her long torso wavered to maintain balance. The branch she used for support snapped above her.

"Ack!" She tumbled, bracing herself to face plant onto the ground.

Instead she landed on an old mattress and a dusty quilt. Her power had kicked in. Finally.

She sneezed and coughed as a cloud of dust wafted around her. Two wasps flew through the open window. She slammed it shut. The nest had partially toppled during her fall. The insects made a beeline . . . or maybe a wasp line . . . to the guard at the edge of the forest where he had been peeing. The man swatted his hands. Another came to assist his friend and cursed as he got stung. Flailing their arms, they whirled around and sprinted to the chopper.

That was a happy accident. She liked it when a plan she didn't intend came together. Although she was stuck inside the cabin, and she didn't know how she accessed her power or how to do it again.

The front door creaked open. This time two sets of footsteps could be heard entering the living room.

Kali pressed against the headboard and slid off the mattress and to the floor, making herself as small as possible. She wasn't sure if she could crawl under the bed without making any noise. The pitched ceiling of the A-frame home carried sound like an echo chamber, which is why she could hear their conversation as if they were standing in the loft next to her.

The Man asked Stockwell to stay outside. He wanted to speak with his grandson in private. From the lawn, the guards continued to curse about the wasps stinging them. Stockwell told them to shut their pansy asses, and then the door closed and muffled his laughter.

A real winner that one.

The floor creaked as they made their way to the center of the room. Kali wanted to disappear. She wanted to pop out of there, but she also wanted to hear what they had to say. Would she learn the truth about Max? Understand what he was doing here, being so friendly with his grandfather—the Man—the one who had milked Kali's power like she was a prized transhuman heifer.

"Nana told everyone you were dead," Max said.

"Instructions I left for Lily, if I ever disappeared. Much easier to transfer assets and collect on insurance policies when it's official."

Kali strained forward to peer between the rails and over the edge. The floorboard under her palms let out a groan.

The footsteps paused along with the conversation. She froze. A few frantic heartbeats later Max said, "We received your message."

"So I see," the Man replied with a deep inhale.

"Mr. Triman told me what I needed to do to get here."

"Mr. Triman, huh? That's the name he chose this time around."

Based on the context of the conversation, Max and the Man were in the center of the living room near the couch where the Three had carved their message.

"He's on DERST's board and is a friend of my father. Growing up I vacationed with him and his family."

"Gabriel has a family? That is wild." The Man took a deep, wheezy breath. "I gather he told you about the Three."

"He mentioned that his sister and her spouses were trapped with you."

His grandfather snorted. "They're the reason I'm here."

"How?"

"They didn't stop me in time."

"Is the Dark talking to me, or are you still my grandfather?"

"It's not evil, Max. It's fate. It's a balancing force. Our universe is imbalanced. Gabriel and the Three and others like them have been keeping Earth alive, limping along on life support for years. The Dark is simply the farmer who burns his fields to create richer soil that leads to the rebirth of stronger crops—what the Earth sorely needs."

"I was told there would be no rebirth after this," Max said.

"Maybe not the rebirth of humans but of new life. You know it's true. I see by your face that you are struggling to come to terms with this knowledge, because you've inherited my tells. It's how I look when I struggle with a concept that goes against my beliefs. I want peace too. However, to have peace, things must die. In this case, humans. The Dark inside you agrees, doesn't it? Don't struggle, my boy, let it flow through your veins. Embrace the liberation and the power it brings."

The Dark inside you.

Kali gasped when the full revelation of this statement stung her with the pain from a hive full of wasps. She cupped her hand over her mouth to keep from shouting at Max, demanding if this was the truth, but his next words cinched it for her.

"I have the Dark under control, where it will stay until Mr. Triman drains it from me."

"You're lying. Like me, you're terrible at it. It's not a bad thing, but it can pose problems for others," the Man said before he raised his voice to call out, "Child, will you come out now that your lover is here?"

Kali pressed her hand tight over her mouth. She screwed her eyes shut to focus inward on waking up her power. She gave it a nudge then a kick. It stirred, threw the covers over its head, and burrowed deeper.

Gah, why isn't it working?

"Who's here?" Max asked, and Kali agreed with the Man on one thing: his grandson was a terrible actor. Even without looking him in the eye, Kali could tell he was lying. He knew she was there. The Three had said he'd make a sacrifice to save them. Their contingency plan. No wonder they never elaborated on the details if it meant Max had to drink the Dark to get here. Kali wouldn't wish that diseased oil on her worst enemy, let alone a backstabbing ex-boyfriend.

Which led to another enigma: If he was such a bad actor, how had he fooled her for so long into thinking that he cared for her?

Probably because she'd been so distracted dealing with her Evil Incident.

"I'm assuming she's the reason you came, and why you were willing to consume the Dark. This letter K," the Man said. "I'm certain Gabriel didn't carve those initials and the heart."

"She's no one," Max said.

Kali's bottom lip trembled. Just like before, she sensed he was lying. Her heart and brain were torn in two, unsure what to make of it.

"Then it won't matter if Stockwell drags her—"

"I'm here. No need to send that asshat after me." Kali clamored to her feet. She peeped over the railing. Max and his grandfather gazed up at her. One bemused, the other . . . what was he doing? Was Max signing to her? He had taught her some signs, but she couldn't remember any of them to save her life—literally.

The Man could be the dude's cousin from *The Big Lebowski*—shaggy salt-and-pepper hair, wooly cardigan over an off-white shirt, baggy linen pants, and sandals. Kali wanted to ask about his rug, but he'd left their universe years before the movie, so the reference would be wasted on him.

His grandfather gave Kali an idea of what Max would look like in thirty years—hair a little thinner, skin wrinkled around the mouth and eyes, jawline softer. But she didn't doubt that Max would look better than the Man when he reached this age. His features were more even, his face open and earnest. He didn't have the demeanor of a person or dark alien entity who thought nothing of using others for his own gain.

Then again, Max had used his looks and charm to deceive her.

Or had she painted him wrong? Because the way he'd handled the Man's questions proved to Kali that he couldn't lie his way out of a paper bag filled with holes.

"Kali, is it? Your friend Robert mentioned you." Hands shoved in his pockets, the Man rocked on his feet.

"He wasn't my friend." Kali squinted at Max, who had given up on the sign language and moved to mouthing, "sorry."

She set her lips and shook her head.

"Don't be a stranger. Join us." Grandpa Martin beckoned.

"I'm good up here." Kali leaned on the railing, attempting to appear nonchalant when every cell in her body wanted to run screaming from the cabin.

"I won't bite," he teased.

"Biting is not what I'm worried about." She pointed to Robert's carcass.

Max turned to take in the man-sized raisin and didn't appear as shocked as she thought he should have.

"It won't happen again. I can assure you," said the Man.

"Then you won't mind if I stay up here," she tossed back.

Don't show fear, she reminded herself. Sage advice for confronting angry dogs and—she was certain—evil alien beings.

"Let her be." Max touched the Man's shoulder.

He threw off his grandson's hand. "She needs to listen to her betters."

The Man leaped into the air. His body soared toward the ceiling like a helium balloon. A scream stuck in Kali's throat. She stumbled against the footboard and tumbled onto the mattress.

He floated in front of the loft, his arms held out to his sides as if he were balancing on a beam. But his aerial display wasn't the most shocking part. Empty black pits, where his eyeballs had been, gazed at her from a serene face. She crab-walked backward on the bed to get as much space between her and the floating man, and only stopped when her head hit the headboard.

This would be a good time for her power to kick in. But life was a bitch like that. When you truly wished for something to work, it didn't.

"Don't touch her." Max bounded up the loft stairs.

His grandfather floated toward the bed, his head inches from the ceiling. Max lunged and grabbed his legs, yanking him onto the mattress. Under their combined weight, the frame collapsed, and the bed pitched to the left. The chest under it kept one side from hitting the floor. Max and his grandfather rolled off in a tangle of limbs. Kali clutched the headboard to keep from landing on top of them.

Max wrenched his grandfather's arm behind him and planted a palm on the middle of his back. "You won't do anything to her ever again."

She gasped at Max's voice that had dropped several octaves. His eyes had darkened as well, not fully black like his grandfather's but a watered-down shade of gray.

She scrambled over the toppled mattress and sprinted to the stairs.

From behind her came a crash. She spun on the second step to find the chifforobe splintered and Max sprawled in its debris.

His grandfather planted his feet in front of Max as she lost her grip on the railing. Her thick snow boots caught on the risers, she tripped. Arms helicoptered to keep from falling. Her power kicked in and she found herself lying on the couch.

"Neat trick, luv." Stockwell appeared over her. He grabbed her upper arm and dragged her from the couch.

The Man floated to the floor with the grace of an aerialist suspended by wires, except nothing she could see held him aloft. Max groaned from under the pile of wood and clothes. Stockwell pulled her toward the Man.

"I thought your power was gone." His black eyes scanned her face as if searching for a clue.

"Comes and goes," she said.

The Man pinched her chin. "Tell me the truth, or I'll resort to other measures, which may or may not kill you."

He drew closer as if for a kiss. She bucked against his fingers squeezing her jaw. She wanted to scream, but an inner voice ordered her to keep quiet for once.

His mouth formed an "o" shape followed by a sucking sound. The air seemed to disappear around her, drawn inside his gaping void of a mouth. She struggled to breathe through her nose.

Black specks floated in front of her eyes from this vacuum forming inches from her face. The Man pried her mouth open by wedging his fingers and thumb into her cheeks until it felt like his nails would rip through her skin. The sucking sound filled her ears. Air from her lungs whistled past her teeth. Her knees buckled. The Man held her aloft by her jaw, Stockwell by her arm.

Then the sucking stopped. The Man let go. His gray eyebrows arched. "You're the real deal."

A smile stretched his lips under his scruffy beard. The oily ink coating his eyes slithered away, revealing muddy gray-green eyes. He laid a hand on her stomach.

She wrenched back, banging her head into Stockwell's jaw. Uttering a curse, the Aussie held her in place.

A heavy object thudded against the floor behind the Man. Stockwell released her arm. Her legs buckled, dropping her onto the braided rug. She gulped at the air as if she'd been drowning.

The recliner tipped over, followed by another thud. This time she was certain the sound came from a body slamming onto the floor. She looked up to find Stockwell sprawled out and Max holding the Man in a chokehold.

A zap then a pop echoed in the room. She smelled burning fabric, hair, and flesh. The Man moaned and slumped into a heap near the kitchen table. Over him, Max held a small square weapon. His eyes were now as dark as his grandfather's had been.

Kali continued to shake, unsure whether it was in shock or fear from having her life force suckled or seeing the Dark possessing Max. However, even with the demon-colored eyes, his face displayed peace, where she felt it should be contorted in fury to match the fierceness with which he'd fought.

"You okay?" He growled, and this primal sound froze her like a scared bunny confronted with the Big Bad Wolf.

Chapter 28

Reunited

She gave Max the barest of nods, her brown eyes so large she could be an anime drawing.

The Dark slithered under his skin, aroused by her fear.

Or maybe not only her fear. His grandfather lay unconscious by his feet. Ripe for the reaping.

He forced his feet to step across the room away from his grandfather. The further he walked from the unconscious man, the more he gained control over his movements. Kali pressed herself against the couch as he stalked past her. A part of him wanted to hold her, tell her that he was there to save her. That he was ashamed of what she'd found in his basement. If time wasn't important, he'd fall to his knees to beg for her forgiveness for not being honest with her. But the part of him that was being strangled by the Dark found pride in making her squirm. His mouth twitched, wanting to grin. He chewed on his bottom lip to stop it.

He reached the cabinet in the corner and removed the green bottle and alien dagger from inside.

Drain him and take the power for yourself.

Max ignored the voice as he hurried to his grandfather's prone body. He kicked him onto his back and straddled him.

Take the power. You deserve it.

Max fitted the bottle onto the knife as Mr. Triman had shown him.

Take his power. Use it to protect Kali.

He pressed his palms against his eyes. The Dark was worming its way into his brain, making up lies to control him.

"What are you doing?" Kali asked.

He couldn't face her. He was afraid to see the pain in her voice reflected in her face, and that would stop him from doing what he needed to do.

The thing that claimed to be his grandfather moaned and attempted to roll away. He backhanded him.

Kali stifled a cry.

"Look away." He wrapped his hands around the handle. The letters glowed with a dull light.

"Max," she whispered.

"Look away," he repeated, then lifted the knife in an arc above his head. His body shook with the effort to do it.

"Max!"

"It's the only way."

The Man lifted his arm to block the blow.

"Drop that knife if you don't want your girl missing a brain," Stockwell ordered.

Twisting around, Max found the Man's henchman pressing the barrel of his gun against Kali's head.

* * * * * * * * * * * * * *

Why, oh, why wouldn't her power work when she needed it?

As Stockwell pressed a gun against her head, Kali dug deep again. It kicked up a pile of dust then petered out. Times like these, she wished her power came with an instruction booklet.

With the blade raised above his head about to strike, Max turned to them. The black layer covering his eyes receded. His arms trembled as if fighting with himself to release the blade.

"Max, if this is what you need to do, then do it. Don't worry about me," Kali said because she was supposed to say that, even if she was shaking down to her snow boots, because Stockwell wouldn't hesitate to kill her. He was that kind of bloke.

"A brave one, aren't you?" the Aussie chided, not buying her faux bravado.

She pressed against the scratchy sofa cushion to distance her head from his gun's barrel. That's when she noticed something that gave her pause. His revolver wasn't cocked and the visible chambers were empty.

Prying his hands from the blade, Max dropped it to his side. He rose to face them. The black muck had cleared from his eyes, returning to his normal gray.

The Man remained on the floor with his legs bent. The kitchen clock ticked off several seconds before he lifted his upper body and placed his head between his knees. His muscles spasmed. His limbs twitched. When he raised his head, dark circles lined his eyes. Cheeks were sunken. Tan skin the color of ash.

Using an oak chair for leverage, the Man hefted himself up. He rotated his shoulders, causing a few pops. The back of his sweater and shirt sported a torso-wide hole with the edges singed. His exposed flesh was red and raw.

"Well, my boy, that was a fun tussle." He gave a wheezy laugh, and he put out his hand to Max. "The Triskele Dagger and my prison, please."

Max shot a look from Stockwell's gun aimed at Kali to his grandfather, who took the hint. "Put the gun down. My grandson will cooperate."

His henchman backed off, but he stayed close to Kali. Max handed over the knife and bottle.

"The Dark hasn't seen its old abode in a long time." The Man removed the bottle from the metal ring, which snapped back into place. He raised the bottle to the sunlight streaming in from the windows and peered into it.

"It's empty." He shook it. "You're going to want more."

"I want this sick mess out of me." Hands fisted, Max stood astride with his feet firm on the floor.

"It's a powerful aphrodisiac. You'll miss the high soon enough."

"Never."

"We'll see." The Man handed off the dagger and bottle to Stockwell, who then handed them off to a guard outside the door. Kali watched as the man on the porch placed them in an olive green knapsack.

To her chagrin, Stockwell didn't leave but returned to her side.

"As you requested, I'm here." Max extended his arms. "Let Kali go home."

"Go home? And how would she get home?" The Man chuckled and Stockwell joined in on the joke, even though his half-hearted attempt made it appear that he was only laughing because his boss was.

"She's blocked," the Man replied when Max grew silent.

He shuffled over to Kali where she remained on the floor in front of the sofa, wishing they'd forgotten she was there.

"What do you know about my lack of mojo?" she asked.

The Man lowered himself on the couch with a groan. "When you came through that portal, your power was temporarily siphoned. As you know, stronger energy feeds off the weaker one."

"The Three told me as much. And that this Dark energy inside you is stronger than I'll ever be. I saw what you can do . . . thank you very much . . . and I really wish I'd brought a change of underwear," Kali sputtered.

The Man chuckled and slapped his knee. "Oh, you're a riot."

"Glad I amuse you," she murmured.

"You always did."

"Excuse me?" Kali blinked at him.

"Don't think that I didn't remember you from the time before."

The blood drained from her face. She felt Max's eyes on her. Heard him approach then stop when Stockwell shifted his bulk between them. But she couldn't raise her eyes to look at him. If she did so, she was going to cry.

"You fought me that time. You refused to help. I had to use Stockwell to do what the Dark needed. But he wasn't up for the task. Were you Stockwell?"

"Sir?"

Kali's ears pricked up. In that one word, she sensed a crack in Stockwell's hard exterior. An uncertainty or maybe it was fear.

Fingering the handle of a knife clipped to his belt, Stockwell locked eyes with the Man.

The Man licked his lips. "When I tasted her essence now, I confirmed she was the one who'd been here before. Who I had a PA about."

"PA?" Kali interjected.

"Psychic Alert. Flashes of the future," he clarified. "When we detected the portal opening in Utah, I assumed it may have been you and was disappointed when I found only that." He waved at Robert's husk.

"My memories have been spotty about the time before the reset," the Man said. "But Kali's cleared up my static. Stockwell, you made a mistake when you travelled to the other universe, enabling her to save her other self and causing both universes to reset."

"Is that so?" Stockwell's left hand wrapped around the handle of his knife.

"Now don't get your panties in a bunch. You didn't do it on purpose. It was your first foray into dimensional travel. You get a pass this time."

"Thank you, sir," Stockwell replied, yet he didn't remove his hand from the weapon.

The Man shrugged. "We learn from mistakes, and we won't be making that one again."

"No, we won't," Stockwell replied.

Kali started to shake as the meaning of his words sunk in. The couch became her lifeline. She dug her fingers into its cushion to tether herself to the here and now. But she couldn't stop the images of that fluid-filled coffin from carrying her to places she never wanted to go again.

"You won't do that to Kali this time," Max said. "I won't let you."

Max closed in on the Man. Stockwell shoved him back.

"Even if her power was working, she can't return with me anyway," the Man said. "The Dark's energy negates her own unless it's contained, which I'd learned through trial and error last time. I'm sure Gabriel told you what needs to be done."

"He did," Max replied, and it finally dawned on Kali what needed to happen to Max for him to return home. The Dark inside him needed to be contained as well. That dagger needed to puncture his chest to neutralize the alien energy.

"Holy shit," she whispered.

"Holy shit, indeed. You didn't see that coming, did you?" The Man smirked. "But I did see my offspring infected by this force. It's why I tried to trap the Dark here before I finally saw the light . . . or the darkness rather."

"You foretold the future in that journal," Kali said, recalling the images and names that she could discern from the shifting language.

"My PAs strengthened when I tasted the Dark. But links to the future are constantly in flux. Without being in my universe, the ability has diminished.

But I predicted a few accurate things with the Dark's help, like you." He ruffled Kali's head.

She jerked back and into Stockwell's leg.

"I knew Hugh, your father," he continued. "He lived on my commune with his family—your actual one, not the alternate version you use as a stand in. He was one of the brightest kids I'd ever met."

There were no words Kali could form to say what she felt in hearing this revelation from him. Max's grandfather had known her father. Her real father from their universe.

Max had shared with Kali that his grandfather had studied the metaphysical. He'd traveled the world, learning from various gurus and living with New Age groups. Max had also mentioned that he left DERST and his family behind to purse a peaceful existence. He never said anything about a commune even when she told him about her father and grandparents living on one for a few years.

"Is this where I traveled to visit my father? Well, this universe's version of my father," said Kali.

"Yes." The Man grinned like a cat who not only ate the canary but every bird in his yard.

Which led her to a question that she didn't want to ask, afraid of the answer. "What did you do to the people living here?"

"Don't worry, your father in this universe will go on to great things. In fact, already has. His education is being funded by DERST. He'll make an excellent addition to our R&D department."

"No, that's not right. That's not the path he followed. He was the youngest physics professor at MIT and formed his own consulting firm that worked with NASA."

"So? This isn't your universe. The paths can be different here."

She shook her head because that wasn't right. When she'd traveled to 1998 in this universe, she'd been curious about transhumans. Did they exist in here? It was around that time when her bosses had first met. Ten years later, they'd form the foundation for UltraSecurity, after some humans developed special powers from TransGen treatments and from underground genetic tests. Crimes committed by transhumans began to occur. The police force needed help, and U-Sec provided backup for them.

But in this universe, transhumans didn't exist. Rumors of people with special abilities—like those with telekinesis or mind reading powers—were written off as frauds. Her boss Sean died as a child. The technology never developed to help him live. Gloria was interning with a team of researchers decoding DNA for Johns Hopkins. Pax had been killed while deployed in Afghanistan.

And Kali's alternate-world father was still alive. His early path was the same as in Kali's universe before his heart gave out. In this one, he worked on the SETI program. He wrote for magazines and lectured on dimensional theories and space travel.

He didn't work for DERST. Ever.

"You're screwing with lives," Kali said.

"I might as well move the game pieces to work in my favor. This universe had no chance in keeping the same path after I entered it, let alone after you reset it. There are ripples, consequences for your actions as well, missy."

Kali held her head in her hands. He was right. That future most likely had changed.

But there was a chance it didn't. There was a chance that what she saw in 1998 was after all this happened, and it turned out all right.

Then again . . . even the greatest minds had trouble unraveling the paradoxes of time travel.

"This is a total nightmare," she said.

"No, it's an opportunity," the Man said.

Holding back tears, she lifted her head. "I'm assuming my real father back in our universe didn't know about this thing inside you."

"No, he couldn't have. The last I saw him, he was running off to set the table for dinner."

"No one ever told me about my family's ties to you." She scowled at Max, who gave her blank look as if he didn't know what she meant.

"I feel like all this is a cruel coincidence." Turning from Max, she stared at her hands clasped tightly in her lap, as if they held an answer to this mess.

"It's no coincidence," the Man said with conviction. "Your father, along with his parents, were brought to my commune for a reason. A cosmic force bound them here."

"The Dark?" Kali offered with a snort.

He gave her a condescending smile. "No, not the Dark. It wouldn't have wanted that. In fact, it would've stopped them and destroyed the children living there if I hadn't spirited it away. Although knowing what I know now, I should've let it. The Dark has lifted the veil and allowed me to see the truth."

"Which is?" Kali prodded.

"That humans' time has come to an end."

"I won't let that happen." Black oil slithered across Max's eyes.

"You will come around soon enough as the Dark melds with you. You have potential. As my heir, I want you at my side and your child protected."

"I don't have any children," said Max.

The Man turned to Kali.

Instinctively, her hands went to her belly. "Why are you looking at me?"

She and Max had had sex . . . before Christmas and then after and then the day after that and then . . . oh, crap . . . had she forgotten her birth control pills during any of this?

"I felt its life force when I tasted your essence," he said.

"No, it's too soon. You don't know this for sure." Above her, Max and Stockwell stood with mouths hanging open in shock. Rising from the couch, the Man closed up the semicircle and grinned under his shaggy beard.

"Boss? What are you saying?" Stockwell said, and Kali didn't know why he would sound worried. He didn't just find out he'd potentially (if the thing wasn't lying) be a parent.

"It's the other reason her power is sporadic. The fetus is blocking it. It's using your energy to grow."

Kali doubled over, clutching her stomach. The room spun like one of those hateful carnival rides—the Scrambler—on which she'd vomited over her first boyfriend. She wasn't sure if it was the realization that she was going to be a mother or that the Man admitted to tasting her essence, which sounded both vulgar and intimate.

"It seems to be growing quicker than a normal fetus," he said.

Kali winced at the word "normal." Did that mean what was growing—err, potentially growing—inside her was abnormal?

"As I mentioned before," the Man continued, seemingly not noticing or not caring that Kali was a word away from a panic attack, "the stronger power feeds on the weaker one."

"You're lying!" she spat, even though it felt like the truth. It felt right. It was one explanation for why she'd been feeling off for the past few mornings. Why her power came in fits and spurts unable to recover from the portal's power suck. Any available energy went to feeding another's body and not her own.

She scrambled to her feet and onto the couch. Her only escape route from the three pairs of eyes judging her, watching her, waiting for . . . She wasn't sure what they were waiting for her to do, and she didn't care. She crawled over the back of the sofa and leaped over a small table, knocking photos and knickknacks to the floor.

She sprinted to the front door as fast as she could while doubled over. She needed air. The cabin was too stuffy and oppressive, her body too hot and sweaty. She tore open the door and stumbled onto the porch. The afternoon sun threw the forest into shade. She wanted to run through the trees and keep running until she couldn't breathe, couldn't see, and then maybe she'd awake from this terrible dream.

But she was trapped. Five men from his private army formed a semicircle around the porch. Two lifted their guns. The rest settled their hands on their holsters.

She leaned on the porch banister and gulped at the air, so much cooler and fresher than inside the cabin.

The door slammed open behind her. Arms enclosed her and turned her around, forcing her against a warm shoulder. Tears streamed down her face. Max smoothed a hand down her hair and rocked her.

He hushed her and kissed her cheek. In his arms, she forgot about the Man and the Dark—ridiculous name, really?—and how Max's eyes had been coated with the gross oil. She pictured herself back in his home, sleeping in his arms on Christmas day. Could they ever return to that peaceful bliss?

Unfortunately, she knew the answer.

Nothing good ever lasted for an UltraAgent. Eventually, a Big Bad would turn everything to shit—and she just met hers and lost the first battle.

"Don't touch me," she said, coming to her senses. She wouldn't be tricked into the safety of his arms again.

She threw off his hands. When she touched him, her power churned, kicked in, and they disappeared into the in-between.

Chapter 29

Stuck in the In-Between

She tried. Oh, did Kali try to break through the dimensional wall to go back to her universe. She shoved and pushed into the membrane, pliable but unbroken, like the wall of a womb—an apt analogy considering her current bodily state, if the Man was to be believed.

She shot a look at Max's hand on her wrist. His arm stretched out like a rubber band from his body, which had stretched so much, she could barely make out his white-haired head. The crystal skull she'd released in the void colored the grayish space an electric blue. She considered releasing Max as she had the skull, to see if the Dark inside him was the reason she couldn't push through to her universe. But she couldn't do it. She couldn't leave him to float in nothingness, no matter what he'd done or planned to do or had become with that alien goop in him.

She sensed her power fading. The adrenaline fueling it turning to fumes. It wasn't just the Dark inside Max. It was her. She was being blocked. Her power siphoned as if she was being forced to stay.

Kali turned them around, surging back into the alternate universe with Max in tow. In her subconscious she must've pictured the happy place her alt-grandparents had taken her when she'd visited them. A boulder materialized under her feet. The scent of spring water, fresh dirt, and leaves filled her lungs. Water gurgled over rocks. She wrenched her hand from Max and knelt next to the cool stream. Scooping up a handful of water, she splashed it on her face and neck and poured it over her head, letting it soak her hair.

Max's rubber soles shuffled against the rocky surface. He sank to the ground with a grunt. "That one made me sicker than usual."

"Probably that alien goo inside you." She wiped her face with the bottom of her tank top.

"Probably," he said.

She hazarded a glance at Max sitting a few feet from her, his arm resting on one bent leg, the other leg stretched out. The sides of his head shaved with thick white hair cresting on top like a wave. A few strands fell against his forehead. She wanted to push them back. She wanted his arms to wrap around her and hold her, because she needed comfort, someone to tell her it would be okay.

"I screwed up," Max said.

Kali snorted. "Big time. I can't believe you drank that stuff."

"Not that. I did that to save you."

Oh, he did not just go there. "Don't put this on me."

"I'm not putting anything on you. Just let me say this, okay? Because I don't know if I'll be able to say it later."

Whether it was his sincerity that cracked her resolve or her curiosity or both, Kali said, "Go on."

"I had no clue your friends would be hurt by that TPC. I certainly didn't consider how it could be used on you, until you told me what happened with S-Kali."

She kept her eyes focused on her blurry reflection in the water. She didn't want to look at Max and see how truly sorry he was. She wanted to hold onto this anger longer because it was the one thing that kept her grounded, fueled her focus.

"I'm sorry," he continued when she wanted him to shut up. "I should've told you."

"Yeah, you should've." She hauled herself onto her feet so he wouldn't see the tears leaking from her eyes.

"And why didn't tell me that your grandfather headed a commune? The same one where my family used to live?" She spun around. Her boots kicked up water, splashing him with it.

He held up his arm against the watery assault. "I didn't know it was the same one. I thought your father was from California."

"He was born there, but his parents moved to Maryland when his father got a job with the government." Where he probably met Max's grandfather and was recruited to the commune. "Their picture was next to our bed with them standing in front of the cabin on your property."

Max shrugged. "I didn't recognize the cabin. By the time my father took me there, they'd renovated the structures and leased the camp to the Boy Scouts."

Kali shook her head, annoyed that he could keep this important fact from her.

"Listen, my parents didn't want me talking about what my grandfather had done. I only found out about the commune when I discovered his journals. My father was and is still angry with my grandfather for abandoning the family and stepping away from DERST and leaving him to run it. The Board sought to preserve DERST's reputation, and a peacenik founder doesn't exactly scream defense contractor so our family kept it secret."

"How many more secrets are you keeping from me?" Kali demanded.

"That's all. I swear. I will tell you anything you want to know from now on. I'll be an open book." Max raised his hands.

"Never mention the word *book* again."

Above the trees, a helicopter darted past then circled back. She sent her feelers into her gut. Her power churned then sputtered like an engine with a starter that was spent.

"Dammit." Her power was tapped out by the accidental jump and maybe pregnancy—the jury was still out on that—so she went with a long-shot option and trudged up the hill toward the campsite, hoping against hope that the cabins were still there.

"Where are you going?" Max scrambled to his feet.

"Home," she said, then added under her breath, "my second one."

If she was about to die or get captured or whatever the Man had planned, then she was going to see her home-away-from-home one last time.

Her feet were squishy from the sweat pooling in her wool-lined boots. Although she hated the sensation, she trekked forward, sliding every now and then on the wet leaves. Her boots were not made for hiking either.

"Be careful," Max said when her foot slid and she tipped sideways. Her shoulder banged into a tree trunk.

"As if I'm purposefully trying to harm myself. Are you afraid I may hurt myself, then you can't use me to get home?" She stomped into the clearing where dozens of small cabins circled a screened-in mess hall cluttered with picnic tables.

"I never wanted to hurt you."

"Could've fooled me."

He was close on her snow-booted heels as they passed the large fire pit overgrown by weeds and surrounded by boards overlaying tree stumps, creating rustic benches.

The helicopter circled again. Men shouted and leaves rustled in the distance.

She stopped in front of the cabin where her alternate grandparents had lived.

"I had just learned about your friends being imprisoned in one of DERST's TPCs. I wanted to tell you the day before you left and then we got distracted with . . . you know . . . and then you finally opened up about what happened in the other universe, and I couldn't bring myself to upset you more and—"

"Then it's my fault you didn't tell me?" She twisted the doorknob. It wouldn't budge.

"That's not what I meant."

"*Hmph.*" She cupped her hands over her eyes and peered into the dirty window. Furniture was toppled and broken, dishes shattered on the floor.

"Kali, I care for you. More than anyone I've ever known. I won't keep anything from you again. I promise."

She moved to the side of the cabin, picking her way through overgrown vines and poison ivy to get to another window. Max trailed her like a sad puppy. Good thing she was a cat person. She wasn't falling for it.

Using the bottom of her tank top, she rubbed the dirt away from the bedroom window.

"Oh, no." She stumbled back. Her hand pressed against her mouth.

"What is it?" Max steadied her when her boot rolled over a piece of wood and her knee buckled.

"They're dead. Shriveled up like Robert." She was so distracted by this discovery that she didn't notice Max's arms wrapping around her from behind, drawing her against his chest until his heart thudded against her back.

He squeezed her, at first comforting and then becoming tighter and tighter. Her back cracked.

"Max, that hurts."

With a grunt, he let her go. His eyes were no longer gray with flecks of green but muddy, like tarnished silver.

"You're freaking me out, going all Vader on me." She willed herself not to shrink back from the force contorting his handsome face into a monstrous mask—a hard thing to do when the evil aura slathering his body made her want to run and never look back.

"Kali to Max." She held up her hand and snapped her fingers. "What's going on? Is it the Dark?"

He nodded. His face clenched along with his fists.

"It keeps trying to take over." He rubbed his temples. "It whispers things. Horrible things it wants me to do."

His head wagged from side to side, like he was trying to get rid of a bug dive-bombing his ears. She narrowed her eyes when she noticed his ears no longer held his cybernetic hearing aids.

"You can hear?" she asked.

"Only good thing about it. It repairs any bodily damage. It wants its vessel as perfect as possible."

She cringed when Max uttered "vessel." The bitch goddess used that word when describing Synthia, reducing her from a human being to an object that the goddess could fill and possess at will.

"Why did you ingest that evil oil?"

"To save you."

"Why?"

"Why do you think?" His face softened. Eyes cleared of the dark oil blinked back tears and stared at her as if she was the most precious thing to him, more precious than his own life.

A lump formed in Kali's throat. Either she was going to be sick or cry or both. The Three had told her that Max was their last resort, but she wouldn't have guessed that he'd sell his soul to do it and least of all to save her.

"Surefire warned me this would happen," he said.

"Surefire?" Kali asked then remembered how Dara said her friend was helping Max.

"She and Raven came to me after you disappeared into the journal. With the help of a family friend—"

"The Three's . . . Dara's brother?" Kali interrupted, piecing it together.

"He never told me his sister's name, but, yeah, the Three. He's been trying to get them back home for decades."

"And this family friend"—she accentuated "friend" as if it were a made-up word because why would a friend encourage Max to do this—"told you to drink the Dark?"

"He suggested it. Reluctantly. They tried to dissuade me from doing it, but I wouldn't leave you to face this alone. You saved me. I owe you my life and so much more."

She dropped her gaze to the ground covered in leaves and ivy and broken branches. She wanted to stay angry with him. Anger kept her focused.

Get hold of yourself. Don't forget that he never told you the truth.

He wasn't tricking her. There was sincerity in his words that he couldn't fake. Not too many could. Her reality star mother, yes, which is why Kali could spot emotional manipulation from across a bedazzled and camera-lined room, and why she'd been so blindsided by Max's betrayal.

The sounds of leaves crunching caught her attention. The Man's guards were closing in. The helicopter looped by once more.

"We need to stop the Dark from doing that"—he stabbed a finger toward the cabin—"to anyone else."

"With that bottle and blade?"

"We plunge it into my grandfather's chest and drain the Dark into the bottle. We then use his body to open the portal."

They'd reached the edge of the campsite. Stockwell ordered his men to fan out and search the mess hall and outer cabins. It wouldn't be long until they searched through the first group and found them standing between last cabins.

"But we have to neutralize the Dark inside you first," Kali said. "The Three kind of explained it." She furrowed her brow. "Not in detail, mind you, but an alien *Cliff Notes* version of it. The Dark can't enter our world inside your body without being neutralized, otherwise, its power will grow too fast."

"I know," Max said.

"Do you really?" She blew out breath. "Because you'll need to turn the dagger on yourself."

He nodded.

"Then how do we get it out of you?" she asked.

"Gabriel might be able to do it when we get back."

"Might? That's insane."

"They may need to leave it in me."

"Even more insane."

Max drew close, and this time Kali didn't shrink from his touch. He placed his hands on her shoulders. She held his eyes when he said in a hushed tone, "If you have a chance to leave, you take it. Forget about me. You save yourself."

"Max, I don't know if I'm pregnant."

He shook his head. "That's not why I'm saying it. Besides, that thing lies, it manipulates. Trust me."

He cupped her cheek. His lips close to hers as he said, "Kali, I love you. I need to say it now in case I don't get another chance."

"Stop." The floodgates opened. An ugly cry racked her whole body.

As she tried and failed to stop sobbing, he cradled her against his shoulder. "I've never said that to anyone besides my family."

"Don't do this to me." Her emotions were stretched to their limit as if they were stuck in the in-between. Max confessing he was sorry, he loved her, he drank the Dark for her was too much to take in.

"I'd rather you live than me."

"Don't say that!" She slammed her palms into his chest. "Don't ever say that." She pushed him again. "We're in this together. Do you think I want you to die?"

Max did a slow blink as if it took a few beats for her words to sink in. When they did, he smiled at her. Relief softened his eyes and relaxed his shoulders. He knew she felt the same.

"Over here," a man shouted.

Kali and Max whirled around to face the speaker who held a rifle and was joined by another rifle slinging man.

"You know what to do, mates." Stockwell rolled up behind them.

Before Kali could utter a word, a wasp stung her neck. She reached up expecting to find a dead insect, but came away with a small dart. A drop of blood coated her fingertips and the needle.

Her knees shook. Her arms flopped at her sides. The numbing sensation spread up to her neck, then to her face. She tried to keep her eyes open as the world spun like a kaleidoscope.

She was vaguely aware of Max catching her and easing her to the soft ground. He spoke her name, but she couldn't form a reply.

"What did you do?" Max launched to his feet. His legs blocked her view of the shooter.

The spinning world funneled into blackness. A gunshot echoed in the void.

* * * * * * * * * * * * * *

Stockwell took a wide stance behind the guards, his hands resting on both holsters. He rocked on the balls of his feet. "She can't take you anywhere now."

Max leaped at the smirking man. He'd rip the lips from his face. The men fired off dart after dart into Max. They struck him in his chest and arm. He batted away another. He tore the rifle from the man on his left then swung it at him like a bat. It cracked against the mercenary's cheek. A tooth shot out from his bloodied mouth as he hit the ground. Max whirled on the balls of his feet, moving faster than the other guard could shoot. He slammed the rifle's butt into the man's chest, knocking the wind from him and slamming him down.

He tossed the rifle aside and strode to Stockwell. His palms itched for the feel of his neck crushed under them.

The Aussie had both weapons out but hesitated on taking the shot. Max's grandfather appeared between them.

"She'll be fine. She's only sleeping." A sliver of oil slithered over his eyeballs.

Max lunged at his grandfather. His hands wrapped around the elder man's neck.

Drink his essence.

His grandfather's eyes rolled back into his head. His mouth formed an "o" shape. Max inhaled to drink . . . drink . . . drink . . . as the voice became a chorus of chants ordering him to consume the senior's life force.

Stockwell rammed his shoulder into Max's side. Arms snaked around his neck, locking together to form a chokehold. But the Dark gave Max the strength of ten Stockwells. The lead henchman might as well be a toddler trying to tackle his father.

A needle jabbed Max's side. Whatever it contained was more potent than the darts, two of which stuck from his torso. Lava burned through his system. His fingers released his grandfather's neck. His arms and legs quaked like Jell-O until he couldn't support his own weight. He toppled onto his grandfather.

"That'll do you," Stockwell said between huffs of breath as he kicked Max off his boss.

Green leaves and the blue cloudless sky swirled together like paint on a palette. Max couldn't move his limbs or his head. He was paralyzed.

"I'd hoped it wouldn't come to this." His grandfather coughed from the ground beside him. "I assumed Robert would've satiated me for a while, but that weapon of yours took a toll on me, and the Dark inside you is strong. It wants to reunite in one body. I can feel it pulling on my essence even now."

"You need to stay away from him. It's too much for you, sir," Stockwell said.

"I know, but it's not too much for *his* body to take. It's now or never. We need to prep my grandson."

Max couldn't move his lips to ask what his grandfather meant. He drifted into a nightmarish sleep of nothingness.

And that's exactly what the Dark wanted him to become.

Nothing.

Chapter 30

Kali in a Happy Place

Kali tilted her face to the sun's rays streaming through the trees. Their warmth blanketed her skin. Refreshing water trickled between her toes. She lifted her arms, longing to hug the trees, hug the air, hug the stream cascading over mossy rocks. It was all so perfect, and she was perfectly content. She didn't want this feeling to ever end.

Feet splashed in the water behind her. She squealed in surprise when Max's arms caught her around the waist. He scooped her up and kissed her. His lips soft against her own, she wanted to melt into them.

He carried her from the water and lowered her onto a bed of moss. He planted a trail of kisses down her throat.

"I love you," he whispered and she'd never get tired of hearing him say that. His breath tickled her ear. She giggled at the sweet sensation.

She would do anything for him in this moment. Because in this dream, Max wasn't infected with the nasty alien goo. His possessed evil grandpa didn't exist. The TPC in his workshop never existed.

Only the two of them existed.

He stared at her like she was the most precious thing he'd ever seen. "I need to say it, because I need you to know it's true."

She framed his face with her hands. Her thumbs caressed his cheeks, prickly with morning stubble.

"Okay." Tears stung her eyes. "I believe you."

Stretching out by her side, he draped his arm across her stomach. She snuggled into his bare chest, running her fingers over the smattering of springy white hair. She drew in a breath and drew in a scent of leaves and soil and the spicy cologne he wore that made her mouth water. He laced his fingers with hers.

Something splashed in the stream at her back, big enough for a few droplets to land on her bare arm.

A young boy cried, "Mom!"

She snuggled closer to Max. He squeezed her hand.

"Mom," the boy cried again, "that's not Dad."

"What?" Kali rolled over to see who this child was.

But instead of a boy, she saw the edge of a bed covered in a cream and blue quilt.

"Have a nice snooze, luv?"

She threw her legs off the bed, but her upper body didn't follow. Instead, her shoulder jerked back with a crack. Stockwell was squeezing her hand. A steel cuff would be less painful and definitely less sweaty.

"No going anywhere until you know the rules." His sun-worn face broke into a grin.

Being this close and personal, she noticed his scars, which had criss-crossed his cheeks and neck and disappeared under his shirt when she'd last seen him in her universe, were absent. The reset must've changed whatever accident had occurred to wound him like that. Or those scars were from failed attempts at fitting him for the alt-traveling pack, its tubes having been fused into his skin.

She considered her options, which were slim to none, for escaping this cozy bedroom that could pass for a room at any grandparents' home. A cherry armoire matching the bed's headboard and footboard loomed between two closed doors. To her left across Stockwell's legs, a powder-blue Queen Anne armchair, with white doilies over the arms, sat empty between windows hung with lacy cream curtains and roll-up shades. Matching nightstands held more doilies with a windup alarm clock on the one and a Tiffany-style—or maybe a real one?—lamp on the other near a door to her right. A painting of Great Falls from the Virginia side hung on the wall next to another door, which she assumed led to a hallway.

But she couldn't confirm it with Stockwell's hand glued to her own.

"Where am I?" she asked.

"At the Man's home in McLean, Virginia."

"Oh."

The effects of the drug that knocked her out still lingered. She was grateful for her hazy brain and hazier emotions, because they kept her from full-blown panic when he confirmed that they were at her nemesis's house.

Her heart didn't beat out of her chest in fear. She didn't scream and wail at Stockwell to get away. Instead, she sat there, taking in one calm breath after another with a single thought: *I'm so screwed.*

She sought out her power. Only a smoky tendril remained in her core where it usually resided.

Stockwell continued to sprawl on the other side of the bed, his back propped against the polished headboard. He was fully clothed in his fatigues and button-up shirt and fully armed. Only the green beret he'd worn earlier was missing. A *Ms.* magazine lay open on his lap, which didn't shock her as much as it should've. The needle on her shock meter had broken hours ago.

Kali perched on the edge of the bed, her arm extended behind her at an awkward angle. Stockwell wasn't giving her any slack.

"How did I get here?" She smoothed a palm over her bed head.

"The chopper."

"How long was I out?"

"About five hours. It's almost time for dinnies."

"Have you been holding my hand this whole time?"

"Don't think I'm sweet on you. It's so you don't get cheeky and leave us."

She rubbed her right eye then her left. A nervousness scratched at her gut. The more the drug's effects receded the more awake and aware she became. The fog muddying her brain lifted enough for her to realize an important prop was missing from this scene.

"Where's Max?"

"In another part of the house. We'll see him soon."

A soft throbbing had begun between her eyes, which was sure to turn into a migraine-level pounding if she didn't hydrate.

"I need water." She rested her shoulder against the headboard, keeping her back to him.

"No worries."

The bed bounced as he shifted closer. A citrus scent drifted across her face. His cologne wasn't as unpleasant as she wanted it to be. In fact, it reminded her of Max's aftershave, which might explain her dream.

"Here." He held out a glass of water along with two pills.

The water was room temperature, probably because he'd kept it next to the bed while she was unconscious. On closer inspection, the pills were benign aspirins. She recognized the initials stamped on them. The brand her alt-grandparents used to buy.

Instead of taking them, she dropped the pills on the nightstand. Already she'd had a drug used on her to knock her out. If she was pregnant, then she didn't want to introduce more narcotics into her system.

"What are the rules? You said you'd let go of my hand when I knew them." She drank the water.

"Right. You're not to go disappearing on us. We need you here. And so does Max."

"I'm not leaving without him, and I can't take him with me until he gets rid of that alien stuff inside him."

Or the Dark is neutralized with a magical knife sunk into his chest.

She shrank back from this image. No need to think about that now. Maybe the Three will have an alternate plan that didn't include skewering Max.

"Besides, my power and I are on the outs. I can't leave." Even though every cell in her body wanted to flee this nightmare.

"That's good, because the Man wants to eat, and we need to be there."

"What exactly does he plan to eat?" She envisioned Robert's deflated corpse.

"Not you. You're too important now that you're knocked up. But he wants you to join him for a meal before he dies." He released her hand.

"Dies?" She wriggled feeling back into her fingers then wiped her moist palm against the quilt.

"This weapon Max used on the Man did a number on him." Stockwell made a show of unclipping Max's pulse taser from his holster.

"Good." Kali couldn't stop the word from leaving her mouth.

"Not so much for your boy." He inspected the compact weapon in the fading sunlight that filtered through the sheer curtains.

"What do you mean?"

"Max's body will be the Dark's new vessel." He returned the taser to his belt.

"Come again?"

"Vessel, doll. It's what I said. Now let's get you ready for dinner." He shoved off the bed.

She longed for another shot of that tranquilizer, not enough to knock her out but enough to tamp down her emotions again—which were back online at full operating capacity—as this news jumpstarted them.

Kali stayed seated and hoped beyond hope that she was dreaming again. "Is Max okay *now*?"

"The Man's making sure he isn't damaged goods."

She stretched her back. Tilted her head from side to side to crack her neck. She set the empty glass down and tried not to panic, to give herself a task to distract her mind from what he'd told her.

She rose and exhaled a soft sigh that she didn't immediately plop back onto her rear. With the back of her hand, she brushed away a few tears that ran down her cheeks. When she was composed enough to not break down into a sobbing ball of nothingness, she forced her bare feet—someone had removed her socks and winter boots—to walk across the soft blue carpet toward the window, toward her captor.

"How long does he have?" she asked.

"The Man or Max?" Stockwell peeked out the curtain.

"Both."

"Two hours, maybe three tops." His eyes held hers as if gauging her reaction to this news.

"Then I don't have much time."

"No." He propped his shoulder against the wall and continued to watch her.

Kali fought to maintain a calm exterior, which began to crack under his unwavering gaze. Not that his eyes—so similar to Max's that it gave her pause—watched her in a sexual way. Not that she felt he was going to hurt her. There was something more to the way he stared at her that she couldn't understand, as if he were debating whether to trust her or not.

You're losing it, babe.

She parted the curtains to look out across an expansive lawn dotted with leafy trees. A circular drive veered off between a copse of pencil-shaped evergreens twice as tall as the house. From this vantage point, the main road and any surrounding houses were obscured.

She counted two guards walking along the driveway. In Utah, Dara mentioned in passing that they had a mole in the Man's ranks. Were one of those guards the Three's mole? Could they or would they help Max before it was too late?

"There's only one way out of here," Stockwell said.

"In a body bag?" She'd heard this line in countless cheesy action movies given by stereotypical, surly henchman like Stockwell.

He chuckled. "No, but that's a good one. I need to remember it."

A bell tinged from the hall. Kali pictured a white-haired butler wearing black tails standing outside the door, his fingers daintily holding the wooden handle of a brass bell.

"Ay, we hear you," Stockwell shouted toward the door. "That's a thirty-minute warning for dinner. Best get ready. We'll finish this later."

Finish what? she wanted to ask, but he'd already moved away from her and onto the next topic.

"In here"—he opened the second of two doors on either side of the armoire—"is a closet."

Kali leaned to her right to peep inside. It led to a walk-in closet lined with bright dresses, pantsuits, and a shoe rack.

"Yep, sure is." She bobbed her head.

Stockwell removed a peach tank dress and then a pale blue ruffled one. He held them both up to Kali.

He tossed the peach one onto the bed.

"That is so not me." She curled her lip. For a moment, the old Kali, the one without the weight of two universes on her shoulders, made an encore appearance. Fashion—or in this case, lack of fashion—could get this gal going. "Do you have any pieces that Cher or Twiggy would've worn?"

"This color and style suits you, and most importantly, suits the occasion."

"Your job description also includes that of personal stylist?"

"No, but my mum was a beauty queen turned model before . . ." He disappeared into the closet, leaving the unfinished statement hanging in the air.

Kali frowned, annoyed at hearing this tidbit about Stockwell—both that he had a beautiful mother, and based on how much he enjoyed playing fashion plate with Kali, he had a good relationship with her. It brought him closer to being human and not just the bad guy rooting for her demise.

Closer but not close enough for her to forget that he was a kidnapping prick who'd stolen her power in another timeline.

He popped his head out of the closet. "What's your shoe size?"

"Ten."

"You've got big feet."

Kali didn't dignify that with a response.

"Mrs. M is normal-sized."

Again, Kali kept any comments to herself. A true feat indeed—pun intended.

"Your boots won't do." He clucked his tongue. Then he opened the door on the other side of the bed. He stood half in the hall and half in the room. "Hey, Jonesie! See if you can find a lady's pumps, preferably white in a size ten."

Kali couldn't hear what the other man said, but Stockwell chuckled. "Yeah, I know. Big feet, right?"

"Seriously, my feet are not big, especially for my height," Kali said with a shake of her head.

"So you say."

He rummaged through the drawers, tossing underwear and stockings onto the bed.

"I'm assuming you have a bra under your tank. Mrs. M is above average in that area, if you know what I mean." He stood with his hands on his hips in a manly pose in a room with decidedly unmanly furnishings and dresses. He'd be a fish out of water if he didn't appear to be enjoying it so much.

"Right. The bathroom." He moved to the door nearest her. "In here, you'll find towels and a shower."

He hung the dress on a hook and placed the stockings and underwear in the bathroom. Kali crossed her arms, watching him putter about the room in a soldier's uniform with weapons secured to his belt as if war could break out at any minute. At this point, she wouldn't be surprised if he carried a makeup case in a pocket of his cargo pants.

After he was finished, he stretched out, combat boots and all, onto the bed. He picked up another magazine from the nightstand. Situating the pillows to prop up his back, he opened *Harper's Bazaar.*

When Kali continued to stare at him dumbfounded, he said, "Go on. Go shower and get dressed. Dinner's ready in twenty-six minutes. Mrs. M. left her makeup case. But you don't need much. You have nice skin."

Did he give me a compliment?

"Where is Mrs. M?" she asked, worried she'd suffered the same fate as her alt-world grandparents.

"In Europe somewhere with her son. The Man encouraged her to travel as much as possible. Keeps down the snooping that women do."

A real charmer this one.

"You're going to wait here, while I'm in there?" She jabbed a finger at Stockwell then toward the bathroom.

He looked her up and down. "I can go in with you, if you prefer. However, I didn't think you'd be up for any messing around in your condition."

"Trust me. Not in this or any condition."

"Suit yourself." He shrugged and flipped the page. "You can lock the door, but it won't stop me if you don't answer. Every few minutes, I'm yelling your name. Answer back and I don't come in."

She flicked a look toward the door that led to the hall.

As if reading her mind, he said, "You won't get far. Two men are out there, two more patrolling the property. They're trained soldiers. I served with a few of them. Do your vanishing act, and you'll guarantee the Dark will be wearing Max's body by tonight."

He crossed his ankles and settled in as if he were her hubby waiting on her to get ready for a night out, or possibly to go deer hunting, given the way he was dressed.

He lifted the magazine over his face, giving her a view of a short-haired brunette with a toothy smile and a bold-faced headline touting *The Fitness Craze.* Right below that read *Couples in Trouble: How to Stay Together* followed by *Can Your Job Wreck Your Marriage?*

"Oh, universe. You are a bitch," Kali murmured.

"What?" Stockwell piped up.

"Nothing. Only the universe mocking me."

"Would you prefer I do it?"

She glowered at him.

He chuckled and flipped to another page. "You have twenty-four minutes now."

The bathroom was surprisingly large. A square shower to her left, with frosted glass trimmed in gold, stood across from a sink with a tiled vanity lined with decorative soaps and sporting a matching gold faucet. The clothes Stockwell had chosen were hung carefully on a hook near a makeup case. Next to the shower was the toilet and down from that, perpendicular to the room, was a soaking tub under a shaded bay window. Royal blue towels and washcloths hung from racks opposite the toilet.

She glimpsed her reflection in the mirror. She didn't want to look too hard, afraid of what she'd see. Afraid that she'd find someone different looking back, because she certainly didn't feel the same as when she was sucked into the smoky rabbit hole.

She rummaged through the cabinet under the sink to find something to defend herself with. A can of Aqua Net could throw a fireball if she had matches, which didn't appear to be here.

With a dejected sigh, she straightened up. A gold flash caught the corner of her eye. She turned, expecting to find sunlight bouncing off all the gold plating. Instead, the Three appeared in front of the toilet. Surprised, she jumped and banged her elbow into the door.

"Is everything all right in there?" Stockwell yelled.

"I'm fine. Just tripped over the rug. Didn't realize how tired I was."

"Hurry up. And I better hear that shower running."

Kali flipped on the exhaust fan then turned on the shower. She herded the Three to the bathtub as far from the door as possible.

"How did you know I was here?" she whispered.

"Kali," Stockwell bellowed.

She clutched her chest at the sound of his voice.

"Polo," she yelled back.

"Ha, I see what you did there."

She rolled her eyes then turned back to the Three.

"You left me at the cabin." She wanted to scream the accusation but had to settle for a harsh whisper, which didn't come close to conveying her anger.

"We did," Dara replied, which wasn't the reply Kali was expecting.

"And . . .?" she prompted the alien.

"A reason?" Dara's eyelids fluttered in confusion as if it were obvious.

"A reason would be nice." She folded her arms tightly over her chest.

"The Dark would have killed us," Dara stated.

"We're too weak. With his men, he would have overtaken us," Tomas added.

"We used our reserves to teleport ourselves," Gilroy said.

"Far enough so he couldn't find us," Dara continued.

"You left me alone to face the Man!" Kali said.

"That was unexpected," Dara said.

"We assumed he'd remain at his base in Utah," Tomas said.

"Our source assured us he wasn't well enough for travel," Gilroy added.

"Yet he came and I'm a prisoner once again and Max—" She stopped when she remembered what they'd said at the Man's cabin about how she needed to respect Max for his sacrifice.

"You knew Max would do that." She stabbed a finger into the middle of Dara's chest. "That was the sacrifice Tomas talked about. Max's life is over because of you."

Dara gently pushed her finger down. "We made the recommendation. Gabriel requested we wait."

She understood the unspoken message between the alien's words. They had waited for Kali to save them. But her power was a no show. She failed and now Max was condemned to be the Dark's next vessel.

"After they took you away, we went back to the cabin. We saw what was written to Gabriel. The Dark demanded Max in exchange for you," Dara said.

Kali took a breath to process this news. It didn't make it any better. "Did you leave me behind on purpose?"

"We assumed if you were taken by the Man, then Max would have to come and save us," Dara replied.

She pressed her hands on either side of her head to keep it from exploding.

"You sneaky bitch!" she exclaimed then shot a look at the door, expecting Stockwell to burst in.

The two men moved in front of Dara. Body guards protecting their mistress.

"Our mole promised to protect you until Max opened the portal," she said.

"He was only to take a drop," Tomas said.

"He took more," Gilroy added.

"Psst." She shook her head, annoyed that Gilroy was blaming Max for his fate. "We're already trying to stop one guy possessed by the Dark. Now you let Max become infected?"

"It was a chance we had to take or risk worlds being destroyed. He hadn't consumed as much as his grandfather. There is time. He is able to handle it for now. He is still in control," Dara explained.

"Barely," Kali spat.

"We need the strength the Dark has gifted him," Gilroy said.

"We needed the bottle and the dagger, which he brought with him," Tomas said.

"We aren't strong enough to defeat the Dark without his aid," Dara said.

"It was our contingency plan," Gilroy added.

"Then we're going to need a backup-contingency plan because the Man is going to use Max as a vessel. And I'm pregnant, I think."

They froze, conducting their mental conference call.

"Another reason your power is off." Dara came out of their psychic meeting with a knowing nod.

"With this new bump, what is the plan? How will this go down?" she asked.

"Kali!" Stockwell yelled, and before she could respond, he threw open the door. "Well, lookie here. Was wondering when you blokes would show."

Chapter 31

Max in a Happy Place

Max woke from the emptiness where the Dark had shoved him, to being wrapped in Kali's arms at his favorite spot on his property in the Shenandoah Valley. Sunlight streamed through the leaves on the tall trees. It was the beginning of summer. Not too hot or humid. A perfect day to hang out by the falls.

Had he finally awoken from that nightmare? He must've been asleep for months. Or perhaps he'd been in a coma, which was why he couldn't remember up to this point. Had he been infected by the Dark? Had he traveled to the other universe? Had Kali forgiven him?

Her large brown eyes stared into his. The way she looked at him as if he were the only man for her made his heart ache. He told her he loved her. He wanted her to know it was true. He'd never felt this content with anyone else. Didn't believe he ever could.

He rolled onto his back and stared past the green leaves to the blue cloudless sky. Kali snuggled next to him. Her long legs rubbed against his. Her fingers danced along his chest. He adjusted his swim trunks. If she kept that up, they'd have to make love here. Max couldn't make it back to the cabin.

A fish jumped in the water.

He raised his head to peer over Kali's shoulder toward the sound and found it wasn't a fish. It was a child.

The toddler's little hands were clenched, his mouth wide open as if he were shouting, his face flushed with the effort, the muscles in his small neck drawn tight. His voice was faint as if he were yelling from far away and not feet from them.

Max looked down at Kali to see if she saw him.

She was gone. He hadn't felt her leave. Had she used her power to pop away? Why would she do that when she seemed as happy as he'd been?

He turned his attention back to the boy, who was pointing upstream. Maybe he knew where Kali had gone.

The boy's shouts filled his ears as if his hearing aids had finally tuned into his frequency.

" . . . leave! You have to leave now!"

"Who are you? Where are your parents?" Max's bare feet gripped the mossy rocks. The icy water bit into his toes. He squatted in front of the child.

His tiny chest heaved with heavy breaths as if he'd run a long way.

"You have to go," he said in a child's tiny voice, yet with an authority that surprised him.

"Why?" Max studied his soft round face and dark brown eyes with flecks of yellow.

Just like Kali's.

"Because it's not safe here."

"What happened to the woman I was with?"

His long dark eyelashes fluttered against his freckled skin. "She's gone to save you."

"Save me?" He glanced around, expecting to find the Man and his troops gathered behind him.

"This is fake. The Dark created this dream to keep you locked up. You need to go now." His tiny palms shoved into Max's chest, hard enough to push him onto his rear into the shallow water.

"Hey!" Max drew himself up, careful not to slip on the rocks, and found the boy gone.

"This way." He reappeared farther up on the path and beckoned Max to follow him.

When he hesitated, the boy said, "I'm here to take you back."

Max took off on the path, trying to keep up with the surprisingly quick child. Rocks and sticks cut into the soles of his feet, but he soldiered on. Max's long strides couldn't catch him up to the boy, who would disappear then reappear farther up the path until they reached the clearing at the side of the cabin.

"You need to go into the cabin." The boy stuck out his arm and pointed at the front porch.

"Why? Is Kali in there?"

"It's the only way home."

"I don't understand." Max shook his head.

"Go!" The boy threw up his hands in exasperation. "I'm losing my mojo. Just listen to me, geez."

Afraid the child would have a meltdown, which Max wasn't equipped to handle, he followed his orders. He shouted Kali's name. No reply. He called for her a few more times as he climbed the porch steps. The wooden boards creaked under his feet. He peered in the wide front window and didn't see any movement.

He poked his head around the corner. "She's not . . ."

The boy was gone, having disappeared into the trees or wherever odd kids hung out.

Max stood with his hands on his hips. He replayed the weird conversation with the boy. The nearest home was miles away unless his parents had been camping along the trail. Maybe he was lost. Although he didn't seem lost. In fact, he appeared to know the woods as well as Max.

And why would this child send him back home to his cabin when he asked about Kali?

Because it is a dream, the logic part of his brain spoke up.

No, he shook his head. He couldn't believe this. Then the precious moments spent with Kali, how she felt for him, loved him, had forgiven him, wouldn't be real.

And the Dark nightmare would be.

He felt a tug at his core, an encouraging push to go back to the waterfall. It drew him like a moth drawn to a bright light. His feet moved of their own accord across the creaky wooden porch to the steps. He was going to make love to Kali as he had wanted before the child interrupted him. Under the canopy of trees, next to the waterfall, they'd—

He paused with his foot lifted in mid-step.

There would be no making love to Kali. She was gone. And the boy said she had left to help him, which didn't make sense, but nothing about this was making sense. He turned on his heel and opened the door as the child had demanded.

"Kali," he called out.

The stain on the wall across the room drew his eye. It appeared to be moving, growing wider. A black substance oozed from it. He needed to clean it. Make sure it wasn't mold. He couldn't have Kali or their baby in here with that poison.

He strode across the room. The stain widened to the width of Max. He touched his finger to it and his whole body pitched forward into a black hole.

Chapter 32

Three Aliens and a Henchman

"Bernard," Dara said in greeting.

Kali's eyes ping-ponged back and forth between the four of them.

"Bernard?" For whatever reason—possibly because this was another example that her mind was lost—learning his first name was Bernard was more shocking than Stockwell *not* going all commando on these alien intruders.

"What of it?" He folded his arms.

"You don't look like a Bernard." To punctuate her impending madness, she snickered.

"It's a family name." His heavily lined brow deepened. He jerked his bristly chin at Gilroy and Tomas. "I see you brought Tweedledum and Tweedledee here. I guess these wankers didn't share when you were *supposed* to get here after things went south."

Gilroy's lip curled. Dara touched his arm as if to rein him in.

"We weren't at full capacity. Our powers are fading more quickly, and we needed more rest between teleports."

"We drove here. Ate dinner to reset our mojo." Tomas gave Kali a small smile, seemingly proud to use her slang.

"Wait a minute. You're working together?" she asked, her voice louder than she planned.

Stockwell and Dara both shushed her.

He closed the bathroom door.

"He's our inside person," Gilroy said.

"But . . ." She shook her head, although no amount of shaking would make sense of this twist. "Stockwell kidnapped me. He kidnapped Max and others from my universe. And he stole my power to do it."

"Another life, another time. With the reset, it technically never happened," Dara said.

"Oh yes, it did. I remember." Kali tossed up her hands in exasperation. "I remember everything this asshat did to me."

"Sorry," Stockwell replied with a shrug.

"You held a gun to my head at the Man's cabin!" she whisper-yelled at him.

The shushes returned.

After two beats and a long intake of the steamy bathroom air, she regained control of her volume and said to the Three, "Just hours ago this douche put a gun to my head after you left me in the Man's cabin."

"Wasn't loaded," Stockwell said.

"Babe, I'm an alt-traveler, not a mind reader. And your men shot Max and me." She was in his face now. Either the Three being in the room to protect her—although why she believed they'd protect her when they'd left her in the cabin was ridiculous—or Stockwell admitting he was playing on their side emboldened her. "Back in the cabin, Max had a chance to take down the Man, and you stopped him. You pointed that gun—loaded or not—at my head."

"I couldn't let you take off without the Three." Stockwell didn't flinch but stood his ground. "They gave me their word I could tag along. They're my ticket out of here."

"Don't tell me you're from our world too," she said.

"No, but I have nothing left here." He looked everywhere but at Kali. He was clearly uncomfortable with revealing this much—which wasn't much by her standards—but was probably a lot for him to admit.

Kali said, "When my mojo is back online, I could've come back for them."

"I didn't know if your power was gone for shit. And even you don't know why it's bloody fizzled. What I do know is that tea is in minutes, and the Man will be as mad as a cut snake if we're late. We go and keep the old bloke busy while the Three stick the guards," Stockwell said.

"I understood maybe like 50% of that," Kali retorted. "And didn't you say he was serving dinner?"

"Tea is dinner." He shrugged. "And also tea but you know what I mean."

"Not at all." She shook her head, wondering how they could both be speaking English.

Setting them back on course, Gilroy spoke up, "We need the Dark's prison and the Triskele Dagger."

"In the storage area in the basement," Stockwell replied.

The Three nodded.

"We need a few moments to regroup before we can begin," Dara said. Their brown complexions had turned ashy. A gray sheen dulled their skin.

"Regroup in the bedroom. She needs to shower," Stockwell said.

Kali sniffed at her tank top and crinkled her nose. He was right. She did need a shower. If she was going to die, she didn't want to go out smelling like a stinky wet sock.

Stockwell herded the Three from the room.

"Be quick about it." He slammed the bathroom door.

She didn't take time to pause and collect her thoughts. If she did, then her brain may break apart, her neurons overloaded with this change of events that blindsided her and made her question everything that had happened since the *Real Life* dinner party.

The Dark was planning to use Max as its new vessel. That was the only thing that mattered. The faster she arrived for dinner, the faster the Three could disable the guards and take out the Man and stop it from happening.

Getting home to her universe could wait until Max was safe.

Kali undressed and hopped into the shower. She concentrated on washing her important bits and hair. It did feel good to scrub the dirt, sweat, and other nasty things she didn't want to think about from her skin. She turned off the shower and grabbed a towel.

"Five minutes," Stockwell said with the authority of a drill sergeant.

She flipped the bird at the door.

"Right back at ya," he shouted.

She inspected the door for a peephole or a camera but couldn't find a way he could see in, which meant Kali was more predictable than she thought or Stockwell was a good study.

Go figure.

Once dry, she slipped on the silky slip and underwear he'd left for her. She unzipped the polyester peachy-keen, sleeveless dress and tugged it over her shoulders. It was a bit big in the chest and short in the legs, the hem hitting a several inches above her knees. Otherwise, it fit even if the style was more in line with a country club maven who hosted afternoon bridge games. At least, he hadn't given her pearls to dress up the outfit. She tossed the stockings aside. She hadn't worn those since junior high, and she wasn't going to start again. She rubbed her short hair with a towel to get it somewhat dry.

The door swung open. "Time's up."

"You could've warned me before barging in," Kali snapped.

"What would be the fun in that?" he replied with an obnoxious grin, actually his default grin.

She flattened her body against the vanity as he forced his way in.

"Where are the Three?" She felt better knowing they were close, as if he wouldn't try anything shady with them nearby.

"Napping."

Kali leaned out the door, and sure enough, Tomas and Dara were spread across the bed. Gilroy sat in between them with his back propped against the headboard. Each hand clasped one of his spouses. A pale yellow light pulsated from his hands along the others' skin.

"Will they be able to help us?" she asked. Although the color had returned, their skin wasn't as vibrant as before as if they were recovering from a long illness.

"One way or another." He rubbed his hands over his dark blond buzz cut and situated himself next to Kali at the sink.

"Are you planning to put on foundation too? Maybe do a mud mask to clear your pores?" Kali asked as she dusted her face with powder she'd found next to the sink.

"Crikey, I could use it." He studied his reflection in the mirror, turning his sun-weathered face from side to side.

"Here. I brought you these." He set beige heeled sandals on the vanity next to the decorative soaps. They looked brand new. If she cared, she would've asked where he'd found them.

But what she did care about was, "Why the charade? Why are you acting like we're a couple going to a dinner party? I'm not a guest here. I'm a hostage."

"Turn around, let me zip you up."

She obliged because Stockwell offering to zip up her dress felt normal, and she found comfort in this normal act.

"The Man likes to keep things civilized. He wants you to be at ease in his home, and we need him to believe that you are."

Her shoulders tensed when his rough fingers found the zipper at her lower back and yanked it up.

She plopped down on the toilet lid to sit and pull on the sandals. As he waited for her, she considered asking how he'd remembered the timeline reset. Then she reconsidered. He probably wouldn't know since she didn't understand why only those who'd traveled between the universes and the aliens recalled the events before the reset.

But there was one thing that he could explain.

"What changed your mind about helping us? Because you did the opposite in the alternate timeline."

He leaned on the doorjamb. His thumbs hooked into his belt. "I don't remember coming to blows with you."

She jammed her feet into the shoes and buckled them. "You didn't have to physically attack me to hurt me, although you must've strong armed S-Kali to get her inside that power-draining device."

"I'm sorry," he said, and she couldn't tell if he was saying this to keep her quiet and move her along or if he meant it.

"You don't sound sorry." Kali stood and smoothed down her dress. She kicked out her feet, testing the sandals. They fit well enough.

He scowled. "You're asking me to apologize for a dream."

"It wasn't a dream."

"That's what it seems like to me. I was a right wanker in the time before. I'll admit that I fucked it up. And now we get a chance to make it right."

"I didn't make things wrong the last time, so don't include me in this 'we' business."

He swept out his arm to the open door, indicating the end of the conversation.

"No stockings?" He gave her bare legs a pointed look.

"It's bad enough I'm wearing literal granny panties. I'm not going to toast my nether-region with stockings."

He chuckled. "You're a strange bird."

The Three didn't stir when they passed through the room. The yellow light over their skin had dulled yet continued to throb as if keeping beat with their hearts.

As she stared mesmerized at the Three, Stockwell admitted, "I created the paradox on purpose."

"Say what now?" Kali cut a confused look at him over her shoulder.

"I didn't know you were stuck in that chamber. I didn't know how the Man was getting this power to travel to the other universe. He recruited me for a special DERST project. I was consulting for one of the Man's defense companies in Australia after I left the British military."

"Wait . . . Why were you in the British military if you're Australian?" Max and Kali had researched Stockwell's uniform when he appeared at the *Real Life* dinner and discovered it was worn by British commandos, which was confusing since he sounded Australian, although Kali sucked at guessing accents.

"My mum was an Aussie. We spent half of the year down under with her family, which is why I got the better accent. My dad was British. Well, the bloke I thought was my dad before I learned the Man was my real—"

"Hold up?" Kali came to a jolting stop in front of the door. "The Man's your father?"

"Not him. The real Maxwell Martin from here, not the possessed one from yours. The one the Dark keeps as a souvenir in the chest under the bed in the cabin."

"In that long wooden box?" The one her body pressed against when she'd hid under the bed.

"Yeah, that one."

She squeezed the doorknob. If she had Pax's strength she would've crushed it. "Then I was hiding under the bed next to a dead man."

He squinted at her. "Huh?"

"Never mind." She longed for another hot shower to scrub away the creep factor. "When did you learn that the Brit wasn't your real deal?"

And here she thought Stockwell was a one-dimensional henchman, kissing up to the Man for power. In this short time, he was revealing more layers than a Smith Island cake.

"He visited my mum after my dad died, and I saw him a few times after that. I thought he was another hotshot that followed her around, wanting a piece of her. After I stopped being a Digger, he hired me for DERST's security team. That part follows this time line too. But in the other, he trained me to use the pack containing your power. It exploded on me once. Left me raw. Took months to heal before I got back to it. But I didn't know how he was powering it, and I didn't care. It was a thing of beauty being able to teleport like that. He told me I was saving the world. I would be a hero."

He stopped talking. He set his jaw and cracked his knuckles. Kali wasn't sure if he was waiting for a response or an indication from her to go on.

Then he said, "I started thinking something was shonky with him. Then I found that shriveled corpse in the cabin. The one of my real dad. It was there Dara paid me a visit and told me the truth. The Man had already killed her one mate Gilroy. After our meeting, Dara and Tomas tried to rescue you, the Man killed them too. Then it fell on me to stop him, so I reset the timeline."

Kali leaned her head against the door. She never imagined this man would side with her, let alone help bring about the paradox that saved the universe.

"Thanks," she said even if it didn't feel adequate.

"No worries," he brushed her off.

Kali looked toward the bed to find the Three were no longer sleeping. Gilroy and Tomas peered out each window. Dara stood at the bottom of the bed, watching Kali and Stockwell.

"That was the fastest catnap I've ever seen," Kali said.

"There's not much time. I sense the Dark's vessel is weakening, and its new one is strengthening," Dara said.

"Max," Kali murmured.

"Keep the Dark distracted. Meet us in Max's room in an hour. We will dispatch the exterior guards and ready our weapons," Dara said.

Stockwell nodded. "I'll take care of anyone on the inside."

A bell rang once more from outside the room.

"That's our signal." Stockwell's hand rested on Kali's lower back.

She opened the door and took long strides into the hall ahead of him. Her mouth watered at the familiar savory smell.

"That bastard," she said.

"What's that?" Stockwell caught up to her and grabbed her wrist.

"Split pea soup," she said as they reached the stairs that circled down into a grand foyer.

"You don't like?" He led her down the red-carpeted stairs under a glittering chandelier.

"It's her grandfather's recipe. Her favorite." The Man appeared at the bottom of the sprawling staircase.

Chapter 33

Obligatory Dinner at the Villain's Home

She would never eat her favorite comfort food again without thinking of the Man. Only a truly evil force would go to such lengths to ruin everything she loved.

The split pea soup was delicious with the right balance of salt and ham stock, like her family made it. It smelled like home so that for the duration of the meal, she didn't give another thought to the alien force presiding over it. And if her mind wandered to where Max was being kept, she slurped down the soup with extra gusto to remind herself that she needed strength to save him. She hadn't eaten in nearly a day. The questionable jam and stale crackers at the cabin didn't count.

She took a second helping, using crusty bread to sop up the bottom of the bowl. Maybe if she ate enough and kept this meal down, then she'd kick-start her power and save them all.

"I've never seen a woman eat so much." Stockwell shook his head as he took a third—or was it fourth?—helping of soup and bread.

"You've been around the wrong women." She wiped her mouth with a napkin then sipped her ginger ale, which helped settle her stomach. "Or maybe by wearing an arsenal to dinner, you leave them without an appetite."

"I've never had any complaints about my guns," Stockwell said between chews.

"Kali, I must admit that I'm surprised at how you're taking everything in stride." The Man saluted her with his wine glass.

She lifted a shoulder. Since she'd entered the room, she'd made an effort to focus on her food, avoiding conversation as much as possible with the Man aka the Dark aka Max's possessed grandpa. Pretending, as circumstance would allow, that this was a normal meal at a boring dinner with her mother's reality show friends.

Her improv training came in handy for something, at least. And her ostrich-like ability to bury her head helped too.

"I've come face to face with humans possessed by Aztec gods. Having dinner with the dark lord and his *Mad Max* sidekick doesn't faze me much."

"Saw that film last month back home. Liked it all right." Stockwell downed his glass of wine.

The Man folded his arms on the table and his eyes, swimming with the black, held hers.

She refused to look away, didn't want to show fear. So she dabbed her lips with the napkin and lounged in her chair.

"What is it?" she asked when he continued to stare.

"You mentioned an Aztec god?"

"Yes." Her mouth suddenly dry, she took another sip of her soda.

"Did someone raise him using a crystal skull circle?"

"Tried to but we stopped him." She wasn't sure how much information she should give. She was concerned she'd already spilled too much.

The Man stuck out his bottom lip as if turning over these facts. "Then a team of transhumans has already formed in your time to stop him."

"I wouldn't call us a team, more an agency. Transhuman security for hire, or something like that. I only became an agent recently to help out when the case calls for my expertise."

"But you combined your powers to stop this entity from entering your world?"

"We didn't go all Power Rangers, but yeah, we each had our part. But you know this already, right? The Dark—or was it you and your PA system?—transcribed those events in the journal."

"I only placed a taste of it on my tongue hoping to enhance my PAs and reveal my true path." He touched his index finger to his lips as if miming what he'd done.

"But this exile was not foretold. My PAs are unpredictable and weren't any more predictable with the Dark." Wistfully, he stared into his wine as he twirled the stem between his fingers.

His use of pronouns confused her. "Are you Max's grandfather or are you the Dark?"

"Both. The Dark has altered me."

"Brainwashed is more like it," she said into her glass as she took another drink.

"More like a change of consciousness."

An imagine of Max from her dream popped into her mind. His arms wrapped around her. His lips kissing her neck. His voice saying he loved her. Was this dream to be the last memory she had of him before the Dark corrupted him, blackened the way he viewed the world?

She found herself standing. Her faux calm cracking. "What's going to happen to Max?"

Stockwell cocked a grin, looking from Kali to the Man then back to his meal.

"With the small amount he's ingested, it would take several years and him feeding the Dark for it to fully meld with him. But I'm not going to make poor

Max wait that long. He'll soon carry the Dark that's within me, and then he'll reach full enlightenment within a few days."

"He'll resist."

"Then he'll die. No matter how much or how little of the Dark is within him, it will feed off Max's own life force if he doesn't give it the sustenance it needs. The human essence in this universe won't sustain the Dark." He gestured at himself to make his point. "He needs something more substantial only found in our world. I imagine Max would survive in this universe longer than I have since he's younger and healthier from the start. But you'll be taking him home. I've seen it and he will be more powerful than the Custodian who started it all."

"Then Max . . ." Kali couldn't say it. He was doomed.

His hand spasmed, knocking over his wine glass. He dropped it to his lap out of sight.

"You good, boss?" Stockwell wiped his mouth and stood, throwing his napkin onto the table.

"Not now. Sit, sit." The Man motioned with the hand that wasn't shaking.

"Sir, I think—"

"I'm fine, Stockwell," he said, then addressed Kali, "He worries about me. Dotes on me too much. It's quite endearing but it can be annoying."

With his napkin, Stockwell sopped up the spilled wine then sat down.

"He told me I could see Max if I behaved," she said.

"So I did." Stockwell frowned at her, as if to remind her she wasn't sticking to the script.

As he looked her over, the Man cocked his head. She worked hard not to squirm or bat an eyelash. She sensed he was assessing whether she had an ulterior motive.

"Please," she said with a dollop of sugar for effect. "If what you say is true, and I'm pregnant, then he's the father of my child. I'll sleep better knowing he is safe."

For dramatic effect, she placed her hand over her belly, which felt different. It had changed, a change only she would notice about a body she'd been intimate with for almost thirty years.

It had to be a trick of her mind.

She'd been told that her pregnancy was real, and now she was hypersensitive to subtle oddities like her stomach's strange shape. No way her body could change that quickly. Or could it? She'd never been pregnant before. Plus being a transhuman upped the danger factor. Would the child be an N-T or be born with powers? Could her alt-traveling body even carry a child to term?

And could she be a good mother given her own experience? Her mom and dad had recently graduated when Kali was born. Her mom would joke that she'd trapped Kali's nerd of a father because she assumed he'd be successful. Kali never found it funny. And now, she had gotten pregnant by a rich man she'd just met.

Like mother, like daughter?

No, she'd never be like Deandra, because she'd never force Max to do what he didn't want to. She could take care of herself and the baby, if it was real, which every cell in her body screamed was so.

Just like the boy in her dream.

She couldn't shake the sense that he was real too. But she didn't have time to think too hard about it, because the Man and Stockwell were both staring at her as if they'd asked her a question and were waiting for an answer.

"What did you say?" Kali asked.

"I told the Man that you'd be more pliable if you saw Max. Isn't that right?" Stockwell lifted his brows.

"Pliable." She bobbed her head. "That's my middle name."

"Then let's make that happen." The Man's face stretched into a fiendish smile.

A gun went off outside the dining room window and startled Kali. She banged her knee into the table. Men's shouts followed.

Stockwell leapt to his feet. The Man seized his forearm.

"Sit, son, sit. They have it under control," he said.

"What's going on?" Stockwell looked to Kali, who was closer to the windows.

Unable to see from her seat, she hurried to the window. She pressed her cheek to the warm glass. Boot prints on the plush lawn were the only indication that his guards had been there.

"Intruders," the Man said with a dismissive wave.

"Then I need to—" Stockwell tried to leave, but the Man kept his hand firmly on his arm.

"I said sit. Both of you. I didn't dismiss you yet." His tone carried a threat that chilled Kali down to her borrowed sandals.

She scooted back to her seat. Stockwell gave her a side-eyed glance, and she wished they had the mind-conferring powers of the Three, because then he could tell her what to do. Although if his expression was any indication, he hadn't a clue what his next move was either.

"How about I make good on that promise to Max? I'm famished for dessert." He picked up the delicately carved handle of the dinner bell from the buffet and shook it.

Stockwell was riveted to the entranceway of the dining room from the kitchen. But the sound that followed the ring—squeaky wheels turning on a cart—echoed from the foyer behind Kali. She peered over the high back of her chair. Every squeak of the wheels was like pointy nails scratching at her heart.

That sound didn't come from wheels on a dessert cart.

She recalled what made the squeaky rolling sound with horrifying accuracy, as if she were twelve-year-old Kali watching the nurses wheel her father from the ER for surgery, one from which he'd never return.

Two guards pushed the gurney holding a semi-conscious Max into the room. Leather straps were buckled around his wrists and ankles. His glassy, heavy-lidded eyes stared at the ceiling.

"Oh, hell, no." Kali shoved out of the chair to her feet.

The men parked Max in front of the cherry buffet behind Stockwell's chair. They locked the wheels into place.

Max's head lifted as if seeking out Kali. Either he was too weak or too drugged, because he couldn't hold it up. It sunk back onto a small pillow.

Hands gripping the edge of the table, Kali fought with her desire to help Max and her instinct to run and hide and let Stockwell and the Three, wherever they were—weren't they supposed to take care of the guards?—handle this situation. Despite her mandatory U-Sec training, she wasn't a fighter and swore she'd never need it.

Kali wanted peace and love and all that shit.

She sent a silent plea to Stockwell to employ whatever backup plan he had. But his attention was centered on the Man who was rubbing his hands together with glee like a child about to unwrap a new toy, which in a twisted way, the Dark was about to do.

"Boss, what is this? I thought the transfer wasn't happening until later." Stockwell's right hand dropped below the table.

With a moan, Max's head lolled to the side. Underneath closed lids, his eyes snapped from side to side in rapid movements that didn't seem like normal REM sleep.

"My energy is rapidly depleting. I can no longer heal this body." The Man lifted his shirt and peeled back the medical tape securing the gauze to half of his torso. The large wound oozed blood mixed with a black oil.

"I can no longer contain the Dark within me," he continued. "And if I let this foreign energy decay here—"

"It will destroy the universe with a black hole," Kali said.

"Precisely," he said.

"You're not doing this." Stockwell rose with Max's pulse taser in his hand.

The two guards stationed at either end of the gurney reached for their weapons.

"Yes, I am, and you can't stop me. And neither can the Three," he tossed out, unfazed by the taser. "I know about your betrayal, my son. To say I'm disappointed in you would be an understatement."

"Stockwell!" Kali cried when the guards aimed their guns at his back.

But she didn't need to worry about them. The Man raised his empty hand, and Stockwell flew past Kali, through the room's entrance, and into the foyer.

The Man planted his palms on the table as if it were a lifeline. His breath came out in spurts. He fell into his chair and mopped his flushed forehead with a napkin.

"I didn't want to do that, but I was so angry to learn my own flesh had betrayed me," he said between gasps.

The guards holstered their guns. As they watched the Man struggling to hold himself upright, they glanced at one another and appeared confused over what to do. They were trained soldiers, not doctors.

Finally the taller one asked, "Do you want help?"

"Just give me a moment, will you?" the Man replied.

The guards nodded.

"May I say goodbye?" Max's taser was inches from the gurney. It must've dropped from Stockwell's hand when the invisible foot booted him from the room.

"You may." The Man rewarded her with a small smile.

"Thank you." She poured every ounce of politeness into those two words.

If she'd play nice, talk nice, she might convince the Man she wasn't a threat. Considering he still retained his Dark powers, a mosquito would pose more of a threat than she, but being nice may buy her time until the Three showed up, if they weren't dead.

The shorter guard, standing closest to her at the head of the gurney, backed off as she approached. He craned his neck to look off into the foyer, as if checking on Stockwell to give her privacy.

A sheet and a thin blanket covered Max's body up to his shoulders, which were bare. She could see the outline of boxers under the covers.

"You tied him up." She ran her fingers over the leather strap on his wrist.

"The Dark has made him stronger, unhinged. You saw how he attacked me at the camp. This is for my staff's protection," the Man said.

As the side of her shoe touched the weapon, Kali touched Max's hand. It was cool but not inhumanly so. She slid her hand into his and squeezed. No reaction. Not even a facial twitch.

She leaned over him and ran her fingertips along his cheek. It was warmer than his hand and held a flush of color. When she brushed white locks from his forehead, his eyelids fluttered but didn't open.

"Max." She bent closer, wanting to be the first thing he saw. "Max, babe, can you hear me?"

There was movement in the skin around his eyes. A squint maybe. Slowly, she touched his brow, caressed the side of his face. She lifted his eyelid, hoping to force him awake.

A line of black slime oozed from the corner of his eye then withdrew under the lid.

She bolted up and gaped at her fingertips, certain the black goo had gotten on her, but her skin was clean.

"That living oil slick tried to get me," she stammered.

"You need to consume it for it to get inside you, and you don't have any cuts. Although . . ." The Man appeared to mull something over. "Maybe it senses your child. He would be a healthy carrier."

"He?"

"You'll have a boy," the Man stated.

Kali trembled at his revelation. "What do you know about him?"

"As I said, things come and go with my PAs. Sometimes it's as if I see the possibilities rather than the complete picture like a transhuman traveling to this universe or my grandson becoming one with the Dark."

"And our child is one of those possibilities?" Kali wasn't sure why but this made her sad, as if being told someone she loved may not have a future.

He tapped his index finger against his chin then said, "I think it's more than that. I saw him in a dream. Not a PA but a dream."

Impossible.

"What did he say to you?" she asked.

The Man hesitated again. His milky eyes stared past her. "That I need to transfer the Dark into Max."

"Bullshit." Kali dropped to her knees. She snagged the weapon next to her foot and aimed for the Man.

The guards unholstered their guns.

Backing up, she kept the weapon trained on the Man. Her bottom hit the gurney's metal rails. Safeties clicked off the guards' tranquilizer pistols. The same ones they'd wielded during the standoff at the cabins.

She hesitated in pulling the trigger. The Man was looking at her, his eyes no longer black but gray like Max's. They looked human, no longer like a demon. His lower lip trembled.

"Don't shoot her," he told his men.

What would happen if she shot the Man now? Would he die and the universe implode? Or would it disable him enough so they could remove the Dark and get back home?

"She won't do anything. She can't take the risk that I would die and take the universe with me. After all, she's a peace-loving gal." He used her own words against her. Words he most likely sucked from her brain when he sucked on her life force.

"Kali," Max said so softly she assumed her ears were tricking her.

"I'm here." She glanced down to see his head turning from side to side as if seeking her out.

He hadn't become the Dark's bitch yet.

 And he wouldn't on her watch.

She aimed the taser at the Man's arm. Slid her finger to the trigger and pulled.

The blast rattled her bones. The force grazed the Man's shoulder. The impact burned a hole in the wallpaper behind him. In shock, he wrapped his hand around the oozing wound and slid from the chair. The nearest guard tried to catch him.

She stared at his slumped form. Her hands shook. She dropped the weapon. Max shouted at her but her ears were clogged. He jerked one hand free.

The guard tried to prop up his disoriented boss as he shouted to his partner to shoot Kali. The other man refused and tossed his weapon. He shouted that he wouldn't do it knowing Kali was pregnant. He sprinted from the room.

With a curse, the remaining guard raised his gun from the floor where he'd tossed it to help the Man. She held up her hands, closed her eyes, and cringed.

Two rounds went off.

She waited for the sting of the darts.

"Take that, you rat bastard," Stockwell said.

She opened her eyes to find the guard sprawled on the floor, and Stockwell standing next to her with the smoking gun.

Chapter 34

Not How Max Wanted to Wake Up

A man said Max's name in the pitch-black void where he hovered. It was muffled, like an adult voice in the *Peanuts* cartoons.

The stained wall in his grandfather's cabin had sucked him inside this void. He didn't know up from down. He couldn't see his hands, legs, or body, like when Raven and Surefire made the truck invisible—except in that case he could see his surroundings. In here, there were no surroundings, just a black space of nothingness.

He concentrated on the voice. His whole being—whatever was left—honed into the jumbled sound. A lifeline to the real world.

The dark void lightened to a gray. He smelled body odor and cheap aftershave.

The man became two distinct men. One with a mid-Western twang in contrast to a hard, abrupt Brooklyn accent.

Their conversation was low, tinged with urgency.

"He rang the bell. He wants him now."

"Is it time?"

"If he says so, then it is."

A jolt vibrated the air where Max floated. No, not floated. Where he lay on a hard mattress. He winced at a squeaking sound as the bed—not a bed, a gurney—rolled along.

"Do you know what he's going to do?"

"Nope."

"What the hell is he? I mean, he's not human. Did you see what he did to that guy we bagged in Utah?"

"He pays well, that's all I care about. Besides, I'd rather be on his side than not."

Max moved his hand to scratch an itch in the corner of his eye, but he couldn't raise it. He could only move it as far as his stomach. He tried his other hand, the same. Both were tethered by what felt like a leather belt.

"I don't know, man. It just ain't right. He's a demon. I swear he is. Is money worth our souls?"

The gurney came to a jerking stop. "Don't say that. He might hear you."

"What about that chick and those two dudes? Did you see their eyes before Jonesie took them out? They were gold, like angels."

"Angels don't exist."

The gurney started moving again.

"But demons do."

"Shut up. We're here."

Max's blurry vision cleared. He found himself staring at a white ceiling edged with crown molding.

"Oh, hell, no," Kali exclaimed.

He tried to turn his head to see her, but it was too heavy for his muscles to move.

The guards stepped back as the Man approached Max. He stood at his feet and rubbed his hands. He looked giddy. Gleeful. A kid who had been brought his favorite birthday cake and couldn't wait to sink his teeth into it.

Stockwell spoke from Max's right. He hadn't seen him there. Couldn't raise or turn his head to see where he was. His consciousness was fading again. The Dark burned under his skin through his veins up to this neck until the oily mess snuffed out his vision.

Kill him. Consume him. Become one.

The hissing chant filled his ears, drowning out everything else. He pushed back and summoned all his will, all his strength, to swim against the churning current until he broke through the surface.

Kali was leaning over him, saying his name. The Dark tide receded to reveal her face lined in horror. She pulled back in disgust. What had she seen?

She reeled on the Man, her words coming in and out like a weak radio signal but enough for him to understand the message. She was scared of the Dark inside him, of what the Man planned to do to him.

He watched her hand lift his pulse taser and point it at his grandfather. He wanted to stop her, tell her to put the weapon down.

"Kali," he said her name like a prayer. He wanted her to wait for him. Not do anything rash. Not get shot. But he could only say her name.

He watched as her finger tightened over the trigger.

"I'm here," she replied.

She pulled. The blast from the weapon blinded him and sent the Dark scurrying inside his core.

Moment by moment, control returned to his limbs and mouth. Max yelled for Kali to take cover. He yelled to the guards to put their weapons down. A pulse of heated power shot from his chest out to his limbs. His legs kicked out and burst through the restraints.

The short guard, who resembled Squiggy, lowered his weapon.

His tall, gangly partner dropped to his knees to help the Man. He shouted at the other man to shoot Kali.

The short man shook his head. His beady eyes darted from each person before he sprinted from the room. Kali dropped the weapon. His partner gone, the guard on the floor sprang to his feet and drew his gun.

"Stop!" Max's right arm pulled up and over until the leather cuff tethering his hand to the bed snapped.

Pop. Pop.

Kali dropped to the floor. Her long arms covered her head.

A dart hit the guard standing over the Man. Staggering, he fell into the doorjamb then face-planted to the floor.

Max ripped the final restraint from his left wrist. He swung his legs off the gurney to find Stockwell trying to catch his breath as he propped himself against a chair. His face and arms were bruised and battered.

Whether it was his adrenaline or having Stockwell—the one who'd kidnapped him and used Kali's powers—so close to Max, the Dark's power grew. Its hellish tentacles reached out from the abyss, wrapping around Max's mind with greater strength than before.

Kill him.

The dark energy raged inside him. He flew from the mattress. His shoulder knocked into Stockwell's chest, forcing him to the floor. Max wrapped his hand around his throat.

Stockwell's sun-creased skin turned red. His deep-set eyes bulged. Max wanted to stop. He wanted to let go. As much as he despised this man, he didn't want to kill him. But the Dark possessed his body and was fighting to possess his thoughts, his emotions.

Nails dug into his arm. Someone was trying to pry him off.

Kali's voice cut through the gurgling sounds coming from Stockwell's gaping mouth.

"He's on our side. He's helping us," she pleaded.

Max pushed back against the tide. Inch by inch, control returned to his fingers, his hands. He released Stockwell.

Holding the Dark at bay, he watched as the Aussie rolled onto his side into a fetal position and hacked.

Kali's arms slid around Max's torso, simultaneously holding him back and soothing him. He closed his eyes and sunk against her chest. She rocked him and hummed a lullaby . . . no, not a lullaby . . . the *Star Wars* theme next to his ear.

His heartbeat slowed. His muscles relaxed. The urge to kill Stockwell nearly vanished.

"He's working with us?" Max asked.

"A long story. Trust me on this." She kissed the top of his head. "I thought I lost you."

"You will, if we don't get that dagger and bottle." Stockwell rubbed his neck. Red finger-sized welts appeared on his flushed skin. He stretched out on the polished wood floor across from them.

"What about the Three?" Kali asked.

Stockwell shook his head. He coughed and spat blood.

"I don't even know where the dagger and bottle are or I'd try to pop there," she said.

"Downstairs in the basement. Where you were held in the alternate timeline," Stockwell replied.

Kali went still. Her heart thudded against the back of Max's head.

"She doesn't have to go. I can do it." Max sat up.

The Man moaned and the Dark inside Max surged in response, butting against his resolve.

"I need you here," Stockwell said.

As if on cue, boots pounded against the floor as the outside guards entered the home. A man, who could've been a linebacker in a former life, appeared in the doorway to the kitchen. Another one, who could've been his younger and slightly smaller brother, stopped between the front door and the foyer.

"Go!" Stockwell stood to face the men.

"I got this," Kali said.

Max moved to shield her, but she was already gone.

The refrigerator-sized man started toward Max and Stockwell. The Man grabbed his leg.

"Forget him, Jonesie. Get the girl. Downstairs in my storage room, and have the Three brought to me now." The Man's voice was full of gravel. It sounded painful for him to speak.

Jonesie nodded and ran into the kitchen, calling on his walkie for backup.

"Kali," Max started after the guard.

Stockwell's hand gripped his shoulder to stop him. "She can handle herself. I need you to handle him."

He flicked a look at the Man sprawled on the floor.

Stockwell held his hands up at the imposing guard in the hall, who now had a pistol aimed at them. Max couldn't tell if it was loaded with darts or bullets. Stockwell motioned for him to raise his hands too.

"Jim, put the gun down. There's been a misunderstanding," Stockwell said.

"Sir, what do you want me to do with them?" Jim stepped closer. He peered past Stockwell into the dining room at his real boss.

"Kill Stockwell."

Chapter 35

Kali Faces Her Nightmare

Kali found herself in an unlit room. It smelled of dank basement, sour chemicals, and her worst nightmare. She stumbled around until her head banged against a metal surface. Running her fingers across it, she discovered a handle and a lock, then a seam of a door and a door jamb butting against a concrete wall and light switch.

She flipped on the light and squinted as her eyes adjusted.

With a groan, she muttered, "Maybe I don't have this."

Not much had changed in the room where she'd found S-Kali imprisoned. Same single bare bulb illuminating its center. Same square shape with a damp concrete floor. Same creeping chill that stung her bones.

Same glass coffin in the far corner. The only difference being it wasn't filled with slimy liquid or S-Kali. It was in a state of semi-repair or semi-build, the wires sticking out like a spiked mohawk hairdo. Missing were the connectors and lengths of tube that had attached the unit to the alt-travel pack.

Even after the universe reset, the Man had been waiting, as S-Kali had warned he would be.

Her heart thumped double time. Her lungs couldn't take in enough air that grew denser, making it harder to breathe.

I need to get out of here.

She stopped herself from tearing open the door while screaming at the top of her heaving lungs. With a deep inhale of musky air, she rested her forehead on the cool metal door. She clenched her fists. Dug her nails into her palms until the pain took her focus from this room, and she was able to think.

Get it together.

She rolled to her side and leaned against the door, which had become her anchor. Its cool surface was keeping her frosty. When her ear settled against the door, she heard a small sound. She held her breath and listened.

Did someone whisper "help?"

Pressing her ear against the door, she heard it again. She wrapped her fingers around the nickel-plated knob. She opened the door a crack and peered into the dim hallway lined with similar doors. At the far end was a service elevator.

Dara called to her from one of the other rooms.

"Dara." Kali tiptoed into the hall, leaving the door open behind her.

A knock came from the room to her right. Carefully, she turned the door's knob. It was locked. She peeked into the small rectangular window in the middle of the door. The room was lit in a sickly orange. Beyond the window, she noticed an empty space.

From the floor above came shuffling sounds and bangs as if from a fight.

"Let's try this." She sucked in the air and sucked up her power from the center of her torso into her chest. The warm tendrils spread up her neck and into her brain where she pictured the space on the other side of the door.

As soon as she materialized inside the room, her breath caught in her throat. Three glass containment units on rollers lined the room. They weren't filled with liquid, but each held one of the Three.

Dara smiled in thanks when Kali threw off the latches of her prison. She released the rest and stepped back as they pushed open the lids.

"I was worried you were dead," Kali said.

"I was shot in the leg." Dara rose from her prison. Her red hair was askew. Her Valentino pantsuit a wrinkled mess with a hole in the thigh surrounded by dried blood.

"Oh." Kali hurried to help her. Dara batted her away.

"The leg repaired itself while I was unconscious." She tossed a bullet on the ground, which Kali assumed had been embedded inside her thigh.

"They ambushed us." Gilroy hopped out.

"They knew we were here." Tomas threw his legs over the edge and jumped to the floor.

"We fought back but our strength had depleted." Dara leapt over the edge. When she landed on bare feet, her knee buckled. Not fully healed as she'd said.

Tomas steadied his wife. Gilroy joined on the other side. A golden glow bathed their bodies like it had in the bedroom, where Gilroy appeared to recharge the others. But now he appeared more tired, drained. Dark circles deepened his eyes. The golden light became a muddy yellow.

"How did they get you in these things?" Kali asked.

"They drugged us. Shot us with vials," Dara said.

"What they used on Max and me?"

"I assume so." Dara pulled away from the men. Her light brown skin was not as vibrant as when they first met. Her red hair had turned dull and brittle.

"They used a lot to disable us." Tomas turned around to show off a series of holes in the back of his leisure suit.

Kali pulled a face, "Not to be morbid, but why didn't they just kill you? Why keep you alive?"

"The Man will feed us to Max," Gilroy said.

"Once the transfer is complete," Tomas finished.

Kali wished she'd never asked. The Man was storing these aliens as a chef would keep her best cut of meat, saving it for a special meal. This thought filled her with dread. Max would become a supernatural cannibal once this Dark took hold.

"Stockwell's trying to hold off the guards with Max. But I'm sure Grandfather Dark will try the transfer as soon as he can. We need to find the bottle and dagger," Kali said.

The ceiling vibrated. Furniture or bodies or a combination of both banged against the floor above.

"Shhhh!" Kali flattened herself against the wall next to the door.

"Someone's coming." Gilroy pulled Tomas toward the containment units.

A guard in a thunderous baritone, which Kali feared matched an equally thunderous body, bellowed to another, "Roll them out to the service elevator. I'll check on the girl. He thinks she's down there."

"Yes, sir," his partner replied.

They were talking outside the door. Kali held her breath. One set of boots marched down the hall.

The Three opened their prisons, presumably to hop in and pretend to be locked up to buy time, but they weren't fast enough. The door swung open. The guard took two steps inside before he halted and reached for his gun.

His attention focused on the Three, he didn't notice Kali flattened next to the door behind him.

Mojo, please work. We need you.

Kali lunged and grabbed his neck, cutting him off in mid-yell. She took him to the in-between. His legs stretched into oblivion behind her. She dug her nails into his neck when he started to slip. He might be working for the Man, but he didn't deserve this forever prison. She pictured the overgrown lawn outside the Man's cabin in this universe, in this year and time. The grass formed under them. The crickets sang and the frogs croaked. Stars blanketed the sky.

The guard fell to his knees and vomited.

"Stay," she said before she popped away again.

The split pea soup seemed to be helping, or maybe it was the forced rest she'd had when shot with the dart.

Or maybe it was something else.

Maybe this child potentially growing in her womb was guiding her, giving her strength when she needed it.

It was a ridiculous thought, but somehow it comforted her to feel like she had a guardian angel—and just like with supernatural creatures, the miracles were sporadic and unpredictable.

The room where she'd left the Three came into focus.

They were gone.

She listened against the door. The deep-voiced guard was speaking into a walkie, which clicked on and off with static.

"No one down here. Three gone. One man missing. Need backup."

At the sound of the man bounding up the basement stairs, Kali opened the door. She dashed to the room where Stockwell said they'd find their weapons—and where she'd encountered S-Kali trapped in the containment unit.

The door had been left open. She stuck her head inside. The light was on but no sign of the Three. She entered and closed the door.

I'm not going to panic again.

Across from her was a cabinet, which took up the entire height and width of the wall. If the Man was going to hide mystical objects, it would be in a nondescript office supply case. She yanked on the cabinet doors with no luck. A cypher lock held them in place.

"You found it," Dara announced.

"Ack!" Kali plastered herself against the cabinet doors and nearly choked on her heart flying into her throat.

The Three stood in the room's center under the single light.

She clutched at her chest. "You want to knock next time?"

"We didn't come via the door," Dara replied.

"It's an expression. Man alive, I almost had a heart attack." She shoved away from the cabinet.

"But you didn't. Your vitals are strong," Gilroy noted with a nod.

"Good to know. Hanging around with the likes of you, a gal needs strong vitals. And speaking of vitals, you don't look so good even after your recharge in the bedroom."

Their skin had turned sallow again.

"We've used up the last of our power to materialize from that room so the other guard wouldn't find us," Tomas explained.

They fell silent, and she assumed they were doing their psychic convo.

"You said that I found it. I didn't find anything, except this locked cabinet." Kali hitched her thumb over her shoulder at it.

"What we seek is inside." Dara raised her chin, hands clasped in front of her.

"It's locked." Kali jiggled the handle to make her point. "Anyone know the code? I won't Q-T into an object I don't know."

Tomas nudged Kali aside. He extended his arm behind him. Dara took his hand and then Gilroy's. The alien placed his fingertips on the lock. Their signature gold emanated from his hand. His jaw clenched in concentration. In sequence, the silver pegs depressed. A lock popped and the cabinet opened to reveal a small chamber lined with shelves containing various objects. Its doors were heavy and thick like ones on a safe, not those used for a typical cabinet.

Tomas caught himself on a cabinet shelf when his body wobbled. Kali took his elbow to right him.

"We scraped the bottom for that." Dara put her arms around her husband. Gilroy hugged the two of them.

Gold sparks flashed then dimmed along the Three's skin. But this recharge didn't have the same effect as the others. They moved out of the embrace with the sluggishness of someone who'd donated too much blood for the cause.

Inside the safe—the size of a large walk-in closet—shelves held rows of artifacts, relics from around the world. Spearheads. Axes. Statues of bronze, silver, stone, marble. And one item she was very familiar with.

"That's Xochi's crystal skull." Kali stuck out her hand then yanked it back, afraid she might activate it and summon the goddess.

"It merely represents the goddess in this universe and does not contain her energy." After sucking in a long breath, Dara held up her hands, palms facing out. Releasing her breath, she dropped them back to her sides. "None of these contain any power."

Kali let her fingers stray over the smooth surface of the goddess's lavender-colored skull. Dara was right. She felt nothing, not even a tingle indicating untapped energy.

"You might've said this before, but I'd like a refresher. Why don't they contain any mojo?" Kali asked.

"The deities birthed in our universe were never born here. The elemental energy that created them doesn't exist here. However, you will find artifacts in homage to them. Our legends have bled into this neighboring world."

"Then those like Xochi are also fueled by this light energy that you rely on," Kali said.

"Precisely," Dara replied.

Kali's foot kicked a duffle bag shoved under the bottom shelf. The same style and color she recalled the soldiers using for the dagger and bottle.

She unzipped it. "I got it!"

"Stockwell kept his word. He didn't let the bottle be destroyed." Based on the way Gilroy said this, he'd been on the fence about whether to trust Stockwell.

She handed him the duffel bag.

"And these are coming with me." Kali nabbed her burner phone and Robert's and Max's along with her passport, which must've fallen from her jean pocket when she was knocked out. "One less thing to cause change in this universe." She tucked them inside her dress pockets.

They hurried from the safe and into the center of the room.

"Take us to Max." Dara put out her hand to Kali.

Before she could pop them away, the door crashed open. Two men—one frightfully large —barreled inside with guns literally blazing.

A bullet grazed Gilroy's arm. The next one hit the duffel as he flung it in front of himself to block the shot.

The bag fell from Gilroy's hand and gaped open. What remained of the bottle fell to the floor. The bullet had shattered it.

"No!" Kali screamed.

Without another thought, she leaped on the large man's back when he turned his gun on Tomas.

Within two blinks, Kali and the brute were in her alt-grandparents' cabin. She deposited him in the living room among the broken dishes and furniture and odors of decay.

"Think about what you've done." She kicked the guard with Jonesie stitched on his uniform with her size ten foot. He rolled onto his hands and knees and started to dry heave.

Before he could recover, she was back in the room with the Three and the less-intimidating guard unconscious and propped against the cabinet shelves.

Dara and Tomas crouched by Gilroy sprawled on the concrete floor. Their hands hovered over his blood-soaked arm and then moved to his side. The bullet must've passed through the duffel and bottle, hitting him there.

Their fading yellow light flickered then dimmed. In unison they looked at Kali and lowered their hands.

"We don't have enough mojo," Tomas said.

"We need to get him home to our universe," Dara said.

Gilroy struggled to take in the shallowest of breaths. His spouses stared at Kali unblinking and looking to her for direction. Normally, she'd run to her fellow agents to back her play, tell her what to do, take over the case.

But they weren't here. Communication was cut off. She was left adrift on a stormy sea with the motor puttering and her backup seasick. It fell on her to end this situation, and she couldn't live with herself if the universes were destroyed.

Which was a moot point but still.

"He's not dying on my watch. And you'll see Willie Nelson sing if it kills me," Kali said with more confidence than she felt.

"How?" Tomas asked.

"He's alive and touring in my time."

"Yes." Gilroy shut his eyes.

Buoyed by this forced bravado, Kali removed the dagger from the bag.

"But we don't have the bottle," Dara said as if reading Kali's thoughts.

"There has to be another way."

Dara hung her head and Kali didn't ask why.

The transfer could happen at anytime—could be happening now—and they'd been delayed enough. She stole the unconscious guard's gun and checked the safety as Synthia had taught her. She tried to figure out where to holster it. The dress's pockets were full of phones and her passport, so she was stuck holding it.

With her feet wide apart, Kali positioned herself in front of the Three, who continued to stay on the floor.

"Grab a leg," she ordered.

"Max will become the new vessel now," Dara stated.

"Just grab a leg." Kali didn't want to discuss what she feared as soon as the bottle broke.

"We can't remove it from him before we leave," Dara continued, not getting the hint to stop talking about it.

"Yeah, I know."

Tomas took her leg and held Gilroy's limp hand against her skin.

"He will need to take it all in. He will be consumed," Dara said.

"Thank you Dara Downer for the pep talk that we all needed," Kali shot back.

"You're welcome." She wrapped her fingers around Kali's ankle.

She rolled her eyes and said, "Don't let go."

In a few blinks, they were in the dining room. The Man's shriveled body sprawled across the table next to Kali's empty soup bowl.

Max straddled him, his hands planted on either side. He lifted his head and greeted Kali with a smile only the devil would appreciate.

Chapter 36

Max Faces His Nightmare

"Don't do this, Jim. The Man's not what you think." Stockwell tried to reason with the guard, who responded by raising his pistol and following his boss's orders to kill him.

"Get the Man!" Stockwell shoved Max into the dining room as the guard fired.

Max whirled around, expecting to find Stockwell bleeding on the ground. But somehow Jim had missed, and he wouldn't get another chance because Stockwell was tackling him. Limbs flailing and shoes shuffling, they moved from his line of sight into the hallway.

Inside the dining room, Max threw the gurney aside. It crashed into the buffet, shattering the crystal goblets and plates laid out on top. He stalked to his grandfather. His face was calm in stark contrast to the turmoil burning Max's every vein. The Man knew what was coming and had resigned himself to it. In fact, he seemed to welcome it.

"I won't do this." He stood over his grandfather.

"You don't want this power?" The Man winced as he lifted his body to a seated position.

"I don't believe the real Maxwell Martin—my grandfather who I hope is still in there—would have wanted me to bear that burden," Max said.

"How do you know? You never knew him."

"I read his journals and pieced together what I could from things my father and grandmother shared."

"What did my Lily say?" he asked with a hitch in his voice when he spoke his wife's name.

"Both she and my father said you were a good man. That you turned inside yourself for the peace the outside world couldn't give you."

"They said that, after I abandoned them?" His black eyes focused past Max on wherever his thoughts were.

"They were hurt by what you did. My father is still hurt. Sometimes I wonder if that is why we never bonded, because he didn't learn from you how to be a father."

Max bit his lip against the ache in his heart from admitting this. He didn't realize how deep the pain went until he dug it up and held it to the light.

"I'm sorry he wasn't there for you. My son took after his mother, aloof and materialistic. They refused to seek enlightenment."

"But my grandfather did seek enlightenment until the Dark corrupted him." Max squatted in front of him.

"That so-called enlightenment made me believe I needed to save our world by taking the Dark though the portal. But it needed to remain there. In coming here, I condemned this one as well."

"You only drank the Dark to trap it here?" If this were true, then his grandfather was a hero. One who had willingly allowed this entity to possess him, not for its power but to force it from his universe to save everyone.

A shadow passed over this grandfather's face, casting deeper creases around his eyes. As if recognizing its counterpart, the Dark inside Max bubbled to the surface. Max hugged himself tight to rein it in.

The Man shook his head and said, as if it were the most obvious notion, "You can't protect the world by exiling the Dark, any more than you can remove lions from the Sahara to save gazelles. There's a reason predators are needed. They keep the balance—the delicate ecological balance. It's a balance that will be upset once the new gods come into power."

"What new gods?" Max flinched as the Dark slithered up from his gut under his skin. He hugged himself tighter.

The Man chuckled. "You call them transhumans."

"No." This thing was playing with him, trying to confuse him.

Yes, the hideous voice rose again inside his mind.

The Man planted his elbows on his knees. His face inches from Max's. Lines dug into his dry skin, its baked-in tan fading away along with his life. Broken blood vessels stood out along his nose.

"You will be their greatest nemesis. Imagine how much stronger you'll be when the Dark inside you consumes a transhuman."

Yessss.

"From those who can handle the Dark, you will make your own army. You'd be unstoppable."

Do it! Join the Dark. The voice grew to a cacophony. It was frantic, hungry for the power being offered.

The hairs on Max's arms stood on end. Energy collected around his grandfather, a gathering thunderstorm of metaphysical proportions.

"I won't do it." His body convulsed with the need to do the opposite.

"I've seen the future. It will happen."

The fight between Stockwell and the guard had grown silent. Max glanced into the foyer. Stockwell was gone. It was only him against the Man.

"We're draining you into the bottle and taking you home," Max said with less certainty as the minutes ticked away and Kali didn't return with the dagger or bottle.

"You will give in. I saw it. This vision is what tipped my hand to open the portal. But I can't stop the inevitable."

From the kitchen, he heard someone running up from what Max assumed was the basement. At first he thought it was Kali but then realized the footsteps were too heavy. Once they reached the top, a man shouted for backup.

Kali is in trouble.

With a roar, he stamped the Dark back inside. He was on his feet in one swift movement. But three steps toward the kitchen, his limbs froze. He sputtered and struggled against an invisible wall. His bare feet slid backwards along the polished floor. He was a chess piece sliding across the board to a certain checkmate.

"What's happening?" he ground out.

The Man drew himself into a cross-legged position with no indication that he was manipulating Max. "The Dark needs a new host."

"I don't want it."

"You already have it."

"But it doesn't have me." Max's body came to an abrupt stop then spun to face the Man.

"Don't make this more difficult than it needs to be." He put out his hand to Max.

He grunted, trying to hold himself back from the Man. He refused to touch him, even if his body had other ideas.

It won't hurt. I promise. You will feel so strong, so good, the Dark whispered.

"You'll know all their secrets. Don't you want to understand our universe?" the Man asked.

"I already understand it more than I care to."

Taking in a ragged breath, his grandfather hoisted himself from the floor to stand eye-to-eye with him. The black oil had retreated, revealing the senior's gray-green eyes that had faded to a milky soup.

Max strained to remain upright and not bend closer to his grandfather, but he would have better luck fighting against a tidal wave.

"Stop, Poppy. Please."

The Man paused. His eyes seemed to refocus on Max's face.

"I'm sorry." A tear slid down the Man's gaunt cheek. His jaw quivered. "I never meant for any of this to happen."

Max didn't question if this act was a trick of the Dark, because his gut told him he was seeing his actual grandfather.

"I know." He rested his hands on his grandfather's shoulders.

"I thought by drinking that damnable stuff, I could hold it long enough to take it far from our universe where it couldn't hurt anyone again. I didn't mean for it to survive in another and destroy life there. And yet here you are, as I'd feared."

"We can stop it."

"Not me, you." His grandfather's legs buckled. Max caught him before his body hit the floor. He helped him onto the table where the older man stretched out on to his back, knocking the dishes, bowls, and silverware onto the floor.

In Max's ear, he whispered, "I didn't have the strength to fight it but you do. I sense it, and the Dark does too. Just don't let it feed."

Max leaned over his grandfather, whose fingers gripped Max's arms with the ferocity of a man at death's door.

"Poppy," he uttered, but the Man's eyes had gone blank. They no longer saw him.

A high-pitch exhale issued from his opened mouth like a deflating balloon. His grandfather's grip slacked then tightened again. His entire body grew rigid.

"Pop." Max shook him.

The oily film slid across the Man's eyes again. Max tried to pry his arms from his grandfather's tenacious hold. He planted his hands on the table to wedge himself free. But the Man wouldn't release him. Instead, he yanked Max closer. The inky substance bled from his eyes and slid down his cheeks. The oil's trajectory then changed. It flew off his flesh and smacked onto Max's lips.

He sucked in his lips to seal them shut. Shook his head to dislodge the oily splatter. In response, a cold, wet mass snaked along Max's spine. It coiled around his neck like a soggy rag before it spread over his jaw to force his mouth open to the Dark.

He fought against this power that possessed his muscles and bones until they no longer belonged to him. Sweat broke out on his forehead. His heart beat with the force of a frightened animal, trying to escape its cage before the monster consumed it.

A bitter taste touched his tongue, slid along the center, and down his throat. At first, it constricted to expel the foreign object then relaxed, giving up and giving in, until Max feared he'd drown from the vicious substance filling it.

The Man's fingers loosened their steely hold then flopped onto he table like two dead fish. His cheeks were paper-thin on either side of lips fading from a healthy pinkish tint to blue. His eyes fogged over with cataracts. In Max's arms, his body went deathly still.

"Pop?" Tears burned Max's eyes and rolled down his face along with what felt like baby oil. He ran his finger under his left eye. Black ink stained his fingertips. He rubbed his thumb and index finger together. A gooey, sticky substance coated the tips. In horror, he watched the smeared liquid congeal into a droplet before sliding under his fingernail. It wriggled beneath his flesh, leaving a black streak along his skin.

A scream tore up his throat. "Noooooooo!"

He turned over his arms. His veins were now tinted black as the Dark spread inside his body. He recalled Surefire's warning, that his life wouldn't be the same again.

His lungs were on fire. His brain was scrambled, disoriented as if he were riding a twisting roller coaster with high then low G-forces. He couldn't discern up from down. The room spun. The floor seesawed. The Dark's roar grew in his head until his skull vibrated with a multitude of voices, like an auditorium filled with thousands waiting for the main event to start.

Then there was silence.

No, not just silence. Time stopped. The grandfather clock by the kitchen's entrance paused with the second hand in mid-tick.

His vision tunneled. The edges spun into a blur, blending into a kaleidoscope of colors until he couldn't perceive details. The chandelier's clear light faded to gray. He floated in the void where he'd found himself after the boy took him to the cabin, after he touched the moldy mark on its walls.

A pinprick of light appeared far in the distance. Above or below? Hard to tell when he couldn't get his bearings.

He pushed through the gray mist, and the light dimmed. He kicked out, or maybe it wasn't a kick but something else entirely, because once more in this empty place, Max didn't perceive his legs or arms or a body.

But he had to try. He had to get to the light. It worked before, so he could do it again, even if the rip tide he was fighting against was a hundred times stronger.

He heard voices, a multitude of languages, and a deep, soul-wailing scream that he'd imagined was only found in hell. But it came from inside his mind.

He focused on the light, which grew brighter, enlarging from the pinprick to the size of a dime.

He needed to tap into his reserves to keep moving, because when he stopped to rest his phantom limbs, he drifted with an invisible current, pushing him several paces back from the progress he'd made.

One voice stood out of the rumble. It called his name and silenced the rest. *Kali.*

She was there, somewhere in that light, and she was scared.

He threw himself into the shining star.

But a force wrenched him back, spiraling him from the bright star until it was snuffed out. He was stuck in a whirlpool that sucked him into a sea of black with the knowledge that Kali was about to face the Dark without him.

Chapter 37

Kali Looks into the Dark

"Max." Kali was unable to register the spectacle, unfolding in the dining room.

Her boyfriend slid from the table. A wide, toothy grin plastered to his face.

"Max," she repeated.

The muscles in his arms flexed then relaxed. His fingers curled like a hawk readying its talons. Dark slime oozed under the surface of his skin. Slug-like globs slithered across his chest, up his neck and cheeks. It filled his eyes turning them into demon-like pits.

"I've been waiting for you," he said in a voice as chilling as his smile.

She shot a nervous look at Gilroy on the floor behind her. Tomas kept pressure on his torso wound. Pale light flickered under his palms, a dying flame trying to ignite another dying flame.

Kali squeezed the dagger's handle. Its curved, rough ridges cut into her palm. Try as she might, she couldn't raise it in defense as Max—or more to the point, the evil possessed version—stalked closer. The blade's weight grew in her hand, or maybe it was the weight of her conscience that couldn't face piercing his chest, where she'd spent many nights resting her head.

The hand holding the gun shook. She tried removing the safety without removing her eyes from Max. But her fingers were stiff with fear. She couldn't bend them to flip the switch.

Strolling toward Kali from the opposite end of the long dining room, he seemed to savor the anticipation and the stress his deliberate movements caused her. So mesmerized by this mad, stalking Max that Kali didn't notice Dara at her side. She barely registered the female alien prying the blade from her hand.

With a slow blink, Kali broke the hold Max's demonic eyes had on her as Dara lunged at him.

A wave of cold energy blasted through the room. It flung Dara into the back wall of the dining room with the force of a cannon ball. Her body busted a hole in the drywall and into foyer. She crashed into Stockwell, as he was attempting to stand.

Tomas used his body to shield Gilroy. When the room quieted, he yelled to Kali, "Behind you!"

Max's arm snaked around her waist. Hot naked arms drew her tight against his equally naked and feverish torso. The gun slipped from her hand as she twisted and tried to escape. But he only squeezed harder. She struggled to breathe. His chin rested on her shoulder.

"You're the reason for this tightness in our chest and below." He ground against her back, accentuating his point.

Ignoring the "our" bit, Kali pleaded, "Max, I know you're in there. Fight it."

"He's in here. Far below the surface, giving up his memories." His hand caressed her arm, traveling up to her shoulder.

She squirmed again. Flung back her head to hit him in the nose but he'd already moved to the other side to whisper in that ear: "So many delectable, sensual memories. We haven't felt this emotion in eons."

Cold lips pressed along her neck. His tongue darted along her skin, giving a sweet lollipop a long chilling lick.

This entity was violating her body, her memories. And with her arms pinned at her sides, she was trapped.

"Max, stop." She shifted her hips in an attempt to throw him off balance. But he was too strong and adjusted his stance as if anticipating her moves.

Pieces of wood and drywall crumbled from the hole in the wall. From the foyer, Stockwell grunted, but she couldn't see neither he nor Dara. She wondered if they were on the floor out of view.

"Max's life beats inside you." He nuzzled her neck. His hands caressed her midsection to make his point.

"Let me go," she tried the soft approach. "Please, you're hurting me."

Broken glass crunched behind them as someone approached. Before Max could react, his body arched. He released Kali.

Legs shaking like gelatin, she toppled against the edge of the table then righted herself and discovered what forced Max to let her go. The dagger stuck out from his back where Dara had stabbed it.

His arms flailed, trying to grab the handle.

Beaten and ragged, with dirt and dust coating her red locks, Dara grasped the handle and pushed it deeper. She must've taken the long way round through the kitchen to surprise them from behind.

Max howled.

"Wait!" Kali tugged on Dara's arm.

It was instinct. She wanted to protect Max, protect her friend. Hearing him cry out in such agony sent her reeling.

Dara knocked her aside. Tripping over her feet, Kali's bottom landed in the chair where an hour ago she'd eaten soup. Now she watched her boyfriend's body buck. His flailing forearm struck Dara across the face. Her hip slammed into the buffet. With a wave of his hands, Max flipped the table upside down, sending the Man's dried husk to the floor along with clattering china, glasses, and silverware.

Tomas dragged Gilroy from Max's warpath as the possessed man trudged into the foyer. Stockwell moved in front of him. He raised his gun and shot off a round. Despite being hit in the chest, Max kept moving forward. Stockwell aimed lower and shot again. The bullet struck Max's knee. His leg gave out.

Dara scampered to the fallen man. She pulled the dagger from Max's back and flipped his body over. She raised the blade above her head.

Kali noticed a change in Max. His arms lifted in defense. His body didn't pulse with the power as it had before. The negative energy had ebbed.

Wailing like a banshee, Kali launched from the chair and tackled Dara.

They tumbled to the floor. The blade dropped from the alien's hand and spun across the floor.

Kali rolled away. Her left shoe flew off, so she kicked off the other one.

"Kali?" Max rasped. His head lifted. In a daze, he peered down at his body. His fingers prodded a bullet hole in his chest.

Chapter 38

Max Takes Control

Max's spirit filled out his limbs like a hand fitting into a glove, one that was on fire.

He murmured Kali's name. At least he thought he did. He raised his head to search her out when he noticed his chest was covered in blood, which pumped from a wound hidden underneath the dark red.

"Max." Kali crawled over to him. "I'd say you're okay, but you were shot and stabbed and shot again. So that would be a lie."

With each breath, awareness returned. His entire body wasn't on fire as he first felt. The pain was concentrated in his chest, back, and his knee, which he couldn't bend without feeling as if a sledgehammer had been taken to it.

"My leg."

"It'll heal," said a red-headed woman who looked as ragged as Max felt. Her hand, gripping the dagger, shook as if it was too heavy to hold. Exhaustion lined her oddly symmetrical face, which could've inspired an ancient Egyptian mural. "But if I stab him—"

"Wait." Kali covered Max with her body clothed in a peach dress that looked like one his grandmother had worn in a family portrait.

The woman is Gabriel's sister, the thing whispered in his mind. *Dara.*

"This has to be done," Dara slurred.

She's weak. We can take her.

Max pressed his hands one either side of his head, forming a vice to squash the voices.

"Gilroy's fading. We need to go home." Dara propped herself against the bannister.

"I know." Kali's eyes swam with too many emotions to count. Although sadness rolled off her in waves. The Dark could taste it and responded with a content purr. It didn't taste as sweet as fear, but it was a close second.

"Where's the bottle?" Stockwell spun on his heel and scanned the area.

"Broken," Kali said.

A moan came from a guard tied up on the bottom step. Stockwell ordered him to be quiet.

"And you don't have another?" the Aussie asked.

Dara and Kali shook their heads.

Good, the Dark filled his head.

"Shit. We're in the cactus, aren't we?" Stockwell said.

"If it means that we're screwed, then yeah." Kali's fingers rubbed comforting circles up and down Max's arm.

The Dark quieted. Her gentle touch appeared to confuse it.

Max took in a ragged breath. As the Dark withdrew, the pain grew again.

Kali enfolded his hand in hers. "Can you talk?"

He nodded and uttered, after a wave of pain passed over him, "The Dark. It took over."

"What happened to the Man over here? Did you kill him?" Stockwell asked.

Max inhaled and got a whiff of floral soap. He cut a glance at Kali. Why did she smell like his grandmother?

"It's okay, Max. Take your time," she said.

He closed his eyes and focused on Kali's touch. The pain subsided from searing acidic levels to isolated throbs.

"It left him and went into me," he said, getting stronger by the second. "The transference destroyed his body."

The throbbing morphed into tingles. Tiny needles pierced his muscles down to his bones. His chest itched. When he scratched at it, a bullet popped from the wound. He wiped away the blood to find a red mark the size of a quarter, the only sign that a hole had been there only moments before.

Kali's mouth fell open in surprise or fascination or horror; it was hard to tell. Maybe it was all three. She gave the area a gentle prod to test the skin.

"Holy healing factor," she said.

Stockwell swore under his breath.

Inch by aching inch, Max lifted his upper body from the marble floor to a seated position. His abrasions were tender as if he was in week three of recovery. Minor pangs radiated from his knee when he bent it. The skin had already formed a scab under the blood and black oil.

"The Dark is buzzing in my veins like one of those static generators. I heard your voice, Kali." He peered into her warm chocolate eyes. He could clearly see the fine lines and dark circles around them.

She smiled in return, but it was a smile given to a sick friend who learned they would never recover. She blinked back tears, because she knew what it meant when he said the Dark had overtaken him. She knew what they had to do to get him home.

He wanted to assure her that he'd be okay. He'd won this round. He'd proven that he could overcome it. "I couldn't do anything. Couldn't move. Speak. I was locked in a room at the bottom of an ocean. But you called my name, and I found the light. Your light."

Her smile widened but instead of being happier, she appeared sadder. Tears trickled from her eyes. She wiped them away.

"So this sheila brought you back from the abyss?" Stockwell tossed out with a snort.

"Impossible." Dara scooted closer to them.

"I heard a voice and otherworldly ones. Some are still running around my skull." He screwed his eyes shut and rubbed his temples.

"What're you talking about?" Stockwell asked.

"Memories," Dara explained. "When the Dark possesses a being or feeds on its essence, it absorbs everything they saw and experienced."

"Like body snatchers? As in invasion of?" Kali shuddered.

"Except with enough power to take over the world, if we don't keep it contained," Dara said.

"Or keep it from consuming transhuman energies," a dark-haired man in a leisure suit chimed in from the dining room floor. He held his hands over another man who was unconscious.

Tomas, the Dark hissed. *Gilroy.* Dara's husbands.

"I won't let that happen," Max stated.

"You don't have a choice," Dara said.

"And we don't have a choice." Kali gave the alien dagger on Dara's lap a worried look.

The redhead sat with her legs tucked under her and back bowed. She appeared on the verge of sinking to the floor and falling asleep as she slid toward Max's side.

Kali made shushing sounds when Max convulsed. He fought against the Dark's rising hold. The closer Dara moved, the more it sensed weakness in her. And saw an opportunity to strike.

He told the Dark to screw off. Cursed it back to hell. They weren't eating Dara. He put a metaphysical foot down.

His pushback worked. Or at least disoriented—if that were possible—the Dark. It wasn't used to being made to back down.

"What is this?" Dara pointed at his tattoo.

"What I thought was the Martin family's crest." He faced away from her when the oil made another play up his throat.

Her broken fingernails scratched along its surface. "It's a symbol from our culture used to protect and bind."

"So I've been told," he ground out. The liquid burned the back of his throat.

"What about the tattoo?" Stockwell narrowed his eyes at it.

"Is that why this symbol was on the journal and on the wine bottle Robert had brought to Syn's place?" Kali asked.

"It's a ward against the Dark," Dara continued.

Max flinched when she grabbed the side of his face and forced him to look at her. Eyes the color of wheat stared into his. Gold glittered within the dark yellow. Her skin was a lighter brown than Gabriel's, but their wide faces and angled cheekbones were the same.

He held his mouth closed against the slimy bugger that slithered onto his tongue. Clenched his jaw until he feared his teeth would crack.

"The tattoo may be weakening the Dark and enabling you to regain control, but I'm unsure how long it will last."

It won't, the Dark whispered.

"Shut up!" Max grounded out.

Kali caressed his shoulder. "What's happening?"

"It's trying to break me down," he said between clenched teeth.

He swallowed and swallowed, forcing it from his tongue. The slimy substance receded into the middle of his throat. It settled there, burning his esophagus like the worst case of acid reflux.

"Get the body," Dara called to Tomas in the dining through the hole in the adjoining wall.

He left Gilroy's side and climbed over the toppled table to retrieve what was left of the Man. The dried up corpse appeared more like a haunted house prop than a real body. And this thought brought some relief to Max. If the thing Tomas was carrying didn't resemble his grandfather, then Max wouldn't be reminded of what the Dark, using him, had done.

As if afraid that any jolt would destroy what was left, Tomas carefully bent his knees and laid the remains next to Max.

Dara attempted to rise to help him retrieve Gilroy, but Stockwell put his hand on her shoulder and offered to do it. He held the limp man up by his shoulders while Tomas took his legs.

After depositing Gilroy by his wife, Stockwell took a long, hard look at the Man's shriveled corpse. "Can't say it doesn't bring a tear seeing my old man reduced to this a second time."

It took Max a moment to understand what he meant. "The Man was your father?"

"This one killed my real dad and took his place."

"Then you're my uncle in a way," Max said.

Invigorated by Stockwell's claim, the Dark's voice split into several similar voices. Once again, Max rubbed his temples to tamp them down, but they grew louder, regaling him with tales from his grandfather's past.

"I'm getting his memories about the affair he had with your mother." Max pieced together the words reverberating in his skull. "But also I'm getting memories from my own grandfather. He had a son, too, by an Australian in my universe."

"There's another me in your world?" Stockwell said.

"As if one wasn't enough," Kali said under her breath.

"I can't believe I never knew this." Max lowered his hands. His vision focused once more in the present.

"It's not like a cheater brags to their family about fathering bastards," Stockwell said.

Bastard. A woman screamed. Not in the foyer but inside Max's head.

"No." Max pressed a palm against his forehead, wishing he never uncovered this memory. "The Dark killed your mother."

"What did you say?" Stockwell asked in a quiet tone.

"It's all in my head. The memories of this thing and what it did to her." The Dark dripped down his throat, giving him the ability to speak freely.

"Shut up." Stockwell's wild eyes landed on the dagger on Dara's lap.

Before she could react, he swiped the blade and lifted it above his head.

No one moved. No one spoke. As if they were afraid any sound or movement would set him on a rampage.

Stockwell's arms shook as if he struggled whether to strike or not. In mid-swipe, he stopped, dropped the dagger to his side, and cursed.

"Fuck all." His shoulders shook as he sobbed.

"About a year after you took the security job with DERST, your mother passed. You were planning to leave the company. She'd asked you to come back home," Max said.

Kali shushed him. "Don't say—"

"He needs to know," he cut her off, fueled by the need to tell this tale. It was important. He was certain of it. This man needed to know what happened to his mother.

"She'd been sick with ovarian cancer," he continued. "The Dark saw her as a threat to its plan, one that relied on you."

Max was so focused on what the Dark was whispering to him, that he didn't see Stockwell squat on the floor across from Kali. He didn't see him raise the dagger until it was too late. He plunged the long silver blade into Max's chest.

"Stop!" Kali screamed.

His lungs filled with blood. He gasped for breath. Black spots floated across his vision. The back of his head bounced against the marble floor.

"Get off." Kali struggled against Dara and Tomas. Both held her arms back.

"The Dark has to be contained inside Max when we cross over. The blade is the only way to do it," Dara said to her.

"That's right, you fuckin' bastard." Stockwell straddled Max holding the blade in place.

Max realized he'd been played by the Dark. It wanted to get home. The only way home was with the dagger neutralizing its power so the Three would transport him there.

Pinning Max's left arm under his leg, Stockwell took Max's right arm and placed his hand on the Man's parchment-like skin.

"Now what?" Stockwell looked to Dara.

"Home," Max whispered, and the Dark echoed the sentiment, focusing the full force of their will to call forth the portal.

But nothing happened.

Chapter 39

Kali—Their Last Hope

"Why isn't it working?" Kali looked from one weary face to the next.

None of them replied. Instead, they stared at Max's fingers touching the brittle arm as if their gazes concentrating on that single area would force the portal to open.

"Take . . ." Dara panted as if she'd just barely finished a race. "the knife . . . out."

"But I thought—" Stockwell began and Dara interrupted with, "I did too. It's not working."

The alien planted both her palms on the marble floor. Her words were slow and slurred. "Maybe he's blocked."

She took another gulp of air before soldiering on, "When one possessed by the Dark opens the portal in our world, they are not impaled by the dagger."

"Then how do they get back to their home universe?" Kali asked.

Dara gave her a blank stare. Either she was so weak she was going to pass out or—

"You've never done this before," Kali stated.

The alien wagged her head. "The first traveled here and back because she had the gift."

"The Custodian whose flesh"—Kali's upper lip curled at the memory of holding it—"bound the journal?"

She nodded.

Kali flung up her hands. "The Man's flesh isn't this Custodian's. It doesn't contain the same DNA as her tanned hide binding the journal."

"We assumed the Dark had transferred enough of her DNA to the current host," Tomas explained. His voice came out stronger than his wife's but not by much.

"You assumed!" Kali bolted to her feet. "You don't assume when lives are at stake." She flapped her hand toward Max. "In fact, you're supposed to know what could happen, because you created this sentient blob that's possessing my man."

"Your man?" Max hacked so hard, she feared a lung would come out.

"Don't move, and don't talk until we figure out what to do next," Kali told him.

"Okay." He coughed again, causing the dagger to bob in his chest.

She cut him a look for him to keep quiet. He gave her the thumbs up that he understood.

"Then should I take the dagger out?" Stockwell directed the question at Kali this time.

She wasn't sure if she should be flattered or anxious over Stockwell turning to her for leadership. She blanched at being responsible for solving a life-or-death, world-shattering situation like this. Her shoulders were too narrow for this kind of weight, as her mother was apt to point out. But given how Gilroy was involuntarily checked out, Dara looked as if she'd consumed a six-pack of Cokes, Tomas was sprawled on the floor with slightly more energy than his wife, and Max was possessed by an evil entity, she was the best and only choice.

Kali folded her arms. After a deep, not-so-calming breath, she said, "Okay, but be—"

Stockwell ripped the dagger out sending a spray of blood into the air. He launched himself out of its way. Dara scooted across the floor to the steps. Kali jumped over the Man's shriveled legs. Tomas rolled over, sliding an unconscious Gilroy alongside him.

Max issued an earth-shattering scream. His hands clamored across his slick flesh to squeeze the hole shut. Red streams spewed along his chest to his stomach. Streaks of black pulsated from the wound before turning course and returning into the gash.

"I wasn't finished." Kali whirled on Stockwell, who was inspecting himself for traces of the Dark.

"You said 'okay,'" he argued.

Shaking her head, she moved back to Max. The blood was beginning to coagulate. Whatever Dark leaked out had retreated inside its vessel.

"Touch the Man. Now." She hated to order Max after he had a knife ripped from his chest, but she didn't want to give that black goo time to possess him.

But it was too late.

Black tentacles radiated from the knife wound. They blazed thin trails up his neck to form a dark spider web over his face. An inky film coated his eyes. His features relaxed. Burgundy smears coated his teeth.

With a casual flick of his arm, Max's hand flopped onto the Man. The brittle flesh crumpled. His other hand drummed its fingers along his chest.

"You knew it wouldn't work, didn't you?" Kali was sick of playing games with supernatural beings. She'd been doing it for the last year, and it was never fun except for the otherworldly assholes.

"We learned the lesson before," Max said, but it wasn't him speaking. Kali doubted he could ever sound that much like a smug prick.

"Before the reset, the Man forced you to alt-jump with him. But it didn't work," he said.

"Without the dagger, his energy couldn't be neutralized for the jump," Dara said with a yawn.

"I'm remembering bits more." Stockwell frowned. "The Man forced the Dark into Gilroy then killed him. He wanted to use the bloke's body to open the portal. But that didn't work either."

"The Man then wanted you to alt-jump for him," Tomas said to Kali.

"You refused," Dara said.

"I did?" Kali choked.

"Which is why he gave your power to me." Stockwell glared at Max, whose lips stretched into a I-got-one-over-on-you grin.

"After I grabbed Max, the Man wanted me to snag the dagger from your world. Then the Dark would possess Max, and we'd neutralize him so I could take it back home—in a healthy body—and release it there. But then the reset happened." It was Stockwell's turn to grin.

"I was a ripe whacker for helping it at first." Without ceremony, he straddled Max and plunged the blade back into his chest.

"What are you doing?" Kali screeched.

"You need to get these three home," Stockwell motioned to the aliens growing weaker by the minute. "We need to get this Dark shit out of this universe before it destroys it. The Man's corpse didn't open the portal with and without the blade in your boy, so it's up to you to give it a go."

"He's right," Max whispered back to his old sweet self.

"I can't do this." Kali dropped to her knees.

"You can," he said.

She sensed Max wanted to tell her more but couldn't. The letters on the blade pulsated. His eyes screwed shut as if the pain had intensified.

Dara slid off the step where she'd propped herself up. She crawled over and collapsed by Kali's leg. Stockwell helped Tomas slide Gilroy to her other side.

"Seriously, I don't think I can do this," Kali said.

"Don't think, do," Stockwell retorted.

He did have a point, however brusque it might be. She had been able to access her power to trap the large guards at the commune. Maybe it was strong enough to take them home. She had nothing to lose by trying.

Except the lives of the Three and this entire universe.

Cold fingers dug into her calves. She grasped Gilroy's limp hand and took Max's with the other. Stockwell wrapped his calloused, warm hand over her bicep.

"Here goes everything." She inhaled, expanding her chest as far as it would go. As she released the breath, she visualized her power growing like vines into her chest.

Heated energy vibrated from her torso. It crept out to her limbs. Slow and lumbering like a train running out of steam halfway up a steep hill.

If she didn't have five people to carry, then she would have made it home. But the energy required to alt-jump a group of aliens, herself, two people, and a sentient evil blob wasn't there.

Stop taking my power, Kali screamed inside her head. She was grasping at metaphysical straws. As if the small bean growing inside her would understand that he was stealing her mojo.

"Tomas," Dara said.

A blast of hot air streamed up Kali's calf from under Tomas's hand. Dull yellow light coated her knee and thigh and continued under her dress.

"You're going to die," Kali said. "Stop."

Ignoring her pleas, Tomas appeared unconcerned at losing his life for the cause.

Jumpstarted by his energy, her power surged outward to her limbs. But she needed it stronger. This amount of juice could carry three of them but not all.

Tomas issued a strangled growl as if he was coming to his final burst before he'd pass out or worse.

Max's back arched. His teeth clenched. The alien letters were so bright on the dagger it hurt her eyes to look at them.

She needed to get Max home and this dagger out of him.

"Come on. Just a little more." Kali closed her eyes and focused deep, scraping a spoon against the bottom of a burnt pot.

If it was her baby taking her power, then the little bit had explaining to do.

Someone touched the middle of her back. She jerked forward but the hand—a small hand—pressed harder against her skin, which was impossible because the dress zipped up to the base of her neck.

A child murmured in her ear, "I got your back."

"What?" She looked over her shoulder to find no one there.

"Close your eyes," the bodiless voice said.

She did and was transported to the waterfall on the Man's property. Her skin was moist from the humid air. She wore a bikini top and jean shorts. A picnic blanket strewn with snacks was set out on the mossy ground next to the refreshing water.

The small hand remained pressed against her back.

She turned to find the same boy from her dream. The boy who'd warned her to wake up when she was asleep next to Stockwell.

"What's happening?" she said.

"I'm giving you back the energy that I'm now stealing."

Kali tried to make sense of what he meant, but would have better luck solving a Rubrics cube while blindfolded. "I don't understand."

"You're pregnant with me. I'm growing at a faster rate than other fetuses. The energy in the portal jumpstarted my growth when you went through."

"Then you're my child and you're talking to me from the future."

"Right."

"And you're sending me vibes from the future to power me up."

"Yep."

It was possible that this was a hallucination, but she had to ask, "How are you doing this?"

He slung his small arm over her shoulder and patted her on the back like one encouraged a teammate to go for the goal. "It's just what I can do."

The way he acted wasn't how a child his age would respond. Kali wondered if he was using this guise to appear less threatening—or shocking—as it would be to see him as a grown man.

"Did you visit your great-grandfather in his dream?" She recalled what the Man had said at dinner.

"Yes," he said, going very still and sounding very sorry.

"And you told him to give the Dark to Max."

"I did."

"Why?" Kali wanted to shake him, scream at him, but he was a just a kid. He didn't know better.

Except he did, because he was from the future. He knew what had to be done. And the fact that he was alive to travel back in time to help them meant that she survived this and hopefully Max did too.

"I can't tell you anymore." He gave her an aw-shucks, childish shrug. "If I do, it will affect the future. But you know that."

Without warning, Kali was back in the foyer. The sounds of water trickling and birds chirping morphed into labored breathing and Stockwell yelling for her to get on with it.

The invisible hand on her back gently pushed her to move forward.

"Where to?" Kali asked no one in particular. Her power was awake, fully operational and powered by a thousand preternatural espressos. She felt strong enough to take the whole planet with them.

"My cabin." Max sighed with his eyes closed, as if he were already there in his dreams.

She focused on what the cabin looked like in this universe and hoped it looked the same in theirs. Then she directed all of them through the in-between and back into their world.

Chapter 40

No Place Like Home

He wished so hard for his cabin in the valley that he wasn't sure if he'd made the wish aloud when Kali asked where to go. One moment he was on the marble foyer, and the next he was draped across the oak dinette table in his cabin staring up at Stockwell. His face was contorted as if he were trying not to be sick.

Stockwell hurled himself off Max. From under the table, the Aussie coughed and spat but otherwise kept his dinner down. Max was glad he missed the alt-jump. He must've passed out before they took off.

A woman yelped. Max raised his head in her direction to find Surefire with her hand clasped over her mouth. She stood between Raven and Mr. Triman outside the basement's stairs where they'd disappeared before he opened the portal.

Raven stepped toward him. Mr. Triman put out an arm and shook his head for him to wait.

A multitude of groans rose from the floor around the table. Kali's brown halo of hair appeared over the edge to his right. She hefted herself to her feet. Her blood-shot eyes took stock as if she'd woken hungover from an all-night party.

Max couldn't manage any movement other than turning his head. The blade rendered him paralyzed.

"Did it work?" Stockwell scrubbed the back of his palm across his mouth.

"We're back home . . . well, not my home, but my universe," Kali replied then noticed her friend and squealed, "Synthia!"

She ran over to Surefire and Raven and hugged them both.

"What happened to Gilroy and Tomas?" Mr. Triman hurried from the doorway and dropped under the table below Max's feet.

"Gilroy was shot and Tomas gave his last reserves to help Kali. I don't know if he'll survive." Dara's brittle voice came from somewhere near Max's head.

"Tomas doesn't have a pulse. Gilroy's is barely there," Mr. Triman said.

"Do something," Kali pleaded.

A yellow beam exploded upward from where Mr. Triman sat. The bright light hit the ceiling and fanned out. Dara clutched a wooden chair that wobbled under her weight. She hobbled toward the golden light. She stuck her fingers into the beam and threw back her head with an "ohm."

The letters on the blade, which had dimmed, began to reflect the sun-like rays. The brighter they grew, the hotter the blade grew until Max's flesh sizzled and he smelled the acrid scent of it burning.

He tried to lift his hands to remove the blade. Both were held down with lead weights. Black spots swam across his vision, blurring out the room. The spots weren't caused by the Dark but from literal searing pain.

"Guys, stop!" Kali shook Dara out of her stupor. "The blade's killing him. The more energy you emit, the more it glows."

As the light over the dagger dimmed, Dara leaned over Max. Gold glimmered in her irises. Her skin was a soft brown with a flush of red. Its ashiness replaced by a healthy shine. Mr. Triman moved to the other side of Max next to Kali.

"Does it still hurt?" Dara asked.

His flesh stung but the smell had diminished. "A little."

"What happened?" Kali looked to Gabriel.

"I was too close while trying to heal them. I was so distressed to see them like this that I didn't think what could happen to Max," Gabriel said.

"It will be fine, brother." Dara reached over Max to lay a hand on Mr. Triman's arm.

A golden spark flared between them, igniting the blade. When Max moaned, they jumped apart.

"Once more, I'm sorry," Mr. Triman said.

"My light energy is so low, it is automatically pulling on my brother's for strength," Dara said.

"If we had continued, we would've incinerated his interior, leaving a shell," Mr. Triman said.

"Like the husk that was used for the book," Kali said.

"But only if we had something to drain the Dark into. Otherwise, Max would be kept alive."

"Let's not do that again, okay?" Kali exclaimed.

Max seconded her assertion with a nod.

"We need to get your spouses out of here. Away from Max to help them heal. There are rooms downstairs," Mr. Triman said to Dara.

"I'll help," Raven offered.

Before picking up Tomas, he put his hands on his hips and gave Max a once over.

"I'm sorry, dude. I really am."

"You were right," Max whispered.

"I wished I hadn't been." He lifted Tomas as if he were a petite woman, not a man packing more muscle than he.

"Welcome to the freak club." With a half-hearted smile, Raven bowed his head and took off into the basement.

Mr. Triman, cradling Gilroy, made his way to the stairs. His golden aura spiked to cover the unconscious man, but he'd moved fast enough that it didn't set the dagger ablaze. Dara trailed behind. She tripped only once to show that she wasn't fully healed.

"What do we do now?" Surefire put her arm around her friend.

Kali laid her head on top of hers. "I honestly don't know."

"I could use a drink." Stockwell stomped out of Max's field of vision.

The door to his grandfather's old liquor cabinet creaked open. A cork popped. Since only the good bottle of whiskey Glen had gifted him one birthday had a cork, Max surmised it was what the Aussie had opened.

Stockwell could drink as much as he wanted. He'd earned it. Based on the guzzling noises that made both women gape in his direction, he was doing just that.

"You expecting anyone?" Stockwell asked. The whiskey sloshed in the bottle as he set it down with a clink.

Max craned his head to find Stockwell cupping his hands against the glass.

Surefire peered out the window behind her.

"It's the people in white. The ones who attacked us at the ski resort," Surefire said. "They're coming around to the front."

Mr. Triman threw open the basement door with Dara in tow.

"My friend notified me that the Organization is on the move." Mr. Triman glanced out the windows. "Appears he found out too late."

He proceeded to pull the drapes over the windows. Kali and Surefire helped until all were covered.

Dara closed her eyes tight. "They number at least twenty. But I don't sense upper management."

"Upper what?" Kali asked. "Are you using human terms to simplify your alien ones again? Because it's annoying."

A helicopter flew over the cabin.

Mr. Triman looked up at the ceiling as if he could see through it to the aircraft. "Management won't come near, because they fear the Dark's power. They're testing it first."

"With their low-level contractors in white?" Kali said.

"Something like that," he replied.

"What do they want?" Raven stepped up from the basement.

"The Dark." Mr. Triman's weary eyes landed on Max.

"Then we'll take them like we did in Utah." Raven positioned himself at the front door.

Surefire took his hand. A purple haze grew from where they touched to cover their bodies.

"Dara, go downstairs and guard your men," Mr. Triman ordered.

When she hesitated, he whispered to her in a lyrical yet haunting language. What Max assumed an ancient dialect would sound like.

She smoothed her palm down her brother's cheek, and it flashed with a golden light. After she left the room, Gabriel closed and locked the hidden door behind her.

"What can I do?" Pinned by the dagger, Max was helpless, paralyzed, but he needed to do something. This Organization was after him. He didn't want them to fight without his help.

"Drink." Stockwell put the mouth of the whiskey bottle to Max's lips.

The smooth liquor rolled along his tongue, sending a warm coat of liquid courage down his throat and distracting him from his pain.

Stockwell set the empty bottle on the table. He took out his gun and positioned himself behind the power couple guarding the front door.

Mr. Triman's index finger tapped against his lips.

"I need you to take Max away from here," he said to Kali.

She wrung her hands. "Where?"

"Do you have any suggestions?" Mr. Triman asked.

"My office at U-Sec." She bobbed her head as if agreeing with herself that this was a good idea. "My bosses will be there as backup. We can use one of our secure rooms to keep Max hidden."

"Go." Gabriel left them and headed to the front door then he paused and circled back to her.

"Thank you for saving them." He gathered her hands in his. A sparkle of light passed from his fingers to hers.

Max winced when the blade flashed with heat then cooled as the light went out.

"We are fortunate beyond words to have you. And so is my Max." The genuine way he spoke to Kali made Max want to smile the largest smile. She deserved that praise and much more.

Kali appeared at a loss for words, and Mr. Triman didn't give her time to find them. He left them to join with the others in forming a formidable line across the front room of the cabin.

"You got this," Max said.

"I know." Kali smiled, more to herself than to him it seemed. "I have help from the future."

He opened his mouth to ask what she meant, but she placed a finger on his lips. "Later, babe. I'll tell you later. Because I know there will be a later for us."

A tingle tickled at his heart. The Dark retreated. As if it were a vampire, and this warm feeling was pure sunlight.

"Let's go." She rotated her shoulders, took in a breath and . . . the back window blew out.

A cold shot of air gusted into the room, blowing the lamp dangling above the table. The top pane of the window nearest the dinette was destroyed.

"Ow," she uttered.

"Kali!" He whipped his head around to find a trail of blood staining her bicep.

Clutching her upper arm, Kali backed up from the table. Behind her more shots shattered the front windows, sending the others diving for the floor.

Tentatively, she extended her hand to Max. Another shot tore through the shattered glass. This time the bullet splintered the back of the oak dinette chair at her hip.

He said her name again. His words were lost in the commotion in the room. She didn't hear him.

Instead her eyes focused on the outside as she disappeared.

He turned his head from side to side to figure out where she'd gone. From his limited POV, she wasn't in the cabin. Across the room, the others held off a swarm of white ski jackets forcing their way through the front door and climbing through broken windows.

He watched the scene unfold like he was in the audience of an interactive theater, but one that affected his life and those in this room—and even the world if the Dark was unleashed—and he could do nothing about it.

Surefire called up branches from the Azalea bush to wrap around the feet of two assailants and fling them from the room. Raven hefted another over his head.

Gold light bathed Mr. Triman in a full-body halo, making Max wonder if he'd sprout wings next. His halo expanded to cover Stockwell. It acted as a barrier to the shots. Bullets smacked into the light, losing velocity and dropping to the floor.

Stockwell fired and hit two assailants. Blood blossomed across their white coats as they collapsed. He unclipped Max's taser from his belt.

Max didn't see what happened next because a white coat stepped into his line of sight. The owner grasped the dagger causing the tip to wriggle in his chest.

"Don't," he gasped.

"I have to because you messed this up," Mia said. She glanced over her shoulder at a woman who stood behind her with a pistol. "If you'd only done it my way, I wouldn't have to do this."

She started to pull. Her face twisted in disgust. "This is gross."

"Do it," the pistol-packing woman with the build of a pro-wrestler commanded.

"Don't," he pleaded again.

"They're going to kill father and our family, if I don't do this." She cut another look at the stocky woman.

"Glen?" Max asked, attempting to stall her.

"He's alive but he won't be for long if they catch him."

He broke out in a sweat as he struggled to lift his hands to stop her but they might as well be sealed in a concrete slab.

"Just like a bandage. A single pull. Ready?" she said.

Max shook his head.

"One, two—"

"Mia, no!" Her father shouted. His halo darkened to a muddy yellow. The effort to shield him and Stockwell from the shots was draining him fast.

He flew toward his daughter as she yanked out the blade.

Max's back arched with the force of it coming free. His insides twisted. A scream tore up his throat at the agony it left behind.

Mia tossed the dagger down and ran to the hidden door leading to the basement.

As the Dark tide rose in his veins, he watched the barrel-shaped woman body slam Mr. Triman. His halo faltered. She wrapped her thick arms around his neck and squeezed. His dress shoes slid and kicked against the wood planks as they went down.

The pain diminished from white-hot bursts to a mild ache. Max fisted his hands, sat up, and cracked his back. Nervous energy poured from his brain down to his toes. He was in control, and he was going to help his friends.

With one hand he grabbed the large woman's hood, yanked her from Mr. Triman and flung her into the pane of the shattered window.

He turned his attention to the front of the house. Surefire, Raven, and Stockwell had taken the fight to the porch, having pushed back the few assailants who had gotten into the home. Max stepped outside. Snow crunched under his bare feet.

The clouds had parted. It had stopped snowing. The full moon lit up the lawn where Max counted twenty people of various sizes with various weapons, some holstered and some in their hands ready to fire. The fight on the porch had moved to hand-to-hand combat. Those surrounding the property weren't shooting, afraid they'd hit their comrades.

"Max," Surefire called to him.

But he didn't acknowledge her. He kept his focus on the encroaching minions in white. Because when the Dark heard her voice, when it felt the goddess's power being used several feet from him, it took all of Max's inner strength to stop it from taking over and attacking her. It wanted her energy. It salivated to taste it.

He stepped off the porch.

We get them then we get her, the Dark said.

A part of Max realized that the Dark was letting him keep control. It wanted Max to taste its power and be seduced by it.

And it was excited for this fight and to have Surefire as a reward when the battle was over.

A high-pitched whistle broke out. In unison, the group on the lawn turned. They clomped away from the house in the snow. But the Dark wasn't going to let them run away. It didn't care that they'd come to free it. It knew they only did it to gain its trust and eventually control it.

Max launched himself into the air and landed on the opposite end of the retreating group. He reached out to the one nearest him. The knee-deep snow made it impossible for them to run. He grabbed him by the throat and sucked at his life force before tossing him aside and reaching for another then another. A few began to fire, tried to save their friends, but they were no match for the Dark gaining in strength and rage, becoming higher and more potent with each life consumed.

"Max!" Surefire screamed from the porch. Her body glowed in a delicious purple light, which would taste sweet with a touch of lavender and succulent flowers and rich spice.

Smacking his chops, he climbed on top of bodies piled at his feet.

Now for dessert.

Chapter 41

Kali Jumps the Gun

Kali's bare feet sank into the snow below the limb where the sniper was positioned. Her rifle attached to the thick branch, her legs straddling it like she was riding a horse. The sniper leaned forward, eye pressed against the scope pointed to the window. The drapes were slitted enough for her to spy Max on the table.

She was so focused that she didn't hear Kali pop below her.

Kali hugged herself against the cold, but it didn't matter. Her exposed flesh prickled with goosebumps. Toes, feet, and shins numbed. One good thing about the cold was that the knick in her bicep from the sniper's first bullet no longer hurt because she couldn't feel anything.

"Hey, you!" Kali reached up and grabbed the henchwoman—or would it still be henchperson?—by her ski pants. She pulled using all her weight and caught the sniper off-guard. She tipped out of the tree and plopped into the snowdrift against the trunk.

As she struggled to right herself, Kali pounced. Her fingers splayed out, searching for exposed flesh. She wrapped her hands around the woman's round face and hauled her into the in-between then dropped them both into a secure holding room at UltraSecurity in Baltimore.

The lights automatically shot on. Kali rolled off the woman who then rolled onto her hands and knees and started coughing up whatever meal she last had.

"Where . . ." the woman heaved once more then spat. "am I?"

"UltraSecurity," Kali replied.

She sprang at Kali, who popped behind her, holding a pistol she'd nabbed from the sniper's holster when they Q-T'd. Her arm stung again. But the blood was seeping less.

"Give me your jacket and pants," she said, surprised at how calm she sounded.

When the woman didn't comply, Kali made a show of cocking the pistol to prove that she knew how to use it.

"Kali, what's going on?" Pax's booming voice vibrated from the speakers in the room.

"She's working for the Organization. They've surrounded Max's cabin. I got to get back to him." Kali took the warm clothes from the woman with a pleasant, "Thank you."

Just because they were on opposite sides—and this woman had shot her—didn't mean Kali couldn't be polite. She would be the bigger person here, which sucked because this woman's jacket and pants were going to be way too short on her.

"We're coming down," Pax announced, but Kali didn't have time to wait for them.

She popped back to the cabin into the kitchen. She tore off the dress, threw on the pants, and zipped up the jacket over her bra then turned to the oak table.

Max was gone.

She spun around and kicked into something soft.

A leg.

"Ow!" Mia cried.

"Where is Max?" she demanded.

"Outside." Mia cowered in the corner by the refrigerator.

"Give me your boots."

She must've looked completely unhinged because Mia didn't hesitate but kicked off her plush snow boots and handed them to Kali.

Thankfully they had the same big feet, but weren't really big, but screw Stockwell for making her think that.

She trudged through the eerily quiet cabin to find a frightening scene in the snow outside.

Max was playing king of the hill with a pile of white clad bodies. They looked like smushed marshmallows layered on top of one another.

His chest had fully healed. He stretched his back, tilted his head from side to side, and shook out his arms like a fighter warming up for the next round.

"Max," she said. His name echoed across the eerily silent night. She heard no animal calls, no wind, no footsteps, no shouts.

Where were her friends?

She stepped onto the snowy porch, and that's when she saw them.

Surefire, Raven, Stockwell, and Gabriel stood unmoving, unconcerned about the threat hiking through the snow toward them.

But they weren't in shock. They were frozen by the Dark.

As Max sunk into the drift at the bottom porch step, he took a small, wobbly step. His legs swayed. His head sagged. Another step, another struggle, as if the snow was waist-high and not up to his knees.

His hand jutted out to Surefire then drew back to his side. It rose again, coming within inches of her friend's throat.

He was trying to maintain control and keep from attacking her friend unable to defend herself. If the Dark took her power, it would grow too powerful and kill Surefire in the process.

With no time to think it through, Kali edged in front of Surefire and Raven and into a front row spot for Max's Jekyll and Hyde struggle. One eye was fully black, the other its lovely gray-green.

The air was charged, heavy with negative mojo. Pins and needles broke out across Kali's chilled skin as if suddenly exposed to a heat source.

"Go," Max grunted through gritted teeth.

She was certain he was holding the Dark's energy in check to keep it from making her one of the living mannequins lining the porch. But his control was wavering. It wouldn't last long.

Still fully charged, thanks to the extra jolt from the future, she grabbed Raven's and Surefire's stiff hands and took them into the in-between with her.

Chapter 42

The Dark Strikes Back

The sweet food disappeared inches from Max's fingertips. Had the Dark fed on the couple's energy, it would've been unstoppable. It would've easily destroyed everyone in the cabin and made its way into this brave new world the Dark had yet to savor.

Now there was a palpable void in their wake.

Its mouth—actually Max's mouth—which had watered in anticipation, emitted a horrifying growl. Rage exploded in Max with an atomic force, blowing his soul back into the gray vacuum. A door slammed and locked from somewhere in front or above or below him. Like before, he didn't sense a floor or atmosphere or anything, not even his body. No smells. No sounds, which shouldn't have fazed him, having lived with deafness until his high-tech hearing aids restored his hearing.

But now he found it jarring, disturbing. Maybe it was the combination of nearly all his senses being extinguished—except that of sight where he was treated to a gray room as if there was a light source somewhere off stage. He wasn't submerged into total darkness.

This gave him hope that he continued to be connected to the outside world. The Dark hadn't fully snuffed him out.

He shoved in the direction of the light source. As he did, his surroundings grew brighter. He traveled through a gray gradient from dark to light, bringing sound with it.

A wooden chair flipped over, bounced against the floor. A table cracked. At some point, the Dark had made its way back into the cabin.

Mr. Triman.

The Dark was seeking out Mr. Triman and then it would find the Three. With Surefire and Raven gone, it was going after the next power source, the strongest one to rebuild itself.

Snap, crackle. A current zapped through him. A dull ache grew, as if a pitcher had beamed a baseball at his chest. The lighter the gray became, the more he could feel, hear, smell, and taste the blood and bitter alien oil in his mouth.

He pressed toward the light.

The pain increased in his chest and dropped Max on his knees. In his right hand was the taser, crumpled like a soda can. His left hand was angled up, shooting invisible energy to the ceiling where Stockwell was suspended. His back pressed against the angled ceiling by the Dark's supernatural force.

A yellow light grew in the room like a mythical gold-laden treasure chest had opened inside the kitchen.

Squinting against the building brightness, he found Mr. Triman and Dara holding hands. Their bodies bathed in a twinkling aura like fairy dust.

"Mia," Mr. Triman called for his daughter, raising his other hand to her.

Max wanted to lunge at her. He wanted to let Stockwell go and fall to the ground so he could hurt Mia for doing this to him and for forcing them on this terrible journey. But the gold light paralyzed the Dark. The more it built up, the weaker the Dark became, unable to heal from the chest wound inflicted by the taser.

On sock-covered feet, Mia shuffled from the galley kitchen where she'd taken cover.

"What do you want from me?" She stopped a foot shy of her father's extended hand. She stared at it as if she'd never seen a hand before, and she didn't know what to do with it.

"Take my hand."

"Why?"

"We need your power to add to ours."

"I don't have any."

"Of course, you do. You're my daughter." He touched her and Mia gasped as the light jumped from his body to cover hers.

"I didn't know." Mia closed her eyes and smiled.

"You weren't ready. But now we need you. Picture our combined energy growing, like you are blowing air into a balloon to expand it," Mr. Triman said.

The Dark grumbled inside Max's mind. Focusing its power inside, it lowered Max's arm, releasing Stockwell.

Dara shot out a ray of light that caught Stockwell and lowered the flailing man to the couch.

"Get the dagger," she ordered him.

In sync, Dara, Mia, and Mr. Triman stepped toward Max. Behind him, Stockwell was flipping over furniture and fallen attackers searching for the blade.

Max released the crumpled taser and shifted back as they drew closer. Their light expanded to create a protective bubble around them. The Dark rallied its forces and focused all its energy to pop the magic membrane.

He pressed his palms against its golden edge. The soft light burned his palms like a handle on a hot pot, but the Dark didn't fall back. Instead, it dug in his nails to tear it open. When that didn't work, he punched and bit and kicked it.

Feed on it.

Those words sent him into a frenzied state the louder the Dark spoke.

Feed. Feed. Feed.

The compulsion to feed on their energies grew as the protective balloon grew. It wanted to destroy them and consume their power at any cost.

I've become a vampire, Max thought.

This morbid idea didn't stop him from seizing on a finger-sized hole in the membrane and ripping it open.

He launched himself through the tear and plowed into the weakest link, Mia. They fell and scattered like bowling pins. The Dark's force pitched Mr. Triman through the broken window, above where Stockwell had knelt to search for the dagger. Dara was flung in the opposite direction into the wall next to the front door, wide open and falling off its hinges.

Max dragged Mia through the cabin, through the broken front door, and onto the pile of bodies, barely alive, writhing under him.

He wedged open her mouth. Like squeezing a tube of sweet icing down his throat, he tasted her half-alien essence.

Chapter 43

Help from an Unexpected Place

Kali considered the choices of where to take her friends. Her condo. U-Sec offices. Their boss Pax's home.

But those places wouldn't provide immediate solutions to the hot mess unfolding at the cabin—or provide answers to save Max from the Dark.

"What's with the blue streak?" Synthia's question reverberated in the abyss. Both her body and Raven's stretched and flapped behind Kali like rubber bands.

"Crystal skull. The one Robert brought to the condo," she replied.

"That's why I'm sicker than normal with this jump," Synthia said.

"Why is it taking so long? Usually, we're in and out," Raven asked.

"Can't decide where to go."

"Pick anywhere, or else you'll be traveling through streaks of vomit. Not sure how much longer I can contain it." Synthia gagged as if to make her point.

Contain it. The words hit a switch in Kali's mind, giving light to an idea that was far-fetched, but considering the current state of things, not out of the realm of possibility.

She pictured Max's home lab and pointed them to that location.

As the room materialized, Kali sensed a disturbance in its vibe. The air felt oppressive, the energy prickly. Not from the broken bits of glass and plastic that crunched under the soles of her stolen snow boots. Not because the room appeared as if Dorothy's tornado had made a pit stop here on the way to Oz.

No, there was a negativity weighing down the space. It wasn't supernatural but—

"Oh, no," dropped from Kali's lips when she noticed Synthia's father sitting where the screen used to hang.

"Synthia." St. John rose from the rolling seat in front of the computer console that was littered with shattered glass and frayed wires.

Her friend bent over Max's work table and clutched her stomach. Raven rubbed her back as she panted to keep from being sick.

"I'm fine." She held a hand up to Raven. He stopped rubbing her back and gave her space. His eyes never left St. John as if daring him to make a move toward them.

Synthia rose. Her head gave a hard shake as if shaking her senses back in place. She cut Kali a look that made her knees wobble with guilt.

"Sorry," she mouthed to her friend.

Synthia cleared her throat before saying, "Kali, why did you bring us here?"

She slumped against the edge of the table. "Max has something that I hope can help us."

Raven draped his arm around his girlfriend's shoulders. Kali was learning this action wasn't meant to shield Synthia but as a show of strength. In attacking one, you attacked both, and in turn, would have to fight both.

Large jagged pieces of glass hung suspended from the ceiling where the screen used to be. She concluded that the glass littering the floor was what remained of it.

"What did you do?" she said to St. John, assuming he was to blame for this destruction.

The man kept his intense gray gaze seared on his estranged daughter, without a glance in Kali's direction to indicate he heard her question.

"The journal is what happened. Its power threw Synthia across the room and into the screen," Raven replied when St. John didn't.

"Kali, get what you need and let's go." Synthia kept her arms crossed and offered her father the same unreadable expression he was giving her.

"Where is it?" Raven asked.

The silence between his girlfriend and her father was stretching to a terminal breaking point. Kali knew that Raven feared what she feared. If Synthia grew angrier, the goddess would take over. And she had even less love for St. John.

"In there." Kali pointed to an unlit room off to the side. The door was wide open as when she'd left.

"If you're here, then the Dark has returned." St. John broke his visual standoff with Synthia.

Kali stopped herself from asking how he knew, because she didn't care and because she'd never get a straight answer from General Everything-Is-Classified.

And also, they didn't have time.

"Yes, the Dark is back and almost made your daughter its main meal," she replied.

"Then you don't have it neutralized?" St. John asked.

"That's why we're here." Kali checked her watch as she hurried to the containment unit. It had been five minutes since they'd left. It felt like hours.

As soon as her foot crossed into the storage room, the lights came on. She steeled herself against the inevitable anxiety at facing this monstrosity again.

But she felt nothing. It held no power anymore over her. It was a cursed object that had lost its curse. Maybe because she knew it wasn't going to be used on her this time.

The others gathered around her as she drew closer to understand its inner workings. Reflected in the glass, she saw Raven and Synthia standing behind her. St. John's bulldog face appeared behind them.

Wondering what pieces may go with it, she checked the controls and the wires and plugs.

"It's self-contained," St. John said.

"How do you know?" Synthia demanded.

Kali guessed her friend knew the answer, but she wanted her father to finally admit it.

"A Black Books project. Outside of DERST's official project list," he replied.

"Like what Lucinda worked on for you?" Purple light sparked across her eyes.

The hair on Kali's head stood on end. A metaphysical lightning storm began brewing inside her friend. Fortunately, St. John defused his daughter—and a lightning strike—by saying something no one expected.

"I made a mistake." He hung his head.

"You did so much more than that," Raven said.

For the first time since Kali had met St. John, he appeared less of an authoritarian and more of a remorseful father seeking forgiveness.

The purple flashes in Synthia's eyes mellowed. She screwed up her mouth and appeared confused as to how to respond.

"Did you plan to use this one on me, if I didn't agree to work with you?" Kali asked.

After Kali stepped out with her power to help with Synthia's case, St. John had hounded her for months to get specialized training, to work with his black ops forces. She declined. She had no desire to work on secret missions where she wouldn't be sure that she was helping the good guys.

"This was never intended for you. This TPC was created to contain the Dark," he said.

"How do you know about the Dark?" Raven asked.

"I saw it. Firsthand. I was living on Maxwell Martin's property with my mother after my father died." St. John took two steps toward the couple then stopped when Raven glowered at him.

"No one knows about our years there. Not even your mother," St. John continued. "After Maxwell disappeared, the commune disbanded. Your grandmother took over our family's horse farm. I joined the Army."

His thick hands twisted together. On anyone else it would appear like a pleading gesture, but St. John never pleaded for anything. He ordered, took, did what he needed for the supposed greater good.

"I never forgot what happened that day. I vowed never to let that evil enter this world again. When I learned of your ability," he nodded at Kali, "and where you could travel, I'd hoped you could work with us to monitor it in the other universe."

"That didn't go as planned. Maybe you should've told me, and you know, we could've discussed it." Kali finished inspecting the unit. St. John was right. It was self-contained.

"I didn't know if I could trust you," he said.

Did St. John, the bogeyman of conspiracy theories, say he didn't trust her?

"Man, that is the wildest thing that's been said all night. And that is saying something, babe." Kali laughed and looked to Synthia and Raven and even they chuckled at this unbelievable assertion.

"Get in." Kali pounded the top of the containment unit with her fist.

Synthia and Raven stopped laughing. Both their mouths dropped wide open at her request.

St. John didn't budge to follow her order. This didn't surprise her one bit.

"I said." Kali unlatched the lid and threw it open. "Get in."

St. John went still as a tiger before a strike. He tried to stare her down with his steel-colored eyes.

Wasn't working this time.

"We've wasted enough time chitchatting," Kali said. "The Dark is going to use Max to snack on this world. The longer we wait, the more chances it has to use him to expand its power. You know how to set this up and use it. So shut up and get inside, so I can Q-T you and this thing to the cabin."

"Kali—" Synthia began and she stopped her.

"You two stay here and call Pax. Until we have the Dark contained, I don't want you near it." Kali was surprised at how confident she sounded in giving orders, and she was surprised to discover how much she liked it.

"My team's been notified of the breach. They should be at his cabin soon." St. John drew a stepladder over to the unit.

"Have you Q-T'd with something this size and with someone in it?" He asked as he slid inside.

"You'll be my guinea pig. Imagine that?" She slammed the lid down and locked it.

"Are you sure about this?" Synthia laid a hand on the arm of the sniper's puffy coat that Kali had forgotten she was wearing and was just now noticing how much she'd been sweating underneath.

"No." She slid the jacket off and tied it around her waist. She'd forgotten that she only wore a bra underneath, having shed her dress.

At least it will give her more skin to press against the unit, exposing it to her power.

"I don't know about this." Raven scrubbed his hand down his face.

"I'm doing it. I can't give up on Max." She climbed up the ladder and threw her leg over the top portion of it. "Especially after he drank that Dark to save me."

Before her friends could argue anymore, she tapped the glass. "You ready?"

St. John nodded. A strange look of worry passed over him that made her happy.

She wrapped her arms around the thing and rode it into the in-between.

Chapter 44

Truth in the Darkness

The Dark fed on Mia's alien energy like a black hole feeds on surrounding stars, its mass growing with each meal.

Max pried himself away. The feeling was too intense. His thudding heart was going to ram through his rib cage if he didn't stop.

A scream stuck in Mia's throat. She wedged her hands against his chest to free herself. Her fear amused the Dark as it took over the driver seat and jammed Max's fingers into her mouth to hold it open.

He inhaled her essence. The sweet, earthy flavor of pot coated his tongue. Adrenaline pulsated under his skin. His gut swirled with a euphoria akin to a child surrounded by birthday gifts.

And he was unwrapping one satisfying gift. Mia's tasty life force strengthened the Dark, and in turn, made Max feel more alive than ever. He was strong, powerful, invincible.

He succumbed to the allure of its power. With it, he could do anything, have anything he wanted.

Right now, as he drew in Mia's life force, he wanted answers. In this state, she couldn't hide the truth from him.

When he'd drained the Organization's soldiers, he didn't think to search their minds. He was blinded by anger that they'd attacked his home. Shot at the woman he loved. His only concern was to stop them.

Why did you do it? He shoved every ounce of his desire to learn the truth into that question.

A mist blocked out his vision. Piece by piece, an image appeared inside the haze. He became a fly, riding Robert's shoulder as he led Mia inside a nondescript brick building found in any business park. She followed him past an empty reception area and through another door where the neutral walls and thin carpet stopped abruptly, and a vastly different room took shape.

Too large and elaborate to be housed in that one-story building, this domed chamber belonged in a medieval castle Max had seen once in a photo, or maybe he'd visited—he couldn't access the memory.

A high-back antique chair sat alone in the middle of the room positioned in front of a mahogany table that took up half the space where twelve people sat, their faces obscured by shadows that—based on the brightness of the room—shouldn't be there. Robert motioned for Mia to sit.

These shadowed faces spoke to her in voices equally distorted, as if her memory was a video that they'd scrubbed to keep their identities hidden. They unveiled their plan for the Dark. They wanted to use it, access its powers. They revealed her father's part in the accident in Max's lab.

The more they spoke, the angrier Mia became with her father. And the more she considered offering up herself to the Dark. From their alien father, Glen had developed a talent. But her alien genes had given Mia nothing that she could find. The next big splash in reality television would be a transhuman star. She wanted it to be her. That was the initial reason she didn't want Max to be infected with it. When it became clear to her that this power was unstable—that the Dark would possess Max until he no longer existed—she wanted to protect him.

He was family.

Family.

Pop! Pop! Pop!

Three bullets struck Max's back, embedding into the flesh around his spine. The opulent meeting room disintegrated, and Max again stared at Mia's slacked face. Her eyes had rolled in the back of her head. Her arms hung loose at her sides.

He tossed her into the snow. He was done with her. She'd given all she could to him. Maybe if she survived this, then the Dark would make her a vessel. Grow its army. Give her the power she craved.

The snow crunched as two people drew nearer. Without looking, Max knew one was Stockwell, who toted the dagger. The gun he'd fired into Max's back lay on the porch. Its chamber was empty.

Max bowed his back. The bullets slid from the wounds. Skin itched as the holes closed up.

Mr. Triman's golden aura reflected in the snow and grew wider as the two approached. The Dark shrank from it, but not as much as before. It was stronger, and with this strength, it could deflect more of this alien's light power.

"Family," Max spat when Mr. Triman was in earshot. He wiped the back of his hand across his lips.

"Allow Dara to take my daughter," he said.

His pleading tone touched Max's heart, momentarily displacing the Dark like a stone dropped into a puddle of water.

Above him, Dara descended like an angel from heaven. Body sheathed in a glittering halo. Her energy surrounded Mia and floated her limp body into the alien's arms. She flew into the house, cradling Mia with more care than Max felt she deserved.

"Family," Max repeated.

His arm struck out to his side. The men stopped walking. The glow over the snow flickered.

"Then you know," Mr. Triman said.

Max turned to the two men. The Dark cemented them in place. Stockwell's knuckles had turned white from grasping the dagger. Tendons in his neck protruded as he tried to move. Mr. Triman's protective gold bubble thinned.

"How many wives did you have over the centuries? How many women did you fuck?" Max reeled on him.

Mr. Triman blanched at his words.

Max continued, "How many of us are related to you and your kind?"

The Dark was enjoying the show. It rewarded Max with more control and pumped power into his limbs.

Take him. It wanted Max to kill. Make Mr. Triman theirs. Consume his essence so it would reside within them forever.

The longer Mr. Triman took to reply to this accusation, the more Max wondered whether he knew how many women there had been. Over thousands of years, it would be easy to lose track.

"I loved your great-grandmother," he admitted.

"You abandoned her," Max spat. "She was a single mom raising a son during the Depression."

"I supported them from afar and ensured they were comfortable. Your grandfather, my son, was special at a young age, and he grew to exceed even my expectations."

"Then he became the Dark."

The light shielding the men wavered. Mr. Triman's gaze lowered. "That's not what I intended. I kept them safe for as long as I could as the rift in the Organization deepened. I feared repercussions from enemies if they realized who your grandfather was to me."

"Yet you started another family."

"By then, I assumed the Organization had left Earth when our government cut support for us. I stayed behind to wait for my sister. And I am glad that I did." Mr. Triman set his lips into a defiant line and tilted his head to look down his nose at Max.

His prideful stance enraged the Dark. It surged forth to possess Max. It would make Mr. Triman pay for his arrogance and for not giving it the fear it demanded.

But Max tamped it down and stopped it from taking him over. Maybe it was the shield knot tattoo. Maybe it was the ability he received from his special strands of DNA that allowed him to hold the Dark at bay and construct a metaphysical brick wall to contain it and protect Mr. Triman from what the Dark wanted to do to him.

"I will tell you anything you want to know. But first, let us contain the Dark before we lose you forever," Mr. Triman said. "I see you're holding it back. You are indeed strong, but it will not be enough if the Dark continues to grow."

To prove his control to Mr. Triman, Max focused on the energy used to hold the two men in place. He pictured it withdrawing.

But as Max released the invisible chains, Stockwell lunged at him.

"No!" Max swung his arm and batted Stockwell and the dagger into the air.

Mr. Triman pivoted. His aura shot upward to stop Stockwell from crashing through a tree.

In the distance, came the sound of multiple helicopters approaching.

Max grabbed Mr. Triman by the shoulder. He slammed him to the ground. His bald head bounced against a chunk of ice. The gold glow faded, leaving an ordinary man in its wake.

Max closed his eyes to seek out what was coming for him. Friend or foe.

It doesn't matter, the Dark whispered. *Both wants to use you. Study you. Contain you.*

Max wasn't going to be anyone's lab rat or weapon. He'd destroy them and syphon Mr. Triman's power to do it.

He forced the alien's mouth open and inhaled. Mr. Triman tasted like dusty old books, grilled steak, sweet cola, and a savory power that was more potent than his daughter's. Max shook with ecstasy. His heart rate accelerated, but this time, he knew it wouldn't burst his chest. He was sturdier now. The Dark coated his skin. Every bone and muscle was fortified with this intoxicating substance.

The Dark shared its secrets, and the more it shared, the more Max believed it to be right and true and the universe's savior. He experienced in vivid Cinemascope the pain and horror humans inflicted over the centuries. This world needed a reboot. The Dark would purify Earth and use the dead to fertilize the soil. Given multiple chances to restore peace, humans had failed. Through Max, the Dark would use DERST's resources and wealth—

From far, far away, a woman called his name.

Mr. Triman's hands slid from Max's forearms. His struggles slowed from the strength of a healthy man to that of a dying one.

"Max," the voice spoke closer this time, near his ear. "Max, you're killing him."

The Dark's whispers faded into incoherent mumbles. He became aware of the frigid air and his numb feet, which were planted in a knee-high snowdrift over the shriveled, dead vegetable garden. His surrogate father hung from his hands like a sock puppet.

What have I done?

The Dark started its whispers again. A drone filled with hateful rhetoric urged Max to finish the job.

But its urging was distilled, watered down.

"Stay back," Kali said.

He assumed she was speaking to him, but as his eyes refocused on the scene, he found Dara floating from the edge of the forest with Stockwell. Kali had changed into white snow pants and jacket. The hood pulled over her head.

She touched his shoulder.

The Dark cowered from her light touch, recoiling deeper into his torso.

It hated what she brought out in Max. A tingling in his chest, flittering butterflies that tickled his stomach and made him squirm with giddiness. Max craved her warmth, her scent. He wanted to laugh with her, gaze into her large brown eyes, kiss her soft lips.

He missed her—her laugh, her voice, the feel of her skin.

And the Dark didn't know what to do with these feelings. They didn't fuel it but repulsed it. Fear, rage, and violence, it knew intimately. Sex without tenderness, it could get behind.

But love was another thing altogether.

She wrapped her arms around his neck.

"Let Gabriel go," she said against his ear.

Dara floated to the ground and set Stockwell on his feet. The tough Aussie was banged up like he'd come out of a bar brawl on the wrong side. With a curse, he sank into the snow. He struggled to stand, but his whole body shook. Max's eyes zeroed in on the dagger glistening in his hand. It reflected the lights from the helicopter circling the property.

The Dark's defenses reared up. It sent forth a storm of emotion that raged against the love he was feeling. He clutched Mr. Triman's limp body to his chest.

"Focus on me." Kali's fingers entwined in his hair. Her thumbs rubbed circles on his temples. Her face appeared in front of his and blocked out the frantic scene.

"You can beat this," she said.

"How?"

"Together," she said. "But also, that tattoo is helping and probably your own abilities. So I can't really get all the credit."

"Trust me, it's you," he said.

His eyes fell onto what he was holding. No, *whom* he was holding.

Red blotches soaked the snow under Mr. Triman's head. More blood coated Max's arm.

Another feeling emerged in Max, making the Dark cringe and rear back further into its pit.

Guilt.

"I killed him," Max said.

"It will take a lot more to kill this guy. But he is hurt."

Dara extended her arms to take her brother. Max sucked in an icy breath. His arms shook as he wrestled with the Dark to let Mr. Triman go. It helped that Dara wasn't using her power to force him. He sensed that she was holding it in reserve to heal her brother.

Mr. Triman slid from Max's stiff arms to Dara's open ones. Donning a grateful smile, she took her brother and glided into the cabin.

Max narrowed his eyes, peering into the cabin's entrance. A multitude of shadows moved across the living room, where a large object that wasn't part of the decor took up the center stage.

"Who's there?" The Dark rose again, clawing its way from the pit and up Max's torso.

"Hey." Kali planted a kiss on his cheek. She enfolded him in her arms. Her fingers massaged the back of his neck.

Above them two helicopters hovered.

"What's going on?" He started to look up, but Kali held him steady against her.

"Do you love me?" she asked.

He blinked and processed her question, as soldiers rappelled from the helicopter to land in the snow near them.

"Do you love me?" she asked again, accenting each word.

"Yes," he said before he couldn't, before the Dark fed off the small seed of fear growing as the soldiers approached.

"Remember our first night together in the back of the VW bus?"

Max nodded.

"I want you to hold onto that memory. Hold tight to that feeling of our first kiss because it will only get better from here."

Tears stung his eyes.

"With all my heart, my soul, and with this peanut growing inside, I trust you will overcome this."

"Kali, I can't—"

"Shhh. No negative vibes." She put a finger to his lips. "You can and will do this."

"It's too strong."

"You're stronger."

Hearing her faith in him spoken aloud with such certainty ignited a warmth that radiated from his heart. The Dark rallied against it. But Max found that when he focused on the positive vibes, he grew more powerful. His body was converting the negative energy that fueled the Dark and turning it into light.

She pulled away, leaving a void between them.

"I got it, mates." Stockwell shoved off two soldiers, who were helping him to his feet. As soon as they let go, he fell face down in the snow. Either the whiskey or the fight had gotten the better of him. He was down for the count.

And he no longer had the dagger.

Max wondered if he'd dropped it in the snow until he felt its sharp point pressing into the skin below his chest.

Kali held it now.

Another helicopter circled the cabin and forest. Its lights skimmed across the clearing and illuminated Kali and him. More soldiers in black appeared and formed a circle around them. Their weapons were drawn. He knew . . . or the Dark sensed . . . that they worked for St. John, who was inside preparing the TPC for him.

Pressure built in his core like water boiling in a kettle. The Dark was making a last ditch effort to save itself. Its oily tendrils stretched downward to wrap around his legs.

Run away.

The voice grew louder, whispering to Max that they had the power to destroy them. They could fight and leave here and take over the world. All Max had to do was to stop resisting. Tear off the skin holding the tattoo.

Then it would lock Kali in the TPC until the child was born.

Max surrounded Kali's hands with his own. But the Dark continued talking, not realizing its mistake, because Max would rather die than let it hurt Kali.

"Do it," he said.

Her tearful eyes held his as they both shoved the blade inside.

"I love you, Max," she said as he cried out against the hot poker tearing at his insides, neutralizing the Dark, silencing the demon's voice.

"I know," he got out.

She laughed between tears at what he'd said. His body went rigid. He could barely focus on the man looming over him in a wool coat. Gray hair cut in a buzz. Clean shaven jaw.

"Get him to the TPC," he ordered with the confidence of someone used to directing others.

"Stephen St. John," Max whispered.

He recognized him from DERST dealings. The classified connection behind the TPC project. Mr. Triman's military contact.

Two soldiers hefted his prone body onto a stretcher.

Kali appeared at his side and said next to his ear in a conspiratorial tone, "St. John is the original 'The Man.'"

She fell back as they carried him inside the cabin. Where the wagon wheel table used to stand was the TPC. He glanced at Kali, hurrying to stay by his side.

"I brought it here because I didn't know what your basement lab looked like, and we were cutting it close as it was," she said as if anticipating his question.

"Take it to the basement," St. John said to Kali.

She cocked her head at the general. "What do you say?"

He was a few inches taller than Kali, but his authority lent several more. Although that didn't stop her from putting her hands on her hips and tapping her foot while waiting for him to give the response she required.

"Please," he relented.

Satisfied, Kali nodded and sprinted away. She popped back into the room after Max assumed she determined the layout downstairs.

"All systems are a go." With a flourish, she opened the TPC.

St. John's soldiers lifted up Max and slid him onto the cushion inside.

"How are you holding up?" Kali pushed strands of hair off his forehead.

He tried to smile but managed a grimace instead.

"That good, huh? We'll have this evil ink out of you in no time. Don't worry, I did a test run with St. John in this thing." She winked at him. "I don't think he was happy about it, but I taught him a lesson, or maybe I just annoyed him. Either way, it was worth it."

St. John scowled at her from the other side of the case. She shrugged him off then clamped down the lid. Max next found himself staring into the abyss of the in-between, and then at the ceiling in the living room of his basement lab.

"Kali," he tried to say, but it came out as more of a croak than her name.

He couldn't see her and couldn't move his head to see where she'd gone. The TPC vibrated followed by a hiss. They'd turned it on.

She appeared over him and held up her phone with a text that read: "It's warming up now. We're setting up the machine to monitor your vitals then—"

The chamber filled with cryo gas, blasting from the nozzles embedded into the sides that he'd helped install.

Chapter 45

Two Weeks after the Dark's El

Kali stared past the thick glass of the TPC and into the chilled chamber keeping Max's body alive—and the Dark contained.

When she refocused on the glass, S-Kali's sallow face floated in front of Max's.

"Oh!" She jerked back and into Stockwell.

"Steady, girl." He righted her. "Looks like you saw a ghost."

"Close enough." She rubbed her eyes and the eerie image away.

"I got your back." He clapped her shoulder.

"Painfully so." She winced. Stockwell didn't know his own strength, or maybe he did and didn't care.

The latter seemed more likely.

For the past two weeks at the tech lab/bunker-style apartment under Max's cabin, he'd followed Kali around like a lost kitten—one that carried an arsenal around his waist. So maybe kitten was too cuddly a simile for this man. Perhaps he was more like a stray cat that followed her home from a dark alley.

"You're still here?" Gloria bumped Stockwell out of her way as she walked to the controls on the side of TPC that displayed and monitored Max's vitals. "Don't you have a kangaroo to throw on the barbie? Or maybe choke on some vegemite?"

"I don't like kangaroo meat, and you can't choke on vegemite, you daft sheila."

"I'm sure you could find a way."

Kali coughed to cover her laugh.

"What's that supposed to mean? You calling me a drongo?"

Gloria referenced the tablet computer in her hand before adjusting the TPC's controls.

"Don't know what that is, but if it's insulting, then yes." She tapped the screen and began downloading data from the machine supporting Max's body.

"Don't." Kali planted a hand on Stockwell's chest when he cocked his hip, about to lay into Gloria. Last time that happened, Kali had to Q-T them onto separate floors to keep one from killing the other.

Kali laid her bets on Gloria getting in the knockout punch.

"You insulted her brother. Only she gets to do that—and possibly Pax. Although what you called Sean when you crashed the dinner was beyond insulting."

"How was I supposed to know he wasn't Japanese?"

"That's not the point." Kali groaned in annoyance.

Not only had Stockwell made an erroneous assumption about Sean's ethnicity, as if all Asians were the same, but he'd used a derogatory term when he first encountered her boss at the *Real Life* dinner. Sean's adoptive parents had been careful to encourage his interest and pride in his Korean heritage, just as they had taught their adopted daughter, Gloria, about her background.

Based on the uniform Stockwell had worn when he'd crashed the dinner party and his flippant use of the slur, Kali had guessed that he was from an older generation—one that grew up in the aftermath of World War II—as they tracked him through time and space after he'd taken Sean and the others from the dinner that night.

"It doesn't make it right. If you want to live in our world, you need to rethink how you view others and show respect." Kali frowned at herself. This pregnancy was already turning her into a lecturing mom.

Stockwell folded his arms tight across his chest and appeared as if he was going to argue.

Instead, he surprised her by saying, "All right, I will. I see how bad that was."

"You also fought Sean and held him in your universe, which is another reason Gloria can get away with calling you a drongo or whatever."

"I apologized," he said sheepishly. "Besides, it wasn't me but another version of me. I haven't punched him since I've been here. Wanted to, but didn't. Can't I get credit for that?"

"No." Sean walked up behind them.

"Shit on this. I'll be in the kitchen sinking a piss." He stalked toward the door then slammed it open.

When it closed behind him, Kali asked, "Can you at least give him a chance?"

"No," they answered.

"Why did you bring him here? I don't even know what we're going to do with him." Sean shot a sour look in the kitchen's direction.

Kali sighed at once again having to explain this. "As I told you already, he was working with the Three to spy on the Man. He was the one who neutralized Max so we could get home through the portal. He had nothing left in that universe. The Dark used him and killed his mom. I feel sorry for him."

Gloria snorted. "It's like living with a chatty Australian Rambo."

"He needs to get used to our time and universe. With some tough love, he's young enough to change," Kali argued. "Besides, he has military training. We want him on our side. He could help on cases."

"Take it up with Pax," Sean said. "Right now, I may have found something in the journal to help Max."

Kali watched Gloria for a reaction to what Sean had announced, but she continued to pour over Max's electronic charts and didn't appear to have heard—or maybe was too focused on what was in her files to hear—what Sean said.

"Heart rate is accelerated," she began as her eyes skimmed the electronic chart. "His body is constantly being flooded with adrenaline. I have to keep administering vasopressors to keep him from going into cardiogenic shock. He has heart damage from one of the many gunshots. The chamber has slowed the Dark's ability to heal his body. For now, Max is holding up under the pressure. His tattoo and genetic makeup may have lessened the Dark's hold on him, but it also appears the Dark is recoding him."

"As in . . .?" Kali prodded.

"Restructuring his DNA."

"That's what I thought you meant." Her shoulders slumped along with her heart. "Restructuring to what?"

"I confirmed he has a transhuman marker in addition to a percentage of unknown DNA. I believe both combined are allowing this biological substance to take root. Then there was another code in his genes, I've never encountered before in N-Ts or transhumans."

"The Dark was a fellow Custodian and relative of Gabriel before it morphed into the evil oil slick." Kali stuck out her tongue, making a yuck face. "Maybe it's alien DNA from the Dark?"

"I believe it was in Max's code prior to the alien entity merging with his body. Gabriel did mention that he knew Max could handle the Dark after having studied his medical files." Gloria's lips twisted as she mulled over what this meant.

Kali had a hunch, based on Mia's excuse for saving Max because he was "family." But it was only a hunch. She wasn't about to spread rumors now, especially with Gabriel not here to provide any answers.

"And Gabriel hasn't returned my calls for a few days," Sean said.

"They blew out of here before I could get a blood sample to compare with Max's. Apparently, these Custodians are fine with experimenting on us although . . ." Gloria arched her brows. "I did find a few hairs that the redhead left behind, so we'll see what I come up with."

After ensuring that Max was stable and properly contained in the TPC, Gabriel had left the following day, taking the Three and his daughter with him. He'd played intermediary with Max's parents by telling them that their son was in quarantine after being exposed to a chemical agent in his basement lab that caused an explosion. With Glen's help, his parents were persuaded that Max was getting the best care, and they needed to wait until he was allowed visitors.

Glen appeared to have this silver-tongue gift down pat. Kali hoped he would be there when she told Max's folks about the pregnancy, which Gloria confirmed with a test the day after Max was put on ice.

"I think the Three plan to hitch a ride to their home planet. The substance that can hold the Dark is not found on Earth, so maybe they've left already?" Kali said.

"I'll confirm that with Glen once he's back up for air. We're supposed to meet, but he's been overwhelmed with DERST's PR department, helping them craft messages and field interviews about Max taking a sabbatical. Then there's Mia's tell-all web series about her alien father," Sean said.

"Haven't you heard? Mia's disappeared," Kali said.

"When? Because they just released details about her upcoming *Real Life* alien edition special." Sean folded his arms.

"The story was streaming on the web news and gossip channels this morning." Kali held up her phone to show him the headlines scrolling across the feed.

Sean shrugged. "I never watch that nonsense, which explains why I missed it."

Kali rolled her eyes at his comment, because she'd caught him watching those channels when he thought no one was looking. "It could be a publicity stunt for all I know. I can't reach her. Her phone is out of service. With Mia claiming in the show's ads that she has secrets to share about a shady network of aliens, Gabriel may be forcing her to go underground."

Or even St. John could be behind her disappearance. Mia had mentioned a black ops team in her promo for the web series.

Currently, St. John was gathering his specialized team. Putting aside their past differences with the retired general, Pax and Oracle offered to help track down the Organization before it targeted other UltraAgents. They started by interviewing the sniper Kali had deposited in U-Sec's holding cell. Like Robert, she'd been a former Olympic athlete.

St. John hadn't divulged much to Kali about the Organization's military force—or low-level contractors, as Gabriel referred to them—who ambushed the cabin. He never mentioned Max accruing a pile of bodies after the Organization attacked. Never said whether they were dead or had survived. His team removed them and even cleaned up and repaired the cabin. After a new snowfall, only broken tree limbs gave any sign of the destruction that had taken place.

"Although, we should keep an eye on this story," Sean said, bringing Kali out of her thoughts and back to the conversation. "See if Mia turns up. As annoyed as I am over what she's done, she doesn't deserve to die over it."

"True." Although she'd cursed Mia's name since the dinner, Kali didn't want her to die and didn't want her *Real Life* web series to go forward either. She was certain Mia would highlight Kali's and Max's story. She only hoped they hadn't filmed any episodes before Mia had disappeared.

"Sean, you found something in the journal?" Gloria turned the conversation back to her brother's earlier statement.

"Trying it out now." His hands were on the metal box that housed the TPC's switchboard. A blue current sparked from them, melding his nerves with the machine holding Max.

"What are you doing?" Gloria said.

"I'm trying to get a read on the Dark using the TPC. That thing is a biological database of knowledge, and right now, Max is its server. Based on what I uncovered in the journal, we might be able to tap into it." Sean removed his hands, rubbing them together as if trying to return feeling to them. "I can't go deep enough through this TPC. If I can insert a biochip inside him, sync it to the Dark, then I could possibly re-program it to not destroy all humans. But I don't know what it will do to Max."

"That is so farfetched." Gloria shook her head then stopped. If she were a cartoon character, a light bulb would've appeared over her head. "It might actually work."

"All I care about is getting this thing out of Max and to preferably not have to wait for whenever Gabriel can get back here with another bottle." Kali rubbed her hand over the cool glass lid under which Max slept peacefully.

Laying her forehead on the TPC, she sighed. She needed Synthia more than ever, but she wasn't going to derail her from making amends with her father. After talking in Max's basement for the first time since Xochi, using Synthia's body, had wielded her power to cover his crew and a billion-dollar submarine in flowers and vines, St. John apologized. He wouldn't admit he was responsible for Lucinda, the unhinged scientist he had at one time employed, and who had kidnapped and drained Synthia's powers. But it was enough to gain a centimeter of his daughter's trust back. She and Raven even pledged themselves to the cause of fighting the Organization.

As if sensing her sadness, Gloria stated in her brusque way, "You can stay with me. I wouldn't want you to go through this alone."

"That's nice of you," Kali said and meant it.

"No problem, really. Plus, you should be monitored—day and night. Already, you're further along than you should be. With your ability, I'm not sure what that little bugger may do inside there." Gloria mimed her hand exploding from her chest and making screeching alien sounds.

Kali was going to be ill right there on Gloria's expensive boots. No one with her power—because there had been none—had birthed a child. Most transhumans with abilities were sterile. Those who had children weren't high up on the power spectrum. They had low-level abilities like enhanced vision or hearing. And just like the genetic lottery, some abilities were passed down and others weren't.

"It's just a joke." Gloria nudged Kali and laughed. "Besides, it wouldn't be chestburster because it's too low."

"You can stop now." She scowled at her boss/doctor, who shrugged her shoulders as if Kali had no sense of humor.

Fortunately, Sean interrupted them before Gloria could make another "joke."

"I also found a section in the journal that details how to transfer the Dark to another host. It's similar to how the Man transferred Kali's power to Stockwell via the pack he wore," Sean said. "Doing it slow like that would give Max's body time to adjust and allow us to control the flow of the Dark, so it doesn't kill the old host or overrun the new one."

"I'll do it." Stockwell strutted into the room with a beer in his hand.

"Really?" Gloria appeared to consider his offer. Her eyes roamed over him, taking stock of his physical form to determine if he was strong enough to handle it.

"Absolutely not. I will not trust you of all people with this kind of power. Look at what it did to someone who's not a sociopath." Sean flapped a hand at the TPC.

Stockwell glared at him. "Put me on ice then do the transfer. Then take the dagger out of Max and neutralize me with it. No worries."

"Do we have another TPC?" Kali looked to Sean.

"I can check with Glen. DERST held the plans and the prototype for it. I'm sure they could devote resources to creating an identical one, if it means getting their CEO back sooner," he said.

"I'll need to run tests on you." Gloria inclined her head at Stockwell. "See if you can handle it."

Sean huffed. "Really, Glor? You're going to give *him* this power?"

"As you said, he'd be a server for it like Max is now. Maybe it would give you time to figure out how to reprogram it. And we'd keep him in cryo for as long as it takes."

"Stockwell was able to handle my power," Kali spoke up. "In that alternate timeline, he used my ability to cross over."

"Which is why he can't be trusted." Sean wagged his head.

Stockwell's lips twisted into a cocksure smile, which Kali recognized as him about to launch a verbal attack.

She pulled him aside before he could start a war of words with Sean. "Why are you volunteering to do this?"

"Because." He punctuated the reply by crossing his arms.

When she realized he wasn't going to elaborate, she said, "This is dangerous. You could—"

"Die?" he said. "By all rights, I should be dead already. I've been a regular wanker. I've made poor choices. I've hurt people in my past and apparently also in an alternate timeline, even when I thought I was helping. I was misguided and I aim to atone."

"There are other ways."

He shook his head hard. "That baby of yours should know his father. I don't want the Dark corrupting another good person and depriving another child of his old man. That child is my family too via a different universe, so I'm his great-uncle in a way."

Kali's nose started to run. She sniffled. This damn Aussie was driving her to tears and for the first time in a good way.

Stockwell looked everywhere but at her face. His jaw worked back and forth as if deciding whether to say more.

"I looked up myself on your Goggly thing," he said.

"Google?"

"Yeah, what I said, and I found out who I could've become."

"There are so many variables that define this universe and yours. Don't—"

"My mum in this universe died in her eighties of natural causes. She survived the cancer and wasn't killed in her fifties by the Dark. This Stockwell married after the service. Ran a security agency with offices in Sydney and London. Just retired and handed the company over to his daughter. I saw what could've been. My alternate future. I didn't think a future like that was even possible for me."

"In your universe, this future may not have been possible," Kali said.

"I'm helping you, because I've gotten a second chance. It may kill me, but that's the risk I'm willing to take for the next generation." His eyes flicked to her belly.

He wasn't going to change his mind. She'd seen that look before. It was the one that Max wore when he told her he'd taken the Dark to save her. It was full of determination and knowledge that what he was doing was right.

She dragged him into a hug. He stiffened, so Kali hugged harder until he finally lifted his arms and embraced her.

"Do I call you Uncle Stockwell?"

"Uncle Bernard is fine."

Kali laughed as she pulled away.

"What's so funny?"

"You don't look like a Bernard."

"It's a family name."

"Can I call you Bernie?" she asked between snorts, trying to regain her composure.

"No."

"Nardo." Oh, man, she needed this laugh.

"Don't press your luck."

"Uncle Berry it is."

"Can they stuff me in that box now?"

Chapter 46

A New Year, A New Hope

Willie Nelson's voice serenaded Max in his cabin. The song was one of his favorites and Mr. Triman's too, who sang along to the record and serenaded his wife sitting next to him on the couch. She giggled at the attention, and Max's father teased him for being a hopeless romantic.

Max hummed along. From outside the window next to the wall with the black stain, a brown-haired boy appeared. Max looked at the others in the room to see if they'd noticed too. But they were busy drinking their cocktails and chatting about work. The boy waved him over. As Max left the recliner and drew closer, the child rewarded him with a wide smile. Then he pointed to the wall at Max's side.

Confused, he turned to stare at the large stain. He hadn't noticed before that it had the vague shape of a man. The kid flattened his palm against the window. He motioned for Max to touch the wall. When his fingers brushed the blackened surface, Max was thrust into a dark room where he could still hear the record playing.

In the distance a light cut through the blackness. He pushed into it and the room filled with gray. Willie's voice grew louder as Max sung the words with him, "Give me one more chance . . ."

He opened his eyes then shut them against the glare of an overhead lamp.

He lifted his arm to shield his eyes but couldn't get too far with an IV stuck in it. Slowly, he opened his eyes again, keeping his head angled away from the bright bulb.

He was on a hospital bed with the metal rails lifted up on either side. But he wasn't in a hospital. He was in a room underneath his grandfather's cabin.

"He's awake," Kali announced from his other side. A chair creaked. A hand locked with his. He turned to find her standing next to the bed. Her other hand was messing with her phone, trying to shut off the music.

"Hey, you." She smiled. "Didn't know you could sing so well. It was Mr. Triman's idea to play Willie Nelson and a few of your other favs."

"How long was I out?" His voice, brittle as dry grass, sounded foreign to him.

"Almost a year," Kali replied. She adjusted his pillow.

His gaze strayed to her torso covered by a flowing peasant blouse over jeans. Rusty gears ground to life sorting out something important that his grandfather revealed about her.

"Aren't you pregnant?" he blurted before he could process that she'd said he had been out for a year, and before he could process that maybe he shouldn't say anything because the baby may not exist.

"Do I look pregnant?" She laughed, flattening the blouse against her non-pregnant belly.

"A real rocket scientist you got there." A dark-haired woman with angular features strolled in wearing a white doctor's coat .

She flashed a penlight in Max's eyes. The harsh light distracted him from other questions bouncing around his foggy mind. The doctor's cold hands prodded and poked at various places on his neck and abdomen. "He'll be groggy and will need physical therapy to get used to using his limbs again."

The last thing Max remembered was the TPC shutting over him. And Kali's face as the cryo jets sent him to sleep.

"What happened?" Max tried to sit up, but the room tipped sideways. He grabbed the rails to keep from falling.

"You just came out of cryo, and the Dark was successfully transferred into a new host," the doctor replied.

He finally recalled who this doctor was. "You're Gloria Vivas."

"Maybe you are smarter than the average CEO," she said with a neutral face so Max couldn't tell whether or not she was joking.

"She's been monitoring you all these months, and she'll be overseeing your therapy," Kali said then whispered in his ear, "She's the best, but she's also a bit of prickle puss, so don't mind her."

He plowed his free hand through his hair only to find his hair wasn't there. Someone had shaved his head. He touched his ears and found no hearing aids.

"I can hear. Is the Dark . . .?"

"It's still part of you. We can't remove it. It's embedded in your DNA, and it made some upgrades to your body. Some are obvious and others we'll have a wait and see about. Good news is that you can't pass it to others. See this?" Gloria pulled down the sheet, exposing Max's body covered in a hospital gown. She flashed a penlight containing a black light over his skin to highlight white tattoos on his legs and arms.

"What are they?"

Kali raised the bed and adjusted the pillows behind his head to prop him up.

"Before they took off for their planet, Mr. Triman, Dara, and Gilroy left Tomas behind to tattoo these symbols onto your body after we siphoned off what we could of the Dark. You're now the bottle with the genie trapped inside you, which sounds really gross and weird, I know," Kali said.

"How did you get it out of me?"

"The same contraption that the Man used on Kali to siphon her power. It was a workaround. Sean uncovered the directions in the journal. Engineers at DERST were able to design a similar system while you were in stasis," Gloria said.

"Where is the rest of the Dark now?" Max looked from one to the other.

"In Stockwell," Kali said.

Max stared at her, waiting for a sign he'd misunderstood.

"Believe it or not, he volunteered. And after a few months of testing, Gloria determined that he could handle it," Kali explained.

"But he's—"

"A bit of a bastard?" Kali finished for him, donning what Max assumed was supposed to be an Aussie accent. "He wanted to make up for past mistakes."

"When the aliens return with the elements to construct a new bottle, we should be able to safely drain Stockwell of the Dark," Gloria said.

"But he'll still have some left," Max said, trying to follow the conversation. His drowsy mind struggled to catch up with all the information being fed to him.

"We'll cross that preternatural bridge when we get to it. Sean is working on a way to reprogram the Dark, so we'll see how that goes. Kali insists Stockwell wants to do right, and it was either take a chance on him or accept that you wouldn't see your son until he started preschool or maybe not until middle school. And kids are annoying enough when they get to pre-teens, they just suck, which is why I didn't have any—"

"Son?" Max interrupted Gloria's rant. His heart ached as he looked to Kali.

"Yep, we're bona fide parents."

"Then we need to make us bona fide." He took both her hands in his.

"On that disgustingly sappy note, I'm leaving. But no sex until I give you the all clear." Gloria wagged a finger. "Obviously, it may be hard for you two."

Kali rolled her eyes as the door shut behind Gloria.

She dropped the metal rail and hopped onto the bed. "Will you be okay with this? I mean, I don't want you to think I trapped you into—"

He stopped her with a kiss on the cheek. "Kali, I knew when you kidnapped me from the dinner that we were meant to be together."

She arched a brow at him. "Hold on, buddy-boy, I saved your butt from said kidnapper. I didn't kidnap you."

"Admit that you wanted to though." He gave her a smile, pouring into it all the love he felt for her.

"I'm pleading the Fifth." She tried to slide from the bed, but he wouldn't let her.

"No matter what life throws at us, we'll handle it as a team." He laced his fingers with hers. "How is he?"

"He's normal, as normal as any kid of mine could be." She laughed.

Max didn't want to insult her, didn't want to insult their child or think that he would love him less if he was a transhuman, but he had to know.

"Is he okay? I mean, does he have powers?"

"I think you know that he will," she said with a conspiratorial wink as if he should know the answer. "Both parents have the transhuman marker. One has powers and another is related to an alien."

Max pressed into the pillow. His head was starting to pound as he recalled another momentous reveal when possessed by the Dark. "Mr. Triman is my great-grandfather."

"We know. Gloria analyzed Dara's hair and pieced together that you were related. Tomas later confirmed." Kali took a plastic cup from the nightstand. She held the straw to his lips. "Here. Have some water."

He slowly sipped the cold fluid, taking his time, getting used to drinking again.

"Where is he now?"

"Heading to the District, their home planet. He was a bit dodgy on the space flight details."

"No, I mean our son."

"Our son," Kali repeated with her smile growing bigger, brighter. "I like hearing you say that. Drink again, your throat sounds super dry."

He did what she asked.

"He's with your parents."

"Excuse me?" Max started to cough.

Kali leaned him forward and patted his back. "On second thought, I should've told you that before you drank."

It hadn't occurred to Max to ask about his parents. Alone in this room with Kali, it felt like it was only the two of them in the world.

"When your mom realized I wasn't like Deandra, who by the way is persona non grata after trying to sneak little Bernie on web TV, so we're not talking to or about her right now. Anyway, when your mom learned that I was an UltraAgent who saved your life and had your life growing inside me, she welcomed me to the family. It also helped that Glen did most of the introducing and talking. In fact, your parents cancelled the rest of their trips to spend time with their grandson. I think almost losing you made them realize how important you were to them. Your sister even flew out to meet me and help me get the nursery set up, which gave me a break from Gloria . . . and you could see why I would need a break.

"Anyhoo, he's bonding with your parental units and Tomas, who is a perfect babysitter when I'm off to work or in here with you. He's so cute with Bernie, and I've taken him to see Willie Nelson twice. Got me this authentic Stetson too." Kali held up a beautiful cowboy hat that was sitting on the back of a chair near the bed.

"When can I see him?" Max asked, feeling a pang of jealousy that so many people have spent time with his baby, whom he had yet to see.

"When Gloria gives the okay, which should be in a couple days. Don't worry." She rubbed his hand. "He knows who you are, and I think you'll recognize him too."

Max's eyelids grew heavy. He fought the urge to doze off. Obviously, it was going to take time to get back to his old self. Just this short interaction—albeit filled with incredible details—was exhausting him.

"Get some rest." Kali lowered the bed. "Once you're strong enough, you can start PT and then we can talk about our next steps."

"Getting married for one," he said, forcing himself to stay awake. He didn't want her to go away again.

"Yes, that too. But I need to talk to you about our next moves. Synthia and I are going to train with St. John's special team. I need to know how to defend myself and our family. The peace-loving gal in me would prefer to take a non-violent route, but this new mama bear needs to learn how to use her claws."

Max wanted to fight her on it, insist that she stay out of harm's way, but the fierceness with which she spoke communicated loud and clear that it would be moot to argue. She had defended herself against him and his grandfather when the Dark had overtaken them. She'd be an asset to St. John's team.

"Besides, I'm the first and only alt-traveling transhuman. I can only guess what our baby may be able to do." She drew up the cover to his shoulders.

"I'm sorry I wasn't there." Max couldn't stop feeling guilty for not being there for the birth.

"It's not you're fault. I had Gloria, for better or worse, and Bernie came nearly two months early, and he was healthy. He's growing at an average pace now, but the team at TransGen is keeping tabs on him with my explicit instructions that he's to be treated as a child not a science experiment. Gloria grumbled about it but relented."

"And I know he'll turn out fine," she added, turning serious, "with a man like you for his father."

Max's heart became so full that his eyes watered. He'd never felt so honored.

"And with a geeky mother like you," he said.

"Watch it, buddy. You're one too. I've seen your comic book collection."

As he drifted to sleep, he said what he wished he'd said before being placed in the TPC, "I love you."

"I know." She kissed his forehead.

A Surefire Way • UltraSecurity Book 1

UltraAgent Surefire always hits her mark. Well, almost always.

During the Olympic trials, she missed it—a screwup that sidelined her athletic career and vaulted her twin sister into gymnastics stardom. Ten years later, Surefire sets the bar high again at UltraSecurty, a niché security firm which solves crimes committed by transhumans (genetically enhanced humans). With determination and a sure shot aim, she rises through U-Sec's ranks and lands an assignment on which two other agents have failed: capturing the transhuman thief Raven.

Then she misses her mark a second time.

Dama X • UltraSecurity Book 2

After Surefire's case, UltraAgent Oracle takes time off from using her mind reading abilities—until a horrific transhuman crime forces her back on the job at UltraSecurity. At the same time, an old promise forces UltraAgent Pax to confront a new villain on the scene—Dama X, a Mexican cartel leader with a gender-bending way of dispatching her enemies.

The Grandfather Paradox • UltraSecurity Book 2.5

Is it the end of the world if an UltraAgent takes a vacation—in another universe?

Someone is threatening UltraAgent TimeTrap's good vacation vibes. Her holiday plans include visiting her peace-loving grandparents who only exist in the 1960s in an alternate universe. Fortunately, she can travel to the past within the universe parallel to hers where she turns on, tunes in, and drops out of her crazy life.

But TimeTrap keeps popping into the wrong era as if pushed off course. Her fellow UltraAgents are disappearing with no record of their existence. When she saves the CEO of a billion dollar defense company, things get really freaky–professionally and personally. Her universe is changing with each passing minute. She'll need to stop whoever is messing with her world before it no longer exists.

Learn about J.T. Bock's latest adventures,
cool contests, book research, and fun facts.

Go to **www.JTBock.com**
and subscribe to her e-zine today!

www.ingramcontent.com/pod-product-compliance
Lightning Source LLC
Chambersburg PA
CBHW082105090726

47910CB00009B/2604